FLESH AND BONE

BLOOD OF KAOS SERIES

NESA MILLER

CONTENTS

Acknowledgements   vii

1. Enter into Darkness   1
2. A Greater Evil   17
3. Portal to Hell   31
4. Castle of Blood   45
5. Salvation   67
6. Affliction   87
7. Aftermath   109
8. Investigation   127
9. Abomination   147
10. Restoration   169
11. Family   193
12. Robes of Valor   207
13. Krymerian Valor   227
14. To Say the Least   253
15. A Black Blade for a Black Blade   269
16. Escort Service   287
17. Unanticipated   305

Also By Nesa Miller   325
Note from the Author   327
About the Author   329

Visit the author's website at www.ladyofkaos.com.

Cover Design: Amy Queau – Q Designs
Formatting by Serendipity Formatting:
https://www.facebook.com/SerendipityFormatting/

First Edition

ISBN-13: 9781916063723

To my Mom, she never read my books but supported me all the same.

I miss you.

ACKNOWLEDGEMENTS

A special thank you to –
Meredith – you're always there when I need you.

Kim Young – my guardian angel who edits like the devil.
https://www.facebook.com/EditorKimYoung

Amy Queau of Q Design – my angel of graphic delights.
http://qcoverdesign.com/

Erica Alexander of Serendipity Formatting – you make the magic beautiful.
https://www.facebook.com/SerendipityFormatting/

Thank you to my beta readers and friends who have advised and provided their invaluable assistance.

Special thanks to Derek Barton who helps me out no matter how mean I am to him. I promise to be nicer in the future.
https://rivyen.wordpress.com/

1

ENTER INTO DARKNESS

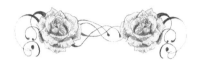

I couldn't save her. Nothing I did. Nothing I said. None of the gifts I gave her – ring, sword, cloak, my name, even my blood – proved strong enough to overcome her most dangerous enemy. Me.

Midir was right when he said I didn't deserve her. Her light illuminated the world and warmed the coldest of hearts. Her determination inspired us all. She made me a better man, showed me how to feel again. She saved my life.

Now she is gone. Murdered by my own hand.

I repeatedly ask myself why? Why was she there? How was it possible for her to be right behind me, *right…behind…me*, and not feel her presence? Was I too caught up in the bloodlust? Did my need to kill the flame-headed demon cloud my senses?

Everything has turned to dust.

My sweet Etain, *a chuisle*, please forgive me.

All that's left to do is prepare. Let the demon's abuses to my flesh purify my soul, cleanse me of the evil that darkens my heart. I didn't deserve her love, but she loved me all the same. Once I am purged, I know her beautiful soul will find mine and take me home.

Dathmet slammed shut the porthole in the cell door. "Damn the man. Is that all he does? Lie there?"

"He hasn't moved or eaten, milord. He stares at nothing, muttering nonsense," said the guard. "Don't see any reason for the shackles, sir. His mind is gone. Won't be long before the rest of him joins it."

"They're a gift, made especially for him. He'll be buried in them." Dathmet turned to leave, then stopped. "In the meantime, he can provide some needed entertainment. Pain has a way of bringing out unique qualities in a person. Get him to the yard and strap him to the stones."

"It will be done, milord."

The guards dragged Dar's limp form down the stone hallways to the main yard, leaving a bloody trail in their wake. Two black stones stood at its center. Tall as a man and spaced the width of a man spread-eagled. Each had two iron rings – one at the top, the other at the bottom. In the days of old, they served as icons, cleansing the souls of traitors to the realm. In present days, they mainly served as reminders of past tortures. Today they glowed in expectancy of fresh blood.

Dathmet watched the guards chain the High Lord to each of the stones. Satisfied his prisoner was secured, he dismissed the guards but allowed them to stay and watch. The red-skinned demon grabbed Dar by his hair, glaring into his golden eyes. The fierce fire that once burned in them was now extinguished, his will to live lost. The pride of generations of great warriors, which had been handed down from father to son throughout the entire history of the VonNeshta family, broken.

"The mighty fall hard," Dathmet said, releasing Dar's hair, letting his head fall forward. He moved to a nearby table set up with various knives, whips, and other tools in the trade of a Master Torturer. "All from believing he murdered the one he holds most dear." He pulled out a pair of steel-enforced black gloves, sliding them onto his hands. "Now, almighty High Lord…" His voice sounded cool and collected, "there are a few questions I want answered."

His fist slammed into Dar's mid-section. "Where have you sent the precious High Lady?" Stepping back, he waited for an answer, but only a grunt passed Dar's lips. A hard blow to the side of the head made his body shake and slump. "You must have sent her away." His voice was calm, yet laced with anger. "If you don't tell me where I can find her, I will tear the flesh from your body and wear it as a mantle."

Drawing his fist back, he drove into Dar's head again. His anger amplified as he hit the once handsome face over and over, ripping into the skin, splattering blood across the ground. Dar's cheek gave way under the constant battering and his eye began to swell. The relentless attack raged on until the master was breathless from the effort. Enraged by the man's silence, Dathmet threw the gloves to the ground and grabbed hold of the arrow still embedded in Dar's shoulder. The demon twisted and turned, pushing it deeper until the tip broke through the skin of his back. Dar's body shuddered, but he did not scream.

"Stubborn idiot!" Dathmet returned to the table and picked up one of the nastier cat-o'-nines. He admired his new toy. Three narrow tails, their tips encased by pieces of curved metal. "This should make an impact." He turned his attention back to his victim. The cruel weapon raked across the High Lord's back, the sound of ripping flesh music to the demon's ears. With every lash, the tips dug deeper. Dathmet laughed, watching the blood flow, bits of flesh littering the ground.

Screams of agony poured from Dar's swollen lips each time the whip burrowed into his back, cleaving the flesh away in chunks. Blood pooling at his feet, he cried out, "*Maith liom, mo ghrá (Forgive me, my love)!*"

Dathmet threw the whip to the ground, then grabbed a small metal rod, crashing it across Dar's arms and the backs of his thighs. Dar's body convulsed and jerked, his screams reduced to small grunts.

The master carried on until he heard bones in the prisoner's forearm crack. The sound made him realize his critical error in tricking Dar with the glamour. He tossed away the rod as he stormed off, yelling at the guards to take the excuse of a warrior back to his cell.

The guards replaced the enchanted shackles on the warrior's wrists and dragged him back to the dark cell, dumping his butchered body on the cold stone floor. Blood darkened his hair to a dull brown, plastering it to his lacerated scalp. The left side of his face swelled to the point he could no longer see out of his eye.

To the prisoner, it didn't matter. In *his* mind, he had been purified.

The first light of day broke weak and gray at Castle Laugharne, cold wind blowing with the promise of more rain. Inferno, chieftain of the UWS clan, walked out into the courtyard and stopped, eyeing the seven who stood in front of him.

"Where's the rest?"

"Asleep in their beds," answered Linq.

"Are ya bloody daft, ya damn elf? We don't know what's out there or who has Dar and Etain…if she's even alive. I won't take any more chances. Pure force is what's gonna take the day and get everyone home safe."

"Pure force is what will get more people killed," argued Linq. "We must be quick. In and out. Going in with more than this will draw attention to us and, if they're both alive, could get them killed."

"Inferno," Wolfe said, coming forward, "we agree with Linq. We've all fought enough battles to know we need to be covert."

Inferno eyed them all again. His clanmates, Wolfe and Elfin; Linq, a former clanmate and Dar's best friend; Arachnia, cohort of the Alamir Ambassadors – *what the hell she's doing here, I don't bloody understand*; Freeblood, *a bloody nuisance with no apparent loyalties to anyone*; and two Black Blades he'd not yet met.

"Are all of ya in this?"

Each of them nodded, speaking their agreement.

At that moment, Spirit walked out the front doors. Like her husband, Inferno, she eyed the seven, then glanced at him. He merely shrugged. "Makes no bloody sense to me either." Hands on his hips, he cocked his head toward the group. "Well then, say yer bloody prayers to whatever god ya believe in and let's get on with it."

Outfitted against the weather and seated in their saddles, Inferno and Linq led their small band through the main gates on the quest in search of Dar VonNeshta, the High Lord of Kaos, and his wife, Etain. They headed toward the only clue available – a circle of blood-stained earth a few miles from Laugharne, where Dar's twin scimitars were found after an ugly battle with the *Bok*.

At the circle, Spirit slid from her mount and approached her husband, who still sat in his saddle. She placed a gentle hand on his leg, capturing his gaze with her own. He covered her hand with his and leaned down, sharing a quiet moment with his wife. Even the horses, seemingly affected by the gravity of the group, were silent.

After a brief time, Inferno broke the connection, dismounted, and retrieved the twin scimitars from the pack on his horse. Spirit gave him a sad smile and turned toward the clearing. He followed, carrying the blades. The toes of her boots at the edge of the black stain, a cold wind lashed through the trees, whipping the ends of her cloak. A quiver ran up her spine as her stomach turned. She closed her eyes, breathed in a calming breath, and slowly released it through her mouth.

Feeling more in control, Spirit crouched and scooped a few grains of the blood-encrusted dirt into a small crystal vial. She stood and murmured words of protection, then stepped into the clearing. Within moments, she felt her throat go dry and broke into a coughing fit. Linq grabbed his canteen and tossed it to Inferno. At her side in two steps, he held the canteen while she took a small drink. With a grateful smile, she tried again, this time with a stronger voice and greater will.

"Goddess who is our Mother Earth, grant me sight. Make it worth the time we waste, the time we've burned. Reveal to me those we would have returned." Her body trembled, making the crystal vial dance madly, and her eyes rolled back.

Inferno noticed movement from the corner of his eye. A group of Elven War Wizards had gathered in a circle around the clearing, their lips moving in sync with the mage, a choir of voices united in a scrying chant. He'd not heard them following or seen any sign of them until this moment, but their presence lightened his heart. They might have a fighting chance if the wizards stayed and lent their magic until the end of the quest.

An elder war wizard, distinguished by his purple leather armor and metal staff topped by a large crystal shard, stepped forward and joined Spirit within the circle. He handed his staff to another wizard, then took the crystal vial from Spirit's hand, looped a leather thong around it, and tied it around her neck. Next, he motioned for the scimitars, which he dipped into the stain, one at a time, and placed one in each of the mage's hands, then crossed them over her chest. Retrieving his staff, he remained close as the chanting increased in speed, changing from English to Gaelic to Elven.

Not as enthralled by the magic of the War Wizards, Arachnia sensed something entirely different approaching from behind. She'd felt the wizards in their march toward the clearing, but had recognized them for who they were and hadn't raised an alarm. This was different. Whatever this new thing might be, it was too far away to decipher if it was friend or foe, but it definitely headed their way. She looked to her right. Freeblood was preoccupied with the wizards. She looked to her left. Inferno was intent on the mage. She checked the others in the group and saw all eyes on the happenings within the circle. It was apparent no one else noticed what she did. Slowly, she stepped back, turned, and disappeared into the trees.

The War Wizards melded their magic with that of the mage, using her body as the scrying tool. Lifted by the pure white magic, Spirit rose into the air and hovered over the stain. When her eyes opened, a soft golden light shone like that of a lighthouse.

After several turns, her body slowed to a stop. "He is not of this world. In the east is a portal to his dark realm. She can save him, but the unicorn and the panther must show her the way. Protect her – protect the unicorn – protect the panther – save the legacy."

All those around the circle exchanged glances, none of them certain what her words meant.

Her message complete, she closed her eyes and floated into the safe arms of the wizard. He wrapped her in his cloak and gently handed her to Inferno. "She is well. Give her a moment to reconnect with herself. She will rise of her own will in a small fragment of time."

Inferno lay her in a pile of soft leaves, then sat and placed her head in his lap, stroking her hair. Within a few minutes, her eyes opened. *"Bore da, golygus* (Good morning, handsome)."

"Bore da, fy ngwraig hardd (Good morning, my beautiful wife)." He reached into a pocket for a small chocolate bar. *"I chi* (For you)."

Spirit sat up, kissed him on the lips, and snatched the chocolate from his hands. *"Eich bod yn gwybod i mi mor dda* (You know me so well)."

"Yn unig chariadus ydych, fy cariad (Just loving you, my love)."

Two silent warriors, tired and dirty, swords drawn, walked into Laugharne's deserted compound. They stopped in the center of the yard, their watchful eyes tuned for any sudden movements.

One whispered, "Do you think anyone's here?"

"There's always someone here. Let's go around back." They walked past the corner of the castle toward the back garden.

A man dressed in a red, white, and blue robe stepped out the kitchen door. Seeing the cloaked intruders, he stopped, holding onto the door handle. "Who are *you*?" he asked, speaking with all his Ambassador authority.

"Cappy, it's me. Etain," she said, pushing the hood of her cloak off her head, hoping the Alamir Ambassador remembered her.

A skeptical look on his face, he didn't move. "You can't be. Etain is-"

The skies still somewhat dark, she stepped into the light that shone through the window of the kitchen door. "I'm right here." Hearing his gasp, she felt the hairs on the back of her neck rise. "Where is everyone? Where's Dar?"

The back door opened, surprising Cappy. He dipped with the movement of the door, then caught himself and quickly regained his dignified persona.

However, a not so observant body collided into him, dropping a mug in the process. "Oh… Sorry, Cappy," Thoric said as his gaze landed on the blonde. "Etain! Where did you come from? Is Dar with you?" He stepped into the back garden, standing next to the Ambassador.

She sheathed her sword. "Thoric. Why would Dar be with me? Where is everyone?"

He looked past her at the other cloaked being. "Who is that?"

"I sensed something was wrong, so I had to come." She jerked a thumb back toward the elf. "Taurnil insisted he come along."

Cappy recovered from his initial shock. "You were in Nunnehi."

"And now I'm not."

Thoric raised a brow. "I don't know of any Taurnil in the Alamir. How do we know you're really Etain?"

She blew out an exasperated breath. "I was in Nunnehi, where Taurnil is from, and now I'm here. What's happened to Dar? Was he hurt in the fighting?" She took a step toward the door, but Thoric, as well as Cappy, purposely blocked her.

"Convenient, don't you think?" Thoric asked. "To show up *after* the fighting's done? Neither of you look like you've been in battle. Your cloaks are spotless."

As he came forward, Taurnil threw back his hood and released his cloak with one hand, baring his teeth with a hiss, making the Alamir recoil. "We stepped into hell." Patches of dried mud showed on his dark leathers and boots.

Etain placed a hand on Taurnil's arm as she explained. "We came down from Torfaen Pass and ran into a band of young Alamir, who let us fall in with them." As she spoke, she unclasped her own cloak, letting it fall to the ground. "We fought long and hard, mostly trying to keep them alive." Her leathers and boots were also muddy. "The cloaks are Elven. Nothing adheres to the fabric."

Thoric and Cappy exchanged a look.

"If you like," she continued, "I can come closer so you can smell the blood. Maybe then-"

Cappy held up a hand. "That won't be necessary."

"Why didn't these Alamir you speak of come with you?" asked Thoric.

Taurnil's glare forced the men back another step. "Most are buried. Those who lived chose to go home."

Etain finished the story. "They live only because something made the *Bok* turn. So, I ask again, what is going on and where is Dar? Where's Inferno?"

At this point, Zorn and Felix came around the corner. Zorn stopped dead in his tracks. "Etain?" Felix bounded to her, whining and pushing against her leg.

Seeing Zorn bandaged from neck to hip made her heart flip. She'd not seen him since the wedding. Swee had told her of how the young man chased after Inferno's two wolfhounds that went in hot pursuit of an uninvited guest. It obviously had not gone well, but at least he was on his feet and appeared to be recovering. She greeted Felix with a smile, giving him a good rub behind the ears.

"Hello, boy. How ya doing?" She looked at Zorn. "Any sign of Ruby yet?" Felix suddenly barked and ran back to the young man.

Zorn shook his head.

Etain straightened and faced the other two men. "Is that proof enough?"

Cappy cleared his throat before speaking. "We experienced the same as you. The *Bok* stopped fighting and left. We aren't sure what happened to Dar. Inferno and a few others have gone to find him."

"We thought you were with him," Zorn added.

She noticed the paleness of his face. "You should go inside, Zorn. You're not looking too good."

At that moment, his legs gave way. Taurnil, quick on his feet, caught him before he slumped to the ground. "Whoa, there. Etain's right. Let's get you inside." Thoric met them halfway, slipped an arm around Zorn, and walked him inside.

"Which direction did they go?" Etain asked the Ambassador.

"Straight out to the east. You should find them rather quickly. They haven't been gone long."

A sudden weight squeezed the air from her lungs. Her heart felt ready to explode. She reached for Taurnil, who wrapped an arm around her waist, letting her lean against him. "We should go," she whispered to the elf.

"You need to rest, E."

"No. I won't rest until I find him." Feeling stronger, she gently pushed away. "Thank you, Cappy." With that, the two left the Ambassador standing in the yard.

Arachnia followed her instincts, zigging and zagging through the trees. As long as she kept going in the general direction, she saw no reason to make a beeline into what could be a hornet's nest. Her lips curled in a satisfied smirk at the silly pun.

Bees. Hornet's nest. I'll have to remember that one for Thoric.

The niggle in her senses elevated. So much so she slowed down, her pitchfork in the lead, and inched through the forest, her senses on high alert.

"Who are you?" a voice asked from behind.

Arachnia stopped cold. Obviously, her alert wasn't high enough. *Damn. I won't be telling anyone about this part.*

She turned to two figures in black cloaks, their faces obscured by hoods. The bit she could see didn't appear to be demon but there were plenty of *Bok* who weren't. "In light of recent events, I think it best you state who you are first."

A scream pierced through the forest. The fastest in the group, Freeblood and Elfin, took off first. Inferno was on his feet in an instant, reluctant to leave his wife. Spirit waved him on, saying she would catch up. He and Linq followed the other two at a dead run.

What they found made them pull up short. Arachnia, pinned against a tree, a dagger at her throat. Elfin and Freeblood exchanged curious looks just as Inferno and Linq arrived. Inferno reacted immediately. A flaming fireball in his hand, he released it just as Linq yelled, "Inferno, wait!"

A second black cloak threw itself in front of the flaming mass, taking a hit to the shoulder. The impact slammed the figure into its twin, virtually crushing the other into the tree. As a result, the dagger at Arachnia's throat cut into her flesh. The cloaked strangers fell in one direction as Arachnia collapsed in the other, blood soaking her front.

Elfin and Freeblood ran to her. Linq ran to the cloaks. Inferno stood frozen in place. Spirit appeared next to him, a concerned look on her face. "What is it, love? Are you all right?"

He gave her a stunned look, then turned his gaze on the cloaks, watching as Linq kneeled next to them.

"Inferno, love, what's wrong?" Spirit asked, trying to catch his eye again.

"Dar?" he said in a small voice. Ignoring the protests of his wife, he stumbled over to the elf just as Linq pushed back the hood of the cloak. "Holy shite."

"Taurnil? Taurnil!" Linq said, giving him a good shake.

One golden eye opened and rolled. The young elf moaned, touching his left shoulder. "*What* in the stars was *that*?"

Linq breathed out a relieved sigh. "*That* was Inferno." He looked up at the Alamir. "Inferno, meet Taurnil of Nunnehi."

"Are ya sure of what yer saying, elf?"

Linq's laugh was more of a grunt. "If this were Dar, do you think he'd lie here moaning like a baby?"

The golden eye glared, soon joined by the other. "You'd moan, too, if you took one of those in a direct hit."

"I don't understand," Inferno said. "Yer an elf."

"Sometimes I don't understand it myself."

Arachnia managed a croak. "She has a…dagger." All three men looked in her direction.

"She?" Linq asked.

"By the stars!" Taurnil exclaimed and rolled away. A low moan came from the cloaked heap beneath him. "E." He gasped at the painful movement of his shoulder as he reached for her. She cried out when he touched her arm. Linq and Inferno stared in silence as Taurnil gingerly pushed the hood from her head and grimaced at the bark burn on the side of her face. "Ouch."

"I think my arm is broken," she moaned, favoring the one she'd fallen on.

"Sorry, E. I was trying to save you from the fire blast."

Inferno pushed his way between the two. "Bloody fucking hell, lass!" He picked her up, crushing her to his chest, making her cry out again. "Thank the heavens."

Spirit shoved through the men. "Goddess of us all. Let me have a look at her." Inferno carefully lowered Etain to the ground, leaning her against the tree. "Etain…" Spirit shook her head. "I can't handle much more of this."

"What?" she said, giving Spirit a strange look. "The woman waved a pitchfork in my face. Who the hell is she?"

"Lady E!" Wolfe exclaimed, having run up with the others. "You're here!"

"Taurnil, Your Grace," Elfin said, giving his prince a respectful bow of his head. "I wasn't expecting to see you here."

The young prince smiled. "It's as much a surprise for me as it is for you, believe me."

"Your Grace?" Inferno echoed, staring at Taurnil. Another moan from Etain shifted his gaze to her.

"How about someone tell me what's going on," Etain muttered as Spirit moved her arm. "Ow!"

"Tck…," Spirit admonished. "'Tis nothing more than a wee bruise. You'll be sore a few days, but nothing serious. Let me see your cheek."

"That hurts!" Etain cried.

Spirit sat back on her heels. "Give me strength. I've not heard this much whining since Inferno had the man flu."

Etain ran a hand through her hair. "Well, it *does* hurt," she said, looking rather bewildered.

Inferno crouched in front of her. "I take it ya never met Arachnia." Etain shook her head. "She came in with Cappy and Thoric a couple days ago."

"Oh, aye." Etain sighed. "Cappy told us where to find you."

He gave her a good look over. "Where's yer husband?"

"*You* had him last. What did *you* do with him?"

He took hold of her good hand and placed a ring on her palm. "We found this in a clearing east of here, along with his scimitars."

Etain stared at the ring. "How did it get there?" She looked up at Inferno. "Are you telling me you've lost my husband?"

"Hey, Spirit," Freeblood called out. "If Etain's okay, we could use your help over here."

Spirit placed a hand on Etain's leg and gave it a squeeze. "When we get to the house, I'll whip up a potion for your face. Let me get to Ara."

Etain nodded, giving the other woman a cursory glance. She waved at Freeblood, then turned to Inferno. "What's happened to Dar?"

He cocked a brow and stood, crossing his arms over his chest. "*You* tell *me* what yer doing *here* when yer supposed to be in Nunnehi."

"I told Dar he couldn't keep me away if I felt anything odd. And what I felt…" She shivered. "Where the hell is he?" she demanded, grabbing Taurnil's hand so he could help her to her feet.

Glances were exchanged throughout the group, but it was Linq who spoke. "We have a general idea in which direction he was taken. We found his scabbard about a mile away from the clearing. But as to where he is physically, we don't know."

Etain bit her bottom lip. "Okay. Okay. He's gone, but at least he isn't…" Taking a deep breath, she ran a hand through her hair. "I'll find him."

"We'll do it together," Inferno said.

Holding her injured arm to her chest, she breezed past him. "Give me a few minutes alone."

Linq grabbed Inferno by the arm before he could follow. "She won't go far. Give her the time. Maybe she *can* find Dar."

"I'm not leaving her on her own."

"She won't be." Taurnil walked after her.

Inferno shrugged out of Linq's grip. "You coming?"

Linq glanced at Spirit and left, as well.

Etain slowed her pace as she approached the spot. Her chest felt heavy. Finding it hard to breathe, she placed a hand over the mark she shared with Dar. The hairs on the back of her neck prickled and her skin seemed to crawl. She almost turned back, but upon seeing the dark stain, she fell to her knees and reached out. Her trembling hand inches above the blood, a slight tingle in her palm quickly spread to her fingertips, encompassing her wrist and traveling up her arm. The blood acted as a magnet and pulled her hand down into the dirt. She tried to pull away, but the attraction was too strong. It held her fast.

Dar's face, twisted in a look of horror, exploded into her mind. Blood and bodies were strewn everywhere. She watched him fall to his knees, tears streaming down his bloodied cheeks. Her heart pounded at seeing him grab his dagger and raise it over his chest.

"No!" she screamed. Sickened by his despair, she took no notice when Taurnil ripped her away from the circle of blood. She murmured Dar's name over and over, trembling in the young elf's strong embrace.

Inferno placed a hand on Taurnil's shoulder. "Hold onto her, lad. Let her know she's safe."

The elf nodded and tightened his arms around her. "I've never known the *Bok* to leave such a presence."

Clinging to Taurnil, Etain whispered so only he could hear. "This is worse."

"What could be worse than the *Bok*?" he whispered back.

"Midir."

"But he's dead."

"Aye. But there was another. An apprentice, I'm sure." She looked into his golden eyes, her nails digging into his arms. Her voice steadily grew louder. "I can't find him, T. He's gone. Holy hell! He's gone!"

The same wizard who had charmed Spirit rushed to Taurnil and invoked a sleeping spell on the young woman. Etain's grip loosened as her eyes closed, collapsing in Taurnil's arms. The wizard turned to Linq and Inferno.

"Make your plans while she sleeps. Our High Lord lives, but I fear not for long."

Nonplussed, Inferno turned on the wizard. "How the hell do ya know where he is when me girl can't find him?"

"There are many dimensions between our worlds, milord. Not even one as old as I can access them all. How can we expect as much from one so young?" He smiled at the sleeping girl. "Our High Lord has chosen well. She is strong but has much to learn. There are times the life force does not wish to be found. However, we have seen shimmers of our High Lord's preparation to pass into the Netherworld. This is perplexing as the bond between these two souls is undeniable. An atrocity must have happened to make our High Lord long for death. We must work quickly."

15

2

A GREATER EVIL

While Etain slept, the group set up camp. Once the horses were unsaddled and tethered, Linq and Inferno assigned various tasks - fetching water, tending the fire, cooking.

Taurnil's concern for Etain increased as he watched her toss and turn, mumbling indistinguishable words in her troubled sleep. At one point, her eyes opened. Reaching up, she held his face in her hands.

"You must listen to me. I'm trying to get to you, my love. Please, show me where you are. Show me the way."

Taurnil's heart twisted, seeing the love in her eyes. *To be loved this passionately...* He knew not to wake her but felt the need to respond. "I will show you when the time is right." He gently took hold of her hands and held them within his. "For now, take a drink to refresh yourself and sleep." She accepted a drink from his flask, coughing when the strong liquid hit her throat. He made her drink once more before telling her to lay down. Once she fell asleep again, he stood to grab a bite to eat.

"We know there's a bloody portal to the east, but how far?" Inferno asked, looking at the faces around the fire. "Do we have any ideas on how to open the damn thing when we find it?"

"I believe we'll have to leave that one to Etain," Linq said.

Taurnil sat down between Linq and Elfin. "I'm pretty sure she's been communicating with him."

"If she's found Dar's mind," Spirit said, "we'll have our open portal in no time. However, her love for him may blind her to things she should see. In order to save his life, she'll fight with no regard for her own." Her gaze fell on Taurnil. "He is her strength and her weakness. Do not let it be the death of them."

"Be assured, I will protect her with my life, milady," Taurnil said. "Unfortunately, she seems to be having trouble getting him to respond."

Everyone stared quietly into the fire.

Wolfe broke the silence. "None of this makes sense to me. I've always heard how strong Dar is. How he overcomes the odds, no matter how great. Can anyone explain what's happening here?"

Inferno looked at Linq. "You've known him longer than any of us."

Taurnil offered a possible explanation. "What Spirit said about Dar being Etain's strength and weakness... Wouldn't it be the same for him?"

"Aye." Inferno sighed. "I have a newly remodeled lounge to prove it." He told the story about the day Midir paid them an unannounced visit and Etain's attempt to get away from his influence. "Dar destroyed that corner of the house to get to her, then did his best to tear his brother limb from limb."

"Who would have a vendetta against him?" asked Wolfe. "What could they possibly hope to gain by defeating him and dragging him off to another realm?"

Linq gave a short laugh. "Vendetta? Name any demon from here to Tartarus."

"Whoever it is knew to use Etain." Arachnia joined the circle. The cut on her neck was nothing more than a slight red line now thanks to her ability to heal more quickly in her scorpion form. She, Freeblood, and the Black Blades found seats around the fire.

"What makes you say that?" Inferno asked.

She shrugged. "It's simple. Her ring was found at the site…" Arachnia's gaze passed over everyone around the fire. "Her *missing* ring. If it's true she's his weakness as well as his strength, then they've used her in some way to weaken him."

"But he knew she was in Nunnehi. He sent her there himself," Taurnil said.

"Why else would such a great warrior drop his blades but to save someone close to him?" she retorted.

"Bloody hell." Inferno jumped up. "The man went near daft when we thought Midir had killed her before." Placing his hands on his hips, he glared at the group. "If the *Bok* have found a way to bring down our strongest warrior, what's to happen to the rest of us?"

"Etain said it isn't the *Bok*," said Taurnil.

"The wizards said the same," Linq added. "Remember, Inferno? They said this evil is not of the *Bok*."

"For fuck's sake! Maybe not, but they're involved, somehow, and it doesn't change the fact that Dar's down."

"We're overlooking something," Arachnia said. "Whoever this is knows of the bond they share. They must know she'll do whatever it takes to get him back."

"A trap then," said Elfin.

"But to what end?" Taurnil asked.

The group fell silent again, dwelling on their own thoughts.

"Well, consider this…," Wolfe said, thinking out loud. "If all that power could be harnessed, imagine the havoc you could cause."

Inferno gave him a skeptical glare. "Dar or Etain harnessed? There's no power in the universe could do that."

"Somehow this foe has managed to take Dar out of the equation and is using it to lure Etain," Elfin added. "And we're serving her up on a shiny silver platter."

"That's just it," Arachnia said. "What if whoever it is wants Etain, not Dar?"

Linq exchanged a look with Inferno. "We have to find out who we're up against before we go any further."

"Let's start with the unicorn and panther." Inferno canvassed each face, either met by a shake of a head or a blank stare. He turned to his wife. "Do you know what it means, love?"

Spirit shrugged. "I only pass on what the spirits tell me. It doesn't make sense to me."

Linq looked across the campsite. "Most esteemed wizards… Can you help us interpret this riddle the fates have laid at our feet?"

The elder stepped forward. "These beings must be significant to the High Lord, the High Lady, or both. Unicorns are light and love and offer hope. In this situation, those qualities would be highly prized." He shifted his staff to his other hand as he circled around those seated at the fire. "The panther can symbolize courage, valor, and power. However, it can also symbolize the understanding of death. The fact that it is red-"

"Red?" Inferno bellowed. "No one said anything about it being red."

"I assure you, milord, it *is* red."

Inferno looked at Spirit, then at Linq and back at the wizard. "Is it bad?"

"Not necessarily…" the wizard said. "It could be a symbol of love…or a warning."

"But-"

The wizard held up an index finger. "Or it could be an indication of anger."

Inferno crossed his arms over his chest and glared at the man. "Basically, yer telling us ya don't bloody know. Ya don't know if he's alive or dead or who the bleedin' hell has him. Ya don't know a goddamned thing!"

Etain, accompanied by a red panther, found her way to her husband. In the far corner, a faint golden light illuminated his form. With one arm wrapped around his knees, the other limp at his side, his head hung low. He shuddered as the red panther nuzzled his matted hair. With a grunt, he raised his good arm and placed it across its neck, scratching its head and murmuring a soft greeting, as if it were perfectly normal for the animal to be in the cell.

Etain stepped into the soft light. "Dar," she whispered. "Look at me."

Thinking he didn't hear, she started to say it again, but he raised his head. She gasped, seeing the dark circles beneath his eyes, swollen face, and filthy hair.

"Oh, baby," she breathed.

"Who are you?" he mumbled out of the side of his mouth.

She crouched in front of him to save him from craning his neck. "It's me, a chuisle. Etain."

He continued to stare at her, but it was clear he didn't recognize her. "My sweet Etain has left me." A slight smile lifted a corner of his dry lips. "But I will be with her soon."

She swallowed hard, pushing back the tears. "Dar, I'm trying to get to you. Can you help me?"

"She's waiting for me on the other side."

Etain took a deep breath. Despite her best efforts, her voice wavered. "Dar." Her eyes roamed over him, trying to take in the damage done to her sweet savage. Seeing the bone protruding from the arm at his side, then the shaft in his shoulder, she bit her bottom lip to keep from crying out. Then she noticed the pool of blood beneath him.

The panther moved toward her. "We will come again, milady. Next time will be better."

"I can't leave him like this," she whispered harshly. "Look what that monster has done to my beautiful Dar."

"You cannot help him presently, sweet lady. Only your physical presence can save him. You must go back and find the path to Da."

"Find the path," she repeated under her breath, unsure if it were possible. "My love…" She reached out and gently touched his good arm. "I will return soon. Please stay strong. I'm not far." But he didn't notice her

step away. Wavering on the edge of wakefulness, Etain looked at the panther. "What did he mean…on the other side?"

The panther merely stared at her with its blue eyes and faded away.

Etain floated back to consciousness, tears in her eyes. *Who would do this? How do I save you?* She needed time alone. Time to think and find her way to Dar.

Muted voices pulled her from her thoughts. She carefully opened her eyes, hoping no one would notice, and was relieved to see most of their backs turned. Those facing her wouldn't see anything beyond the flames of the fire. Slowly, she eased onto her back, watching them. Taurnil suddenly turned toward her. Etain closed her eyes, forcing herself to breathe slowly in the illusion of sleep. No one seemed to notice. She opened her eyes, happy to see he had turned back to the fire.

Quietly rolling onto her other side, she scoped out the perimeter of the camp. The horses weren't far away. *Perfect.* Quiet as a ninja, Etain inched her way to the nearest tree, eased up into a crouch, then scuttled in the direction of her horse. The line shifted, one stallion jerking his head back, knocking into the gelding at his side. Etain froze. *Damn.* She looked over her shoulder. Several heads turned, but Wolfe slapped someone on the back with a boisterous comment about squirrels and ghosts, making everyone laugh.

Etain blew out a breath and approached the horses in a more civilized manner. "Hey, y'all," she whispered. "It's just little ol' me. Gonna take Razz for a ride." She sidled up, stroking Razz's nose as she slipped her tether from the line. "I've missed you, pretty girl. Wanna get out of here for a bit?" The horse nuzzled into her, then backed away into the darkness.

Etain grinned, grabbed a handful of mane and vaulted onto Razz's bare back. "Let's see if we can find us a Krymerian."

Spirit stood. "I think it's time the wizards take their leave, and me with them."

Inferno's face fell. "Love, I wasn't-"

She smiled and touched his cheek. "I know you're angry and frustrated. I'll take them back with me and leave you to do what you do best - save the day. Be safe and come home soon." Her gaze went around the campfire to include every face. "All of you be safe and come home." She stepped up to Taurnil, taking his hands in hers. "You carry the same strength in you as our Dar. Do not be afraid to use it. She will need you to be strong when she falls." Kissing his cheeks, she turned and joined the wizards.

Before leaving, the elder wizard had one last thing to say. "We send you with our blessings. Upon each of you, we have cast a protection spell to keep you safe. Be forewarned. Once you leave this realm, its protective properties could be greatly diminished. It is a great evil you face. May the stars watch over you and guide you well."

Linq came to his feet. "I imagine we'll find out what it all means soon enough. We should follow the High Lady's example and get some sleep. We'll need every ounce of energy we can muster in the coming days."

The group broke away in different directions, ready to settle in for the night as best they could. At least the rain had stopped, but the chill remained. Wolfe, Elfin, and Taurnil volunteered to take the first watch and keep the campfire burning.

"Let me check on Lady E first," Taurnil said. "Make sure she's all right."

Wolfe waved him off. "Gather some firewood while you're at it. It's going to be a long night." Taurnil nodded and disappeared into the dark.

"Maybe not as long as you think." Elfin grinned, holding up two small jugs.

"Mate!" Wolfe laughed, accepting what he knew to be Inferno's best home-brewed ale. "I knew I liked you for a reason!"

The men pulled the corks and tapped jugs. Just as the aromatic liquid touched their lips, a frantic shout wiped the smiles from their faces. Shoving the corks back in, they set down the jugs and reached for their swords.

Taurnil dashed into the firelight, his eyes bright. "Did she come this way?"

"No one's passed by us," said Wolfe. "Who're you looking for?"

"Etain! She's not where I left her."

Linq walked up. "I should've checked the horses when we heard them stir earlier." Taurnil gave him a questioning look. "Razz is gone."

"Bleedin' hell," Inferno murmured, joining the group. "God knows where she's headed."

Freeblood edged his way through the group. "Didn't Spirit mention something about Dar being in the east?"

Inferno held his gaze, then looked at Linq. "She said there's a portal."

"Do you really think she would-" Linq started.

Taurnil was already on the move as Inferno threw up his hands. "Hell! You know how she is!" He and Linq caught up to Taurnil at the horses. "Saddle 'em up quick, boys. Maybe she hasn't gotten too far."

Taurnil untethered a white gelding and jumped on its bare back. It didn't take much provocation to set the horse in motion.

"For fuck's sake," Inferno cursed, saddling his mount as quickly as he could. "Linq…"

Astride his own mount, the elf said, "Stay here, Inferno. We won't be long." He left the Alamir in his dust. Arachnia appeared suddenly, throwing a blanket and saddle on the first horse in the line. "I'll ride with you, Inferno. Freeblood's taken off, too. Said a horse would only slow him down."

"No need for all of us to chase after her." Inferno stomped away. "Someone's gotta keep the bleedin' fire going."

After a couple miles, Taurnil pulled up, having spied something unusual. With a slight nudge of his knees, he walked his mount toward a blue light. He passed a horse grazing on a small patch of grass, then saw Etain, encased within the blue glow, atop a small rise, her hair billowing in the wind. As he dismounted, she turned and watched him walk toward her.

"They cut him to make him weak, then put him in shackles and dragged him to the portal. The bastard could've shimmered him there but preferred to brutalize my love, treating him worse than demon scum." Taurnil looked up into her tear-stained face. "I will track this animal down. He will pay for these abuses."

"E…," he said softly. "I understand your outrage, but don't let it cloud your mind. You have to focus on Dar. Any other thoughts can interfere with your link to him. Forget revenge and concentrate on finding your husband."

"Have you ever lost someone you love, T?"

He shrugged and looked away, unable to meet her glare. "No."

Her gaze returned to the eastern horizon. "Believe me, my mind is perfectly clear. The portal isn't far from here."

Even though it was too dark to see, Taurnil followed her gaze. "Once we get there, do you know how to open it?"

"Not yet. But I will."

Linq and Freeblood, having arrived shortly after Taurnil, overheard their conversation. "Tell me how, Etain," Linq challenged her.

She continued to face east, as though the portal would appear on the horizon. "How what?"

"How did they make him bleed?" He walked around to stand in front of her. "Why did a Krymerian warrior allow himself to be shackled and dragged off like a common criminal? Why didn't he fight? This must be a powerful force to bring down a warrior of Dar's caliber. Taurnil is right. You must forget your vengeance."

"I agree, Etain," Freeblood said. "You have to think this through. *If* you find the portal, you can't just storm in there."

Her blue glow illuminated her eyes. "I will do whatever I deem necessary to save my husband."

Freeblood held up his hands in surrender.

Not Linq. "What makes you think they won't slit his throat the second you arrive? Can't you see how vulnerable he is, letting himself be treated in such a way? I don't know what magic has been conjured, but it may take more than your precious sword to save him."

She stared at him for a long, intense moment, a fire burning deep in her eyes. "Bloody fucking hell!" she screamed and stormed off into the darkness, blue sparks flying like hot spots on the sun.

When Taurnil started to follow, Linq grabbed his arm with a slight shake of his head. They listened to her mutterings and witnessed an occasional stomp of a foot, the wave of an arm. After a short time, she walked straight up to Linq, her blue glow fading with every step.

"Damn elf. Why do you always have to be right?"

"For once, I wish I weren't. Let's get back to camp. We can discuss strategies in the morning."

In the darkness, she heard a quiet stirring, a labored breath. His pain washed through her, making her moan. Although his eyes were open, he saw nothing, but her mind registered what he refused to acknowledge. Blood covered his chiseled arms and elegant hands. She shivered from the cold of the stone floor, felt the pain of the shackles cutting into his bruised skin. The man was lost in his dreams, impervious to the abominations perpetrated on his mortal being.

A unicorn stepped out from the dark corner. "Talk to him, milady. He will hear you."

She extended an arm along his and pressed up close, hoping the warmth of her body would stop him from shivering. "I'm here, a chuisle," she whispered, pouring her love into him. "You're not alone, my sweet."

"My fiery vixen." She heard the smile in his voice. "Make love to me like the last time we were together. I can never get enough of you."

"Dar," she breathed. "You will be in my arms soon. I promise. Please hold on. I'm coming for you."

• • •

Etain woke just as the sky began to lighten. Unsure of her surroundings, she remained still, listening to the sounds of the outdoors. Slowly, she turned her head, her eyes constantly on the move. Her heart skipped a beat when she saw the man lying beside her. As he shifted in his sleep, his blond hair fell back, revealing his ears. She closed her eyes.

Taurnil.

She quietly got up, tip-toed around her sleeping companions, located Dar's scabbard with his black blades and walked away from camp. Strapping on the scabbard, she muttered to herself, "If you're in a demon realm where better to start the search than in a demon's castle?"

Drawing Day Star and Burning Heart, she crossed them over her head. "Mighty blades of the High Lord, a part of you once belonged to the dark Midir. Search your past and take me to his realm."

A small whirlwind formed at her feet, spinning faster and faster. As it grew, it darkened and lengthened, engulfing her legs, continuing up her body until she was consumed completely. She disappeared in a black cloud.

Then appeared in a familiar courtyard. As she sheathed the swords, she looked around the compound, remembering the last time she'd been here. Midir had stabbed her in the chest, just missing her heart, and stolen her away to this place, his castle. Once Dar discovered where she'd been taken, he'd come for her. Thanks to Midir's mind games, she nearly took Dar's life that day, but he understood his brother's dirty tricks. His love and faith in her saved them both.

The place appeared well kept, not at all as it looked when they'd left. The windows were clean and gleaming, the racks of training swords set out for someone's morning practice. She shivered, happy to know they weren't waiting for her. The stones looked perfect, not one out of place or damaged. The huge doors were whole and on their hinges. She smelled the fragrant scent of a wood-burning fire. Stepping farther back, she noticed smoke wafting from one of the large chimneys.

Nothing stirred when she opened the door and stepped inside. The interior was as clean and dust free as the first time she'd been brought here. She continued down the hallway, peering into each room as she passed, each one the same. In the kitchen, she found a simmering pot on the stove and noticed a bubbling dish in the oven.

Apprehensive, she walked up the stairs and stopped at the room she was forced to share with Midir. Like everything else, the door had been repaired and stood open. She walked into the room. The bed was turned down and the balcony doors open, letting in a fresh breeze.

Just another day in the life of a-

She heard running water from the adjoining room. Walking around the bed, she looked through the bathroom door and found Midir's housemaid, Lilith, bent over the tub, testing the water. Seemingly content with the temperature, she turned off the flow and straightened.

A small shriek made Etain jump. "Oh, my word!" Lilith exclaimed, patting her chest. "Milady, I apologize. You surprised me."

Etain eyed the tub. "You were obviously expecting someone. Or is this for you?"

Lilith laughed nervously. "No, milady! We've been expecting you. Just not…well… We weren't sure *when* you would arrive. I run a bath every day."

"Why?"

"Because the master has ordered it."

Etain raised her brows. "The master? But Midir is dead."

Lilith laughed again. "Yes, milady, I know. I speak of my master, Dathmet." She busied herself with setting the towels just right.

"Dathmet? Who the hell is he?"

A dreamy expression softened the maid's features. "A most wondrous master. There has never been one better…or more handsome. He's far exceeded anything his father ever hoped to attain. And he's much nicer."

"Father?"

Lilith looked at her as though she were simple-minded. "Midir, milady."

Etain shook her head in disbelief1. "Midir…is Dathmet's father? When would Midir have had-"

"It is not my place to know of such things. Perhaps you can ask the master upon his return." She motioned to the tub. "Shall I assist milady into the bath?"

Etain stared at her. "No. Milady will *not* be taking a bath."

Her eyes widened. "But the master has demanded it."

"Lilith, is there anyone else here?"

Wringing her hands, she couldn't look Etain in the eye. "There are servants everywhere, but Mr. Raum runs the house."

"Oh, aye. Raum. Where would he be?"

"He should return shortly. Wouldn't you like to relax with a bath while you wait, milady?"

Etain turned away, speaking over her shoulder. "Forget the bath, and don't run any more." She left the room.

At the foot of the stairs, the set of black doors to the library caught her attention. They made her think of the doors to the Black Blade training hall in Nunnehi and *Megiltura* Rana. She smiled in spite of the current situation and stepped into the room, finding it pristine like the others. The red chaise made her shiver. Her eyes cut to the books lining the shelves, particularly the one she had browsed through before, the one containing VonNeshta in gold.

Reaching for the book, she suddenly felt as though something vile crawled over her skin.

You must leave, milady. Do not waste time.

She shrugged it away. *After I speak to Raum, I'll go.*

Get out now! Hurry!

The strength of the message staggered her into the shelves. She jammed her hands into her hair, grasping her head. She took a breath and shook it off, then drew the black blades, crossing them overhead. "Forget your past. Forget the dark. We belong to the High Lord. Take me to the light."

This time, white smoke swirled up from the floor, circling around her. Although her heart beat like a bass drum from the urgent warning, the white magic made her feel protected, as though she were safe in Dar's arms.

Just before she disappeared in the swirl of smoke, the door opened and Dathmet stepped in. Seeing Etain, he froze. His black hair and green eyes accentuated the blood red of his skin. Were she not in mid-transition, she would have frozen, as well. Fortunately, the spell saved her from making that mistake.

She returned a small distance from the campsite, sheathed the swords and made her way back, walking the circumference of the camp in search of a particular face. But her mind was on the demon. The last she'd seen him, his eyes were black and hair in flames. Could he be a shapeshifter?

She found who she'd been looking for. "*Bore da*, Linq."

"*Bore da*, Etain. You're up early."

She smirked. "Oh, aye. I need to get moving. How soon do you think we can have everyone ready to go?"

"An hour, maybe sooner. Has something happened?"

"Just a dream."

He seemed to understand and turned. "I'll see to it."

3

PORTAL TO HELL

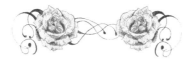

In less than an hour, the whole troop was packed and in their saddles. This being her first time seeing everyone together, Etain turned to Inferno. "This is it? I thought we'd at least have a platoon of Blades."

Inferno shrugged, nudging his mount next to hers. "Covert is what they said." He nodded in Linq's direction. "Limit our casualties."

She met the elf's casual gaze. "Are you fucking kidding me? This is Dar. He thinks of you as family." She addressed each one as she spoke. "We only have one chance to save him and this is what you decide? This guy is a psycho! We'll be lucky if we don't *all* become casualties." With that, she jerked the reins. Giving Razz a strong jab, she broke into a full-on gallop, easily widening the gap between the others. Etain disappeared into the distance, her hair waving in the wind like a silver flag.

"By the stars!" Taurnil jerked his reins and nudged his mount into a run.

Inferno glared at the others, then spurred his own horse. Try as he might to catch them, he finally gave up and watched as Razz barreled toward a small inlet, Taurnil not far behind.

The elf caught up to her just as they reached the water's edge. Etain reined in the chestnut, jumped from the saddle, and ran into the water.

"Etain!" Taurnil was by her side in a split second. "What was all that about?"

"You tell me!" She turned on him. "The High Lord of Kaos has been kidnapped and tortured. Every fucking Blade should be here. Instead, they send out a handful of...of..." She threw up her hands. "I'm so angry I can't even think straight. They have no idea what he's fighting."

"Maybe you should tell them. No one has seen what you have."

She ran a hand through her hair. "It's too horrible, T. I don't know if I can say the words to make them understand."

Inferno reined up and dismounted, grabbing a blanket and a flask of whiskey. "Get yer arses out of the water," he yelled.

"The only way they'll understand is to tell them, E."

After kicking water at the elf, they walked onto shore. Inferno handed her the blanket, then opened the flask. "I'm of the same mind, lass. But we were losing time."

Etain took a drink. "It's too late now. Dar can't afford for us to waste any more time." She handed the flask to Taurnil. "We have to get him safe. We can deal with the bastard who took him later."

"I like the sound of that." Inferno turned, hearing the others. "Let's set up camp."

"Y'all go ahead. There's someone I need to talk to." The two men stood their ground, doubtful looks on their faces. She rolled her eyes. "Someone in camp. I swear. I'm not going anywhere."

Inferno pointed at his eyes, then at her.

"Yeah, yeah. I know. I'll be along in a bit." She watched as the two reluctantly walked away, each one glancing back at her now and then. Once they were otherwise engaged, she went in search of Linq for the second time that morning. She was glad to find him with the horses...alone.

"Would you walk with me?"

He raised a brow, then nodded and walked with her toward the shore. Etain looked around to ensure they'd not been followed. "Do you remember any of the chants Dar used to open the demon portals?"

He shot her a sideways glance. "Why?"

"I have to find a way to him. He's so traumatized, he's not any help. I'm totally lost."

"Are you not going to rant and rave at me for the decision we made?"

She placed her hands on her hips. "I have more important matters to deal with, like the words to open that godforsaken portal."

"What makes you think it's a demon portal?"

"You'll have to trust me on that one."

Linq raised a brow. "What do you wish to know?"

Her hands dropped to her sides. "Whatever it takes to get to Dar."

His eyes darted here and there, as if the right chant would appear in the air before him. "Let's try this."

Etain copied his every syllable, every movement, but nothing happened. Same thing with the next chant. And the one after that.

They spent the rest of the morning working on various chants. Linq suggested mixing words from different ones, changing the emphasis, altering the timbre of her voice. She sang. She whispered. She screamed. The only things they accomplished were raw nerves and dry throats.

"God!" Etain stomped her foot. "What the hell am I missing?"

"Let's take a break." Linq draped an arm over her shoulders. "Perhaps some lunch, then a little distraction? Give our minds a rest."

"A distraction? How do you propose to do that?"

"Dancing."

With a furrowed brow, she pulled away. "I think you've spoken one too many chants, my friend."

A glint in his eyes, he laughed. "Perhaps we can pick up a sword or two? Make it interesting?"

A knowing smirk came to her lips. "That, I would be happy to do, milord."

Taurnil caught up to them as they entered camp. Etain smiled and shared with him their attempts to open the portal. As they walked toward the rest of the group, he offered his assistance with the next set of trial chants. Sharing a light lunch around the fire, the conversation soon turned to the dilemma they faced.

"Dar gets weaker every time I speak to him," Etain said. "Whatever pushed him over the edge must have been intense. I've never seen him this way. And how he's been treated…" She looked away, running a hand through her hair.

Taurnil gently bumped his shoulder against hers. "Tell them straight, E. Don't hold back."

She closed her eyes, took a deep breath, then eyed each one as she shared what she'd seen. The blood, his broken arm, his busted face… his back in shreds. "He won't heal himself. At this point, I don't know if he can. If we don't find him soon, I'm afraid I'll lose him."

"We won't give up until we find the right words," Taurnil said. "Don't worry. We'll find him in time."

"Aye," agreed the others.

Done with the midday meal, they broke into groups to work with their weapons. Etain practiced with Dar's black blades, certain they would give her an edge. Her first partner, Taurnil, zigged and zagged, striking with a parry here, landing a foot to her backside there. At one point, he knocked Day Star from her left hand, circled around her back, and struck at her right side. Rather than making the expected move of turning to her left, she blocked his blade from the right. They staggered apart, staring at one another. Taurnil shook his head and raised his sword into a downward slash. Etain moved to her left, bringing Burning Heart up in another loud clash. They pushed each other, neither gaining an advantage. In the end, they called it a draw and parted.

After a refreshing drink of water, Etain engaged with Linq while Taurnil worked with Elfin. They all spent the afternoon trading partners in preparation for the battle sure to come. Toward the end of the day, Arachnia and Etain faced each other. It took every ounce of Etain's skill to fend off Arachnia's attacks. The two completed the practice in a draw, Etain's blades locked in the tines of her opponent's pitchfork, both breathing heavily, a glare in their eyes. Everyone else stopped what they were doing to watch the two women, waiting for something…violent.

With narrowed eyes, Etain pushed her swords at Arachnia. "How about a brew?"

Her expression just as fierce, Ara lifted her pitchfork a small degree. "Something with a kick?"

"Would I offer anything less to such a worthy opponent?"

"Sounds absolutely fabulous."

Suddenly, the two laughed and disentangled their weapons. Etain draped an arm over Arachnia's shoulders as they walked off. "Impressive moves, milady. Care to teach me a few?"

The others in the camp looked at one another, shrugged, and went back to what they'd been doing.

The next few days were spent much the same way - working on portal chants in the mornings, weapons practice in the afternoons, discussions of strategies in the evenings. Sleep came quickly at the end of the day. Constantly haunted by Dar, Etain visited him as often as she could, accompanied by either the white unicorn or the red panther. Although Dar never recognized her as his wife, he eventually accepted her as a comforting spirit. Despite his acceptance, his condition worsened with each passing day, the dark circles under his eyes turning into black bruises. The open wounds on his back oozed as his blond hair darkened to black.

One good thing did come from the heart-wrenching moments. Dar unwittingly provided her the chant to open the portal.

Realizing the importance of the words, she woke. It was early morning, the sky dark. All except the sentries were asleep. Not wanting to disturb anyone, she quietly stood up and shimmered to the shore.

At the water's edge, she closed her eyes and repeated the words she received through Dar.

She opened an eye, hoping to find a change in the air in front of her. Nothing. Closing her eyes again, she increased her concentration, raised her hands to the sky, and turned to the water. She adjusted the emphasis on different words, chanting repeatedly.

Linq showed up at one point to tell her of his communication with Alatariel. He contacted her in the hopes she could shed light on the right incantation for a demon portal. Unfortunately, she wasn't able to help.

"Dar gave me the words." At the hopeful look on the elf's face, she held up a hand. "Not on purpose. I was able to link into the moment the portal opened. It didn't last long, though. It only just occurred to me this morning the importance of the words, but I must be missing something. I've been saying them over and over, but nothing happens." As she pushed her hair from her face, she dropped down, sitting on the ground.

"Take a break, Etain. Have you eaten?"

"I can't eat." She popped up, pacing along the shore. "I know where he is," she said, her voice getting louder, "but I can't bloody get to him!"

"Etain, keep your wits about you. You won't be any help to him if you lose control."

She whirled on him, eyes flashing. "Maybe that's just what I need to do. Lose control. Go nuts. Start my own war in every demon realm I can find until someone tells me how to get to him."

"That would not be wise."

"I don't care about anything except getting Dar out of that hellhole. Every passing second, he slips farther away from us. I can't get through to him."

"You *do* care. That's why you're driving yourself so hard. It's not an easy task when faced with such an adversary."

She growled. "I don't want to hear common sense. You haven't seen him. He's killing himself because he thinks I'm dead. I want to annihilate the fucking bastard who's done this." She stopped pacing. The intensity in her voice increased with each word. "I want to see *his* blood stain the ground. I want to lay the fucking whip to *his* back until it hangs in shreds. He has no right to do this to him! To us!"

Hearing her declarations, the others ran to the shore where they found Linq having a hell of a time fighting to hold onto her. "Let me go, Linq! I have to find him. I have to-"

Inferno moved in. With one swift right to her jaw, he knocked her out. "That should do it."

Taurnil glared at him. Linq rolled his eyes. "Well, it's done now. Let's get back to camp." He handed her limp form to Inferno, who hoisted her over his shoulder like a sack of potatoes.

Indignant, the younger elf bellowed, "That's not the way to treat the High Lady, sir. Give her to me."

Inferno walked away, his package in tow. "When she starts acting like the High Lady, then we'll see about it. But I'm not making any promises."

An outraged Taurnil turned to the older elf. "Linq!"

"Don't worry," he said. "He'll take good care of her."

At the camp, Etain peacefully slept in her bedroll near the fire. Inferno sat close by in conversation with Wolfe. As Linq and Taurnil approached, he motioned them to sit. "What was that about?"

"According to Etain, Dar thinks she's dead and is ready to end his life," Linq said quietly.

Inferno stared into the fire. "One thing's been bothering me. The blasted ring. How the hell did it get to the clearing?"

"Maybe it has something to do with that Faux woman," Arachnia said, joining the men. "Maybe she passed the ring to the one who's taken Dar."

Sitting on the other side of the fire, Freeblood came to Faux's defense. "How the hell could she do that? And why? Besides, no one else could've entered the compound without one of us seeing."

"Come on, Freeblood," Arachnia said. "Do you honestly believe she was talking to herself in Spirit's herb room? We all know she was destroying the protection spell around the castle. Who knows what happened while it was weak."

Freeblood jumped to his feet, but Inferno stepped in. "Calm down, boy. We'll find out soon enough what happened there." He looked at Arachnia. "The girl isn't such a bad sort. Maybe she thought she was doing something to help."

Arachnia's eyes nearly bulged out of her head. "Are you *kidding* me? You weren't there. You didn't hear what I heard." She glared at Freeblood. "He did and knows damn well she was up to no good."

A prudent Linq changed the subject. "You know who we haven't seen for some time? Etain's brother. With everything going on, I'd forgotten about him. Has anyone seen him?"

Inferno stoked his chin. "Bloody hell. I think the last time I saw him was the night Etain and Dar returned from LOKI. He's either lying low or dead somewhere."

"Can he be trusted?" Freeblood asked, sitting again.

"Well, the boy did give me the twitch when I met him," Inferno said.

"I have to agree," Linq nodded. "Something's not quite right there."

"He needs to be found…for Etain's sake," Taurnil said. "Inferno, can you get a couple of your clansmen to search for him?"

"I can send a message to BadMan."

"Thank you. If she mentions it, at least we can tell her we're searching."

Arachnia turned the conversation back to the main reason for their journey. "I'd still like to know why this…demon, for lack of a better word, wants Etain rather than Dar. He's the strongest but he's been tossed aside. What is it about her that makes her more valuable?"

Everyone around the fire exchanged glances, but no one had an answer.

"Okay… We'll save that for later." Arachnia stood, turning to each one as she spoke. "Should we get this portal to open, what then? We've had a lot of conjecture flying around the campfire the past few nights but nothing concrete."

"Linq and me were talking about this earlier," Inferno said. "We don't know what to expect once we step through that portal. I'm thinking we should break into small groups and spread out, make it harder to pin us down. It's all up for discussion, but…" He looked directly at Taurnil. "You will stick to our girl like glue. Understood?"

Taurnil displayed a Dar-like grin. "Oh, aye."

Inferno raised a brow. "Yer smilin' now, laddie, but if anything happens to her, it'll be yer head we come for."

His grin never faltered. "Aye, milord."

"Hmph. Time will tell." Inferno's gaze roamed over the others. "Anyone have anything to add or a better idea?" Murmurs of "no" and "sounds good to me" carried through the group. "Good. For the rest of us, our main objective will be to clear the way for 'em. I don't know who we're up against, but it's safe to say they aren't gonna be happy about us treadin' in their territory. So, until we get the all-clear for the portal, keep working on yer skills. We're gonna need everthing we got."

In the next moment, everyone around the campfire jumped, hearing Etain's blood-curdling screams.

"Holy shite!" Inferno yelled, running after Taurnil, who was the first on his feet.

Sliding to his knees, the young elf wrapped his arms around her to keep her from hurting herself. Despite his efforts, her body jerked with every scream. A scratch appeared on one cheek, then the other, and she held out her hands as though they were bound together. Bruises formed on her wrists and tears poured from her eyes.

Taurnil looked at Linq. "What do I do? This is insane!"

While the allies discussed their plans, Etain fell deeper into her dreams, calling for the white unicorn to take her to Dar. Before long, she found herself immersed in his being, overcome by his weakness and despair.

"Dar, my love. I'm trying to find my way to you, but the words don't work. Something's missing. I need your help."

"My Etain waits for me, waiting until I come to the end of my road to join her. It will not be long now."

"Dar, I am Etain. I'm trying to rescue you from this hell."

His chuckle sounded more like a groan. "I saw her die by my own hand. Thank you for your kindness in my last days. I do not deserve it."

Etain closed her eyes, biting her bottom lip. How can he believe he killed me?

She took his face into her hands. "Ionmhain, tá tú a chur ar ghaiscíoch láidir. Tá do chroí sin de leon. Nuair a bhíonn an t-am ceart, beidh mé tú a leanúint chun báis agus ina dhiaidh, ach ní lá atá inniu ann, mo fhear céile milis (Beloved, you are a strong warrior. Your heart is that of a lion. When the time is right, I will follow you to death and beyond, but not today, my sweet husband). Show me what happened that day."

Dar took in a ragged breath. "She is gone. I will not relive her passing. It is too painful."

"Show me so I can prove to you that Etain lives."

"Do not ask this of me. I cannot bear it."

His heartache ripped into her, but she had to break through his despair to save him. Her jaw clenched, she pushed him with her questions. "Do you think your death will end the terror? What about your friends and their families? Do you think this monster will stop once you're gone?" She paused, letting her words fall where they may. "He'll keep killing until all the good is extinguished. No one will be able to stop him."

"No..."

"What about Inferno and Spirit? Think of their beautiful children. Seth. Molly. Dylan. Tegan. She's only three years old, Dar. Can you imagine a beautiful three-year-old little girl? Her chubby little legs and round, red cheeks framed by brown curls... Shall she suffer the same fate as

your Victoria? Should Spirit have to suffer like Alexia, witnessing the deaths of her children?"

A growl came from deep within his chest. "You are a harbinger of misery, the devil's witch come to torture me until I die."

Breathing shallow breaths, she waited. This has to work. I know his heart. Minutes passed, her resolve weakening with every tick of the clock in her head. Eventually, a dim light appeared, brightening onto that horrible day.

Dar slammed the hilts of Day Star and Burning Heart together, spinning his lethal blades through the throng of demons. With the expertise of an accomplished swordsman, he separated the swords and turned with Day Star in the lead, slicing through a body set in their deadly path.

Her heart stopped. She saw her image slide apart in pieces, just as her mother had all those years ago. She couldn't breathe. Darkness threatened to steal her resolve, but she sensed Dar sinking with her.

No! Pull yourself together, Etain! This is not his day to die.

She pushed down her grief and willed him to remember the rest. His body jerked at the intrusion, but he returned to the scene.

His beautiful wife dead by his hand, his black blades fell to his sides, blood running down his arms while tears flowed over his cheeks. Etain could hear the ugly taunt spoken by someone nearby. Infuriated by the gloat in the words, she tried to turn her head, but her efforts were hampered by seeing everything from Dar's perspective. Her gaze returned to the butchered image, watching smoke rise as the demon body disintegrated. An object, tossed amongst the ashes, caught her eye. She saw what Dar refused to acknowledge - her ring. Had he seen it, he would've quite possibly realized the game played at his expense.

Circumstances didn't allow her to dwell on its significance. Dar raised his dagger above his head. The blade plummeted toward his heart, but strong hands grabbed his arms, preventing its completion. Shackles, clamped onto his wrists and ankles, cut into his flesh, making him drop his instrument of salvation. He took no notice. His empty gaze rested on the pile of ashes.

They dragged his body across the clearing and strapped him to a contraption she couldn't see. With a great lurch, his body jerked forward, then stopped. A demon appeared and ripped the scabbard from his back and tossed it aside. They started off again. His brain immune to the pain, Dar lost himself in his fantasies. Etain screamed in his stead, the dirt and rocks cutting into shared flesh

Dar's body jolted to a sudden stop, his bloodied head dipping to the side. His eyes open, nothing registered, but Etain saw everything. An imposing demon with radiant red skin surveyed the road before them. She gasped, recognizing him from the tunnels beneath Midir's castle. The castle she now knew belonged to this...son of his. "Dathmet."

Facing his prisoner, his red eyes gave her a start. She was confused. They were black when she first met him, green more recently. Salivating over his prize, Dathmet spoke the words to open the portal.

"Dar," she pushed into his dark mind, "you hold on a little longer, baby. Don't you die on me."

Coming back to herself, she woke to a pair of strong arms around her and a multitude of eyes staring at her. She looked over her shoulder into Taurnil's golden eyes. Her lips moved, but her throat constricted.

"Water," Taurnil said, looking at the group. "Someone get some water."

Freeblood pushed through, canteen in hand. "Here."

The elf put it to Etain's lips. "Take it slow."

Somewhat better, she found Linq's concerned face. "I can open the portal," she croaked, pushing against Taurnil's arms. His grip tightened as Inferno placed a hand on her shoulder.

"Yer not going anywhere right now, lass."

"But I have to-"

"Ya have to get some food in yer belly and rest. We'll tackle that portal in the morning," Inferno said.

"You don't understand…"

"You have no idea what you've just endured, E." This time it was Taurnil. "Look at your wrists."

She gasped, seeing the dark bruises. But just as quickly, they began to disappear.

"This didn't happen to me." Her tears returned as she looked at Taurnil, then Inferno. "This happened to Dar."

"Well, if you've discovered the secret to the portal…," said Taurnil. "you'll want to be in your best form. You're going to need all your strength to face whatever's on the other side." His gaze roamed over everyone around them. "We all are."

She sighed, leaning against the young elf. "You're right."

"Eh?" Inferno placed a hand around an ear, leaning toward her. "What was that? I think me hearing's a bit off. I coulda sworn I just-"

"Aye! You're right," she said and stuck out her tongue.

Inferno and the others laughed. "That's me girl. Let's get our lass some food. We have plans to make."

Everyone except Taurnil returned to their seats around the fire, sharing in the evening meal. Freeblood soon came back with enough food for three. Taurnil let her sit on her own, but not too far away.

"I heard y'all talking about the portal earlier." She picked at the food, letting the men eat most of it. "Has Inferno or Linq cooked up any hare-brained ideas?"

"We're just gonna cut a trail for you and Taurnil," Freeblood said. "But, if you don't mind, I'd rather go with you two."

She looked across the campfire. "Inferno, Freeblood's going with us. You all right with that?"

"That leaves Arachnia on her own."

"It's okay, Inferno," Arachnia said. "I like it that way. In my transformed state, I'm harder to detect and can move faster."

Inferno shook his head. "No one is going in alone, not even an undetectable scorpion. I'm willing to bet Elfin and the Blades won't have any trouble keeping up with ya."

She opened her mouth, but the look in his eyes made her think better of it. "Fine." She turned a skeptical gaze on Elfin. "I'm not waiting for anyone. I don't care what the excuse." She stood and tossed the remnants of her meal into the fire. "If you can't keep up, you're on your own." Adding her dishes to the pile, she stalked off into the dark.

Wolfe gave Elfin a fair impression of Arachnia's evil eye. "If I were you, I'd start now."

"You're telling me. I think I'll sleep on my horse to make sure," Elfin said, laughing with him.

Done with their meal, the group cleaned up and settled in for the night. Etain was one of the first to fall asleep, warm and cozy in her bedroll. Linq pulled Taurnil to the side for a private conversation.

"Pardon for speaking my mind, milord, but I don't understand why you're here. You should be in Nunnehi." He held up a hand to silence the young elf. "However, since you are, I hope you realize how serious your charge is. We cannot fail. *She* cannot fail."

"I've known you all my life, Linq. If you didn't speak your mind, I'd be worried." The shadow of a smile crossed his lips. "I am aware of what's at stake. She will not breathe that I won't know the length and depth of it." His expression turned solemn. "This is my family. I won't let anything happen to either of them."

Linq considered him for a long moment. "Aye. I've known you since you were born, watched you grow into an impressive young elf. There's always been a strong resemblance to Dar. Not only in your features, but in your mannerisms, as well. If I hadn't personally known your father, I'd have sworn… Well… Never mind." He clapped him on the back. "Let's get to sleep. Tomorrow will be a long, tedious day, especially for you and Etain."

"Thanks, Linq. I won't disappoint you or the lady."

They parted company for the evening. Taurnil placed his bedroll next to the sleeping Etain, while Linq bedded down not far away. Silence soon fell over the site as the warriors closed their eyes on the peaceful evening.

4

CASTLE OF BLOOD

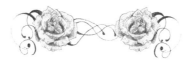

Before sunrise the next morning, Etain was the first to wake. She quietly walked away from camp toward the inlet, left her clothes on the shore, and slipped into the cold water. Her body came alive as she floated on the tiny waves, the chill raising gooseflesh over her skin. Lulled by the rocking motion, she kicked her feet and swam to a small outcropping of land. As she pushed up onto the rocks and stretched out, she noticed the translucency of her skin.

Maybe it's another side-effect of becoming the High Lady of Kaos.

An hour later, when the morning sun peeked out from behind the horizon, she dove into the water and returned to the shore, dressed, and headed back to camp.

The smell of bacon frying made her stomach growl. Intent on breakfast, she didn't notice the young elf until he stepped in her path.

"Taurnil!" She laughed. "Where'd you come from?"

"I've been behind you since you stepped into camp. Where have you been?" His perusal of her was somewhat curious, mainly affronted. "I hope this isn't an indication of how the day's going to go."

She appreciated the stern look on his face and tried to wipe the smile from hers. "Don't look so grim. I needed to clear my mind, so I went for a swim." Linking an arm with his, she turned him toward the campfire. "Let's get some breakfast."

"*Bore da*, Etain, Taurnil," Inferno said upon their approach. "Ya look to be in good spirits this morning, lass. Have a good sleep?"

"*Bore da*, Inferno, everyone." Etain smiled at every face around the fire. "It was peaceful, thank goodness." Accepting a full plate, she sat next to Taurnil, across from Linq. "After breakfast, I'll need a little time to limber up with Dar's blades, if that's okay."

"Tell us when yer ready." Inferno sat next to Linq, dipping his bread into his eggs.

"There's something I need to tell you before we open that portal." Etain's serious tone caught their attention. "The bastard who has Dar was at Midir's." She took another bite of food, letting her words sink in.

Inferno looked at Linq, then back at Etain. "What're ya saying, lass?"

She chewed the food in her mouth, then swallowed before she answered. "I saw him when Dar came to save me. You know…" Suddenly, she lost her appetite and set her plate on the ground. "The whole Midir debacle. I haven't told anyone, not even Dar."

Taurnil touched her arm. "The more we know, the better prepared we'll be."

She nodded, giving him a slight smile. "Midir disappeared into a labyrinth of tunnels beneath his castle. I went after him, intent on ending his life. He was supposed to be *my* kill." Her gaze met Inferno's. "Dar killed the assassin who murdered my family, but it was Midir who hired him."

A flame lit in his eyes. "And ya didn't think it important enough to tell me?"

"No." She saw past the anger in his eyes to the hurt that burned more brightly. "Yes. Shit!" She stood up, running a hand through her hair. "A lot was going on when we returned to Laugharne - the High Council, Freeblood, then the wedding and the stuff afterward. There just wasn't a good time."

"My bloody-"

"Inferno…" Linq cut off his ensuing tirade. "Let's not waste time rehashing the past. Let her talk." Inferno huffed, giving the elf the dirtiest look he could muster, but he didn't say another word. Linq gave her a nod. "Go ahead, Etain."

She stared at Inferno, who wouldn't meet her gaze. "Dar fell into a nasty trap Midir had set for him. Some creepy monster from Krymeria." Her eyes slid to Linq as she returned to her seat. "Midir thought he was dead, but Dar killed the creature, caught up to us, and started a fight. In the end, Midir ran again. Dar went after him." Etain blew out a breath. "I was gonna go after them when this…demon appeared. He had to be a demon. His skin was the color of blood and his head…" She pushed the hair from her face. "The top of his head was covered in flames. Flames! And his teeth… They were like fangs. All of them."

Taurnil took hold of her hand. "It's okay, E."

Inferno looked at her. "Did he hurt ya?"

"No. He laughed and went back the way he'd come. I didn't see him again."

"He's the one who's taken Dar?"

"Aye."

"How the hell did that happen?"

"A glamour." The three men shared confused looks. "He glamoured a demon, made it look like me. Once Dar believed he'd killed me, the asshole tossed my ring into the ashes. I don't know how he got his hands on it." Etain came to her feet again. "If we don't get to Dar soon, he'll be dead. Let me get warmed up, then we can go."

Inferno clapped his hands, setting everyone in motion. "Let's get ready to move."

Within a half-hour, Etain retraced her footsteps to the shore, the others following. She closed her eyes and increased her height to her full seven feet, her great wings spanning out behind her. When her eyes opened, she cast a dazzling silver glow over the company. They all stared, some staggering back at the impact of her change. Even Inferno and Linq, who had seen her change before, watched in awe. Taurnil was completely mesmerized.

Arms lifted to the skies, Etain chanted the words so recently discovered from Dar. The winds stirred, the waves rolled onto the shore. A shimmer formed to the left of her, spreading into an oval of glimmering darkness. She lowered her arms and turned to the group. "Y'all take care. I'm gonna need every one of you when this is over… and so will Dar. Let's go get him."

Etain stepped through the portal. Freeblood motioned Taurnil and the Black Blades next, then Arachnia and Elfin, followed by the others. As they stepped onto the grey dirt, puffs of dust drifted toward the murky clouds overhead. In the distance, a dark stain of a castle stood out against the desolate landscape.

"Cheap and cheerful, it isn't," Inferno said, shielding his eyes from the dull glare off the clouds.

"Gives hostile a whole new meaning," Wolfe quipped.

Elfin grimaced. "Glad we aren't staying long."

At the head of the group, Etain turned. "It looks pretty straightforward, but let me scope it out with a quick fly-by. Knowing the lay of the land will give us some advantage."

"Something tells me there's nothing straightforward about this place," said Linq.

"All the more reason-" Prepared to lift off, a hand caught her by the arm.

Taurnil's gaze bored into hers. "Not without me."

"We don't have time for this."

"Then stop wasting it."

She looked at Linq and Inferno, who merely shrugged. "Fine. Come closer."

When she wrapped an arm around Taurnil's waist, he placed an arm around her neck. She spread her wings for a quick takeoff but couldn't generate enough thrust to lift from the ground. "For a mythical creature, you're awfully heavy."

Taurnil feigned insult. "Mythical?" He looked down at his frame. "This, milady, is pure legend."

She rolled her eyes and released him. "Either way, you're too heavy to just pick up. Step away from the others and prepare yourself."

Taurnil watched her soar into the sky. "For what?" In the next moment, she swooped down, grabbed him around the waist, and they were airborne.

"By the stars!" he exclaimed, watching the ground speed past them.

She smiled. "How's the legend?"

Somewhat manic, he laughed. "Awestruck."

Closer to the castle, they discovered details not readily noticeable at a distance. The walls, constructed of a red stone, stood at least three stories high, their corners tapering into four turrets. The rooftops of the turrets were covered in skulls, blackened by the elements. As they came around from the north, the setting sun emblazoned the red walls, making them appear like freshly spilled blood. Etain shivered, sensing the evil contained within the walls themselves. Seeing the manicured courtyard and the two large, black stones at its center, she and Taurnil exchanged a look.

"Do you see what I see?" she asked, circling around.

"Rather unusual."

"They must know we're here. We have to be extra careful."

"Agreed."

The couple returned to the others, landing softly on the dead earth. Etain released Taurnil, who stumbled a few steps before he found his footing. "The walls are at least three stories high with a courtyard in the center. We didn't see anyone, but I suggest we move with great care. If this demon trained with Midir, he'll use surprise. And do not, under any circumstances, touch the red walls. They're pure evil."

"Aye," Inferno said. "We're ready, lass."

"I have one trick that may help us get into the castle." Etain reached into her shirt, pulling out a small vial from between her breasts.

Linq recognized it immediately. "A glamour?"

She flashed a conspiratorial smile. "If that bastard can use one on Dar, we can use one on him." She turned to Arachnia. "You want to work alone?" Arachnia gave her a quick nod, anticipation in her eyes. "Then work as my double. Take on this glamour and give me the time I need to locate Dar."

"Allow me to transform before you douse the potion over me. My touch will be more lethal."

"Good thinking, Arachnia," Etain said, uncorking the vial.

"Please, call me Ara."

Everyone stepped back, giving the young woman the space needed to transform. A great black stinger extended from her backside as her rib cage expanded, allowing two more sets of arms to elongate, each hand equipped with five claws. Her teeth lengthened to dagger-like fangs. Intense black eyes peered back at the group.

Etain poured the sparkling glamour into one hand, then held out her other to Ara. "We're going to switch places. You'll be me and I'll be you. The real you…not the scorpion."

The creature gently took her hand in one of her clawed ones and gave her what Etain interpreted as a grin. "Good thinking, Etain."

"Call me E."

She tossed the granules into the air, chanting as the glitter dusted over their bodies. Ara transformed into Etain's twin and vice versa. A gasp ran through the onlookers as the black eyes turned ice-blue and the talons disappeared into human hands. Looking at Etain, she now had Ara's brown hair and deep blue eyes.

"Godspeed." Etain gave her a hug. "Please, take care and come back alive."

Ara answered with a wicked smile and turned, taking off toward the castle. Linq cocked his head at Elfin, who was after her in a flash, then turned to Etain. "We wouldn't send our High Lady out alone, would we?"

"I guess not. We need to move quickly. I have to find Dar before they realize they've been duped." Taurnil, Etain, and Freeblood moved toward the right side of the castle.

The rest headed toward the left, all with the intention of meeting in the center at the large gates.

Commander Thamuz stepped into Dathmet's quarters. He found his master busy at his desk, scribbling on sheets of paper. "Have a seat, Thamuz." Without looking up, Dathmet motioned him to one of the chairs in front of the desk. "I have a few things we need to cover before everything goes down. Is there any change in the prisoner?"

"Not for the better, milord. He sinks deeper into his delusions and refuses to eat. My men have tried to force-feed him, but he still has enough strength to fend them off. He is impressive."

Dathmet's head snapped up. "There is nothing *impressive* about a weakling who breaks over the loss of a woman. He's pathetic."

Thamuz steepled his hands, eyeing the young demon. "A woman you're willing to risk everything to possess, milord."

Instead of anger, he was met with acceptance. "You have me there, Thamuz. I suppose if I were to lose such a woman, I would break, too. Thankfully, she'll be here soon and we can get rid of him."

The commander's lips curled in an evil smile. "Yes. Then we can begin."

Dathmet folded the papers, sealing them with his waxed seal - a winged serpent spitting fire. He handed the papers to his commander. "This is for Raum, should things not go quite as planned."

Thamuz raised his brows. "Surely, you don't expect to lose. Everything is set for a perfect execution. We've already obtained two of the Alamir stones and are working on a third. Our hit squads are in full swing, creating havoc in the human realm, as well as the Alamir. And now our prize is about to walk through our front door."

"I fully expect to be the victor. However, never underestimate your opponent, especially in this instance." Standing, Dathmet turned toward the massive window behind his desk, his thoughts on his most recent encounter with the lady. "She is a magnificent being, much more than a mere woman. In her demon persona… My god, she's breathtaking." He turned, his hair of flames glowing brighter than usual. "The blood, the sheer power coursing through her veins... We will be unstoppable."

"I look forward to meeting her, milord."

Dathmet cocked his head, as though listening to something in the air. A sudden knock interrupted their conversation. "Come," he commanded. The door opened and a young man stepped into the room. "Ah, Togor. Have you news?"

"Yes, milord." The lieutenant saluted his commanding officers. "They have split into groups. The lady you seek comes directly toward the castle. Alone."

A delighted smile spread across Dathmer's face as he mulled over the information. "I seriously doubt she comes alone. Keep a close watch. There's sure to be an escort of some sort."

"Yes, milord."

As Togor turned to leave, Dathmet asked another question. "Lieutenant, has our honored prisoner been relocated to the great hall?"

"Yes, milord. Shackled and submissive."

"Excellent. Notify me once she has discovered our little surprise."

With a salute, Lieutenant Togor returned to his duties. Dathmet flashed a smile toward his commander. "Let's set our welcome in motion."

Since the land was flat and devoid of vegetation, the teams were able to keep each other in sight. Their movements were quick, hoping to cover as much ground as possible before detection.

Arachnia and Elfin slowed to a walk as the great black gates came into view. "It's too easy, Elfin."

"It's not what I would expect from a demon like this." They stopped, examining the castle from across the barren land. All appeared still and quiet.

"Well, we've come this far. I suppose we'll deal with whatever comes." Arachnia led the way to the huge gates. "Now what?"

A sudden war cry made them turn. A double row of demons dressed in armor rose up from the ground. The first row held unlit torches, while the second carried swords. A demon at the end breathed a flame, lighting the torch of his neighbor, who shared his flame with the next until all the torches were alight.

The fires reflected off the finely sharpened swords as the demons beat their weapons against their armor, creating a hair-raising ruckus. Arachnia and Elfin looked at each other. He drew his sword as he sprinted into the fray, then looked to his side to ensure he and Arachnia were in sync. Instead, he found himself alone. He looked to his other side, thinking she'd gone behind him.

"Damn!" Intent on retracing his steps, he turned, but demons blocked his way.

Elfin lunged with an upper cut, slashed to his side, then jabbed at those closest to him, slashing at anything that stepped in his path. His sword raised for another kill, he came face to face with a familiar grin but was too far into his move to stop. Wolfe proved the quicker of the two and deflected the attack.

"There you are, ya wee pup. Thought you'd run off to hide with the girlie."

Horrified and relieved, Elfin realized he'd broken through the line of demons. "Cheeky bastard. I couldn't leave you out here alone. I know how bad you suck with the sword."

They laughed and turned, standing back to back. Elfin grounded another demon with a hard kick to the knee and a well-placed elbow to the head.

Wolfe stabbed out, sending another demon to hell. "Ha! We'll see who sucks at the end of the day."

They swept through the throng, clearing a path for their friends. One by one, they slipped through, coming up on the rear of their attackers. With the castle now at their backs, the allies slowly advanced, fending off the demons.

Having been dragged through the main gates, Arachnia, still disguised within the glamour, was taken through the front courtyard and to the main doors, down a large hallway, then unceremoniously dumped in the great hall. The demon escort left and locked the door behind them before she had the chance to take a slice at either one. Infuriated, she slammed her fists against the door and let out a high-pitched screech.

Her keen senses picked up the smell of blood and filth. She covered her nose as she scanned the room for the source of the foul stench. Eight stone columns carried the room, four on each long wall, evenly spaced. Small sconces, two between each of the great columns, cast a soft light throughout the room. The walls sported various accoutrements of weaponry and tools of torture, graceful ivory-handled katanas, rapiers, huge axes with wicked blades, whips of all designs, and an array of swords the young Alamir had never seen.

A faint rustling of chains drew her gaze to the far end of the hall. She slid behind the nearest column and peeked around it, then moved to the next one, slowly making her way to the end of the room. The smell grew stronger with each step. The chains clinked again, followed by a heavy breath. Inching her face around the final column, she peered at the grotesque figure chained to the wall. Her breath caught in her throat.

"Dar?"

The shabby beard on the man made her unsure. She'd never seen Dar unshaven, but it had to be him. The stench forgotten, she raced across the divide and slid to her knees, her only thought to free him. She tried to catch his eye, but he didn't notice, even as she gently lifted his chin. Sudden tears stung her eyes. "Oh, my dear friend. They will pay for this."

His one good eye stared off into an unseen distance. The once beautiful blond locks hung in dark strands over his face. Noticing one arm at an odd angle, she shifted for a better look, finding it broken with no attempts to repair the damage. A black rage rose within her when she saw the cruel lashes across his back.

She cupped his face in her hands. "I know the monster is to be Etain's kill, but I'm going to save her the effort. *I* will kill him for you, my sweet friend, and the woman you love so dearly. Watch as I shred him into tiny bits."

"Who the hell are you?" a voice boomed from behind.

Her anger flashed, but the sight of Dar cooled her blood enough to regain her composure. She slowly stood and turned, lifting her head high. What met her gaze made her stagger. Dressed in a dark suit and finely-pointed shoes stood a flame-haired, red-skinned demon, his eyes as dark as his suit. Her gaze took him in from head to toe and back again. Her brain raced, doing its best to control the hammering of her heart.

"I am the Lady Etain and have come for my husband. Release him at once."

Laughter barreled through the large hall. "A lady you may be, but you are *not* the Lady Etain."

Further enraged by his behavior, she walked toward him, lusting to slash his throat. "What are you laughing at, you red-faced hyena? Release my husband. *Now*."

His eyes narrowed. "Your glamour does not fool me." With a wave of his hand, the illusion dissolved, pooling at Arachnia's feet. "Now, who the hell are you?"

"I am your grim reaper," she growled, rolling her shoulders.

"Yes, I see the grim." He eyed her from head to toe. "Come get me, reaper."

The bloodlust surged through her veins. Arachnia pounced, every talon aimed at the devil's throat. Dathmet transformed into a tower of flames. She passed through his form and landed gracefully on her feet. Spinning around, she launched again. This time, the demon jogged out of the way. As he turned, he drew a finely made katana, its blade blood red.

"I do hope the Lady Etain is as entertaining as you." He grinned, deflecting her talon strikes, then delivered a blow to her chest.

Ara dropped to the floor. He stepped closer, looking down his nose at her. Two of her hands grabbed his legs and pulled as another set interlocked with the blade, rendering it useless. The third pair swiped at his throat as he fell, but he ducked his head, the talons only grazing the side of his face.

"You'll join your friend in hell tonight, bitch." Able to pull free, he jumped to his feet, and purposefully strode toward Dar.

"*Noooo!*" she screamed, lunging at his back. The attack caught him off guard. His sword flew across the room and came to rest next to Dar. Close enough for the High Lord to grasp. "Dar!" she yelled. "Help me!"

Dathmet grabbed and pushed in his efforts to throw off the banshee screeching in his ears and tearing at his skin. He slammed her into a column as he shouted for his guards. The impact having no effect on the Alamir, Dathmet flamed his body. Arachnia yelped and collapsed.

"Dispose of this garbage." Freed from her clutches, he straightened his jacket and checked the cuffs. "Watch out for the fangs."

Seven guards surrounded the burnt Arachnia. Her black eyes darted from face to face, her lips curled over fanged teeth. Six took hold of each arm while the final guard grabbed a handful of hair and pulled her head back, rendering her fangs useless. "No!" she screeched, fighting to free herself. They lifted her and quickly exited the room.

Dathmet looked down at Dar as he grabbed his blade and put it away. He rolled his shoulders, then twisted his head from side to side. Hearing the pop of his neck, he took his time to crack each knuckle, one by one. By the time he was done with his exercise, his wounds were healed, seared by the flames of his body.

· · ·

Outside the great hall, five dark figures froze, their bodies pressed into the wall. Each one held their breath, hoping they would not be discovered by the guards who escorted a writhing Arachnia down the hall. After a concerted release of breath, Etain sent the Black Blades after them, their mission to rescue the courageous young woman. "Make sure no harm comes to her. Once she's free of her captors, head to the main gate and get out as quickly as you can. When I have Dar, we'll shimmer out. May your blades be swift and sure."

Riko and Sion saluted their High Lady with fisted hands over their hearts. "May the Krymerians of the past aid you in this darkest hour." They disappeared down the hall.

Etain, Taurnil, and Freeblood inched closer to the great hall. She placed a hand on the knob, giving her cohorts one last look before she opened the door.

It took several moments for their eyes to adjust to the dimness. The room reeked. All three covered their faces with their hands, trying not to gag.

Etain closed her eyes. *It's your time to be the savior. Don't let him down.*

Scoping out the large hall, she spied Dathmet standing over Dar. Quietly, she pulled the dagger from her boot, then hurled it. The blade sank deep into the demon's left shoulder.

Dathmet hissed, spinning on his heels. "Lady Etain. You're already more exciting than the last piece of meat I roasted." He pulled out the dagger and tossed it to the floor. "Come closer, *mon petit*. Let me smell you."

"You will not get near her," Taurnil growled through clenched teeth, stepping in front of her.

The demon of fire laughed. "My, my, Etain. You do have a way with the men. Who is this young pup?"

The young elf lifted his chin and spoke with great authority. "I am Taurnil of the Black Blades. You will not address my High Lady in such a manner."

Dathmet's gaze slid to Etain. "Black Blade?" He sneered. "An elf."

A fireball flew into Taurnil's stomach, heaving him across the room. Immediately, a flamed barrier rose up from the floor, trapping him inside. "Since you're so full of vigor for our High Lady, I'm willing to let you watch as I transform her into my genesis of eternal power. Then I shall enjoy watching her eat your heart."

Taurnil slammed his fists against the flames and screamed for his release, but no sound passed through the wall. The young Blade had to stand by helplessly and watch the events unfold.

"I hope she works up a big appetite," Freeblood said, making his presence known. "Cause *this* pup has a lot of heart." Dathmet's gaze snapped to the Alamir. "Weren't expecting me, were you?" Freeblood grinned. "Looks like I get to show you first-hand how well I handle this." Holding his hand in front of him, the blue glow in his palm spanned out into a fine-edged katana.

"A slight hiccup I'm sure we can dispose of." Dathmet twirled his sword from its hold.

"Freeblood," Etain kept her eyes on the red-skinned demon as she drew Day Star and Burning Heart. "Get Dar out of here. I'll take care of this."

"Etain-"

Her gaze jerked to Freeblood. "Get…Dar…out."

Dathmet laughed. "You can try. But…" Several guards came through the doors, "we've grown fond of the High Lord. His sense of humor is beyond compare."

Etain stepped closer to Freeblood. "Whatever happens, you get Dar out."

"I can't leave you here-"

Her glare left no room for argument. "Do it."

They turned toward the oncoming threat, blades flashing left, right, up, around, down.

"The woman is mine." Dathmet strolled closer to Dar. "You can kill the others."

The guards systematically split the pair apart. One group pushed Etain deeper into the hall, while the other worked Freeblood toward the door. Once he realized their plan, Freeblood fought even harder to get back inside, to no avail. Those who'd cornered Etain lowered their weapons and joined the others, ensuring the Alamir could not come to her aid. When the doors slammed shut, Etain knew she was on her own.

Dathmet exhaled. "Ah... Sweet silence." His gaze captured hers as he stroked the top of Dar's head. "I knew you'd come to save your precious pet." She watched the demon lift his blade to Dar's throat. "One more dream you'll never realize."

"No!" she said, taking an involuntary step forward. *Shit!*

He laughed. "I wouldn't dirty my hands with this filth. I'll leave it to my guards to rid me of this worthless piece of flesh." Dathmet raised a brow as, step by step, he distanced himself from the prisoner. "He is, you know. Worthless, I mean. Look at him." He motioned toward the Krymerian. "Clueless to where he is or what's happening around him or even *to* him. He has quite literally come to his end."

As the demon moved away, Etain maneuvered closer to Dar's tortured body, but forced herself to keep her sights on her adversary. "No thanks to you... Dathmet."

"I'm flattered that you've shown so much interest in me. You know my name. You've visited my home." He watched his blade as he arced it through the air. "You'll be calling me master before this is over, Lady Etain." His black-eyed gaze fell on her. "You must know none of you will *ever* leave this realm. Those who live will become slaves to my demons and wish for death every day after."

"Midir taught you the bullshit, I see."

His eyebrows lifted. "Little bitch, I won't let you destroy what my father and I started." He stayed in constant motion, keeping his distance, his sword poised for play.

The smell of Dar's blood made her head reel and her own blood race. She swallowed hard, fighting the urge to scream, and rolled her eyes. His words rang a familiar bell in her head. She'd heard them before, spoken by another. "Why?"

He stared at her and stopped his circulation of the room. "Why what?"

"Why me? Why murder my family?" Etain stepped toward him. "Why take my brother? What did either of you hope to gain?"

He looked at his sword, then sliced it through the air. "I asked him the same questions many times." His lips curved into a smirk. "Midir had an incredible mind and the heart of a lion. Together, we planned the destruction of the Alamir and their stupid Council. We marked our targets long ago." He pointed his blade at her. "Until he found you...again. An Alamir who intrigued his black heart and distracted him from his true purpose, his birthright."

"*Damnation* was his birthright. He stole everything he ever possessed."

"I followed his path, obeyed his every command." Dathmet spit the words, his hate apparent. "When the time came to strike, what did he do? He gambled it away on a *woman*. One with no concept of what he offered. A woman in love with his brother." His eyes burned an intense flame as he circled the room. His skin shimmered from the heat just beneath the surface. "His obsession took over." Enraged by his memories, he released a fireball.

Etain easily dodged the attack. "Tell me why!"

"Stupid woman," he huffed. "All you had to do was submit. You would have been the queen of it all."

"All I want is my husband."

Dathmet stopped. "You get what *I* want you to get. This is my house."

She glanced around the room. "Looks more like a big ol' tomb to me."

He suddenly laughed and placed his sword on the floor, then slowly removed his suit jacket and tie, draping them both over a weapon display. "You are a haughty wench." He brought up his blade. "Show me your strength."

Etain attacked with a downward strike, metal against metal ringing throughout the hall.

Dathmet soon realized his *faux pas*. So far, he'd been able to keep up, but it was clear her speed and skill exceeded his.

"Have you seen your brother lately?"

She skipped back, out of reach. "Stop it."

Dathmet practically preened, knowing he'd struck a nerve. "Have you any idea where he is?"

"My brother can take care of himself."

"Like the day he disappeared?" Seeing her falter, he advanced, bringing his sword around, slashing into her left arm. She yelped but kept hold of Burning Heart. "I could've sworn I saw a dark-haired green-eyed man in the dungeons."

"You lie like your mentor." She swiped at his head, but he saved himself with a bend of his knee.

A misstep on Etain's part gave him the opportunity to approach her from behind, crashing his elbow into the back of her head.

"Give up, Alamir. You were made to be my fount of power." With another turn, his sword sliced into her side, making her stumble and fall forward. "Submit to me, Krymerian whore."

She landed on her hands and knees, Dar's swords beside her, and peered at him from the corner of her eye. "Your what? I'll take Krymerian whore any day." She rolled away, grabbing her blades, and onto her feet. "Or did you not learn anything from Midir's demise?" She ran at him, both blades in action, slicing into the demon.

He lurched aside and checked a wound to his chest. "His whore, not mine." Regaining his balance, he moved toward her, his blade before him. "You will serve me your blood, nothing more." She dodged his first attack. "*I* will conquer the Alamir." And his second. "I already command the *Bok*." The third found its mark, cutting into her thigh. "*I* will be the only Krymerian. They will all look to me as their master."

"You speak of the VonNeshtas as though you're better than them. I can't imagine why a woman would subject herself to his touch…" She took a steadying breath. "But if Midir truly was your father, then you're as much a lowlife as him."

Etain lay siege on the demon until they were both drenched in sweat and blood. Her rampant attacks not only pushed him beyond his limits, sheer exhaustion chipped away at hers. Yet she continued to fight.

Dathmet came at her again with renewed vigor, his sword relentless, slicing into her flesh at every opportunity, driving her back against a wall. The black blades slipped from her trembling hands, clanging when they hit the floor. She stared at her tormentor, rivulets of sweat and blood running down her face.

He gave her an evil grin. "On your knees, whore."

She grimaced as her wings extended. At her full seven feet, her white talons slid out from her knuckles, aglow in the soft light. Bringing her wings in tight, a single step had her in his face. She drove her talons deep into his mid-section. "After you."

Dathmet roared from the assault. "You will not leave this place, bitch." Flames in varying shades of red, orange, and yellow blazed across his skin.

"Neither will you." Etain drove her other set of talons into his neck.

He dropped his blade and appeared frozen for a brief moment, then came back to life. "Get the hell off me!"

She encased him within her wings, giving him a bloody smile. "Taste my fount of power."

"Damn you, Etain," he growled, completing his transformation into total flame.

"Don't…" Smoke swirled off her wings as she collapsed onto the floor.

Dathmet backed away and grabbed a great bullwhip from the wall. Circling the leather strip over his head, he cracked the tip into her back. Etain grit her teeth, but despite her efforts, a growl escaped. He snapped the whip again. This time she screamed. His aim was impeccable, striking along the edge of the scabbard on her back. It ripped through leather top, nipping at the vulnerable flesh beneath. She gasped for breath as she crawled across the floor, shielding her back with her wings as best she could.

Another crack of the whip forced her headlong into the wall, smashing the side of her face and splitting her lip. A powerful rage gave her the power to push up. Just as she got her feet underneath her, the whip cracked again. She collapsed onto her knees. Jaws clenched, she swung out with a wing and slapped the demon, knocking him to the floor, then pushed away from the wall, moving toward Dar.

Dathmet staggered to his feet. He spun the whip with all his strength and wrapped its length around her waist. With a vicious jerk, he pulled her to him. "I'm not done with you."

She was imprisoned within her wings by the brutal whip. "This is how submission starts." He ran his fingers through her tarnished hair. She jerked her head, but he grabbed her chin and forced her to look at him. "Thank you for reminding me of my heritage. You're right. I am as much a VonNeshta as that lump in the corner. He doesn't appear to have much use for you anymore. You can be *my* bitch now."

She spit in his face.

He swiped at the spittle with his sleeve.

Feeling the slight release of her bonds, she worked through the pain and pushed out with her wings, freeing one hand enough to cut the whip with her talons.

"Fuck you. Fuck you. Fuck you!" She lashed at his face.

He leaned out of reach and retaliated by shoving the handle into her stomach, continuing to hit her wherever he could find an opening. Once more, she found herself pinned against the wall. Dathmet grabbed hold of the leather straps of the scabbard and yanked her to him. "In time, whore."

A belligerent glare in his eyes, he took hold of her hand, then used one of her own talons to cut the straps. She met his dark grin with a defiant stare. A strike to her jaw knocked the warrior off her feet. Her mouth bloodied, she retracted the talons and curled into a ball. Dathmet ripped the scabbard from her back and flung it across the room.

. . .

His favored bullwhip destroyed, he set his sights on a new instrument of pain. From the other side of the room, he lifted a lethal cat-o'-nine from its display.

"Let's see how you perform under *my* tutelage." He snapped it in the air. "I have to say, I couldn't get anything worthwhile out of your husband…but he *did* scream. I believe I will enjoy yours much more."

He lashed the cat-o'-nine into her back, twisted his wrist, and lashed again. No sound came from her lips, but tears flowed heavily over her cheeks.

"You *will* scream for me." Although the tips were not curved like the one used on Dar, they did their share of damage, biting into her leathers, bruising and ripping her tender flesh. "I made him scream against his will." He lashed out again. "I will fill this realm with yours."

He brutalized her with the whip until her blood covered the floor and sweat rolled down his back. He tossed aside the bloodied cat-o'-nine, then stomped on a tattered wing, grinding his shoe into the main bone.

She screamed.

Dathmet stomped several more times, laughing with her cries. Finally, he bent and wiped his face with the limp wing. She shuddered, her screams reduced to whimpers. He ran his fingers through her blood, closed his eyes, and licked them clean. So caught up in his delusions, he didn't notice his prey dragging herself toward Day Star.

Every move made her grimace. Tears streaked her face as she inched closer to the blade. Her fingertips brushed the head of the hilt. She heard his footsteps, coming closer. She stretched her battered body, fighting through the pain, and gained purchase of the blade. With a groan, she turned in time to block a new attack. The metal tips of the cat-o'-nine tinkled when they hit the floor.

Although he gazed at her, his focus seemed to be elsewhere, pure hatred in his eyes. She frantically tried to scramble away, but a strong grip on her ankle held her fast.

"Submit."

With one last burst of energy, she turned and kicked him in the face. He grunted, releasing her foot, and grabbed his broken nose. Fresh blood gushed between his fingers.

Etain flipped onto her stomach to make her escape when her gaze fell on…

"Dar."

The sight of her husband, lost and alone, broken and bleeding, drained the last of her resolve. "I'm sorry, my love." She lay quietly, drenched in her own blood, knowing it would end soon.

She heard the faint sound of voices and clashing metal. None of it meant anything to her now. Those things were in another place, another time. She struggled for breath, using what little strength she had to inch closer to Dar. If she could but touch him one last time…

5

SALVATION

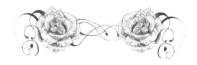

A faint light prodded into Dar's befuddled thoughts. His mind's eye looked up as the inner light grew brighter. His beautiful Etain stood before him, silver hair flowing over her shoulders, ice-blue eyes shining with love.

"I have been waiting for you, my sweet lady."

She walked toward him, a soft smile on her lips. He noticed a great white unicorn and a sleek red panther on either side of her. Peace engulfed him, knowing his family had come to take him home.

The panther stepped closer to him. "Da... She is dying. She is dying."

His eyes remained on his beloved wife. "She's been waiting for my soul to be cleansed. At last, I am worthy. She's come to take me home."

The unicorn went to him. "Da, that was a lie, but this is not."

"She is dying, Da," the panther repeated. "Only you can save her. Only you can save us."

Dar twitched. The words burned into his delusional mind. "I saw her fall. I saw the light leave her eyes."

"Lies, Da," said the unicorn. "Look into her mind, see what happened through her eyes."

Unable to recall the events of that day, he did as the unicorn asked and delved into her memories. His swords were swift, exacting in their quest to rid the Alamir world of the demon's presence. He held his breath, seeing her body fall into pieces, thinking he could not bear to witness it again. But by experiencing it through Etain's perspective, he noticed things he'd missed that day. The blood disappeared. Her flesh turned to ash. The purple ring he'd given her suddenly appeared in those ashes.

The three faded as his mind argued with his heart. Something was off.

Where is her wedding ring? Her sword?

Etain's blood crept across the cold floor as deep a red as the stone of the castle. The hunger deep within the Krymerian instinctively created a vacuum, drawing her blood into his system, dispersing the flow throughout his beaten body. The effect was immediate.

A golden eye peeked out into a strange world. He squeezed it shut and dragged in a shuddering breath. Once the pain subsided, he tried again. Better prepared, he opened his good eye, finding it less painful, unsure of why the other refused to cooperate. His gaze came to the delicate hand next to his thigh and followed the arm to a mass of bloodied, tangled hair.

Etain?

He needed to touch her, make sure she was real. The jingle of the chains at his wrists surprised him. A hiss passed his lips when he moved his broken arm.

Save her, Da. The small voice echoed through his soul.

A frantic eye looked at Etain. The severity of her injuries finally registered - the gashes on her body, the burned and broken wings, her life force fading.

Closing his eye, he centered his thoughts and pushed into hers.

Etain, I am here, a chuisle. I am here.

He waited, afraid he may be too late. Prepared to try again, he heard a faint voice.

Dar…

Strengthened by her response, he sent words of encouragement. We will live, my sweet wife. My body is damaged, but my mind is sound. Listen to my words and repeat them as I speak. They will restore you.

He panicked when she didn't respond. Etain! I am your husband and High Lord. Do as I say.

He felt her sigh. I will…do my best.

In the ancient tongue of the Krymerians, he recited the words of life, the avenue to restore her strength, restore her life force, save their future. Her lips moved silently, chanting in unison with her husband. Dar poured himself into her to strengthen the process.

Her wounds slowly began to heal, the bruises fading. Her wings became whole again and returned to their unblemished state. In time, ice-blue eyes opened and focused on the face of an awakened Dar. A faint smile came to her lips.

Carefully, she pushed up. "Thank you." She sat as close to him as possible, caressing the unmarred side of his face.

"What's going on?" His tongue felt heavy, his voice rough.

"We're going home, my love. Are you ready?" He merely blinked. Rising, she carefully flexed her wings, then picked up Burning Heart. "This is going to hurt. I'm sorry."

With a trusting nod, he braced himself. She raised the sword high overhead, her arms trembling, and managed to bring it down. However, the edge glanced off the chain. She staggered to the side, but quickly regained her footing and aimed the sword for another strike.

A steady hand covered hers. She looked up. "T. How'd you get free? Where's the demon?"

He gently took the sword from her hands. "E, you're too weak. Let me do this." He slashed the chain in two with one strike. "Be ready to catch him." He moved to the other side.

Freed from the wall, Dar cried out as the bones in his broken arm grated against each other and the tattered skin on his back moved. Etain grunted, catching him as he shifted forward, shudders wracking his tortured body.

Taurnil glanced at the shackles. "E, can you get these things off him?"

"I'll give it a try." She tightened her arms around Dar, trying to hold him steady to minimize any further pain, and leaned her head against his. "My love, I need to shift just a little so I can reach the shackles. I'll do the right wrist first. If it works, I'll do the other, then your ankles. Are you ready?"

He groaned, tears trickling down his dirty face. "Do it."

She carefully shifted him back, worried by his ragged breaths, but knew it must be done. She directed a single jolt of her electrical charge to one of the locks. The shackle popped open and fell to the floor. Encouraged by the small victory, she made short work of the other locks.

"Dar, I have to find the others and let them know we have you."

His head came up, a glare in his good eye. "No."

She gently kissed him on the lips. "T will stay here. I'll be right back." With Taurnil's help, she stood. "I'll leave Burning Heart, just in case." She scooped up Day Star and headed toward the door.

Dar growled at the young elf. "Taurnil-"

"E, wait," he said, making her pause. "You're not in any shape to be-"

"Don't worry. I'm sure Freeblood's not far."

She headed toward the door, a confident jaunt in her step. Halfway across the room, she glanced to her side and slowed to a stop, her eyes widening as her mouth fell open. Day Star clattered to the floor. "Noo! No! No!" She darted out of Dar's line of vision, but he could hear the horror in her voice. "Oh, my god! No! Please, no."

Dar shot Taurnil a questioning look. "It's not good," the elf said. "I have to-"

"Go," Dar whispered, a sense of dread filling his heart.

Taurnil ran to Etain.

Tears streamed down her face, her hands frantically roaming over the fallen warrior. The tips of her wings were drenched in blood. She looked up. "T, I have to save him. I have to save him."

"E, there's nothing you can do."

Her eyes brightened. "There is!" Her talons slid out.

Taurnil grabbed her wrist and crouched beside her. "E, it's too late. He's lost too much blood. You can't bring him back."

"I have to try!"

A larger hand stayed her move. "*A chuisle*, he is gone."

"Dar…" Her voice broke. "Please. No. Not Inferno."

"Taurnil, help me down." The elf jumped up, helping Dar sit on the floor next to Etain. Biting his bottom lip, he blew out a breath. "Find the others. Now. We must leave at once."

"Dar-"

"Go!" He clenched his jaw, closing his eye.

"Yes, milord." Taurnil touched Etain's arm. "I'll bring them here. We'll take him home."

She didn't look at him but nodded.

Dar reached for her. "*A chuisle...*"

"I can't take this, Dar. It's too much. First you, now this." She turned to him, burying her face in his chest. He flinched, but wrapped his good arm around her. "It's too much."

"I am here, my love. We will do this together."

———

Linq rushed into the room. "Do we know where the others are? Have you seen Inferno? I lost sight of him…" He trailed off, seeing Dar and Etain.

"You're the first we've seen since…" Taurnil gestured around, then looked down at Etain, "this."

As Linq approached, his mind suddenly registered the blood on the floor. "What's happened here?" Then he saw Inferno's still body. His face paled. He dropped his sword and fell to his knees. "No." He looked up at Taurnil, tears in his eyes. "How did this…" His gaze returned to the fallen warrior.

Freeblood walked in, a battered Robert leaning against him.

Etain turned, her eyes red and swollen. Dar moved to help her up, but she shook her head. "You've done too much already." Taurnil offered her a hand. Walking toward Robert, she broke down in tears, wrapping her arms around him. "What're you doing here?" She looked over his shoulder. "Freeblood, are you okay?"

"A little banged up, but I'm all right." He glanced at the concerned faces. "What's going on?"

She pushed her brother back and held him at arm's length, looking him over. "How bad is it?"

"Not as bad as Dar," Robert whispered, his face bruised and bloody. "Can we get out of here?"

Wolfe and Elfin appeared, carrying Ara between them. "I'm all for that," said Wolfe.

Taurnil went to help. "How badly is she hurt?"

Ara lifted her head, a weak smile on her face. "You should see the other guys."

"Aye," Elfin chimed in. "She was having herself quite a party. Good thing we found her when we did. I think she was starting to slow after the third set."

Her smile disappeared. "Heaven knows, we all fought like madmen."

"The Blades are making one last sweep," Wolfe said. "Where's our glorious leader? I'd have thought he'd be the first-"

"Wolfe…" Etain stepped forward. Her gaze went to the other. "Elfin…" She burst into tears, wrapping an arm around each of them. "I'm so sorry."

"What?" The two stared at the others, confused. It was then they noticed a weeping Linq.

Wolfe pushed away and made his way through the group, Elfin on his heels. Seeing Dar first, he almost smiled, but the realization of his condition turned it into an angry frown. Dar's gaze moved to the body beside him. Wolfe turned his head, following his direction. He eyed his chieftain from head to toe, taking in the broken face and multiple wounds over his body, the worst being the slash to his throat. He looked at Elfin, his face likewise drained of color, and took hold of the elf's shoulder. The two leaned into each other, whispering words of disbelief and sorrow.

Wolfe turned to Dar. "That bastard did this to you? To Inferno?"

Dar could only nod.

Wolfe turned to Freeblood. "There's a room just down the hall. Rip down the curtains." Freeblood nodded and rushed out the door. "Etain, you and Taurnil get Dar out of here. We'll have the Blades take Arachnia." He looked at Linq and Elfin. "We'll carry our chieftain."

Taurnil left the group to retrieve Dar's Day Star still lying by the discarded shackles. As he returned, he also picked up Burning Heart, sliding both underneath his belt.

Freeblood returned, curtains in hand, followed by the Blades. Linq gathered himself, wiped his face, and stood.

"Freeblood, if you will see to Etain's brother…" Wolfe kneeled by his chieftain, saying a prayer as he laid the man's sword on his chest. Accepting the fabric from Freeblood, Wolfe, Elfin, and Linq reverently wrapped Inferno's body.

Covered in his chieftain's blood, Wolfe came to his feet. "Listen to me, and listen well. Once Inferno is laid to rest and the honors spoken, I will hunt down the bastard who did this to him, to Dar, to everyone he's ever harmed. Come with me or not. Doesn't matter. I will make the asshole pay." He swiped at his eyes before the tears could fall. "Let's get out of this shithole."

Having shimmered, Etain, Taurnil, and Dar were the first to arrive at the location of the portal. Taurnil helped Dar to a large boulder where he could rest until the others showed. Leaning heavily against the young elf, he suddenly sat up as straight as he could, crying out at the pain.

On the lookout for the rest of their group, Etain whirled around, her hand going to the hilt of her sword. "What is it, Dar?"

"The shackles...," he whispered. "We need to go back for the shackles."

She shared a look with Taurnil, coming closer to her husband. "My love, we must leave. Now."

"No." He grabbed Taurnil's arm. "We have to get the shackles." He struggled to swallow. "He'll use them again."

She kneeled in front of Dar. "I don't have the time or the strength. I doubt that monster would take the time-"

"Not those shackles." He licked his dry lips. "Water."

Taurnil grabbed his canteen and held it to the High Lord's mouth. After a few sips, Dar said, "In battle."

Etain furrowed her brows. "I don't understand."

Dar growled. "Shackled in battle." The effort proved too much. He slumped against Taurnil.

"Dar!" She looked at Taurnil. "He can't wait until we get back to Laugharne." Reaching for the knife in her boot, she brought it to her forearm, slashing into the soft skin. "Turn him a bit more, T." The young elf maneuvered Dar around to make it easier to access his back. "This should give the healing process a jump-start."

His body jerked, trails of steam rising from his flesh where her blood dripped. Taurnil held him tightly as Etain treated as many wounds as time allowed, chanting a healing spell.

As she continued the bloody application, she asked, "Did you see?"

Taurnil gave her a curious look.

Her bottom lip trembled. "Inferno. Did you see?"

He stared at her for a silent moment. "Yes."

Tears slid down her cheeks. "Did he…"

"That's enough, E. You're weak, too." He turned her arm to stop the flow. Her pained gaze broke his heart. "He fought like a man possessed. I was sure he had the demon by the short hairs, but something distracted him, made him lose focus."

"I heard voices. Did someone else come into the room?"

"No," he whispered.

She swallowed hard and swiped at her tears. "Was it…me? Did I distract him?"

"No! You were the reason he came in and started the fight, but he didn't lose focus because of you. His back was turned to you. There was something at the other end of the hall. I don't know what, but it was enough to give the demon time to creep up from behind and…"

Hearing the others' approach, she quickly rubbed her bloodied forearm across Dar's lips, forcing some into his mouth.

"E, I think I understand what Dar meant," Taurnil said.

"What're you talking about?"

"We wondered how they were able to drag Dar away so easily."

She cauterized the cut in her arm with a blue charge. "Shackles. I remember hearing the click of the locks. But shackles wouldn't be anything for Dar to rip apart. Besides, I wouldn't know where to start the search, T."

Linq, Wolfe, and Elfin walked up first, Inferno's body held between them. "Apologies for taking so long," Linq said.

"Apologies have no place here. It's given Dar time to rest. Linq, would you be willing to leave Inferno to Wolfe and Elfin? Taurnil will need your help with Dar."

He gave her a doubtful look. "You're not planning on going back, are you?"

"Not today. I want to make sure everyone is through the portal before I close it." She looked at Wolfe and Elfin. "You go first, but please, wait for me." As Etain recited the words, gleaming rays of sunlight poured into the dull realm as the portal opened.

Linq carefully relinquished his hold on Inferno's body, then joined Dar and Taurnil. Wolfe and Elfin stepped through the opening, moved a few feet away, and laid Inferno's body on the ground.

Etain turned to Arachnia and the Blades. "You're next, milady."

Once they were on the other side, she looked at Freeblood and Robert.

Freeblood shook his head. "You take Dar next. We're still on our feet."

Etain gave him a ghost of a smile. "It gives him more time to rest. Please, go ahead. We'll be right behind you."

With a nod, the two shuffled through the portal.

Taurnil stood. With Linq's help, he raised Dar to his feet, ushering him into the Alamir realm. Etain looked back one last time.

"I *will* be back, and I *will* win." She was the last to step through.

As the portal closed, Etain approached Arachnia, noting the deep cuts and bruises over her body. "We'll have you home soon, Ara." She walked a few steps away and turned, facing the others. Sinking to her knees, she spread her wings and held out her arms, then looked at Taurnil. "Bring him to me."

He and Linq carefully placed Dar within her right arm. Pulling him close, she embraced him with her wing. She motioned at Freeblood to bring her brother. Safe within her left arm and wing, she turned to the Blades.

"There's room for one more, Ara."

"I can ride a horse, Etain," she protested. "You should take Inferno."

"Nonsense. The sooner you get medical attention, the better. Kneel behind me and wrap your arms around my neck."

With some help, she walked over and placed her arms around Etain, leaning her head against the warrior angel's. "Thank you." Etain leaned into her, quietly accepting the sentiment.

The High Lady addressed the group. "Thank you all for your help. Wolfe, Elfin, once I have these three situated, I'll be back for Inferno." Her eyes flashed with violet light and the small group disappeared.

Spirit, Swee, and others at Laugharne ran to meet them as soon as they materialized in the courtyard. Etain gave Spirit a sad, albeit grateful, look. "I wasn't sure I could get through to you."

"Aye, lass. You came through loud and clear." Spirit smiled. The Black Blades at the castle quickly surrounded Dar and lifted him to transport him into the house as Spirit instructed them to his room. Swee followed the group to render first aid. The Dragon Clan, still battered and bruised, lifted Robert and carried him to his appointed room. Finally, Thoric and Cappy helped Arachnia.

Spirit yelled as the small groups walked off. "Make sure to strip them down and burn those nasty rags."

Thoric raised an eyebrow, giving Ara an evil grin. Eyes narrowed, she quipped, "Forget it, bub. I'm perfectly capable on my own."

"I don't know…," he said, his voice full of doubt. "You look pretty weak to me. I'd consider it a service to strip off those rags." He and Cappy laughed as they carried their charge into the house and to her room.

Spirit turned to Etain. "Where's the rest?"

Etain struggled to her feet, trying not to look her in the eye. "On their way. I wanted to get the worst of the wounded here as soon as possible."

"You're not looking much better than them, lass. Come inside. Let me give you a good look." The mage started toward the house, looking over her shoulder. "You coming?"

Etain shook her head as she pulled her wings in close. "Not yet." She had to bite her lip to keep from crying. "There's one more thing I must do."

Spirit gave her a curious look. "What's wrong with you, girl? What's happened?"

Finding the courage to finally look her in the eye, a tear rolled down her cheek. "There's one more thing…" Blue charges around her, she disappeared.

Sitting as sentries around Inferno's body, Linq, Wolfe, and Elfin looked up when Etain appeared. "Where are the others?"

"We sent them ahead," said Linq, swiping his red eyes as he stood. "The wizards will need the information they have about this…this…"

Etain wrapped her arms tightly around the elf.

"Etain…" His voice was barely audible, his body shaking.

She struggled to hold it together, wanting to be the pillar of strength, but when Wolfe and Elfin joined in a group hug, sharing their grief, she broke, too. Each one cried on the shoulder of the next, holding onto one another, afraid to let go lest they drown alone in their sadness.

After a time, Wolfe lifted his head, his eyes red, giving his comrades a brave smile. "Look at us…" He sniffled, wiping his nose on his sleeve. "If Inferno saw us now…" Tears slid down his cheeks.

Elfin picked up the thought. "'For fuck's sake, stop yer catterwalling,' he'd say."

"Crybabies," Etain said, swiping away her tears. "He'd call us all 'soddin' crybabies.'"

"Then slap us with the side of his blade…," Linq carried on, "and tell us to get on with it."

The four shared a weak laugh, remembering Inferno's gruff manners, each one knowing it was to cover up his true emotions most of the time. The memory lifted their spirits for a moment.

Etain cleared her throat as she ran a hand through her hair. "I need to take him home. Spirit doesn't know. I-I couldn't…" She swallowed rather than give in to the desire to cry again.

Linq shook his head. "It's not an easy thing to tell." They fell silent again, their thoughts with Inferno's wife and family. "You're not doing it alone. Can you take Wolfe with you? Elfin and I can be there in a flash."

"Aye," she whispered, tears in her eyes. She turned, spread her wings, and kneeled beside Inferno's body. "Come sit beside me, Wolfe."

"We'll meet you in the courtyard," Linq said. "Let's go, Elfin."

With Inferno and Wolfe safely encased within her wings, she watched the elves sprint away as she and her charges disappeared in a blue instant.

Kneeling on the ground, her wings at rest on her back, Etain watched Spirit run toward them, the UWS clan behind her. Tears streamed down her face, seeing her friend go through the same emotions she herself was still experiencing – confusion, fear, the horror of realizing someone you loved had been taken from you all too soon.

To know Inferno was gone was almost too much to bear, but to see Spirit's heart break and her pain…

Goddamn!

Etain couldn't breathe. Her stomach churned. Her heart felt as though it were being squeezed dry. She wrapped her arms around her body, watching the clan encircle their fallen chieftain and his shattered wife.

They lifted him and carried him into Laugharne. Spirit had to be carried, too. Once she was safe within Linq's arms, he followed the clan, Elfin at their side.

She remembered Taurnil's words about Inferno being distracted. If his back was to her, what made him lose focus? Surely it wasn't T. What else was in that room?

Alone in the courtyard, Etain took in the grandeur of the castle, remembering the first day she'd come to this place. It felt like ages ago.

Inferno had happily taken her in, made sure she felt at home and that her Alamir education continued. He and Spirit shared so much with her, treating her like one of their own. The kids had come to see her as a big sister, although they called her auntie. She'd been happy here.

Her thoughts moved to Freeblood, Faux, Dar, the dynamics of those relationships, and even to Midir and her brother. Turning her head, she looked at the place where she and Dar became husband and wife. A smile came to her lips as she remembered seeing her handsome savage waiting at the altar while she nervously strolled to his side on Inferno's arm.

Wrapped within her wings, tears trickled down her cheeks, quickly turning into a torrent. Her body shuddered as grief and anger poured out. Tears flowed for Dar's pain and suffering, for her own, for that of their friends, especially Spirit and her precious children. Loss of those in battle ripped at her heart. Fallen heroes who would never know how their efforts preserved the future of more than just one race. Black Blades and Alamir who would never fulfill whatever promises life had offered. Finally, the incredible love shared between her and Dar bubbled up, filling her with so much joy she couldn't contain its glory. She rocked within her winged shelter, feeling as though her heart would burst.

Footsteps crunched on the graveled pathway. Her hair fell over her face as the great wings flattened over her back. She didn't need to look past the neon green Converse to know who stood over her.

"What a mess I've made of this."

Freeblood shifted. "How do you figure?"

She brushed her hair back, sniffling as she swiped at her swollen eyes. "If it weren't for me-"

"If it weren't for you…" He kneeled in front of her, "Dar would be dead, lost in a spirit world, never finding solace." He scooted closer so their knees touched. "You can't take responsibility for Inferno. He chose to walk into that room, to take on the demon."

"But-"

"You can't control the actions of others, Etain. Consider the good you've done. You saved your brother. You saved Linq. Hell, you saved *me*. I'm sorry for Inferno, but the rest of us made it out, alive, because of you."

"But if I hadn't gone to Nunnehi in the first place-"

"Forget it, Etain. Shed your tears and say your goodbyes to those we've lost. Your future lies up there…" Freeblood cocked his head toward the castle, "fighting for his life. A life he's looking forward to sharing with you." He placed his hands over hers. "You have become my family. You, Dar, and Faux. I know we don't all see eye to eye, but what family does? Don't destroy it with undeserved guilt. Get your butt upstairs and be with Dar. You know he'll rest easier with you beside him. And get some rest yourself. Spirit's going to need a shoulder to lean on."

"Damn. When did you get to be so philosophical?"

He laughed. "You tell anyone, I'll deny it."

"Think I'll save it for a rainy day."

Freeblood stood and offered her his hand. On her feet, she retracted her wings as they walked to the large front doors.

"It'll be a different world without Inferno. Spirit, the clan, the kids… I have no idea where we go from here."

"We'll figure it out. That's what being Alamir is about, isn't it? Working together?"

Inside the castle, she smiled as they parted company at the stairs. "Where's Faux?"

"Tucked away upstairs, safe and sound."

"Why is she tucked away?"

"We can talk about that later. Go to Dar."

She cocked her head, ready to pursue the conversation, but decided to let it go for now. "Thank you, Freeblood."

Without another word, he quickly turned and left.

She smiled to herself, watching him stride away in a fluster, then walked upstairs. She stepped into her bedroom just as Swee stood from the side of the bed. Dar was on his stomach, his torn back draped with wet cloths. She also noticed his broken arm had been set and splinted. His hair was damp against his head, shorter but back to its golden honey color, and his body was clean.

"Thank you for your help, Swee."

"It wasn't all me. A few of his Blades helped clean him up." She gave her an apologetic look as she rushed on. "I'm so sorry about his hair. I know how much he loves it." She bit her bottom lip. "The Blades had already chopped it off to his shoulders by the time I returned."

"Swee… It's okay. It will grow back." She placed a hand on the healer's arm. "I'm thankful for all you've done. Believe me, his hair is the least of our worries."

Swee gave her a weak smile. "I've done everything I can. I couldn't mend his cheekbone. It's beyond my expertise. Maybe Spirit will…"

Her face fell, remembering what happened. "Oh…Well… I guess not."

Etain gently squeezed her arm. "We'll figure it out. Go get some rest."

She placed her hand on hers, tears in her eyes. "I'm so sorry about Inferno."

Unable to speak, Etain shook her head and shrugged, fighting back tears.

Swee pointed to a wash basin on the side table. "Don't let the cloths dry out. Keep them damp with that solution. It will help his back heal and ease the pain. Mostly, he needs to rest and eat. So do you. I'll check on you both later."

The High Lady locked the door and walked to a wing-backed chair. Sitting, she removed her boots, then sat back to catch her breath. The dagger tucked in the top of her boot caught her eye and made her realize what she had to do…for Dar's sake. She reached for it as she stood, then walked toward the bathroom, placing it on the nightstand along the way. Turning on the shower, she returned to Dar's side to check on him and allow time for the water to warm. She leaned over him, breathing in his scent, and kissed his damp hair.

"I won't be long, my love."

In the bathroom, she looked at herself in the mirror. What she saw made her gasp. Blood stained the tips of her tangled hair. Her leathers were tattered and blood-stained. Dark circles rested underneath her eyes, and her body ached. She slowly removed the ruined leathers, hissing each time she touched a tender spot. Although Dar's chant healed many of her injuries and faded some of her more visible bruises, there were plenty left on the parts of her body no one could see.

As she washed away the blood, dirt, and touch of the demon, Etain sang the healing chant. The words helped her body while the singing soothed her soul. She had to be at her best to pull everyone through this insane debacle.

I wasn't there for Inferno, but I will be here for Spirit.

Turning off the water, she grabbed an oversized towel as she stepped out of the shower. Again, she stood in front of the large mirror, swiped away the fog on its surface, then twisted and turned, checking for any telltale injuries. Those she found were well on their way to disappearing. The bruises were much improved, too.

Wrapped in the towel, she combed the tangles from her hair as she returned to her sleeping love and sat on the side of the bed. Her dirk glimmered from the bedside table, as if it knew what she had in mind. Gingerly, she pulled back the cloths from Dar's butchered skin, wincing at the brutality of the wounds. Taking the blade in hand, Etain held one arm over his back and sliced across her forearm, speaking her own words of magic.

"This cut is for our past that has long been united in blood. Heal for what we have meant to each other..." Another slash. "This cut is for our present. Heal, for it is all we truly have..." A third and final slice. "This cut is for the future we will share. Heal for what we will become." The blood flowed over the tattered edges of his skin, sinking deep into the wounds. Dar shifted in his sleep. Exhausted by the exchange, she took a cloth from the basin and wrapped it around her arm, then reapplied the cloths over Dar's back.

Rising, she walked to the other side of the bed, dropped the towel, and slid between the sheets, gently inching toward him. She draped his good arm over her body and snuggled as close as she dared. In his sleep, he intuitively turned his face to hers and seemed to relax.

"Here we are, *a chuisle*, battered and bruised, but together." Stroking his hair, she kissed his cheek lightly and noticed a small smile lift the corner of his mouth. "We will heal, my sweet savage, then we'll go home."

With Spirit properly dosed by a special brew concocted by Swee and put to bed, Linq left her to what he hoped would be a dreamless sleep and headed downstairs. Hearing voices, he turned toward the kitchen, thinking a swig of ale and time with friends would hit the spot. As he stepped through the door, he saw a tall man wearing a chef's hat, his skin the color of milk chocolate, in conversation with Swee.

"*Við sjóinn og stjörnurnar* (By the sea and stars)!" He approached the man, giving him a ready handshake. "Alaster! What the hell are you doing here?" Before he could answer, Linq looked at Swee. "Alaster's an old friend of mine, Swee."

She smiled. "Yes, I know. He's been here a few days, awaiting your return."

"Then you'll know we ran into each other while in Deudraeth." Linq looked back at Alaster. "I never expected to see you here, but I'm glad you are. What brings you to Laugharne?"

"Just a sec…" Alaster turned to a nearby assistant, giving her instructions and telling her he'd be with her in a moment. He graced Swee and Linq with a shiny white smile. "I never expected to be here, either." His smile slowly fell. "I heard what happened in Deudraeth, the *Bok* chasing you out of town, and thought it odd. They usually don't bother with us Alamir. A few days later, we got wind of the *Bok* rising and thought maybe you could use some help."

"By the toque…" Linq pointed at Alaster's head, "I'm guessing you're a chef?"

"Have been for a while. I've always enjoyed cooking, so decided to go pro." Alaster looked at the other faces in the room. "It looks like I came at the right time."

"You are a godsend," Swee said. "With Spirit…indisposed, I wasn't sure how we were going to manage with all these people."

"If you will excuse me, Alaster, Swee, I'd like to clean myself up," Linq said, indicating his filthy clothes. "It's not been a good day."

Alaster frowned. "I was sorry to hear about your friend, Linq. He sounds to have been a great man."

Linq swallowed, unable to speak.

Alaster changed the subject. "Leave your clothes outside your door. Cherise'll have 'em picked up for cleaning."

He had to clear his throat before he spoke. "Cherise?"

"My beautiful wife." Alaster looked around the room again and spied her in conversation with one of the ladies from Deudraeth. "Cherise! Come meet an old friend." His gaze came back to Linq. "We had a bed and breakfast in town, but since the *Bok* rising, things have gotten too sticky." A young woman came up and slipped into his outstretched arm. "Cher, this is Linq. Linq, meet the lady of my dreams."

"Linq." Her voice was as warm as her smile and as rich as the color of her striking blue-black skin. She ignored his outstretched hand and wrapped him in a tight embrace. "Alaster's been talking nonstop about you since y'all met in Deudraeth. I feel like you're already family." Releasing him, she turned to Swee. "This is such a lovely place, but much bigger than our B&B. We're going to be very busy."

Swee chuckled. "I'm glad you're here."

Cherise came back to Linq. "I'm sure you'd like to clean up. I'll have one of my boys show you to a room. He'll get you a new set of clothes, too. Just leave what you're wearing outside the door."

Alaster's eyes widened. "Cherise, you just met the man and you're already bossing him around like he was-"

She waved him off. "You take care of the cheffing and I'll take care of everything else. Come on, Linq. Let's get you freshened up. I bet there's a handsome face underneath all that dirt. Noah! Noah James!" Cherise hollered across the room to a boy of about ten. "Get over here and show this young man to his room. Make sure you get him a new set of clothes, too."

Linq lifted his brows and grinned.

Alaster laughed. "She's awful bossy, but she's a good one."

"I'd better be off before she starts hollering at *me*. I'll be back soon for a long chat." Linq scooted off after Cherise and Noah.

6

AFFLICTION

T he weather turned that evening, sleet pelting against the windows. Despite cheery fires burning in every room, supper was somber. Those who were able meandered to the dining hall to enjoy a bite to eat. Conversation was subdued, voices low. The absence of the UWS chieftain and his wife, as well as Dar and Etain, was notable.

In an effort to raise spirits to some degree, Swee had the forge cleaned, brought in several tables and chairs, zig-zagged faerie lights across the ceiling, set up a large keg, and hired in a few musicians from town. A large fire blazed in the pit, keeping the space warm.

Most found their way out to the forge. Those who had made the trip to the blood castle needed a distraction, something that would chase away sleep for as long as possible. Nightmares were sure to haunt their dreams. The Dragon Clan and the War Wizards joined the group, all anxious to hear of the excursion to find the demon.

Shared stories invoked memories of the loss of valued friends in battle. Sensing a downward turn in the mood, Linq held up his mug of ale and toasted those who had fallen. Everyone lifted their mugs and drained them in one gulp.

"Once Dar's ready to preside over the lighting of the pyres, we'll honor their bravery and great sacrifice."

Other salutes were spoken around the fire as they remembered their friends and comrades.

Taurnil sat with Linq and Aramis, listening to the tales. In return, he lamented his failure to help Etain in her efforts to free Dar, but the more experienced warriors assured him he did well to walk away with his life and the life of his High Lord. After a toast in honor of Taurnil, they toasted Inferno and every soldier, by name, lost in the battle. Most stayed up late into the night.

When Linq and Aramis finally said their goodnights, they noticed Taurnil asleep in his chair. They shared a knowing smile at the young elf's apparent inability to handle the drink and left him to his dreams.

Before calling it a day, Swee made one more sweep to check on her patients. Except Dar, whose door was locked. She'd left plenty of solution for Etain to reapply during the night, so she moved on. Given a special brew to help her relax and heal, Arachnia was sound asleep. Moving on to Robert's room, she reapplied fresh cloths to his back, noting how much better the wounds appeared already. With a nod at the Black Blades assigned to his room, she left him to sleep.

She walked downstairs, going from room to room, turning off lights as she made her way to the kitchen. Thirsty, she grabbed a glass and held it under the tap as she looked out the window toward the forge. The lights and blazing fire made her smile. There were a few sitting around, deep in conversation. One in particular caught her attention. Taurnil, asleep in his chair, slumped in an uncomfortable position.

Water flowed over the top of the glass, distracting her from the elf's predicament. She laughed at herself, turned off the tap, and took a large drink. Setting the glass aside, she dried her hands on a nearby towel and walked out the back door toward the elf. She placed a hand on his arm for a gentle shake, but he didn't respond. She shook him a little harder. "Taurnil?" Not yet concerned, she pulled back an eyelid and found his eye rolled back into his head. The other was the same.

She touched his neck in search of a pulse and found it shallow, then noticed the heat of his skin. Again, she tried to wake him, shaking him more vigorously. "Taurnil."

Alarm bells rang in her head. Her hands flew over his upper body, desperate to find a wound, something, that would explain his condition. Yet she didn't want to raise an alarm should it prove unimportant, no need to embarrass the young elf.

I've got to get help. Someone he knows in case he wakes.

The first person she thought of was Linq. Although she loathed leaving Taurnil alone, she forced herself back through the kitchen and raced up the stairs to his room, knocking frantically on his door.

"Swee? What is it?" he asked, slipping on a shirt.

"I'm so sorry to disturb you, Linq. It's Taurnil. Something's wrong. Will you help me?"

"Let me get my boots on." In a few minutes, he stepped into the hallway. "Where is he?"

"In the forge. Passed out in his chair. I tried to wake him, but he's unresponsive. His pulse is weak and he's feverish." They rushed downstairs and outside. "I can't imagine what's caused it. I didn't find any wounds."

"As far as I know, he wasn't involved in any fighting."

"Take him to the dining hall and place him on the table. I need to make sure."

With some effort, he draped the unconscious elf over his shoulder and carried him to the designated spot. Swee moved several chairs away from the table as Linq carefully laid him down. "Will you stay with him while I get my things?"

"I'm not going anywhere until we know what ails the boy," he said, busy performing his own investigation.

She ran up to Spirit's herb room to retrieve whatever she could think of that may help. Coming down to the second level, a small voice suddenly spoke in her head.

You have to tell Spirit. She'll know what to do.

I can't disturb her. Not with what's happened.

As she wavered, the small voice boomed in her brain, making her jump. Her hand inadvertently slammed against a nearby door. Swee cringed, her eyes widening when she realized whose door she knocked on.

"Ooh," she moaned, hearing a commotion on the other side.

A groggy Spirit opened the door, tying the sash of a robe, her eyes swollen.

"Oh, Spirit. I'm so, so sorry to bother you." Swee bit her bottom lip. "I know it's a terrible time-"

"What is it, lass?"

The words caught in her throat. *Great. Where's that little voice now?*

"T-Taurnil is afflicted with something. He won't wake up and is burning up with fever."

Spirit thought for a moment. "Has he been drinking?"

"I'm not sure. His pulse is weak. Something told me you may know what causes it. I understand if you don't-"

"Let's go have a look then." Spirit stepped into the hallway, grabbed Swee's arm, and walked her down the stairs. "I need something to do, keep my mind occupied."

Entering the dining hall, Linq had turned up the lights and was in the process of lifting the limp boy to remove his shirt. Spirit leaned close to Swee. "Go get a few pillows from the lounge."

Swee darted across the hall.

"Linq, let me help you."

"Spirit. What're you doing down here? You shouldn't-"

"I'll decide on what I should or shouldn't. This boy needs me help and I intend to do so."

Swee returned, several pillows in her arms. "Put one under his head and set the others down," Spirit instructed. "Once we know what ails him, we can make him more comfortable."

The women got to work, checking for lacerations, bruising, or broken bones. With nothing obvious, Spirit checked his eyes again. They were still rolled back. She looked at Swee, then Linq.

"What?" Swee asked.

"He has symptoms similar to what Faux experienced after Midir ran his sword through her."

Swee looked down at Taurnil. "But there's no wound."

"There's something." Spirit narrowed her eyes. "We're just not seeing it. Linq, please remove his trousers."

As he began to unbutton the fly of Taurnil's trousers, he looked at Swee. "Before I go any further, can we get a blanket?" Noting his intention of preserving the boy's modesty, she scooted down the hall to a nearby linen closet and returned quickly, a sheet in her hand. Once Taurnil's hips were appropriately draped, Linq removed the pants and the women checked his lower limbs. As expected, they found no injuries or broken bones, just a few fading bruises.

Spirit cupped her chin in her hand. "Where was he during the fight?"

"As far as we know, he was in the main hall with Etain," Linq said.

"Swee, you said you found him in the forge." Spirit looked at Linq. "Were you out there, too?"

"Aye."

"Did he tell you anything?"

"Not much. He was imprisoned in a wall of fire after trying to run interference between the demon and Etain." He considered the young elf's fevered face. "He could do nothing but watch she was brutalized by that monster. He was powerless to help."

"Brutalized?" Spirit dropped her hand. "Then how was she able to bring…" She stopped speaking, thoughts of Inferno getting the better of her.

Swee put an arm around her shoulders. "I think I know what you're asking." She looked at Linq. "If that's what happened, how was she able to bring everyone home?"

Spirit pulled a tissue from a pocket in her robe and blew her nose.

Linq crossed his arms over his chest. "Taurnil didn't get to that part of the story."

"Well, then, I guess we'll have to wake Ms. Etain and ask her," Spirit said.

"Ask me what?" Etain asked, standing in the doorway.

Startled by her sudden appearance, Spirit and Swee turned toward her as Linq came from around the table.

Etain walked into the dining hall. "Spirit, what're you doing down here? You should be asleep."

"Sitting in me room isn't helping anyone, especially me."

She noticed Taurnil on the table and rushed to his side. "What's happened?" "We don't know," Swee answered. "We're hoping you can tell us."

Etain touched his cheek. "He's burning up."

Spirit bustled around to the other side of the table. "His symptoms are like Faux's when she was pierced by Midir's sword. Remember?"

Etain gave her a long look. She'd speak to her about Inferno later. "But the bastard confined him in a fire cage. He didn't fight anyone."

"It has us flummoxed, too," Spirit said. "We've had a good look over the boy. There aren't any wounds."

Swee confirmed her observation. "There's nothing to indicate what could be causing this."

Linq scrutinized Etain from the head of the table. "What transpired in that room? He didn't go into a lot of detail; only said he was held at bay while the demon tore you apart."

Etain shrugged. "Dathmet blasted him with a fireball to the stomach. The impact threw him to the floor, but he jumped up straightaway. He didn't give any indication he was injured."

"You're not answering my question-"

"The poison's had plenty of time to spread though his system," Spirit interrupted. With her on one side of Taurnil, Swee on the other, they began a closer inspection. Unable to see anything with her eyes, Spirit turned to touch, laying her hands on the young elf's chest. His skin was hot, but as she moved her hands farther down his torso, she noticed the most intense heat emanated from his abdomen area. She grabbed Swee's hand, instructing her to do the same.

"Can you save him?" Linq asked.

"I can try." Spirit continued prodding the chest and neck in an effort to trace the extent of the infection. "I think a watered-down version of the potion I used on Faux will work. Since there isn't a wound, we'll have to force it down his throat."

"That will take too long," Swee said. "We need to get it into his bloodstream as quickly as possible."

Deep in discussion, Spirit and Swee walked out of the room.

Etain placed a hand on Taurnil's heated chest. "What's going on with you?" She and Linq pulled the sheet in opposite directions, covering his body from neck to toe. "Spirit and Swee will save him. They're a gifted team."

Linq gave her a hard look. "I may not know how things went down in that room, but I can see the pain in your eyes." He cocked a brow. "One day soon, you two *will* tell me everything. Not only for your own good, but for the preservation of us all." Their gazes locked in a momentary standoff, then his features softened. "What're you doing down here anyway? I didn't think anything could get you to leave Dar's side."

"Oh, well, he's sound asleep…" She placed a hand on Taurnil's chest, gazing at his face, "so I went and checked on Robert. I was just coming from his room when I heard voices down here and thought I'd see who was still up."

"How is your brother?"

"He's well…," she reached out and smoothed a few strands of the young elf's hair from his face, then looked at Linq, "or as well as can be expected under the circumstances. His wounds aren't as atrocious as Dar's, but bad enough."

"Did Freeblood mention where he found him?"

"I didn't think to ask." She shrugged. "I will later. I don't even know how he ended up there."

Spirit and Swee returned, their arms full of bowls, herbs, and other tools needed in the creation of magical potions.

"Etain, lass, get back to Dar," Spirit said. "Linq, you need to go, too. Get your rest." She raised a hand at their expected rebuttals. "There's nothing more either of you can do. Let us do our work, and maybe by early morning, we'll have a better idea of what we're fighting."

"Then we will leave you to it." Linq turned to the High Lady. "Mind if I walk with you upstairs? I'd like to lay my own eyes on our High Lord."

"He's probably asleep, but you're welcome to come. Good night, ladies."

The next few days passed quickly as the allies recuperated. Although still recovering from his ordeal, Zorn, Felix by his side, managed to keep most of the Black Blades busy with various chores around the compound, such as doing repairs. He set others to work digging large, shallow holes for the pyres that were to be used for honoring the dead, while some of the less agile were charged with gathering wood. With plans for a big feast to accompany the memorial, Alaster soon had a group together, ready to travel into town for supplies.

The wizards worked day and night, preparing the bodies of those who had passed. When Inferno's time came for preparation, they invited Spirit in the hope it would help her in saying good-bye.

Spirit and Swee took turns trying various potions on Taurnil and checking on their other patients. Swee dressed the High Lord's wounds each day, always leaving a fresh batch of the medicinal solution. The young healer seemed pleased with Dar's improvement, but Spirit remained somewhat conflicted at the speed in which he and Robert were healing.

She was well aware of what was going on with the Krymerian. The bond between Etain and Dar was too strong for the girl not to use every option available. If sharing her blood made him whole again, so be it. What bothered her more was Robert's recovery. He was a completely different kettle of fish. Inferno hadn't trusted the young man. Spirit felt it was plenty reason for her to do the same.

———

Accompanied by the Krymerian healing chant, Etain continued her battery of blood infusions to Dar's back as he slipped in and out of consciousness. She applied as much as she could each time without compromising herself and left his side only twice during those days to check on her brother and Taurnil.

On the fourth morning, Dar opened his eyes, slowly taking in the room. He breathed a sigh of relief and raised his head, but winced when the movement stretched the skin on his back. Pleased his other eye was in working order again, he gazed at his sleeping wife and smiled, his spirits high. Seeing her so peaceful was a blessing to his heart.

You are here…with me.

His gaze roamed down the length of her covered body, his mind indulging in the sweet pleasures she brought with it. A devilish urge came over him. He tested the state of his beard by rubbing it against his bare shoulder. Satisfied, he rubbed his bristled chin against her arm, moving slowly up to her cheek.

A frown distorted her peaceful expression as she swatted at the nuisance, murmuring indistinguishable words.

He rubbed her cheek again and chuckled. A narrowed blue eye opened, then closed. In seconds, both eyes popped open. She laughed at the grin on his face.

"You rascal. How long have you been awake?"

His throat felt dry, his voice rough. "Long enough to watch my beautiful angel sleep."

"Let me get you some water." She threw back the covers.

"No," he croaked, pulling her close. "Not just yet. Stay here and let me drink you in."

"Oh baby…" She relaxed back and gently touched the uninjured side of his face. "It's so good to see you." She lightly kissed his lips. "I know what you need." Careful not to bump him with her elbow, she pulled her hair away from her neck. "Drink me in with your lips."

She nuzzled into his neck as he painfully shifted closer. Intoxicated from her nearness, he bit into the tender flesh at the junction where her delicate neck curved into her shoulder. She jerked from the intrusion but soon relaxed against him, holding him in her arms. The warm elixir flowed over his swollen tongue, dispersing comfort throughout his savaged body.

Etain began to sing, which both comforted his soul and stirred his loins. The blood left a trail of fire in his veins, burning away the evil remnants of the demon and his world.

Even he was amazed by the speed in which his injuries healed, then realized her words were not a sweet love song, but the oldest of the Krymerian healing chants. He pulled back, staring at her. She continued to sing and pushed his head back to the rejuvenating blood. His body's need for sustenance took over, drawing her life force into itself to replenish lost resources.

Perhaps it had been too long since they shared the blood. The taste was richer, more full-bodied, more…gratifying. It consisted of a sweetness he'd not noticed before, an energy that infused him with life and light. He had to force himself to stop, lest he drain her completely. She'd gone limp, passed out from the blooding.

"Damn. I'm sorry, my love." He laid her back into the pillows and rested his head on his own. "Something has changed."

He caressed her hair, admiring the shine and sparkle of the silver strands as they slid through his fingers. Breathing in her perfume, he closed his eyes in a gracious thank you for another chance to make a life with this incredible woman.

"Why the tears, baby?"

He smiled and opened his eyes, happy that she was awake. "A

mere expression of how thankful I am to be here with you, my precious lady."

She placed a hand on his neck, playing with his ear lobe. "There was a point I thought this day might never come."

"You rescued me." Every cell in his body felt alive. He could actually feel the bones in his arm knitting back together. His face no longer felt tight and swollen, but his back would take longer. "You are my savior, Lady Etain."

She blushed, batting her eyelashes. "Well, I had help, you know."

"But it was you who kept fighting to get to me."

"The others were just as determined."

"For some reason, Taurnil of Nunnehi stands out in my mind, or was it another dream?"

She laughed. "No. He came with me. Said he couldn't have his High Lady running off on her own."

"Good man. He's been taught well." Dar propped up slightly on the formerly broken arm and removed the bandages from his head.

Etain gasped. "I forget how powerful our blood is." She touched his once demolished cheek. "Your face is almost back to its handsome self."

He flinched as he slowly pushed up into a kneeling position, but the pain soon passed. "Do you remember the unicorn and the panther?" He removed the bindings on his arm, then the splint.

She watched him, stunned by his transformation. "If it weren't for them, I'd never have found you."

"I dreamt of you," he said as he tossed the remnants of his splint to the floor. He stretched out the arm, twisting it to and fro.

"Dathmet used a glamour. Not only did he have you thinking you'd murdered me, everyone believed I was either dead or also kidnapped. They found my ring…" She held up her hand, "in the ashes."

"I don't know this Dathmet, do I? A lot remains fuzzy."

She looked at him for a long moment, biting her bottom lip. "He's Midir's son." Dar raised both brows. "I guess you didn't know."

"When? Where? *Tartarus*! Who?" He shifted to a cross-legged position. "I never heard of any woman who stayed in his life long enough to bear a child. Are you sure?"

"Quite sure."

Dar thought back to the day of his capture. "I don't remember seeing a man who resembled my brother. I have to ask again. Are you sure?"

She raised up on her elbows. "When you came to rescue me, he was at Midir's…in the tunnels. I didn't know who he was at the time. I thought he was an apprentice or something. Do you remember a man with blood-red skin and a head of flames?"

His eyes widened.

Etain raised a brow and nodded.

Dar shifted again and stretched out next to her, crossing one long leg over hers. "How do you suppose he acquired your ring? A mole? Someone familiar with the demon?"

"Oh, Dar. I hate to think we were betrayed by someone we trust."

"You never took it off. It's the only logical answer, *a chuisle*." He leaned in, gently kissed her lips, then drew back, his eyes intent on her luscious lips. He dipped in again and kissed her more soundly.

Breathless, she whispered, "Only when I shower." The puzzled look on his face compelled her to explain. "The ring. I take it off when I shower."

He kissed her again, devouring her with his enflamed mouth. She moved a hand to his firm buttocks as the other brushed along his side. When her hand touched his back, he groaned and jerked away.

"I'm sorry," she cried, the moment gone.

"No," he gasped. "It will pass. The blood is working its magic. A few more treatments of your sweetness, along with the healing chant, and I will be complete." He shifted down in the bed and pulled her close again. "From where did you learn the ancient Krymerian chant?"

She looked at him as though he'd lost his mind. "Are you kidding?"

"I am not."

"*You* taught me the words, Dar. At *Sôlskin.* After your disastrous flight."

"It was a healing chant, but not the same as the one you've been singing today. Those words are extremely powerful and sacred. They are not to be shared with just anyone."

"Is that who I am? Just anyone?" She tried to push away. "*You* gave me the words, Dar."

He held onto her tightly. "It's far too soon for arguments. Forgive me. I said it wrong. It's not something that's easily shared."

"Well, maybe at the time you thought my life was worth saving."

He heard the hurt in her voice. "Wait. You're losing me here. Save *your* life?"

Etain spent the next half-hour explaining how they came to the castle and the fight with Dathmet. "I was dying, Dar, but then you… woke. At that moment, I knew I could let go."

Memories lit in his mind. "You came to me with the children. Your spirit pulled me from my hell."

"You thought I had come to take you to the spirit world, but the panther and the unicorn showed you the truth. Your connection with them surprised me."

"Aye," he whispered, thinking back. "Bless the children for their tenacity. They get it from their mother," he said, giving her a dreamy look.

"Sounds more like stubbornness, which they got from their father," she snapped.

Smiling, he pushed his face close to hers. "Stubborn? That could be, but they never gave up. That comes from their mother."

She turned her head away. "Do we have to talk about your children right now? I mean no disrespect, but-"

"*My* children?"

"Aye…" She looked back at him. "Henrí and Victoria, the unicorn and the panther. *Your* children." She turned away again. "I know you loved them very much-"

He cupped her chin in his hand and gently forced her to look at him. "*Our* children."

"Huh?"

"Not *my* children. *Our* children."

Her gaze softened as she touched his face. "I think you're still not quite right in the head. Perhaps we should talk about this in a few days when…" Her words faded as he closed his eyes and rested his head on her stomach. "What *are* you doing?"

Turning his head, he opened his eyes. "*Our* children."

"What?"

"Have you been feeling different as of late?"

"Oh, that." She ran a hand through her hair. "Well, sure, but a lot's been going on. I thought it was another side effect of becoming the High Lady of Kaos." Her eyes widened. "Oh."

A smile came to his face. "Oh?" Sitting up, he shifted and leaned across her naked hips, facing her, and placed his hand on her belly.

With a sheepish grin, she said, "I don't think I've touched the seeds Spirit gave me since way before the first trip to Nunnehi."

"Seeds?"

"A girl has to protect herself. I mean, I didn't want any pre-marriage entanglements, then it was our wedding day and I wasn't ready to share you with anyone. When you fell into that nasty trance, everything else was forgotten." She placed a hand over his. "Do you really think I'm pregnant?"

With great reverence, he kissed her belly, humming an old Krymerian lullaby, then pulled up and stretched atop her body, coming face to face. "Aye, Lady Etain. You carry our children safe within your womb. I can feel their life forces pulsing strong inside you."

She smiled, but her mind was elsewhere. "Now that I think about it, I haven't had my period lately. Off the top of my head, I can't remember the last…" Her gaze came back to him. "My breasts *have* been sore, and I haven't felt much like eating. Then the mood swings…" She frowned. "Wait a minute. *Children?*"

He laughed, tears of joy burning his eyes. "Aye, my precious love. I believe they're called twins."

"Oh my," she murmured, engulfed in her loving husband's strong arms. "Twins?" His laughter spilled into her, filling her with his joy. Although stunned by the news, she was soon laughing and hugging him close, albeit carefully. "Twins!"

"I love you, my sweet wife. I look forward to taking you home."

She sighed. "Home." A sudden tear trickled down her cheek.

"Does the idea not make you happy?" He thumbed it away.

"I've thought of this place as home for so long, it's strange to no longer think of it that way. But that isn't what's made me sad." She took his hand in hers. "It's leaving Spirit. With Inferno gone…" Another tear slid down her cheek. "Dar…"

He wrapped her in his arms. "I know, *a chuisle*. I wish it were different, but she must find her way without him." Her tears felt warm on his chest, her body shaking from head to toe. Dar stroked her hair. "Shhh, *ceann beag* (little one). She won't be alone. The clan will rally. They'll choose a new chieftain and will thrive."

"I hope so. The children will need them, too. Those poor babies."

"Children?"

She pulled back, swiping at her nose. "I forget you haven't met them yet. They have four - Seth, Dylan, Molly, and Tegan. I'm sure Spirit'll be bringing them home from their gran's soon. They'll need each other."

"I look forward to meeting the rest of the family." He hugged her again. "For now, I want you to rest."

"Are you going somewhere?"

"Just to freshen up and shave." He scrubbed at his chin. "I won't be long."

"Be careful of your back."

He slid out of bed. "Don't worry about me. Get a little more sleep."

Despite the pull of his back as he shaved, his thoughts drifted to Etain and their expected children. Never in the past hundred years had he dared dream of such a miracle coming into his life again. Unbridled tears of joy flowed as unspoken gratitude poured from his heart for the blessing of this new family. He knew it would be some time before they were able to return to *Sôlskin,* but the promise was there. He could wait.

Refreshed, he returned to the bedroom. Finding his wife sound asleep, he tenderly placed a hand on her belly and hummed the same old lullaby as before.

"For anyone who tries to separate us again, I vow this day to rip out their heart and savor its bitter juices." Straightening, he walked to the wardrobe, dressed, then quietly slipped out of the room.

Voices floated up the stairs as he made his way down to the kitchen. Cappy, Thoric, Arachnia, and Linq seemed to be involved in a conversation of betrayal.

"Anyone I know?" he asked at the door.

Everyone turned, a surprised look on each face. Linq jumped to his feet. "By the stars, man. What're you doing out of bed?"

Cappy joined in. "Here now. Let your body finish healing, Dar. God knows what could happen if you're up and about too soon."

"I thank you for your concerns." He twisted his arm and pointed to his face. "As you can see, I'm all better."

"That's not pos-" Thoric started to say.

"Impossible!" Arachnia said. "Not even you can heal that quickly, Dar

Dar shrugged off their concerns. "If it were impossible, would I look this good?"

"I was there, in case you don't remember." Arachnia grabbed his chin and turned his head this way and that for a closer inspection. "We all saw what shape you were in." She turned her attention to his arm, moving it around. "You're lucky to be alive. I don't care what anyone says. You shouldn't be walking around."

He looked at each one in turn. "I'll take it slow. Does that make you feel better?"

Arachnia gave him an uncertain frown. "Just don't push it."

"Aye, milady." He noticed the bruises on her face and neck. "You look like you had a tough time, too."

She touched her face. "Oh, I'd forgotten about them. Yes. I felt it was time to teach the *Bok* a few manners."

Despite her light-hearted response, Dar felt a pang in his heart at the sacrifice she'd been prepared to make on his behalf. "Thank you, Ara." He bowed his head. "I am most fortunate to have such tenacious friends."

"Well…" She glanced at the Ambassadors. "You're welcome."

"Now, back to the earlier conversation…" His gaze went to the elf. "What betrayal were you talking about?"

"We were discussing something that happened before the battle," Linq said, returning to his seat.

Dar waited for him to continue. When no offering was made, he raised a brow. "And?"

"Well…" Linq cleared his throat. "We, er, found someone on the inside, working with the demon." Seeing the gleam in Dar's eyes, he hurried to add, "We have said person under guard."

"Yes," Arachnia said. "We have everything under control."

Dar considered the two. "What's to worry about then?" He walked to the coffee pot and poured himself a cup. "Besides, I don't think anything could upset me today. I'm back with my loving wife. We're surrounded by friends. From where I stand, the future looks bright. What more could I ask for?"

"You see, that's the point," Linq said.

Dar sipped his coffee, looking from one to the other. "I'm listening."

"Well, old chap…" Cappy pointed at Arachnia. "I think the one who saw it happen should explain."

"Yes. She should be the one," Thoric added.

Arachnia rolled her eyes at the Ambassadors. "The sacrificial lamb thanks you for your support." She turned to Dar. "We should go somewhere more private, and…Etain should be there."

Dar grunted, mulling over her request. "Give me about thirty minutes, then come to our room. We can talk there." Turning, he walked toward the door, coffee in hand.

Arachnia waited until he left the room before she pounced on the others. "How is it *I* was chosen to tell him about Faux?"

"Knowing Dar as we do...," Thoric stated in a calm and cool voice, "and that's to say we apparently don't *really* know him as well as we thought, well... We decided you should tell him, seeing as you were the one who caught her red-handed."

"When exactly did you three decide this?"

Cappy smiled at her. "Just before you came downstairs."

"Great. Thanks, guys. You know how I hate his blow ups," she said, resigned to her distasteful duty. "You three owe me."

"Don't count me in that payback," Linq smiled. "It wasn't me who served you up on a platter."

"Maybe not, but you have the biggest grin," she snapped.

Dar walked into the bedroom toward the bed. "Wake up, *a chuisle.* Company's coming."

Lying on her back, she rolled onto her side, pulling the covers over her head.

He laughed. "Get up, sleepyhead. Ara wants to talk to us."

"Can't it wait till later? Like when the sun is *up?*"

"The sun *is* up. I'm sure it could wait, but I told her to meet us here in a half-hour." He set his cup on the side table. "By the time you drag this lovely peach out of bed..." He slapped her on the bottom.

"Hey!"

"She'll be here. So, get dressed." With a great flourish, he yanked the covers from the bed.

Etain flipped over, fire in her eyes. "What's so damn important that it couldn't wait another couple of hours?" Slipping out of bed, she reached for her robe and wrapped it around her, tying the sash with a jerk.

"She says she knows who betrayed us. I assume it's Freeblood since she wants to tell us in private." After a light kiss, he pulled away, picked up his cup, and walked to the balcony.

She followed him. "It's not Freeblood."

He peered at her over the rim of his cup as he sipped his coffee. "How do you know?"

"I told you before he doesn't tolerate evil." She gave him an indignant glare. "If my word isn't enough, perhaps the fact he went to the blood castle to help save your ass is."

"Of course. I'd forgotten he was there. It's not that I doubt your word, milady." He turned, watching the men at work outside the courtyard walls. All too familiar with the procedure, he knew they were funeral pyres. "So many have lost their lives in the war against the *Bok*." He watched in silence for a few moments. "Had I not fallen for the glamour, there would be far less pyres being built. I've let down all those who followed me into battle." He turned to face her. "I'm so sorry for Inferno."

"That's enough of that talk. Inferno and everyone else believe just like you. They made their own choices."

A soft knock ended their conversation.

Etain glanced over her shoulder as she walked to the door. "If anyone's to blame, it's me." Her hand on the knob, she took a deep breath and opened the door. "Come in, Ara. I hear you have news."

"I'm sorry you have to hear it from me." Ara stepped into the room but remained close to the door. "Before I start, I ask that you listen to everything before you act." Her eyes settled on Dar. "You especially, given the way you tend to overreact."

Dar walked to the fireplace and set his empty cup on the mantle. "When have you ever known me to act without justice?"

"Please listen and think before you take any action." Her gaze returned to Etain. "Someone in the castle betrayed us. There's no easy way to say this, so I'm just going to be straightforward." She looked at Dar. "It was Faux." Ara's gaze never left his, intent on his reaction.

"What?" Etain's outburst made Ara step back. "No! She may only look out for what's in her best interest most of the time, but she would *not* betray this house."

"I-I was there, Etain. She was in the process of reversing the barrier around the castle." Ara gave Dar a frantic look. "She had a black candle and was talking about a pink mist."

"Why would you say that?" Etain yelled in her face. Dar dashed over and grabbed his wife around the waist. "Did she make a move on Cappy? Or maybe she approached Thoric, upsetting your little *menage a'trois*." Turning in Dar's arms, she pushed away. "And you! Why are you taking her side? You above all others should know Faux wouldn't do such a thing."

"I'm not siding with anyone, Etain." Dar looked at Ara, who appeared ready to explode herself. "Are you sure it was Faux?"

"I personally caught her in the act in Spirit's herb room upstairs." She leaned back, just avoiding Etain's attempted right uppercut. Dar pulled his wife farther away.

"Why are you lying?" Etain screamed. "Let me go, Dar! I'll not have her blaming Faux."

"Ask Freeblood!" Ara yelled, flinging herself at the door. "He'll tell you what happened. He was there."

"Let me go!" Etain strained to get to the woman, despite Dar's iron hold.

"Get out, Ara!" He bellowed. "Stay in your room until we clear this up."

Ara ripped the door open and jumped through, slamming it behind her.

"A stupid little door isn't gonna keep you safe!" Etain yelled. "I swear, Dar VonNeshta, if you don't let me-"

He twisted toward the bed, gave Etain a hard push, and positioned himself in front of the door.

She stumbled forward, but righted herself before she fell and turned to face him. "Get out of the way."

Dar crossed his arms over his chest. "We're going to speak to Freeblood first."

"Then I'll go get him." She rushed at him.

He easily stopped her. "This isn't good for you *or* the babies. You *must* calm down." He felt her body relax. He gave her a wary look. It was too easy. "Etain…"

A serene smile came to her lips as her ice-blue gaze turned silver. She disappeared in a blue shimmer.

"Etain!" Dar ran out the door.

7

AFTERMATH

F inally given permission to visit, Freeblood walked through the imprisoned Faux's bedroom door. He'd hoped for a cheerful reunion, but instead, she stormed toward him, demanding why he hadn't been to see her.

"It hasn't been by choice." He looked at the guard and waited until he'd closed the door. "They've only *just* allowed me to see you."

"It's been weeks!" She turned as Freeblood walked past her to the opposite side
of the room.

Hands on his hips, he faced her. "Just long enough for you to forget what was happening, huh?"

She glared at him, crossing her arms over her chest, but couldn't hold his gaze.

"There was a battle, Faux. We thought Dar and Etain were dead, but then she showed up and things got really crazy." The energy coursing through him made it difficult to stand still. "She was able to find Dar," he said, pacing back and forth, "but he was in another realm." He occasionally looked at her as he paced, wishing she would turn her black gaze to him. "It took time to figure out how to open the freaking portal. Man, it felt like it took forever. When we finally found him, he was in pretty bad shape." He stopped and faced her. "We lost Inferno." Still, she wouldn't look at him. "I'm sorry I haven't been to see you."

She dropped her arms and headed toward the door. "I want to see Dar."

"No," he said a bit louder than he intended. Faux stopped, her hand on the knob. "They won't let you near him right now." He moved toward her. "Did you hear what I said about Inferno?"

She shrugged. "What's it to me? I have the right to see the father of my child."

Freeblood groaned. "Fine. Have it your way. But for the record, I'm against this. We both know what you did. It's only a matter of time before Dar finds out."

With a flourish, she turned the knob and opened the door. Two Black Blades filled the doorway, staring back at her.

"Take me to the High Lord. Now."

"You are not allowed to leave your room," said the one to her right.

The other returned her glare. "Our orders are to keep you confined to your quarters."

Faux continued to rave. "You don't have any right to keep me here! I want to see Dar!" Her screams brought Talamain, a Wizard of the First Order, out from his room. He listened as the guards explained.

"That's right," Faux said. "I *demand* to see the *father* of my child."

Talamain gave her a cold look. "Take her to the High Lord. He seems to be in better health. It is his place to deal with her."

Etain suddenly appeared next to them. "We'll save you the trip."

Dar came up quickly behind her, pulling up short to avoid colliding into her.

Stunned by their sudden appearance, and the High Lady's state of undress, the guards quickly recovered with a salute as Talamain bowed his head. "High Lord. High Lady."

"Talamain. Blades." Dar straightened his shoulders. "We're here to speak with the..." Etain's expression warned him to tread carefully. "With Faux." Freeblood stepped in the doorway. "And Freeblood."

The War Wizard bowed his head again. "As you wish, High Lord. Guards, escort the prisoner into her room."

Faux scowled at the Black Blades. Freeblood held his breath, unsure of how to proceed. Etain took matters into her own hands. "Turn your ass around, Faux, and go back into your room."

Her gaze moved to Etain, then to Dar and back. "Hmph." She whirled around and marched past Freeblood. The guards separated and resumed their posts on either side of the door.

Talamain smiled. "You are clear to enter, High Lord."

"Thank you, Talamain." Dar waved Etain in, then followed and closed the door.

"Hello, Faux," said Dar. "It's been a while since we last spoke. The child appears to be doing well."

"We're just fine, despite being locked up." Rubbing her belly, she tilted her head to the side. "You don't look so banged up to me." Her inquisitive gaze slid to Etain. "That's a new look for you. Have you changed your hair?"

"Maybe it's the glare in my eyes," Etain said. "We've had a chat with Arachnia."

Faux stomped a foot, her tail stiff. "Whatever she said, she's a liar! I was only helping Spirit with her herb room."

Etain glanced at Dar. "I see." She walked past Faux, forcing her to turn around. "Why would Spirit need *your* help?"

"Well... It was crazy around here." She looked over her shoulder at Freeblood. "You remember, don't you, babe?" He only stared in return. She rolled her eyes and came back to her sister. "Spirit was really busy with...stuff."

"Was she?" Etain stopped. "What 'stuff' was she doing?"

Faux shrugged. "I don't know. Mage stuff, I guess. The room was such a mess, I thought I'd cleanup for her."

Etain shifted her weight, crossing her arms. "So, she gave you the key?"

"Key? Uh… Yes!" she said with a nervous laugh. "How else would I have gotten in?"

"Do you still have it? Because the room needs to be locked again." Etain noticed Dar at the door, speaking quietly with one of the guards.

Faux patted her clothes, as if looking for the key. "Gosh. I don't recall what I did with it. Maybe it fell on the floor when that whack job attacked me." She turned to Dar, her hands on her belly. "We're lucky she didn't hurt the baby."

Dar stroked his chin. "It's not like Ara to attack without provocation. Are you sure you haven't forgotten something?"

Faux shook her head, sneaking a peek at Freeblood. "I haven't."

"Hmm…" Dar walked toward the young man, his gaze on Faux. "No black candle?" He raised a brow. "Or mist?"

Faux's face turned a shade lighter. "I-I was straightening things. A candle or two might've been involved." She acted as though she were thinking on it. "I don't remember any pink mist."

A smirk came to his lips. "Did I say it was pink?"

"Uh…well…yeah." Her eyes darted from Dar to Spirit, then Etain. "How else would I know?"

There was a knock on the door. "Freeblood," Dar said, turning to him, "would you mind getting that?"

"Sure, Dar." He gave Faux a quick glance as he walked to the door.

Dar already knew who was on the other side. He'd sent a personal invitation via the guards outside Faux's room. "Come in, Spirit. Thank you for coming."

Looking somewhat sheepish, she stepped into the room. "What can I do for you?"

He motioned her closer as he returned to Etain's side. "Come stand next to us. I'm sorry we've had to disturb you, but I think you're the only one who can sort out an argument between Ara and Faux."

"I don't know that I can help," she said, walking toward the couple, "but I'm happy to try." As she passed Faux, her brows lifted.

"First things first…" He took her hand in his, shifting her attention to him. "Inferno was a good man. He will be dearly missed by us all. Whatever you need, you say the word. And should anyone give you grief, you let me know. I'll take care of it."

"Bless you, Dar," she whispered, tears in her eyes.

He gave her hand a reassuring squeeze. "Now, let's give this other matter a shot, shall we?" He waited until she gave an approving nod, then turned to Faux. "I think you can clear this up in a matter of seconds. I'm aware you cast a protection spell around the castle not long after Midir left."

Spirit glanced at Faux. "Aye. I didn't want him coming back to finish the job of taking Etain, or killing you."

"Was the spell visible?"

"A mage or a person who knows magic, such as yourself, would be able to see it," she said to Dar. "But no one else."

Dar glanced at Faux. "Can you tell me what it looked like?"

"It had a pink cast to it, but since coming back from Nunnehi, I see it's deep red. The wizards must've added a touch of their own magic."

Dar smiled again. "Oh, aye. They did." Seeing Faux squirm was almost too delicious. "You say you were in Nunnehi. When was that?"

Spirit exchanged a look with Etain. "You should know, Dar. You're the one who sent me, Swee, and Etain to get us out of the way."

"Actually, it was for your own safety," he said with a raised brow. "However, was that before or after Freeblood and Faux arrived?"

"Considering how shocked I was to see the lad show up in Nunnehi, it was before." She glanced at Faux. "This is the first I've seen of the lass."

Dar stroked his chin again. "Tell me, Spirit. Do you have a key to your herb room?"

With a furrowed brow, her eyes darted from Dar to Etain. "Aye." She reached into a pocket of her skirt. "Here 'tis."

"Is there another?" Etain asked.

Spirit cocked her head. "You know I've only the one."

Dar raised a brow. "Have you had it with you the entire time? You haven't lent it out to anyone?"

Faux made a mad dash toward the still open door, pushing past Freeblood, who stumbled back. The Blades stepped into her path, but she released a blast of fire that threw them across the hall. Both slammed into the opposite wall and slumped to the floor, unconscious.

Dar ran out the door after her, but stopped long enough to check on the guards. Finding they'd suffered only minor burns, he raced down the stairs in pursuit of his prey, Freeblood not far behind him.

At the bottom of the stairs, they found Swee sprawled on the floor, hit by one of Faux's fire blasts. Dar kneeled at her side. "Someone get Spirit. She's upst-"

"I'm here," Spirit said, rushing down the stairs.

With Swee in good hands, he ran out the front doors in time to see Linq fall to the ground, stunned by a blast from the fleeing girl. He turned to Freeblood at his side. "Check on Linq."

Freeblood grabbed his arm. "Please don't hurt her."

Dar searched the courtyard. "No promises." Spotting her near the main gates, he raised a hand.

After the men ran out of the room, Spirit grabbed Etain's arm and faced her. "There's not much time to explain right now…" Her eyes widened at the damage left in the girl's wake. She shook her head as her gaze came back to Etain. "I have to go after them, make sure no one else is hurt, but you need to know. Faux lost the baby not long after Midir's attack. 'Twas the poison. I tried to tell you before, but…" Etain could only stare at her. "Did ya hear what I said, lass? That child she carries isn't Dar's. I have to go." Spirit dashed out.

Etain turned her back to the door, her mind in a whirl. *Not Dar's?* A short manic laugh slipped out. She slapped a hand over her mouth, not sure whether to laugh or cry. *She's obviously pregnant. Could it be Freeblood's? Holy hell, who cares? It isn't Dar's!*

She smiled as the heaviness in her heart lifted. Another thought tumbled through her mind, crushing the momentary thrill. *Oh, Dar…*

Tears burned in her eyes. Then she remembered her good news and swiped away the tears. *We'll mourn the child's passing, but he's no longer obligated to her. We are free.*

Screams from the courtyard drew her out onto the balcony. She saw Faux, standing alone before the main gates, unable to move her legs. Dar walked through the group of onlookers, a glare in his eyes.

What will you do now that you've caught her?

She tried a mind meld with her husband to no avail. His great fury blocked any outside intrusions. Surely, he wouldn't hurt her. Etain wrapped her arms around herself and watched, anxious to see how the High Lord would handle a traitor.

Dar fisted and relaxed his hands at his sides. His gaze dared the trembling young woman to deny the accusations. Her mouth opened, then shut without uttering a sound.

"Shall I share with you the horrors suffered by our men as they took on the enemy? Would you like to see their faces, frozen in death?" He stepped closer, his hot, angry breath raking over her skin. "Or perhaps those are too removed from your demon sense. How about I show you the abuses your sister endured at the hand of that bastard?"

Freeblood stood just behind Dar where Faux could see him. Eyes the size of saucers, her attention snapped back to the High Lord. "I didn't know…"

"Then allow me to enlighten you." His large hands engulfed her head, tilting it back. She squeezed her eyes shut. "Makes no difference if your eyes are open or closed. You will see this and accept ownership of the devastation you have been a party to." His mind bored into hers, sharing the horrors he'd experienced since his return from Nunnehi. The blood shed by so many; the pain and humiliation of torture; the anguish of having his heart ripped from his chest at the death of his precious wife.

Her screams were heard throughout Laugharne. Tears flowed down her cheeks, her body shaking within his hold.

"For your crimes against the people in this castle, against the Alamir kingdom and the kingdom of Nunnehi, it is my duty to ensure you never do such a thing again." From the corner of his eye, he saw Linq and motioned him closer with a jerk of his head. As he stepped up, Dar released the girl and demanded his dagger.

"Are you sure, Dar?" he asked, handing it over. "She placed all of us in great danger, but think before you do this."

"She is a traitor and has to answer for the part she played in this abomination." He displayed the knife in front of Faux, giving her a good look at the instrument of her death before he placed it under her jaw. "Innocent lives were lost. Valiant soldiers who stood against the *Bok* to protect this house, to protect us all." He pressed the tip into her skin, pushing her head back until a small trail of blood trickled down her neck. "The High Lady of Kaos, my *wife*, your *sister*, jeopardized her own life to stop the demon you value over family and friends. Spirit lost her precious husband and their clan is left without a leader. Even your Freeblood fought the bastard. And what part did *you* play? *Traitor*. For your crimes, FauxPas, I sentence you to death."

"No! Please, Dar. I-I was confused. I didn't know what I was doing. You can't hold that against me."

Freeblood approached. "Don't do this, if for no other reason than the child she carries."

Dar shifted, standing behind his quarry, the blade at her throat. "What should I do, boy? Let her loose to do this again?"

"Think of the child. I'm begging you not to take her life."

Several of the Black Blades in the crowd surrounded him.

"What of the children of Inferno and Spirit?" Dar asked the pained young man. "What is *their* fate now, their father dead at the hand of this monster? Did she give *your* life a second thought?" He then addressed the Black Blades. "Hold him fast."

Faux pushed against Dar as best she could. "You would kill your own child?"

He smiled, but there was no humor. He leaned in close to her ear.

116

"Not my child." He emitted a guttural laugh, feeling the shock run through her. "*You* figure out who the father is. It's not mine."

The edge of the dagger pressed into her flesh.

"Dar!" Freeblood yelled. "I know what she did was wrong, but I swear on my love for this woman, she'll not cause trouble again." His words had no effect. He looked at the faces around him, terror in his eyes. Seeing Etain on the balcony, he made another desperate attempt. "Dar! What of Etain? Does she deserve to lose another member of her family? Hasn't she lost too much already?"

The words hit their mark. The Krymerian swallowed past the lump in his throat, pushing down the anger, as he calculated a new course of action. Slowly, he dragged the tip of the blade across Faux's throat, leaving a faint trail of blood. He came around to face the girl, then sliced the sharp blade across each of his palms before sliding the dagger into his belt. A horrified Faux watched as he dipped a thumb into each blood-soaked palm. Taking her head in his hands again, the bloodied thumbs dragged over each of her eyes as he spoke.

"I blind you from your gift and powers. Never again shall you see them or see those of another."

Dipping into the blood again, he dragged his thumbs over her mouth. "I mute you from your gift and powers. You will never again cast a spell or utter the words another has used to cast a spell."

He covered her ears with his hands. "I deafen you from your gift and powers. You will never hear the words of a spell spoken by another with the gift."

He spread the blood down her neck, over her chest and arms, moving over her belly and down her legs to complete the casting. "I strip you of your powers and all privileges in accordance. I strip you of your heritage from those who gave you life. From this day forward, you will walk this world as a mere mortal, an orphan, dependent on others."

Done with this business, he let her go and abruptly turned his back on her. As he passed Freeblood, he stopped, speaking so only he could hear. "Remember this day well. What I've done to her I can do to you...and your child." The High Lord stalked away and disappeared through the massive front doors.

———————

She held her head high, glaring in the faces full of unspoken accusations. But with Dar's departure, the group separated and dispersed. Her glare landed on the only other person in the courtyard.

"How long have you known?"

"Just now," Freeblood said, a smile slowly forming on his lips.

"How could he know?" she asked through clenched teeth, her hands balled into fists at her sides.

He shrugged. "There isn't much he *doesn't* know. Infuriating, huh?" Seeing his humor was lost on the girl, he sobered. "You know, there are a lot of things I want to do in my life. Being a father is one of them, but I wasn't planning on it happening this soon."

"Well, congratulations, Dad. I never wanted a kid in the first place."

"Bullshit. It's all you talked about when we first met. Baby this, baby that. Dar, Dar, Dar. What's changed?"

"That was different," she growled. "That would've sealed my future in the VonNeshta household. That kid would've been the first born."

"Oh, I see." He pursed his lips. "So, it wasn't the *child* so much as the trappings that came with it. You *are* a bitch, Faux. What *am* I to you? Someone to play with and discard when you're bored? Is that what was going on with that Dathmet jerk? Did you get tired of me and decide to move on to something new? Maybe Dar *doesn't* know everything. Maybe you're carrying a demon child."

"It wasn't like that," she snarled.

He spread his arms wide. "Then explain it to me. You flirting with other men doesn't bother me much, I know it's your nature, but what happened with him went beyond flirting. Do you have any concept of what happened here? People are dead because of him!"

"Why am *I* being blamed for all this?" she screamed, waving her hand around the courtyard. "I didn't bring the *Bok* here."

"The cost, you idiot. Do you have any idea how many more could've died if you'd succeeded in lowering that protection spell? Do you not value me any more than that?"

"I did it *for* you," she howled, stomping a foot. "He promised me you wouldn't be hurt."

He smirked in disbelief. "Thanks, Faux. Now I know what you think of me." He turned away and walked in the direction of the stables. He needed time to cool off before things went to a level he wasn't prepared to handle.

"What?" she called after him. "I didn't say-"

Spinning on his heels, he spelled it out. "Didn't think I could take care of myself or you, huh? Just assumed I'd be an easy kill for the asshole?" He purposely strode back toward her. "Dar isn't the only man who can fight." Again, he turned to leave, then said over his shoulder, "I plan on being in my kid's life. I can do it with or without you." In a flash, he was gone.

Left completely alone in the courtyard, she caught movement from the corner of her eye. She looked up. Etain still stood on the balcony, watching her. Their eyes locked for a brief moment, then Etain turned her back and walked into the bedroom. Faux watched a few moments longer, then decided she should leave, as well. Seeing the hurt in Freeblood's eyes had pierced her heart, filled her with an unexpected sadness.

She rested a hand on her belly. "Come along, Rosencrantz." With a sigh, she turned and walked through the gates, meandering down the path toward the small cottage once used by Dar and Etain. "We have a lot to think about."

Storming out of the courtyard and into the house, Dar stopped to check on Swee. He found her and Linq sitting in the dining hall. Spirit was there, too, fussing over them. Someone had righted the overturned chairs and straightened the room. Once satisfied his friends were not seriously hurt, he asked after Taurnil, Etain having informed him of his condition.

Swee took a drink from a glass of ale, stealing a glance at the young elf asleep on the table. "He's no better, but he's no worse."

"Wouldn't he be more comfortable in a bed?"

"I'm afraid to move him," Spirit said. "I don't know how this poison works and it may send it deeper into his system."

"Has Alatariel been told?"

Linq spoke up. "Aye. She'll be here as soon as she can break away, says she's bringing her healer to help."

Dar raised a brow. "What business would keep her from coming to her son?" He gave them a good look over. "Are you sure you two are all right?"

Swee and Linq looked at one another, then Dar. "Aye," Linq said. "We be fine."

"Good. Now, does anyone know anything about this demon, Dathmet?"

By this time, Aramis and Ra had joined the group, hearing Dar's voice. "There's another one on the loose?" Aramis asked.

"Never heard the name," Linq said.

Dar raised an eyebrow at their confused expressions. "I'm guessing Etain didn't share that information with anyone? Or that he claims to be Midir's son?"

Linq jumped to his feet. "By the stars! She mentioned coming face to face with a demon at Midir's, but nothing more. *Fyrir sakir helvítis, Hinn hæsti Drottinn* (For fuck's sake, High Lord)!"

"Who's Midir?" Ra asked.

"Dar's dead brother," said Linq, his body shaking. "Dar, we assumed you gave her the information. Maybe if we'd known, Inferno wouldn't…" He trailed off, remembering Spirit was still in the room. "Spirit, I-"

She walked to him and took him by the shoulders. "Stop. I appreciate your loyalty to me husband. He loved you like a brother." She blinked several times, fighting back the tears, but held his gaze. "Blaming Etain or anyone else in this house won't bring him back. What it does is break us down, make us weak. We can't afford to be weak. Not now, not ever." She gave his shoulders a reassuring squeeze and let go. "Whatever Inferno's reasons for taking on the demon, whether he were Midir's son, or even Midir himself, would *not* have changed anything. We'll never know what drove him to it, but we have to believe it-"

"*He* knows." Everyone looked at Aramis, who cocked his head toward Taurnil. "He was in the room the entire time. He saw what happened to Etain *and* Inferno. Save him and you'll have your reasons."

Dar touched Spirit on the shoulder. "Let's hope Alatariel shows up sooner rather than later." He suddenly staggered.

Linq caught him. "Someone grab a chair."

"I'm fine. Just a little light-headed."

"Sit him down, Linq," Ra said, shoving a chair toward Dar. "Won't help anyone if he breaks those welts open again."

Swee rushed to his side. "Aramis, would you please get some water from the kitchen?" She turned to Dar. "You've done too much, too soon." Leaning over his shoulder, she peeked down the back of his shirt. "There's blood showing through your bandages." She straightened, a glare in her eyes. "You're going to drink that damn glass of water, get upstairs, have Etain change your bandages, and get your ass in bed." He opened his mouth to speak, but she wagged a finger in his face. "No. *I* am in charge right now." Aramis returned with the water and handed it to Swee, who promptly shoved the glass at Dar. "Drink and go."

Dar did as he was told, drinking a good bit of the water, then swiped his mouth with the back of his hand. "I thought *Spirit* was bossy."

Everyone chuckled, except Swee. "Linq, Ra, please make sure he gets to his room."

"Yes, ma'am, Ms. Swee!" Ra said, a grin on his face. Spirit grabbed the glass from Dar's hand before Ra took hold of one arm and Linq the other.

"Gentlemen!" Dar came up quickly. "I'm perfectly capable of walking upstairs without a nursemaid."

"Just following orders, man," Ra laughed, raising his hands.

Dar swayed and grabbed the chair. "I'll take it slow." He breathed in and slowly let it out. "Back to our original conversation… My wife may have learned a few things about this demon through me, but his name and relationship with my brother were *not* included." He looked at the faces around the room before he headed to the door. "Should anyone need me, I'll be with my wife." He stopped. "I noticed the funeral pyres being prepared. How soon do we expect to have the ceremony?"

"As soon as you're up to the task, Dar," Aramis said. "Fortunately, with the colder weather, we've no need to rush."

"Day after tomorrow should be fine. These brave souls have waited too long to be honored." He bowed his head to the room. "Good day, everyone."

On his way upstairs, he considered how to broach the subject without causing too much distress for his wife, or himself. He decided the best thing to do was start with a mundane topic and slowly work the conversation in the direction he intended.

He expected to find her in bed or possibly getting dressed when he walked into the room. He found himself alone.

His hopes rose. A shower, perhaps? The bathroom was empty, too.

Not yet concerned, he walked into the hallway and returned downstairs…at the risk of Swee's wrath. No one he passed had seen Etain. He found Spirit in the garden, conversing with a group of women he'd not seen before.

She smiled at his approach. "Aren't you supposed to be in bed?" Seeing his knitted brows, she became concerned herself. "What is it, love?"

"Have you seen Etain? I left her in our room, but she's not there. I know she's in the castle, I can feel her presence, but I can't locate her."

Spirit thought a moment. "She may be with her brother. You'll find him in the room just before mine and…" She frowned. "Well…" The color drained from her face. "Oh, I can't…"

Dar wrapped her in his arms. Burying her face in his chest, she broke. The ladies pressed around them, patting her on the back, trying to comfort her with soft words.

"Milady…" He tightened his arms around her, wishing he could carry her pain. "I know we're a poor substitute, but we're here for you. All of us."

The group of women split as a striking, dark-skinned woman walked up. "Ms. Spirit, why don't you go lie down for a spell?" she said, patting her on the back. "You've been doing too much. You need to sleep." She looked up at Dar. "Since I haven't met you, I'm guessing you're the man they went to get?"

"Aye, milady. Dar VonNeshta, at your service."

"Good to meet you. I'm Cherise. I'm going to make her some tea, something to help her sleep. Would you mind taking her upstairs? I'll be right up."

"Thank you, Cherise. You know which one is her room?"

"I do, sir. Be right there."

"Ladies…," he said, still holding Spirit tightly. "If you'll excuse us." The women dispersed, leaving the two alone. "Spirit, we're going-"

She collapsed in his arms. He grimaced, the wounds on his back stretching, some ripping open. He felt the warmth of his blood spread over his back. An involuntary cry escaped his lips, but he gritted his teeth, held onto her, and scooped her into his arms. "Someone help!" he yelled as he stumbled backwards.

Thoric rushed toward him, arriving just in time to take Spirit from his arms. Cappy, close behind, grabbed Dar. Linq dashed around the corner to help Cappy before the two of them crashed to the ground. Alaster, Arachnia, and several Black Blades came running, too. Cappy and Linq relinquished their hold to two of the Blades.

Ara saw the blood seeping through Dar's shirt. "Good Lord! Gentlemen, get Dar to the dining hall. Swee's probably there. Thoric, take Spirit to her room. I'll show you the way." She looked over her shoulder. "Alaster, go find Etain."

"Be happy to, but I've never met the woman."

"Look for a silver-haired Amazon. You can't miss her." With that, she opened the door and followed Thoric inside.

"Alaster, I'll go with you," said Linq. He motioned to the Blades. "Take the High Lord to the dining hall. Be careful of his back. Should Swee not be there, find her."

"Aye, sir." The six Blades maneuvered the High Lord, face down, into the castle.

"Never a dull moment around here," Alaster said, joining Linq.

"Not lately. Let's see if we can find the High Lady."

Humming under her breath, Etain quietly closed the door to Robert's room and turned toward her own, hoping to find Dar there. Linq and Alaster topped the stairs before she'd gone two steps.

"Etain," Linq called.

She turned, a smile on her face. "Linq. Hi." Her gaze went to the man at his side. "Is this your friend from Deudraeth?"

The elf looked at Alaster as though seeing him for the first time. "Er… Yes. This is Alaster. Alaster… Etain, Dar's wife."

She held out her hand. "Good to meet you, Alaster. I'm glad you've come."

He shook her hand, returning the smile. "Lady Etain. When Arachnia called you an Amazon, I didn't think she was serious."

His hand was warm, his grip strong, and his smile electric. She liked him already. "All this and I still can't keep up with my husband," she laughed. "Welcome to Laugharne. How long will you be here?"

"He's here to stay," Linq interrupted. "Sorry to cut this short. Dar's downstairs, passed out. We've had him moved to the dining hall."

Her heart skipped a beat. "What? Holy hell! Thank you, Linq." She rushed past the men and ran downstairs. At the dining hall door, she met Swee just coming out.

"Oh, Etain!" She stepped back, hand on her chest. "You scared the life out of me. Come in. I was on my way to-"

Etain pushed past her. "What happened? What was he doing? Is he okay?" She found Dar at the opposite end of the dining table, lying on his stomach, fresh cloths on his back. "Dar?" She leaned over, peering into his face. "Are you awake?"

His eyes opened, a lopsided grin on his lips. "Awake, but indisposed at the moment."

She pulled up a chair. "Crazy man. What the hell were you doing? Traipsing around the castle, commanding the minions to do your bidding?"

His laugh ended in a grimace. "Old habits."

She rolled her eyes as she touched his cheek. "Contrary to your high opinion of yourself, you are *not* a god. You're flesh and bone, just like the rest of us. You have to give your body time to heal."

"I'm of a mind to agree, milady."

She kissed him on the forehead. "I'm gonna check on T."

"I'll wait here."

That made her laugh. "Be right back, my love."

Etain walked to the other end of the table. Taurnil turned his head as she came closer. "E," he whispered.

She placed a finger over his lips. "Shhhh. Save your strength."

"You're okay." He gave her a weak smile, but it faded soon after. "I'm sorry."

Taking his hand in hers, she held it close as she smoothed his hair. "You have nothing to be sorry for. None of us were prepared."

"Dar?"

Etain shrugged. "He's better than he was, but not quite back to his old self."

With a deep sigh, he closed his eyes.

Swee touched her arm. "We should let him rest."

Etain gently laid his slack hand at his side and placed a kiss on his cheek. "Sleep well, my sweet cousin. You'll be back on your feet in no time." She grabbed Swee by the hand and pulled her to the door. "Is there anything we can do for him?"

"Not until someone with more experience has a look at him. Alatariel's coming with her healer."

"Doesn't Spirit have any ideas?"

"Etain, she's not really been in the right frame of mind for something this serious. She collapsed earlier. Dar tried to get her to her room, but it was too much for him. That's why he's in here."

"I had hoped helping Taurnil would serve as a distraction, keep her mind occupied with the living rather than dwelling on the dead. I should go see her."

"Cherise took her some tea. I made sure it had a little something extra to help her sleep. She won't wake until tomorrow." Swee glanced at the table. "I need to step out for a minute or two. Do you mind sitting with Dar for a while? Once he's rested, I'll have him moved to your room."

"Okay." Etain's shoulders slumped as Swee stepped out the door. Facing the room, she could tell Taurnil still slept, his breathing regular. She meandered farther down the table and found Dar asleep, as well. With a sigh, she plopped down into a chair. "I feel useless." Unconsciously touching her belly, a new idea popped into her head.

She stood, names of who would be best to go with her racing through her head. Freeblood could use the distraction, but she'd seen him leave. With Inferno gone, Linq would have his hands full as backup to whomever decided to step up as acting chieftain. Had anyone thought of that? Who was qualified? Who was even interested?

She bit her bottom lip, pacing from one end of the room to the other. *I wonder if…*

Swee's return shattered her thoughts. Etain hurried toward her. "Whenever you feel Dar's ready to be moved, go ahead. I have something I need to do…for Spirit. If he wakes before I get back, tell him not to worry. I'll be back soon."

8

INVESTIGATION

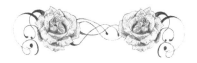

Not long after Etain's departure, Alatariel appeared at Laugharne with Chelri, her Master Healer, Dalos, Taurnil's best friend, a handful of ladies-in-waiting, and half the Royal Guard. Cappy and Thoric welcomed them, doing their best to explain the current situation as they escorted the queen to her son. Having just returned from his self-exploration, Freeblood slipped into the dining hall, unnoticed.

The Royal Guard filed into the large room before Alatariel was allowed to enter. Swee curtsied and quickly informed the queen and her healer of Taurnil's condition. The concerned mother lifted her son's hand to her bosom and caressed his pale face. "I'm here, my son."

His eyes fluttered open and a weak smile touched his lips. Kissing his forehead, she stepped aside so Chelri could perform an examination. He did the regular routine of checking pulse, temperature, and reflexes. He asked Swee a few poignant questions, nodding as she answered. Finally, he placed one hand on the prince's forehead, the other on the area hit by the fire blast, and closed his eyes. In the language of the elves, he asked for the assistance of the old ones in determining the extent of the evil perpetrated on their prince.

Suddenly, his eyes popped open just before he collapsed over Taurnil. Freeblood jumped in, catching the healer before he fell to the floor. Alatariel knelt and motioned for him to lean the elf against her. Swee handed a damp cloth to the queen, who pressed it to his forehead.

Chelri soon woke, embarrassed by the fuss he'd caused. "I do apologize, Your Highness. This is most unusual." Freeblood helped him to his feet as Thoric offered a hand to the queen. Cappy pulled a chair close for the healer.

"Thank you." He leaned back, wiping his face with the damp cloth.

Swee rushed out and returned within a few moments with a mug of ale. "Drink this, milord. It will help."

After a few sips, he took a deep breath. "It's not common."

"It's brewed here at Laugharne. Everyone seems-"

"Not the ale, although it is quite…" He licked his lips and enjoyed another sip, "boisterous."

Swee scrunched her brows. "What's not comm-"

"The poison. This demon knows his history." His gaze moved from Swee to Alatariel. "It comes from an ancient people who no longer exist. Only the oldest of the old remember them."

Alatariel gave him a strange look. "Then how do you have this knowledge? You may seem old to these Alamir, but we elves know you are not."

"My master spoke of such people. He trained me in the ways of old, as well as the new."

Freeblood asked, "What people would that be, sir?"

Chelri eyed him from head to toe, but as he was surrounded by people his queen and prince obviously trusted, he answered. "They were Draconians, said to have evolved from dragons."

He snorted a laugh. "Are you serious?"

Indignant, the healer explained. "They adapted to their environment, developed arms and legs, and their facial features shortened. The Draconians became more human-like, but their wings and scales remained. Although, over time, the scales evolved into smaller versions of the originals." He took another gulp of ale. "They also kept the power of the fire, could blast anything from miles away with either breath or wave of a hand. They were very powerful."

Freeblood leaned against the wall, his arms crossed over his chest. "If they were so powerful, why'd they disappear?"

A baleful light shone in Chelri's eyes. "You would do well to respect those who have passed." He shifted in his seat. "They delved into the Black Arts. The early Krymerians ran into them often and, by trial and error, learned how to defend against their magic. But, in the end, the Draconians destroyed themselves."

Swee crouched beside him. "If you know of these people and their poison, do you know the antidote?"

"I do," he said, then looked at his queen. "It worries me that their arts are still practiced."

"As long as we can save our prince, we'll address that concern another day." Alatariel patted his shoulder and returned to her son.

"What do we need, sir?" Swee asked.

"The blood of the demon who poisoned him."

"Good luck with that," Freeblood said. "We were lucky to get out at all. We may not be so lucky a second time. *If* the demon's still there."

"Then I suggest only the strongest and most experienced of your warriors go. It must be done if we're to save his life."

The Laugharne group looked at each other, but it was Freeblood who voiced their thoughts. "Dar and Etain."

"No," Swee said, shaking her head. "Dar hasn't fully recovered from the first time. Going back this soon would kill him and possibly Etain. They've suffered enough."

Cappy looked around the room. "Speaking of Dar and Etain, where are they?"

"I had Dar moved to his room," Swee said. "Etain had an errand to run. She said she wouldn't be long."

"We need to discuss a few things," Cappy said. "Let's all meet in the living room within the hour. Freeblood, would you track down the UWS clan?" With a nod, he left in search of the various clan members. Cappy turned to Swee. "Queen Alatariel can watch over Taurnil. Would you fetch Linq and Ara?"

"Of course." She left the room.

A forgotten Dalos cleared his throat. "I'll gather up the Black Blades, sir." Cappy gave him an odd look. Dalos smiled and stuck out his hand. "Sorry, sir. I'm Dalos, Taurnil's best friend."

Taking his hand, Cappy accepted his offer. "Thank you, Dalos. Thoric…" He turned to the other Ambassador. "If you will get Aramis and the Dragon clan, we'll meet in the front room."

With a nod, they departed.

Every requested person crowded into the living room, anxious to hear what Cappy had to say. Standing in front of the fireplace, he looked over the group.

"Thank you for coming so quickly. Are we all here?" After several nods and murmured confirmations, he began. "We have a new dilemma, I'm afraid. As most of you know, Taurnil, a new acquaintance to us all, has suffered a grievous injury at the hands of the demon who kidnapped Dar." Whispers went around the room. "Nunnehi's Master Healer, Chelri, has informed us that the only way to create an antidote for the poison is to obtain blood from the demon." Several gasps were heard through the group. Cappy held up his hands. "I know, I know. A nasty piece of work, but that's not the worst of it. Chelri has suggested we send only our strongest and most experienced warriors on this mission."

"We all know who that is," Linq said from the back of the room.

"Yes, unfortunately."

"We cannot ask our High Lord to return," said one of the Black Blades. "He nearly died in that place." Those close by nodded in agreement.

Aramis joined Cappy. "Only he and Etain know what to expect. They would be better prepared than any of us. Etain fought the demon herself. She knows his tricks."

"Easy for you to say, Dragon. It's not *your* High Lord," someone said.

"True, but he's become a good friend. One I don't wish to lose. From what I've learned of Dar, he'd never allow any of you to take on such a dangerous mission unless he were willing to do it himself."

"In case no one's noticed, Dar isn't able to do anything right now," Freeblood said, making his way toward the fireplace. "I heard he collapsed earlier." He turned and faced the group, making eye contact with as many in the room as he could. "And Etain… Well, she may know the demon's tricks, but she nearly died in that room, too. If it weren't for Inferno…" The room went dead silent, all eyes on him. He swallowed, suddenly unsure.

Cappy touched his shoulder. "Tell us, son."

He cleared his throat. "Well, if it weren't for Inferno, Etain *and* Dar would be dead."

"How do you know?" Linq asked, having worked his way to the front. "You said you were shut out of the room."

"I was, but not before I saw him standing over her. The demon, that is." He took a breath, reliving the scene as he spoke. "We heard her scream. Inferno nearly lost his mind, started battering on the door. *Nothing* was going to keep him out of that room. When the door opened…" His voice hitched. "Fuck me," he whispered, running a hand through his hair. He brought his gaze up to meet Linq's and kept his focus on the elf. "She was on the floor, on her stomach, covered in blood. Her wings must've been broken. They were at odd angles. And Dar… Shit. Dar was chained to the wall, just a lump of bloody, beaten flesh." Tears glistened in his eyes, his voice thick. "The demon had a blade, ready to strike what I figured to be the killing blow to Etain." Several tears trailed down his cheeks. "Inferno went in blazing, turned the demon away from her."

Freeblood squeezed his eyes shut, hands fisted at his sides. "I was right behind him, but… Goddamn…" His eyes opened, red and tortured. "The door slammed in my face!" He swiped at his nose. "It wasn't Inferno who slammed it, either."

He took a deep breath and accepted a cloth from Swee, who had come into the room behind him. "Thanks." He wiped his face. "I'll get blood from the asshole. I'll make him bleed real good. You're welcome to come, any of you, but I'm going either way."

"You'll have to stand in line, brother," Wolfe said from the doorway. "I called it first."

"You aren't going alone," said a Black Blade. "Our prince must be saved at all costs."

"For the queen!" another exclaimed.

"For the High Lord!"

"Hold on," Linq said, bringing the bravado down a few notches. "Where's Etain in all this? If what you say is true, Freeblood, is she in any shape to return? I doubt she'd let anyone go without her."

Freeblood shrugged. "She looked all right this morning."

"So did Dar." Ara crossed her arms over her chest. "Look where he is now."

"It doesn't matter anyway," Swee said. "Etain isn't here. She left before the queen arrived."

"Someone must go soon, or we will lose the prince," Chelri said from the hallway, the War Wizards at his back. "Our wizards will do all they can to protect those who go, but it must be in the next twenty-four hours."

"Thank you, Chelri," Linq said. "We'll give Etain until late afternoon to show. In the meantime, we can put together a team. If she's not here by dusk, we'll move without her."

Within a couple hours, Etain shimmered onto the second floor of Laugharne, Tegan in her arms, surrounded by the other three children, as well as Krz and Kane.

"We made it." Etain laughed, giving the little girl a hug. "Your first shimmer."

Tegan giggled. "I wike it! Can we do 'gain?"

"Wow!" Seth and Dylan grinned at each other. "That was brilliant!"

"Can you teach me how to do that, Auntie 'Tain?" Molly asked.

"Hmm… I don't know, Molly. We'll have to ask your mum if it's even possible." Etain became pensive, her gaze moving to the men. "Thank you both for your help. I doubt I could've corralled these four by myself."

"Under the circumstances, it's the least we could do for a fallen Alamir." Krz ruffled Dylan's hair, giving the kids a smile. "I wish you had confided in us sooner."

Etain shrugged. "It didn't occur to me at the time."

Kane picked up Molly, giving her a bright smile and spinning her around. "Family is why we do what we do, Etain." His magnetic dark eyes met hers. "We're all family."

Etain nodded, unable to speak. Tegan took her face in her chubby little hands. "Why you sad, Annie 'Tain? It be okay. I pwomise."

She hugged the little girl. "Oh, Tegan. How can I be sad when I have you? Krz, would y'all mind coming in with me?"

"I don't thin-"

"Yes!" the boys said in unison, jumping up and down. "Please!"

"I could use the support," she added.

After a nod from both men, the group walked down the hallway to Spirit's bedroom. Etain knocked softly, then opened the door. One of the older faeries, Eolande, fluttered toward them. "Milady, she's just waking up."

"I thought the children would-"

"They will be the perfect medicine, milady," she said, a warm smile on her lips. "Hello, Tegan. Welcome home, everyone."

Tegan leaned her head on Etain's shoulder, sticking her thumb into her mouth. Seth, Dylan, and Molly became quiet. "Where's Mama?" Seth finally asked.

"Come with me," Eolande said, fluttering toward the bed.

Upon their approach, Spirit opened her eyes. "Goddess above, look at the blessings I've been sent." Pushing herself up, she held out her arms, engulfing Molly, Seth, and Dylan in her embrace. "I've missed you lot." Tears in her eyes, she reached for Tegan. "Come here, my wee sprite."

"Mama!" Tegan squirmed in Etain's arms, leaning toward her mother.

Spirit pulled her to her chest. The other three climbed onto the bed and snuggled up close to her.

"I thought you should be together." Etain's heart felt ready to burst. "I hope it's okay."

"Aye, lass. Better than okay," Spirit said between kisses and hugs, then looked at the two men standing behind Etain. "Who have you here?"

"Oh! This is Krz and Kane of the Haluci clan. I needed help with the kids and they were available."

Spirit gave them a sad smile. "Thank you, sirs. You're very kind."

The two bowed their heads. "Anything for a fellow Alamir," said Krz. "We are here if you need us, milady."

"Mama…" Dylan tugged on her sleeve. "Where's Da?"

"Do you want me to stay?" Etain asked.

"No, lass. You have your own to tend to. We'll sit here together for a while. Maybe see you tomorrow."

Saying their "good nights", Etain, Krz, and Kane left the family to their private time.

Etain closed the door with a soft click and turned to Krz. "Why don't y'all come downstairs for a bit, meet a few of the folks you didn't get to meet last time you were here?"

Krz gave his brother a sideways glance and smiled. "There *are* a few people I'd like to chat with." He slapped Kane on the back. "Let's go network."

They walked downstairs into a flurry of activity. People Etain had never seen before rushed from the kitchen toward the front of the house and back. She looked at Krz, shrugged, then cocked her head. Krz and Kane followed, making sure they kept to one side of the hallway so as not to interfere with the other traffic. Nearing the living room, they heard several voices.

Etain stepped into the room, which looked like it was filled with everyone in the castle, aside from Dar, Robert, and Spirit. "What's going on here?"

Every head in the room turned to her.

From the back of the group, a face she recognized emerged. A pensive Freeblood came toward her. "Etain, you're back. I was almost hoping you wouldn't show up in time."

She gave him an uneasy smile, her gaze darting over those who stood around them. "Why is that?"

"Taurnil needs the blood of the demon to reverse the poison." He gave the others a cursory glance. "We were just finalizing who should go."

With a lift of a brow, Etain found Linq's face. His stern look told her everything she needed to know. "I assume Alatariel and Chelri have arrived?" He cocked his head toward the dining hall. "I will *not* risk Dar's life again, under any circumstances."

"We all agree on that point, but someone has to go or Taurnil will die." Freeblood glanced over his shoulder. "There's a few of us here who would like a chance at the prick who's caused all this."

"How much time do we have?" she asked.

"You have twenty-four hours, three of which have been wasted waiting for your return," said Chelri, standing a few steps behind Etain.

She shot the healer her classic *go to hell* look, but had more success in controlling her tongue. "There are others in this house suffering from worse wounds. I suggest-"

Linq came over, taking her by the arm. "I suggest we take a few minutes to inform our High Lady of the situation. If you will excuse us..." He bowed his head to the healer and guided Etain down the hall into the kitchen, Freeblood and Wolfe close behind.

Linq gave her a quick synopsis of the poison and the antidote as relayed by Chelri. "Only the blood of the attacking demon will reverse the effects."

"Bloody hell…" Etain ran her hands through her hair. "I caused this by leading everyone into that trap. I'll fix it."

"Hold on a minute," Linq said.

"I should've kept everyone safe. I should've gone alone. I-"

He grabbed her by both arms, making her look at him. "Stop it. Each of us made the choice to go. Taurnil understands the cost of holding such an honor as being a Black Blade. Inferno was a chieftain and fiercely protective. You aren't solely responsible, Etain."

"If I hadn't fried those *Bok* in Deudraeth… Damn, I shouldn't have gone at all." She pulled away. "Then Dar wouldn't… Inferno would be-"

"You also wouldn't have your brother," Freeblood said softly. "You didn't cause this war, Etain. They did. Don't let this demon tear you apart. It's our turn to strike back, to save Taurnil, and show this fucker what the Alamir are about."

"Who's volunteered so far?" She straightened her shoulders and looked at the men around her.

"Everyone," Linq answered.

She almost laughed. "We can't take everyone."

The elf shrugged. "We know… They know… Each of us has our reasons."

"Well…," Wolfe spoke up, "no matter what you decide, the two of us are going." He draped an arm over Freeblood's shoulders.

"What about Elfin?" Etain asked.

Wolfe shook his head. "Not this time."

She exchanged a glance with Linq. "Okay. Wolfe, Freeblood, and me."

"We'll go," said a voice from the door.

They all turned as Krz and Kane came into the kitchen.

"We're here. We're committed. We're ready," said Krz.

Etain gave him a grateful smile. "Thank you. But we aren't going into the human-"

"Not a problem." Simultaneously, he and Kane reached for their belts, coming up with what appeared to be sword hilts with no blades. In the next moment, the blades folded out, extending to their full lengths.

Etain raised a brow. "That'll work."

"Counting me, I doubt we'll need anyone else," said Linq.

"A small, albeit effective team," she agreed, then looked at the others. "Would you gentlemen give us the room, please?"

Everyone cleared the kitchen, leaving Etain and Linq alone.

"Etain. What's this about?"

"I'm pulling rank. As your High Lady..." She held up a hand when he opened his mouth. "You're needed here. You're the only other person who knew Inferno as well as me and Spirit. These people look up to you and know you'll respect his wishes. Until UWS chooses a new chieftain, Spirit's going to need your help and support."

"Zorn's been here-"

"Zorn isn't in any shape to take on the responsibility right now. BadMan will be the first to tell you he can't do it. Elfin hasn't been here long enough and neither has Wolfe. So, my friend, you're it for now." She placed a hand on his arm. "We'll be fine. I won't let anything happen to them." She winked.

"I don't like it, Etain." Linq huffed and puffed for a few moments. "We know how it fares going into that place with a small crew. Take a troop of Blades, at least."

"He won't be expecting us this time." She gave his arm a reassuring squeeze. "A small group of strong warriors is all we need."

His stern gaze locked with hers. "Freeblood saw what he did to you."

Etain bit her bottom lip, breaking eye contact with the elf. "Oh."

"You shouldn't go, either. Let the others take this one."

She turned away, shaking her head. "I have to go. Those gates won't open for anyone else."

"Dar will go ballistic when he finds out."

"Then make sure he doesn't," she said over her shoulder, headed toward the door. "I'm gonna check on T and Dar, then we'll be gone. I'm trusting you to keep it together around here."

Linq saluted her with fisted hand over his heart. "I will, High Lady."

The Royal Guard at the dining hall saluted their High Lady and opened the doors. She found Alatariel virtually alone, except for a few other soldiers of the Royal Guard. The queen rose from her seat with a look of gratitude. "Thank the Elven gods. Etain, how are you?" She held out her arms. "I'm so sorry for your loss."

She stepped into the queen's outstretched arms. "Thank you, Rie." Etain pulled away. "And thank you for coming." She looked at the elf asleep on the table. "I'm sorry for Taurnil, but we'll make him better."

"He's a fighter. He'll pull through." Her smile was melancholy. "Would you sit with him for a few moments? Swee showed my ladies to their rooms, and Chelri has gone off to who knows where. I must make a short trip down the hall, if you don't mind."

"Of course, Your Grace. I wanted to check on Taurnil and Dar anyway."

"Dar was taken to his room. Once Swee knew he was out of danger, she had him moved."

"Well then, I guess I'll be making a trip upstairs, too. Go ahead, Rie. I'll wait for you."

"I'll be back shortly."

Etain waited until the queen left the room, then turned to the elf. She ran her fingers through his hair, admiring his features. "Your resemblance is so striking, T. If what's on the inside is as much like my Dar, you have an interesting future before you."

She leaned down and kissed his forehead, then took his hand in hers. She spoke softly into his ear so no one else could hear.

"This will be over soon. The demon's death will not only get you the blood you need, it will also rid us of his threat for good. It will be over by morning."

As the last words left her lips, Taurnil's tight grip took her by surprise. He opened his eyes and mouthed, *No.*

"It's okay. By the time you miss me, I'll be back."

He worked his lips, trying to get a sound from his throat. At last, he rasped, "No."

"Relax, T. I have an impressive crew going with me." He slowly raised a brow. "I guess you're gonna make me tell you who." She felt his grip loosen. "You're so demanding," she joked. "Freeblood; Wolfe, of course; Krz and Kane. You haven't met them yet. They're brothers from the Haluci clan." She narrowed her eyes. "Both are determined and lethal." Taurnil frowned. "They're cool. Don't worry. Then there's Sion and Riko, a couple Black Blades who apparently know Dar."

Taurnil squeezed her hand again. "A good team." His brows knitted together. "Linq?"

"Nope. Spirit and the clan need him here."

Both his brows raised and eyes widened.

Etain laughed. "I pulled rank. After all, I *am* the High Lady."

Having just enough strength, he pulled her hand. She leaned a little closer. "Take…Blades."Alatariel walked in at that moment and rushed over. "Is he awake?"

Etain slid her hand from his and stepped aside. "I was telling him what we're about to do."

"Thank you for your help, Etain. Please, take great care."

"Don't worry about me. I'll have some of the best with me." Her gaze went to Taurnil. "You hang in there. We'll have you back on your feet in no time."

The young elf mouthed *Blades.*

In the hallway, she took a deep breath to calm her nerves and shadow her thoughts. Last thing she needed was Dar cueing in on her plans.

She found him stretched out on the bed, face down. Hearing her enter, he carefully raised up on one side.

"Hello, beautiful."

She smiled as she walked toward him. "You've caused quite a stir downstairs."

Instead of a shrug, he raised a brow as he lifted a hand. "It's what I do."

She sat next to him on the side of the bed and caressed his cheek. "How're you feeling?"

"Better."

"Lie down. Let me have a look at your back."

"Swee put fresh cloths on not long ago and gave me some awful tea to drink."

Etain peeked under a few of the cloths. "Maybe you need something more…organic."

"No." He raised up again. "I will heal in time…on my own. You have more important things to-"

She leaned in, giving him a kiss. "It means nothing without you."

"I will be fine." He studied her face for a moment. "Swee mentioned you'd left Laugharne. What've you been doing?"

She straightened but kept her eyes lowered. "A family should be together, especially during difficult times." Her gaze came back to him. "I brought Spirit's children home, hoping she'd find some comfort from having them close."

Dar placed a hand over hers. "You are quite special, Lady VonNeshta. And a good friend. How could she not feel *some* peace now her children are home where they belong?"

Etain shrugged. "I needed to do something. I'm not very good at sitting around, doing nothing."

"Resting is what you should be doing. Join me. Let's be together."

A faint smile touched her lips.

"What's bothering you, Etain? Your mind is elsewhere."

"I'm sorry. I guess I'm still trying to process everything that's happened."

"Which is why you should stay here with me."

"I will, but not just yet. I want to check on Robert first. I'll be back in a little bit." After a quick kiss, she left him alone, having no intention of seeing her brother. She would deal with the consequences when she returned.

———

Freeblood meandered along the path toward the small cottage. The place looked deserted, but as he came closer, he saw the open windows and breathed a sigh of relief. However, the sounds of someone sobbing set him in motion. He rushed inside, checking each room. He finally found her in the bedroom, huddled on the floor.

"Faux? What's wrong?"

Tears streamed down her face. "I can't walk. *I can't walk.*"

He kneeled in front of her. "Are you sick? Have you hurt yourself?" He didn't see any visible injuries.

Laying her head on the floor, she continued to wail.

He pulled her up by her arms. "Faux! Are you hurt?" She blinked several times. He took a deep breath and lowered his voice. "Are you hurt?"

She pushed away, turning her back to him.

"What?" Her actions confused him.

Faux looked over her shoulder and down her back. Freeblood raised a brow. She did it again with more attitude. He followed her gaze, then realized what was missing. She no longer had her beautiful tail.

His eyes snapped to hers. "Oh."

"I got out of bed to get something to eat, took one step, and fell down. I've been trying to walk but can't find my balance." She turned away and hid her face in her hands. "I hate that man! I hate him! I hate him!"

"Here. Lean on me." Freeblood moved closer and touched her on the shoulder. "Come on." He grasped her arm, helping her up.

Once on her feet, her hands went to her forehead. "My horns! He took my horns. I swear, I'll-"

He grabbed her flailing hands. "Faux, please calm down. It'll be okay."

"First, I get fat, now this? How can you stand to look at me? I'm horrid." Angry tears trickled down her cheeks.

He thumbed away her tears. "You're beautiful. We'll adjust."

She sniffled. "We will?"

"Yes, we will." The pout of her lips made him smile. "Let's get some food in you."

"Rosencrantz was hungry when I woke. Now he's downright starving."

He furrowed his brows. "Rosencrantz?"

"The baby." She held onto his arm tightly as they walked into the kitchen.

"So, it's true what they say about pregnant women." Freeblood grinned, helping her into a chair at the kitchen table.

"What's true?"

Pulling ingredients from the refrigerator, he turned. "Crazy as loons, every last one of 'em."

"Ha-ha, Mr. Doesn't Have a Clue. You try blowing up like a balloon and finding a comfortable position…sleeping *or* sitting."

"Okay. Fair enough." He cracked a couple eggs into the frying pan, then put bread to toasting. "But Rosencrantz?"

"It's very Shakespearean. I like it." She eyed him for a moment. "Why're you here? I thought you were mad at me."

Freeblood held her gaze. "I'll be gone for a time and didn't want you to worry."

She slipped out of her chair but had to grab hold of the edge of the table to steady herself. Leaning against it, she slowly walked toward the fridge, daring to take the last few steps unaided. "Sure. Why not?"

Although he couldn't see her face, he heard the disappointment in her voice. "I'm helping Etain get an antidote for Taurnil."

"Whatever," she said offhandedly, placing a pitcher of juice on the counter. "You don't owe me any explanations." Her back to him, she reached for a glass from the cupboard.

Freeblood dished the eggs onto a plate just as the toast popped up. Laying the bread carefully next to the eggs, he set the plate on the table. "This is something I have to do. I hope you understand."

She shrugged, pouring juice into the glass. "Do whatever you like. I don't care."

"Okay. Well… Great." He didn't want to leave on a sour note, but had no idea what else to say. "Make sure you take care of yourself and Rosencrantz." Still, she didn't turn. Before he stepped out the door, he looked back at her. "I miss you, Faux."

Juice in her hand, her eyes stung from unshed tears as the door closed quietly. "I miss you, too."

Etain was met by Freeblood at the foot of the stairs, as well as everyone else, who had congregated throughout the living room, hallway, and front entry.

"What's all this?"

"They wanted to see us off," said Freeblood.

Etain swallowed, sudden tears in her eyes. *Damn, Etain. Leaders don't cry!*

Linq stepped to the forefront of the group. "The rest of your team is outside. They knew you'd want some time with Dar."

"Linq…" Her voice broke, overcome by the support shown. *I wish you could see this, Dar.* She bit her bottom lip and tried again. Despite her efforts, a single tear trailed down her cheek. She looked at the others around her. "Please, everyone. Dar can't know until we come back. Let me be the one to tell him."

"I'm proud of you," he said. "I was afraid you'd try something stupid like go by yourself."

"I thought about it." She glanced at Freeblood when he huffed. "But I realized I'm not the only one who's suffered at the hands of this demon. If they're brave enough to go with me, who am I to tell them no?"

Linq surprised her by wrapping his arms around her. "Kick his ass," he whispered in her ear. He turned to Freeblood and shook his hand. "Be safe."

Others patted Etain and Freeblood on the back as they made their way to the front door and stepped into the cool night air. Dalos met them at the bottom of the stairs, two backpacks in his hands. He gave one to Etain and the other to Freeblood.

Her pack in place, Etain looked over her small band of warriors. "Everyone ready?"

Wolfe glanced behind him, then looked at Etain and stepped to the side. It took all her wits to keep from rolling her eyes. "What are you doing here? You should be upstairs, spending time with the kids."

Dressed in violet leather armor, her hair plaited, a crossbow on her back, Spirit lifted her chin. "We had a long chat, and short of all four of 'em joining this little band, they agreed I should go."

"Spirit…"

"You'll not deny me, Etain."

"How did you know we were going?"

Spirit cocked a brow. "It 'tis *my* house. I'm going whether you like it or not."

"I *don't* like it." With a solemn expression, Etain headed toward the gates. "I don't like it one bit."

Commander Crom stepped in her path. "High Lady, your Black Blades are ready to move out."

Taken aback, Etain stopped and stared at him. "Commander…" She watched as every Black Blade in the compound filed into formation, Dalos at the forefront.

Crom came to attention, as well. "We cannot allow our High Lady to go into battle unescorted."

"I *do* have an escort, in case you haven't noticed. You and your men will stay here and protect the High Lord."

Dalos broke rank and approached. "Milady, Taurnil is our brother. We *cannot* stand by and see yet another life lost because of this demon."

The commander turned on the impetuous elf. "Soldier, you forget yourself! Stand down."

"It's okay, Commander," Etain said. "I understand their passion for one of their own. However…" Her gaze went to Dalos, "I will not allow it."

"But-"

"Soldier, you will remember your status and stand down at once," Crom commanded.

Dalos looked from the commander to Etain. His shoulders slumped, but Etain caught the glint in his eye as he returned to the ranks.

Crom turned to her and spoke in a lowered voice. "Permission to speak freely, milady?" She waved a hand. "These men are prepared to defy your orders. They have sworn an oath to protect the High Lord *and* High Lady…" He bowed his head, "and will not allow you to leave these premises without their escort. If you do so, High Lady, they will follow. They were denied the opportunity to save the High Lord. They will not be denied again. This is their prince."

The desire to voice her opinion swelled up in her throat, but she swallowed it down. "Bloody hell," she whispered, remembering Inferno's sacrifice. He would've demanded the Blades go, too.

"Well said." Freeblood leaned toward her and whispered, "But you gotta let 'em go."

She battled with her desire to keep these young warriors safe from unnecessary harm. But the commander was right. They had sworn an oath to not only the High Lord, but to their prince, as well, and would honor it to their deaths.

"We move quickly. Freeblood is as fast as any Blade and knows the location of the portal. Once there, one third of the company will remain outside the portal, one third just inside, and the rest will go with us to the castle itself." She raised her voice to make sure all heard her words. "However, the only Blades who will enter the castle are Sion and Riko. *Any* other Black Blade found within the walls of that hellhole will be stripped of rank and banned from the Blades forever. Understood?"

Commander Crom and the Black Blades saluted their High Lady with a boisterous, "Aye, High Lady."

"Let's move." With that, Krz and Kane moved close to her as she grabbed Spirit and Wolfe, then disappeared in a shimmer of light.

Freeblood dashed around the Black Blades, taking the lead. Within moments, the courtyard was empty except for those left behind.

9

ABOMINATION

O nce at the portal, Etain discarded her backpack as she explained how she must be in her demon persona to open the doorway. The others backed away to give her room. Arms at her sides, she closed her eyes, willing her wings to extend. Several minutes passed with no result, except a nervous sweat trickling down her spine. She opened her eyes and turned, as though in search of something.

"Is this a new technique you've developed?" Spirit asked, perplexed by her actions.

"Huh? Uh, no. It's just that…" She turned one more time, shrugged, and tried again. Rolling her shoulders, she relaxed her mind and envisioned the expansion of crimson-tipped wings, the extension of white talons, and of lifting into the air.

Freeblood and the Blades arrived to the spectacle of the High Lady attempting to open the portal.

Etain's eyes popped open. "What color are my eyes?"

Spirit lifted her brows. "They're…silver."

She gave her a funny look. "Silver? They should be violet." She closed them again.

Intrigued, Freeblood came closer, watching the expressions pass over her face in her attempt to change. It was hard work not to laugh at the comical contortions. Exasperated, she opened her eyes and caught the smirk on his lips. He clamped a hand over his mouth, but unable to hold it in, burst out laughing.

She placed her hands on her hips. "What is so funny?"

"I'm sorry, Etain. Your facial expressions." He laughed, his eyes filled with delight. "I didn't realize they were part of your method."

"You didn't look like that in L.A.," Kane said, chuckling.

She narrowed her eyes. "You stay out of this." She turned away from the group and whispered to herself, "Did you do this, Dar? Did you somehow strip me of *my* powers, as well?"

"What's wrong, lass?" Spirit asked.

"There's some reason I can't change. I have no idea what's wrong!" she exclaimed, throwing a hand in the air and pacing about. "You must be in demon form to open this damn portal."

"Did you have any trouble the first time?"

"Not once I knew what it required."

"Did your eyes turn silver then?" Spirit tried to look into her eyes.

Etain stopped long enough to think it over. "I don't know. I didn't think to pull out me bloody mirror and check. I was a little preoccupied with saving Dar."

"No need to bite me head off," she said. "What do we do now?"

Etain ran a hand through her hair. "Hell if I know."

Freeblood stroked his chin, looking her over from head to toe. "You haven't noticed anything else different?"

She shook her head. "No."

"Maybe it's because of your condition?"

"My *what*?" she said, properly affronted.

Freeblood stepped back. "Well, you *are* pregnant, right?"

Etain placed her hands on her stomach. "How would you know?"

"I've been around Faux long enough to recognize the signs. Maybe that has something to do with why you're having trouble." He let his words sink in for a moment. "It would make sense, wouldn't it?

Maybe the baby doesn't want to return to a realm where you nearly died."

"Freeblood, they can't be more than embryos at this point. How can they exhibit such power?"

"*They*?" Freeblood, Spirit, and Wolfe exclaimed at the same time. Krz and Kane looked at each other.

She realized too late she'd unwittingly exposed her secret. "Uh, well, we wanted to wait a little while before we said anything. We're having twins."

Spirit's shocked expression turned into a huge smile. "Lass!" She took hold of her hands, beaming as brightly as any expectant mother. "I'm so happy for you. Does Dar know?"

Etain felt the burn in her cheeks. "Aye."

"Congratulations, milady!" Wolfe slapped her on the back. "What great news!"

Freeblood shook his head. "No wonder you didn't want him to know what you're doing."

Kane shook her hand, congratulating her, but Krz pulled her into a bear hug, his grin as big as his face. "Wonderful news, Etain! I wish you all the best."

She felt somewhat disconcerted by his sudden outburst. Their relationship had always been friendly, but at a distance. Before she could process what it meant, the Blades raised a great "hurra" in honor of the High Lord and High Lady.

One of the Blades broke away from the group and approached. "High Lady. I am Riko." He placed a fisted hand over his heart and bowed his head. "Forgive my forwardness."

"Riko." Etain dipped her head in return. "I knew you were to be part of our team. It's nice to officially meet you."

"If I may speak freely?"

"Of course."

"Krymerian babes develop more quickly than human babes and are highly sensitive to their environment. You can speak to them, explain what you're trying to do. It might help."

"I don't know if they'd listen to me, but thank you." Biting her bottom lip, her gaze roamed over every face around her. When she came to Freeblood, an idea hit her. "Freeblood."

His eyes darted right and left. "Uh, yeah?"

"You're going to be a father. You talk to them."

"What?" His eyes widened. "I was kidding. Like you said, they're just tiny things."

"Riko is right. *They* led me to Dar." She placed her hands on her belly. "*They* told me what to do." The confused expression on his face compelled her to explain further. "Remember the unicorn and the panther?"

"What?" He shoved his hands into his pockets, pacing back and forth. When he stopped, he turned to Etain. "Wait. The unicorn and the panther are the babies…inside of you…who can't possibly be any bigger than a pea?"

"It may seem crazy, but consider who their father is." She nudged him on the shoulder. "What do we have to lose? Our sterling reputations?"

He chuckled and jabbed a hand through his hair. "It wasn't so long ago I was completely clueless to this world. Now look at me. Involved with Krymerians and talking to babies."

"If it helps any, I've heard babies respond quite well to a man's voice."

"We're losing time here, folks," said Kane. "The sooner we get in, the sooner we get back."

Etain ignored the outburst and concentrated on Freeblood. "Talk to them like you'd talk to your own. Close your eyes and pretend I'm Faux."

He shrugged as he kneeled in front of her. "This feels weird."

"You're fine. Just tell them we have to find the demon to save a life."

"Will they understand me?"

"Just do it, Freeblood."

"Okay! Okay." He breathed in, then blew it out. "Uh, well… Hi, little Krymerians." He looked up at Etain, who gave him an encouraging smile. "I'm your Uncle Freeblood… Well, I hope to be considered your uncle. I'm gonna be a dad soon, too." He grinned. "Hey, I just realized you three'll be about the same age. You're gonna grow up together. That is so cool!" An "ahem" from Etain helped him focus. "Okay. So, right now, we really need your mom to open the portal back to the blood castle."

Etain gasped and placed a hand on her belly. Freeblood looked up at her. "It's okay. Just a flutter."

"Hey, little ones. Don't be scared. I'm here with your mom. There's a lot of people here with your mom, even a whole company of Black Blades, uh…although you might not know what that is yet. You will. Anyway, we have to go back. Our friend, Taurnil… He's an elf, but you might not know what that is, either." He dodged away from Etain's attempted thump to his head. "He'll die if we don't get the blood of the demon. Kinda like your dad's blood saving your mom, except it's to reverse a poison this time. Please, little ones. Help us save someone's life."

Freeblood leaned back on his heels and looked up at her. "Feel anything?"

Etain sighed. "No."

"Try your wings, lass," said Spirit.

Etain moved away to give herself room. All it took was a fleeting thought and her wings extended. She grinned at the others, then turned and spoke the incantation to open the portal. A thin silver line slashed through the air, opening into an oval doorway.

"Remember, a third outside the portal, a third just inside, and a third to the castle, but no Blade enters its doors. Are you ready?"

The Blades snapped to attention. Krz, Kane, Wolfe, and Spirit exchanged glances. "We're ready," said Krz.

Freeblood and the Black Blades quickly maneuvered through, taking their assigned positions. Those Blades left in the Alamir realm surrounded the entryway, forming a double line, one row faced the portal while their counterparts guarded the shore.

The Blades within the demon realm stood in the same formation around the entry. The final group moved toward the blood castle, finding no resistance whatsoever.

A gray haze clouded the already weak sun, leaving a chill in the air. At the fortress gates, Etain easily opened one side, then turned to the Blades. "Do *not* touch the walls of this cursed castle. The evil will penetrate your very being and wither your soul." With a uniform salute, they acknowledged the High Lady's warning.

When she and Freeblood walked through the courtyard, Etain furrowed her brows. "What's going on?"

"Yeah, I know what you mean." He pushed open the castle doors with a sneakered foot. "Why hasn't anyone come out to stop us?"

"Was it this dark the last time we were here?" They stood in place for a few moments to give their eyes a chance to adjust.

"It's like no one's here."

"Shall we split up?" Krz asked, coming up behind them.

"Me, Freeblood, and Spirit will take this level. You, Kane, and Wolfe take upstairs. Riko, you and Sion take the lower level."

"Aye, milady." Riko grinned at Sion. "Let's see if any goblins made it this far."

"Ugh. I'll let you take them. I've had my fill."

"Wait," Etain said. "Look for a pair of shackles. They won't be attached to a wall or anything. They'd be something used to transport a prisoner."

"Aye, milady." The two Blades disappeared into the darkness.

Etain grabbed Krz by the arm as he passed. "Be quick, but don't let your guard down. This demon is worse than the *Bok*. We'll meet here in an hour."

"Got it. Come on, Kane. Let's check this place out."

"Spirit?"

"Aye, lass. I'm here."

"Stay close to me and Freeblood. I have no idea what we're gonna run into."

"Aye."

Etain lifted her *Nim*, channeling her solar into the blade to light their way. A blade of blue light extended from Freeblood's hand as they worked their way through the ground floor, checking each room, saving the main hall for last. Her hand on the knob, Etain hesitated. She glanced at the two behind her, then opened the door, its hinges creaking.

"Stay together." Etain stepped inside and lifted her sword, pouring out more of her light, but not enough to illuminate the entire room. "Freeblood, see if you can find a light switch."

"Right."

She heard the squeak of his sneakers on the stone floor. "Spirit, get closer to me."

"I'm here," she said, touching her on the arm. "Is this the room?"

Etain's breath caught in her throat. "Aye."

"Show me where."

"Spirit, I don't think-"

"Show me."

Etain turned and led her to the center of the room. "I found him here." She lowered her sword so Spirit could see the bloodstains on the floor, but Etain turned her head, not wanting to see it again.

"Are you sure, lass?" Spirit crouched and touched the floor.

"Aye. Do you not see the stains?"

"There aren't any." Spirit tugged on the leg of her pants. "Look for yourself."

After a long sigh, Etain turned her head. "They're right…" She felt her heart skip a beat. "Where'd they go?" She swung her sword left and right. Turning in a circle, she stepped out farther and farther, searching for the stains she knew they'd left behind. "I swear to you, Spirit. He was right here."

"Lights don't work," Freeblood called out.

Etain grabbed Spirit by the arm and dragged her deeper into the darkness. Hearing the chink of chains against her boot, she lowered her sword. Although Dar's bindings still lay on the floor, there were no signs of blood anywhere.

"What is it, love?"

"There should be bloodstains everywhere. The floor was covered in it. Surely they didn't take the time to mop it up."

Freeblood joined them. He studied the area for a few minutes, then transformed his sword into a dagger. "Just a hunch." He dragged the knife across his palm. The blood quickly welled up, dripping onto the floor.

"Did you hear something?" Spirit turned, looking into the dark.

Etain grabbed him by the wrist. "What're you doing?"

"Wait," he whispered. They watched his blood form into a small puddle.

"What do you hope to gain by doing that?" Spirit asked.

"It's just an experiment," Freeblood said, giving her a sharp look. When they looked again, the blood was gone. "Yep. Thought so." He wiped his hand on his pants. "Those walls outside are blood red because they *are* blood."

"Holy hell," Etain said quietly.

Spirit shivered. "Crikey. What does that mean for us?"

"Not a damn thing," Etain answered. "There's no one here, and any spilled blood has been sucked up by this horrible place."

"Oh, Etain…" Spirit gave her a worried look. "Taurnil."

"Bloody fucking hell. Freeblood, any idea where this demon might be?"

"How the hell would I know? I've run into him a couple times, but it's not like we're mates or anything."

Etain's eyebrows lifted. "I thought Laugharne was the first time you saw him."

"*I* didn't see him at Laugharne. I don't know how, but I think Faux did. We met him at a music festival in Germany just before we came to Laugharne." His eyes brightened. "But I'd met him before that. He's the one who taught me how to use the gem in my hand." He jabbed his other hand through his hair. "It wasn't long after I'd turned Alamir. His hair was freaky, and his skin… Man, I thought I was trippin'." Freeblood shuddered, his laugh hollow. "I think it was Japan or somewhere like that."

"You couldn't have mentioned this earlier?" Etain narrowed her eyes. "Like the first time we came to this horrible place?"

Freeblood considered her for a moment before he answered. "I didn't know it was the same guy until we faced him here. I nearly lost my shit."

She looked away and shrugged. "Okay. So, what happened in Germany?"

"Not a lot. After the festival, we ended up in a nightclub. Faux enjoyed herself, dancing and teasing everyone around her, especially him. His flaming hair and green eyes intrigued her."

Etain bit her bottom lip. "Do you think she knew him?"

"No way. Crazy as it sounds, I think she just enjoyed having another demon around."

"Yeah. Crazy is what she does. Still, it's hard to believe she was trying to open the door for him."

"Now that I think about it…" Freeblood rubbed the back of his neck, "she seemed hypnotized, couldn't take her eyes off him. I had to drag her out of the club."

"You said his eyes were green?"

"Yeah. Hard to miss."

"That's strange." She rubbed her forehead. "He keeps changing the game."

Spirit suddenly turned. "Did you hear *that*?"

Freeblood dismissed the noise. "Maybe one of the other teams."

"Let's see if they've found anything." Etain lifted her sword and walked to the door. "There's nothing in here." She turned the handle, but it wouldn't engage. She jiggled it a few times, then leaned down for a closer inspection. "Freeblood, did you lock the door behind you?"

"Why would I lock the door?" He released his sword but kept the gem lit as he and Spirit joined her, both taking a turn at the handle.

"I guess we'll have to shimmer out." Etain tucked away her sword and grabbed them each by the arm. Just as her shimmer began to glow, it reversed, as if her body had sucked it back in. She gasped for air as her knees buckled, but the other two caught her before she fell to the floor.

"What's wrong?" Spirit grimaced, holding her steady.

"I can't shimmer."

With a sigh, Freeblood leaned back against the wall. "Great. Do you think it's the babies again?"

Before anyone could answer, a faint whistling sound made them turn. They glanced at each other, then at the darkness.

Etain yelled, "Get down!" She grabbed Spirit and barreled into Freeblood, knocking them all to the floor.

"What the hell?" Freeblood mumbled from beneath the pile.

A small breeze lifted Etain's hair as something passed within inches of her head. Twisting, she drew her sword, lighting it again. "Holy crap." Embedded in the door, mere inches above them, a handful of throwing knives gleamed in the light.

Freeblood pushed out from under Spirit and jumped to his feet. "Where'd those come from? I thought-"

Etain was up in an instant, grabbed him, and twisted just as a set of throwing stars whizzed past. They heard their flight end at the stone wall. "Spirit, stay down."

"Who's throwing those things?" Freeblood's voice sounded thin.

In spite of Etain's order, Spirit stood. "The castle knows we're here." She looked at Freeblood. "My guess is it hasn't enjoyed the taste of fresh blood in a few days. It wants more."

He exchanged a look with Etain. "Shit."

A faint whistling sound came toward them.

"These walls are covered from top to bottom with all kinds of weapons," Etain said. "It's coming for you."

He gave her a shaky grin. "Well, it's a good thing I can run." He dashed away. Within seconds, a snake of weaponry followed him into the darkness. Etain and Spirit watched his blue sword spark with each engagement.

"We have to get out of here." Etain tried the handle again.

Spirit pushed her aside. "This *I* can do. Give me some room." She bowed her head and closed her eyes, her lips moving in a silent chant. Raising her hands, she spoke out loud. "*Dduwies iâ, clyw fy nghais. Caledwch y drysau hyn, felly fe allwn ni ffoi* (Goddess of ice, hear my plea. Harden these doors, so we may flee)."

A whoosh came from the darkness. Etain leaned back against the wall as a large spear sailed through the air between her and Spirit. "Freeblood! Spear at six o'clock!" Hearing its impact with stone told her he'd heeded the warning.

"Etain!" he yelled. "Get that door open!"

"Working on it."

She shivered, the air suddenly cold. Moving her light closer to the doors, she noticed the wood at the bottom steadily turning lighter in color. The wood creaked and cracked as ice ran up its length.

"Now! Open it now!"

Etain looked at Spirit. "I have to go help him."

"I've got this." Spirit pulled the crossbow from her back, slipped her foot into the stirrup, and cocked the string. "Go." Bringing it up, she loaded a bolt, aimed, then squeezed the trigger. The bolt rammed into the frozen wooden surface.

Etain sprinted away, hearing the crack of the wood and Spirit reloading her crossbow. With *Nim* lighting her way, she found Freeblood, who was holding off a barrage of weapons.

She screamed, "Get out of the way!"

Freeblood dashed out of the circle of death, ran toward a wall, up its surface, then flipped over Etain's head. The moment he made his move, her eyes lit in a white light, melting every weapon in sight. He landed behind her and grabbed her by the arm. "We gotta go."

"Wait. There's something I left behind last time."

"Etain, we don't-"

She disappeared into the dark and soon reappeared, Dar's scabbard in her hand. "Now we can go."

The two sprinted toward the door. Freeblood grabbed Spirit around the waist and pulled her away as Etain's solar shattered the frozen doors. An ear-piercing howl filled the room as a result of the breach.

Freeblood pushed Spirit through the doors. "Get out. Head for the gates."

The castle responded with a new barrage of attacks, intent in procuring the blood it now desperately needed to repair the damage. A volley of weapons, churning in an invisible wind, funneled up toward the ceiling. Curling back around, they shot straight for Freeblood, Etain in their path.

With lightning speed, Freeblood twisted toward Etain. His sword flashed its blue light as he slashed through the air, forming a barrier he hoped would deflect the threat. The knives glanced off the shield and sailed out the destroyed doorway.

Etain blew out a breath. "Thanks. Where's Spirit?"

"Safe. Let's get out of here."

A movement from the side caught their attention. Turning at the same time, they watched as a black-bladed dirk careened toward him. Etain pushed him out of the way but wasn't able to do the same for herself. It sank into her left arm, making her stumble sideways. Her sword and the scabbard dropped to the floor.

Freeblood retracted his sword and wrapped his arms around her. They fell to the floor to avoid the onslaught of a dozen daggers that whizzed past and embedded in a stone column. Knowing Spirit was safe and with Freeblood holding onto her, Etain's mind flashed on shimmer. This time they were able to get out. Spirit ran through the front doors just as they appeared in the courtyard.

"You two stay here," Etain said. "I have to warn the others and get them out."

Spirit reached for her. "Let me tend to your arm, lass."

She backed away. "Not yet. Not enough time. Do *not* go back in." Headed toward the castle, she realized her sword was still in the main hall. "Damn." In her mind, she called to her *Nim*. The crystal blade instantaneously appeared in her hand. Before she could make another move, Wolfe, Krz, and Kane ran out the front doors. "You're okay. Anything interesting?"

Krz gave her a good look over, nodding toward her arm. "Not as interesting as yours."

She shrugged. "Just a scratch. Have you seen Riko or Sion?"

"Here," said Sion, the two coming toward them. "The lower level is clear."

"We didn't find any shackles, but we found this along the way." Riko held up Dar's scabbard. "I thought it important."

Etain gave him a grateful smile. "It is. Thank you, Riko. Will you carry it for me?"

"Aye, milady."

"Let's move." Etain led the way to Freeblood and Spirit. Standing in the center of the courtyard, she watched the group head toward the massive gates, sorely tempted to pull the dagger from her arm. However, she didn't want to chance another blood offering. The castle had feasted enough.

Freeblood stepped over the threshold and turned. "Come on, Etain."

How she would love to tear this place apart, burn it to the ground, and grind it into dust. Her heart beat faster, imagining the screams of the stone and the satisfaction of watching it fall. If only she had Dar's power, she could raze it like he'd done with the LOKI castle. With a shrug, she waved at Freeblood and realized too late it was the wrong arm to use.

The dagger shifted. A trickle of blood trailed down to her elbow. She grabbed the arm with her other hand, cupping it close to her body. More blood oozed from the wound, turning the trickle into a flow. The blood spilled over the cut leather, pooling at her hand until a single droplet fell. Several more followed. The tiny drops rolled over the gravel like molecules of mercury, traveling directly toward the castle.

She looked at Freeblood.

A moan evolved into a loud roar. The earth shook. The walls vibrated. The monstrosity remembered the sweetness of this one. This was the blood the master had sought for so long.

Freeblood took off in a dead run toward her, squeezed between the closing gates, and slid into the courtyard. "Let's go."

Within moments, every weapon within the castle burst from its doors. Etain yanked the blade from her arm and threw it down. Arcing her wings, she grabbed Freeblood and spiralled up into the sky.

The metal snake swirled and curved hot on the blood trail of its prey. Freeblood held on for dear life while Etain swerved and dipped, trying to avoid its bite.

"Etain!" He had to yell to be heard over the wind and clang of the weapons. "I'm weighing you down."

"If I land, it will be certain death for us both."

"Sweep down as close as you can. I'll do the rest."

Several of the pursuing blades nicked at her boots, forcing her decision. Freeblood tightened his hold. She dove straight down, then curved a few feet from the ground, skimming along the surface. "Go!"

Freeblood let go, pulling his legs into his body and tucking his head. The gem in his hand glowed, extending out beneath him, acting as a protective shield as he skidded over the ground. Etain looked over her shoulder. Seeing him on his feet surrounded by the others, she rolled and curved up into the sky, the death squad behind her.

"Did you see that? Whoa!" Freeblood dusted himself off, a smile on his face. "It worked!"

"Are you all right?" Spirit asked, running up to him.

"I'm good, but..." He looked after Etain, "she isn't going to last much longer."

Krz followed his gaze. "Any ideas?"

"It's crazy…"

"Can't be any crazier than what's happening," said Kane.

Freeblood turned to Spirit. "How in tune are you and Etain?"

"We're close."

He nodded. "Krz, you and Kane get her attention, motion her to come in."

"With that metal snake on her ass?" Kane shook his head. "That *is* some crazy shit."

"He's right, Freeblood." Krz watched Etain swoop and dive, making passes around the turrets. Some blades embedded into the stone of the castle, but not nearly enough. "Those things will rip right through us."

Freeblood pulled his shoulders back. "They'll rip right through *her* if we don't stop them! If you can't do it…" He turned to the elves. "Sion, Riko-"

Krz held up his hands. "Just making sure you realize what's at stake. Let's get to work, Kane."

"I'll help," Wolfe said, the three walked several paces away from the group, waving their arms and yelling Etain's name.

Freeblood turned to the mage. "Can you cast a spell on the weapons like you did the door? Freeze them?" At the doubtful look on her face, he reached out and touched her arm. "Spirit, my shield will protect us. Trust me. It *will* work. She means a lot to me, too."

"Aye, I can, but with that many, it won't last long."

He smiled. "It won't have to. She'll finish them."

As Etain came around the western turret, Krz, Kane, and Wolfe caught her eye. Once they realized she'd seen them, they motioned her to land. She shook her head, but they were insistent. She made another sweep around the castle, doing her best to widen the gap between herself and her pursuers. Glancing over her shoulder to gauge the distance, she didn't realize how close she was to the eastern turret. By the time she faced forward, she was just able to twist away and avoid the stone wall by inches, but her wing clipped the edge of the roof. She cried out, lost control, and plummeted to the ground outside the castle walls. The metal snake didn't miss a beat in its pursuit.

Freeblood sprinted across the distance and dove, engaging his gem as a shield. It deflected the weapons, but he felt their power draining him.

He closed his eyes, afraid he couldn't maintain his strength much longer. Suddenly, the bombardment ended. Freeblood looked up, relieved to see ice on the blades. He released his shield and absentmindedly swiped at a tickle on his upper lip.

"Etain!" He grabbed her by the shoulders. "Wake up! You have to blast these things. Etain!" She moaned, her eyelids fluttering. "Etain! Spirit's spell won't last long. You gotta wake up."

"Uh… Oh…" She grimaced as she touched her head. "What?"

"Your solar!"

"My what?"

"You gotta move, Etain. Your solar."

She clearly didn't understand what he meant as her eyes focused on him. "You're bleeding."

"Never mind that! The shiny white light thing you do, like the door you blasted? You gotta hit those things." He pointed toward the instruments of death wrapped in a sheet of ice suspended in mid-air. A drip fell from the tip of the lead dagger, the same one she'd pulled from her arm.

They looked at each other.

"Help me up." She took hold of his hand, but had to lean against him. "Is this Spirit's spell?"

"Yes! You have to hurry."

"*You* have to get out of here. I don't have control of it like Dar. I don't even know if I have the energy."

The metal snake quivered. Small cracks appeared in the ice, running in every direction.

"Go, Freeblood. I can't lose someone else. Get the others to the portal and get out of here. I'll follow if I can."

"No fucking way am I leaving you here alone. We either do this together or we die together."

She ran a hand through her hair. "Bloody fucking hell. You're a hard-headed-"

"Heathen?" He smirked.

"Brat." She almost smiled. "Okay then. Before these things thaw completely, go tell Krz and Kane to get the others out, especially Spirit. Maybe something'll come to me by then." She pushed him away. "Go. I can't focus when there's so many lives at stake."

"I'll be right back."

Watching him race toward the others, Etain breathed in, then turned to the snake. "*Thimpeallacht mé féin le sciath cosanta. Táim sábháilte laistigh de mo spás* (I surround myself with a shield of protection. I am safe within my space)."

Electrical charges sparked around her body. "*Ní féidir le do olc teagmháil a dhéanamh liom. Is mise Ard-Mháire na Kaos. Déanfaidh mé pléascáin ar mhaith leat feithidí* (Your evil cannot touch me. I am the High Lady of Kaos. I will squash you like insects)."

She spread her wings, grimacing with the effort, and lifted into the air. "*Ní dhéanfaidh tú saol eile. Táim ag teacht ar do shon, Dathmet* (You will never take another life. I am coming for you, Dathmet)."

Flying above the castle, she turned in the direction of the portal and was comforted by the sight of her friends, the Blades on either side, dashing to safety. A lone figure stood at the gates of the blood castle – Freeblood. She smiled at him as she slowly descended. His yells washed over her, his fists banging against the massive gates, but she could *not* expose the stubborn man to further danger. She landed within the center courtyard in front of the black stones that still reeked of Dar's blood. Her hands shook as she touched the smooth surface of each one. So contaminated by evil, they turned her blood cold and made her stomach roll.

"*Riamh arís*," she whispered. "Never again."

Withdrawing from the stones, another sound came to her ears. The clank of murderous weapons released from their icy prison. It wouldn't be long now.

She brought her wings in tight to her body, bowed her head, and focused on the abuses her husband had suffered - the mental and the physical. She thought of Taurnil and how he lay suspended between life and death. Zorn, another victim of the demon, was thankfully recovering, mainly due to the sacrifice of Ruby, Inferno's red-haired wolfhound.

Inferno…

The head of the snake appeared from behind the southern turret, its parts clanging off each other and the stones of the castle. It wound its way over her head, coiling its metal body around the northern turret.

Instead of coming for her, the snake shattered a large window on the second floor and disappeared inside. She heard the broken glass tinkle and the whoosh of the snake as it tore through the hallways. Although puzzled by the strange behaviour, she remained calm.

Within a few minutes, the snake burst into the courtyard from the same window it had entered. It had changed, grown larger, and now included an actual head. Etain collapsed to her knees. It was as though someone had physically punched her in the stomach. Bile rose into her throat. Unable to swallow it back, she leaned forward and vomited.

Mistress, I am with you. Fill me with your light. Let us stand together against this darkness.

Nim... My fearless blade.

Mama.

Etain lifted her head, tears in her eyes. The unicorn and panther stood before her.

For Da, said the panther.

For them all, said the unicorn.

"Etain!" She heard Freeblood's voice. "Etain!" His pleas became more frantic, screaming her name, threatening her with everything he could think of.

She dragged her sleeve over her mouth and stood. Head bowed, she unsheathed *Nim* and forced herself to take slow, deep breaths. She waited, her blade at her side.

The snake spun into the sky, whipping a fierce wind that sucked in the skulls from the rooftops and dirt from the ground. It dipped into the courtyard, spinning a wide berth around its prey, as though determining from which angle to strike.

Etain remained still, counting the beats of her heart, her lips moving in a silent chant. *I am the High Lady of Kaos. I will prevail. I am the High Lady of Kaos. I will prevail.*

The line of the snake stretched out, lifting into the sky once again, swept around another turret, then dipped. Etain spread her feet until each one touched a black stone. She heard the clanging weapons make one last pass. Both hands on the hilt, she slowly lifted her sword and aimed it straight in front of her.

The snake whipped around the circumference of the courtyard, then shot straight at Etain. Her wings extended, she lifted her head, her eyes filled with white light. Ruby's severed head was at the forefront, jaws snapping, blood dripping from her fangs. The bile rose up again, but this time, the warrior angel pushed it down.

Ruby is gone. Exterminate this abomination.

Nim simultaneously glowed with the same light as in Etain's eyes. A blue electrical charge crackled around her, bouncing back and forth between the black stones. She aimed her sword at the head of the snake, watching as its light burned into what had been Ruby's head. The metal bits following sizzled into oblivion. Some were thrown back into the walls of the castle, while others were cast so high, they crashed into the rooftops of the turrets, shattering what skulls were left.

The ground shook with the intensity of a major earthquake, huge fissures snaking out from Etain's feet toward the blood castle. She sensed the presence of another power source, working in tandem with her solar, ripping the structure apart. A horrible screech rolled over the land as the walls crumbled and the once proud citadel collapsed.

Etain was airborne with a single thrust, but had one last task. Suspended mid-air, she cast her solar onto the black stones, blasting them into dust.

Job done, she tucked away her sword, then flew to the last place she had seen Freeblood. She found him amidst the rocks and debris. A bit dirty and beat up, but well.

Etain scooped him into her arms and raced to the portal where the others waited. The moment she touched down, another roar boomed over the land. A huge geyser of blood erupted from the center of the rubble and rained down, transforming the grey dirt into pools of red mud.

Etain rushed the others through the portal, she being the last to cross over. Once they were safe on the Alamir side, Spirit murmured a spell that sealed the portal for eternity. A unified sigh of relief ran through them all.

Still dark in their world, Etain unsheathed her *Nim,* lighting her up, to search the Blades for a particular face. "Commander Crom."

He greeted her with a fisted hand over his chest as she walked toward him. "High Lady. Did you find the demon?"

"No. Alatariel needs to be told as soon as possible. Maybe Chelri and Swee can come up with an alternative."

Crom frowned. "She will not take this well."

"There's not much I can do about that." Etain ran a hand through her hair. "Just tell her."

"Pardon my saying, but shouldn't the High Lady be the one to carry the news?"

"The High Lady needs to rest," Freeblood said, standing beside her. "We won't be long."

Crom huffed, looking at Etain. "Just go, Commander. Tell her I'll explain when I get there."

He gave a stiff salute, executed an about-face, and joined his men. After shouting the command, the Black Blades marched away.

Once they were out of sight, Etain released the breath she'd been holding and leaned heavily against Freeblood. "Thanks."

"How about you tuck away those wings and relax?" He slipped an arm around her waist and walked her to a grassy patch beneath a tree. "Let me take over on the light."

"I'll recover faster this way." She sat down and leaned back, but extinguished the light of her sword.

Spirit sat with her, while Wolfe stood over them. "When we get to Laugharne, *you* are going to bed," she said.

Etain closed her eyes. "With pleasure."

"If you're okay here, I need to get back to Faux," said Freeblood.

Etain looked at him. "Why don't you not? She's safe and isn't going anywhere. Make her come to you."

"She doesn't work that way."

"Maybe it's time she did. Make her work for it, Freeblood. Then you'll know her true intentions."

Krz and Kane joined them. "Are we good here?" asked Krz.

"We are," Etain said. "Y'all've been a big help. Thank you."

"Anytime you need us, you know where we are," said Krz. "You take care of you and those babies. I think I'd almost rather face that castle again than have twins." His laughter made them all laugh.

"Send my love to Jackie next time you see her."

"Would you like me to share your good news?"

"No." Etain gave him a sad smile. "She'd worry and want to come. As much as I'd love to have her here, we both know it can never happen…for her safety, as well as ours."

Krz nodded. "Well, we're off."

After they left, Etain stood, ready to get back to Laugharne. "Alatariel will be frantic, wondering where we are. Let's go."

"Are you sure, lass?"

Etain felt a pang of guilt at the worried expression on Spirit's face. "I'm good. Really. Taurnil is running out of time. We *have* to go."

"I'll meet you at the house." Freeblood turned and sped off.

"Do you think he'll take your advice?" asked Spirit.

"Did I ever listen to yours?" Etain wrapped her wings around Spirit and Wolfe. "By the way, thank you for the help." Spirit gave her a curious look. "With the destruction of the castle. I felt your power blend with mine. I couldn't have done it without you." Spirit smiled as they disappeared in a shimmer of blue light.

10

RESTORATION

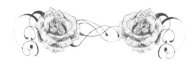

With the arrival of Alatariel's *Nai Turamin* that morning, Swee left Taurnil's side, certain he would be in good hands. Etain's brother, Robert, was the one who needed her more at the moment. Earlier in the day, he was found unconscious at the bottom of the stairs. No one had seen or heard him fall. Not finding any broken bones, bruises, or blood, she had him returned to his room. He had yet to wake.

Seeing no apparent change in his condition, she gently pulled back the covers to check if she had missed something. "Oh, my god."

On his stomach were dark bruises in the shape of a flaming sun. With light fingertips, she touched the skin, which made his body flinch. She looked up to see if he was awake, but his eyes remained closed, his breathing shallow. She placed her hand on his forehead and found it as hot as his body. Determined to bring down his temperature, she rushed into the bathroom and returned with a damp cloth, placing it on his brow.

Her gaze moved down to the unusual mark. In the few moments she'd been in the other room, something new had developed. A crown of swords, seared into his skin, surrounded the flaming sun bruises. She stared at the mark. "Where have I seen this before?"

Swee continued applying cool cloths until his fever lowered to an acceptable level. Certain he'd be all right for a short time, she left him uncovered while she went to stir up a concoction that would further help with the fever.

As soon as Dar's better, I need to tell him.

In the Laugharne courtyard, an elf maiden hurried toward the small entourage. "High Lady, a moment, please."

Etain remembered the young woman. "Erudessa, right?"

Her cheeks turned bright pink, but she smiled as she curtsied. "Aye, milady. I hope you're well."

Etain returned the smile. "I'm as well as I can be."

"Please forgive the intrusion. Her Highness asked to see you in her chambers upon your return. The Royal Sorceress has come with important news about Prince Taurnil. Will you please come?"

Spirit squared her shoulders. Etain stepped in front of her before she could express her opinion. "I'd be happy to, Erudessa." She turned to her friend. "My next stop after the queen will be bed. Go see the kids and get some rest. I'll see you tomorrow."

Alatariel met Etain at the door, giving her a warm hug. "Etain. Please come in." She held her at arm's length. "Was it terrible?"

Etain shrugged. "It wasn't fun. Rie, the demon-"

"Did you meet Sylvan when you were in Nunnehi?" The queen turned to a statuesque female elf. "She is our *Nai Turamin*, our High Sorceress. She's only just arrived."

"Rie…" Etain frowned, concerned by the queen's avoidance of the details of their quest.

"Sylvan, come meet our High Lady." Alatariel waved the woman forward. "This is Etain VonNeshta."

"It is a pleasure, High Lady." Sylvan's voice was smooth, almost hypnotic. "I'm sorry we weren't able to meet whilst you were in Nunnehi." A warm smile on her lips, she reached out and touched Etain on the forearm, then took her hand in hers. "Pardon me for saying, but you look like you've had a hard day."

Etain admired the hands that held hers. Golden bronze against her paleness. Beautifully formed. Soft, yet firm. She met the Sorceress' brown-eyed gaze and realized the chaos swirling in her mind had quieted. "Aye."

"Come sit, High Lady." Sylvan guided her to one of the chairs in front of the fireplace. "Not for too long, as I understand you've only just returned." Etain sat, watching the woman sit in the other chair. She felt a light touch on her knee and turned her head. Alatariel had joined them, sitting on an ottoman.

"Commander Crom told us what happened. Thank you for risking your life to save my son."

Etain blinked, coming back to herself. "But the demon wasn't there."

Alatariel smiled. "It doesn't matter. I wish Sylvan had arrived before your departure, but she came as soon as I informed her that the demon is Midir's son."

She straightened her back. "How do *you* know that?"

"Dar and I had an interesting conversation."

"He was supposed to be *resting*, not having *conversations* about his dead brother." She pushed out of her chair, took a few steps away, then faced the women. "He wasn't even aware of the situation until *I* told him." The High Lady turned to the Sorceress. "I take it there's a connection between this and Taurnil."

Sylvan rested her arms on the arms of her chair. "Midir was a part of Dar. With this demon being Midir's son, they share the same blood."

"*That* is *not* going to happen." Etain pointed at each one as she spoke. "He's lost too much blood." Her gaze went to Alatariel. "I want to save Taurnil, Rie, but I won't risk Dar in the process."

The queen pursed her lips. "Etain, he's already agreed."

"What is *with* you people?" She glared at the queen, feeling as though her brain would explode, then cast her glare on the Sorceress. "We'd lost about four hours by the time we left. How much longer before it's too late for Taurnil?"

Chelri stepped forward from the other side of the room. "Approximately fifteen hours, High Lady."

Etain's gaze darted to the healer. "Chelri, I didn't see you over there. Apologies." He acknowledged her with a bow of his head. "It shouldn't take longer than two, but…" She ran a hand through her hair, "if I'm not back in time, then…*and only then*…will you be allowed to go to Dar. Promise me, Rie."

"Where are you going?" asked the queen as she stood.

Etain stormed to the door, speaking over her shoulder. "Promise me, Queen Alatariel."

Regal in her stance, she sighed, holding her hands just beneath her breasts. "I promise, High Lady. But please, tell me-"

"You remember what I said." Hand on the knob, she turned. "Dar is not to be disturbed unless it's the only alternative." She slammed the door behind her.

As most of the castle settled in for the night, Freeblood was wide awake, unable to rest. He'd not seen Faux since his return from the blood castle. Being apart from her took its toll, but Etain was right. He had to leave it to Faux to make the next move. Then he would know her true intentions toward him. Instead of heading to his room, he stepped outside, hoping the crisp air would clear his head and bring on sleep.

He walked the grounds and checked the gates, then detoured by the stables. Just stepping inside slowed his heart beat, helped him relax. It was another world. Simple, natural – no expectations other than a good nose rub and crunchy apple. If only his life were this uncomplicated.

Satisfied the horses were settled, he slowly headed toward the house, the peacefulness of the night giving rise to a huge yawn. He found the place quiet as he walked through the front doors. Aramis and Ra were in the lounge, speaking in low voices, deep in conversation.

Freeblood heard voices from the kitchen but turned at the stairs toward his room. He walked past Dar and Etain's room, hoping their reunion was going better than his. At Spirit's room, he smiled, hearing her engaged in conversation with her children. It reminded him of his own impending fatherhood.

Rosencrantz.

He laughed as he continued to the farthest corner of the hallway. With a deep sigh, he entered the bedroom, stripping off his clothes for a quick shower.

Once done, he dried off as he walked to the bed, dropped the towel on the floor, and slipped between the covers, hoping sleep would take him before his mind set off on another torturous journey. Eyes closed, he drifted into darkness.

A soft rustling of the covers brought him fully awake. Heart thumping, he looked to his side, straining to focus on the shadows. A familiar scent tickled his nose and a delicate hand touched his chest. "You're home."

Without a second thought, he wrapped his arms around her naked body and pulled her against him. "Faux." He breathed her name, then kissed her on the head, blazing a trail to her waiting lips.

She answered his kisses with the same fervor. "I'm sorry I hurt you-"

"Sshh." He silenced her with another kiss. "You're here. Nothing else matters. Welcome home, my lady."

Alatariel rushed out the door to catch Etain before she did anything rash. The hallway empty, she hurried to Taurnil's room. Perhaps the High Lady had detoured to check on him. At his door, she remembered that Sylvan had him moved not long after her arrival. Etain wouldn't know.

Alatariel stopped at Dar's door and listened. Not hearing voices, she knew she was running out of time.

Sylvan caught up to her. "Your Grace, what are you doing?"

Alatariel took her by the arm and walked away from the door. "I have to stop her."

"I'm sorry, milady. I'm not following."

"Etain!" Alatariel sucked in a breath, looked over her shoulder, and waited for a moment. When no one appeared in the hallway, she resumed in a whisper. "Our High Lady. I know what she plans to do. She can't leave here by herself." She shook her head. "She can't leave…period."

"Your Grace, do you believe she would go after the demon alone?"

The queen headed down the stairs. "Most definitely!"

Hearing voices in the kitchen, she turned and pushed through the door. Linq and Alaster were at the island, ales in hand. Linq stood and bowed. "Your Grace. Good evening."

"Did Etain come this way?"

He glanced at Alaster, who shrugged, then back at Alatariel. "Is there a problem?"

Sylvan stepped into the kitchen. "I'm afraid it's my fault."

"No, Sylvan," said Alatariel. "I'm the one who insisted she be told."

"Told what?" Linq asked.

"I had spoken to Dar-"

"By the sea and stars!" Linq turned to Alaster. "Apologies, my friend. It appears another has a greater need that outweighs my relaxation."

"Sounds like. Just shout if you need me, Linq." Alaster bowed to the others. "Ladies."

Linq followed after Alaster, keen to find Etain.

"Wait, Linq. Let me finish-"

He stopped at the door. "I don't need to hear any more. Dar wasn't to be disturbed. That alone set her off. In which direction did she go?"

"I don't know. She was gone by the time I went after her," said Alatariel.

He came back into the room. "Then *where* did she go?"

"We aren't sure." Sylvan frowned. "But I suspect she's gone after the demon."

"Why would she do that?" He glowered at the two, hands on his hips.

Alatariel had never felt so much like a little girl in trouble. She lifted her chin, reminding herself that *she* was the queen.

"To save me from having to donate my blood," said Dar, walking into the kitchen. "I take it the trip to the blood castle was a failure."

"Dar, you shouldn't be out of bed." Alatariel turned to Linq. "Please help him to a chair."

Linq's glare intensified. "How the hell does he know about the op?"

Dar's eyes narrowed on the elf. "My back is mincemeat, but my hearing works fine." His gaze went to the Sorceress. "Have someone change these bandages and bind me up. I know where she's gone."

Sylvan bowed her head and left quietly.

"If she knows where he is, why didn't she go there first?" Linq blustered.

"I didn't say she knows where he is, only that I know where she's gone."

"Let me go instead, Dar." Linq crossed the kitchen and grabbed a chair, dragging it back to the High Lord. "I'll take our best Blades. Just tell us where."

"Not a chance. This is between me and the demon." Dar straddled the chair, pulling his t-shirt over his head. "He's mine."

"Don't be ridiculous," Alatariel fired at him.

The Sorceress soon returned, Swee in tow. They carefully removed the blood-stained bandages and replaced them with fresh ones.

Swee chastised the lot of them as she worked. "I can't believe I'm doing this again. I could've sworn you wanted to *start* a life with Etain…" She tightened the bandage hard enough to make him wince. "Not end it."

Dar sucked in a breath, sitting a little straighter. "A minor detour."

Alatariel tried again. "You're not in any shape to be running off to fight a demon."

"Don't worry, Rie." Dar grinned. "There will be plenty of blood left over for Taurnil." She responded with a huff. "I won't have the demon do the same, or worse, to my wife. Nor will I expose another living soul to his demented sense of justice."

"I can't let you go off alone," said Linq.

"You can, and you will."

The elf's shoulders slumped. "I have to do *something*."

"Find me a scabbard for Burning Heart. I'm not able to wear one on my back just yet." Dar looked him directly in the eye. "I won't lose you, too."

Linq sighed. "I'll get your damn sword and a scabbard, but there's something I want in return."

"Name it."

"When you return…" He paused for emphasis, "you bring that hard-headed wife of yours to me. I have a few things I want to say."

The grin returned to Dar's face. "Agreed."

Etain appeared in the courtyard of the same castle she'd visited earlier in her search for Dar. The one where Midir conspired to take Dar's life, but lost his instead. Sunshine glinted off an open window upstairs. She lifted a hand to shield her eyes, but didn't see anyone. *Nim* in her other hand, she stalked toward the door, her senses scanning for a hint of the demon. The handle turned easily enough, but she kept her guard up in anticipation of an ambush. She pushed the door open until it banged against the wall, then waited. When no footsteps came, she searched the downstairs. With each empty room, her frustration increased to the point she was ready to raze this castle to the ground, too.

She checked every room upstairs, saving the master bedroom for last. Etain slowly pushed the door open with the tip of her sword and listened for the sound of running water. Lilith had either heeded her warning about the daily bath or she wasn't there.

The bed was made. Etain checked the sheets. They smelled fresh, telling her the place wasn't abandoned, just that no one was home. She walked into the bath. It, too, smelled fresh and clean. The tub was dry, and the precisely folded towels hung on their bars.

Where the hell is Lilith? She never leaves.

Etain returned to the bedroom. The large armoire caught her eye. Curious, she tucked away her sword and opened one of the doors. Leathers in colors of black and dark blue hung inside. She blinked, remembering what Midir had said when she'd scoffed at the different colors in there previously. He swore they would be destroyed and new ones made, but in black only. Why the blue? Why any at all? He didn't have time to order more before…

Maybe they aren't for me.

She pulled a blue set into the daylight. Definitely her size. She rifled through the others. They were the same. Her hand trembled as she returned the hanger to its spot. Her scalp tingled, a flash of heat warming her from head to toe. Rather than keep her anger in check, she let it bubble up into a rage, making her heart pound and body sweat. Powerful, gut-wrenching screams distorted her mouth, as tears of frustration streamed down her cheeks. Her nose ran, her face turned red and puffy, her throat burned. Still, it wasn't enough.

"*Nim!*" she screamed, gripping the familiar hilt as it appeared in her outstretched hand. She wanted to hit, destroy, rip something apart. Anything. Everything. She lashed at the leathers made especially for her, slashed them to pieces, leaving deep gashes in the wood. She hacked at the doors of the armoire, then turned to the vanity sitting next to it.

"I am a warrior! My children will be warriors!" The mirror

succumbed first. Its exploding shards tinkling as they landed on the floor. "My children will *not* be cut down by some cowardly demon intent on taking his revenge on those he thinks weak." One by one, the legs of the vanity gave way. The piece collapsed to the floor.

"My family will not cower in dark corners, waiting for death to find them."

She turned to the bed and climbed onto it, standing tall. "My family will bring the fight to your door, demon." Memories of Midir's attempted seduction swam in her head. "We will cut you down." Over and over, *Nim* stabbed through the covers and the sheets into the mattress. Etain felt a sweet release, imagining him writhing in pain, his screams in the air, the bed drenched in his blood.

It wasn't enough.

It had to burn.

All of it.

She jumped off the bed, sheathed her sword, then lit up both hands with blue electrical fire.

Dar flashed into the same courtyard as Etain had earlier. He also scanned the area and found no other life force, other than his wife's. He sensed the escalation of her anger, felt it simmering just below the surface.

A tiny voice spoke in his mind. *Help her, Da.*

Please, Da, pleaded another.

Then came the screams. His head snapped up, his gaze going straight to the open balcony doors.

Tartarus!

Da!

Dar ran to the open front door, but had to stop and catch his breath. It was more painful than he expected. Never had it taken him so long to heal. If ever he needed to be one hundred percent it was now. He heard her declarations of war and the breaking of furniture. When all went quiet, he knew he'd run out of time.

Rather than run up the stairs, Dar opted to faze into the room. Just as she stepped down from the bed, he appeared behind her, stunned by the devastation. Seeing the blue glow of her hands, he reached for her, felt the skin of his back give way as he wrapped his arms around her, pinning her arms to her sides. He couldn't stop the screams, his blending with those of his wife, as he fought to hold onto her.

"Etain, listen to me!" Involuntary tears of pain slipped down his cheeks. It was like holding onto a wildcat.

"Go home, Dar. You shouldn't be here. *I* must finish this. If Taurnil dies, it will be my fault. I led him into that trap. I led them all into it." She struggled to free herself.

"We each control our own destinies. The Alamir… The Black Blades… All of us…understand…what's at stake."

"I shouldn't have left Laugharne. I knew in my heart it was wrong to go to Nunnehi, to let everyone else fight my battle. It's on me that Inferno is dead, that everyone is dead. I have to save Taurnil without you sacrificing more."

"Please, Etain." He bit his bottom lip to stop another scream, but he still moaned. "*Tartarus*. I can't take much more." Letting go of her, he staggered back.

Etain turned, grabbed his arms, and held onto him. "Damn you." Concern filled her eyes. "What're you doing here?"

"How do I make you understand?" He pulled her to him, pressing his forehead to hers. "You didn't cause this war. Men lust for things that don't belong to them. They seek to possess what cannot be possessed. This is the result of a boy trying to fulfill his father's demented dream. Please, *please*, let this go." His arms wrapped around her. "You can't allow this demon to take your happiness, our happiness. Please, live your life in peace with me, by my side. Make their deaths worth the sacrifice."

"You don't sound like my warrior husband." She pulled away. "We… I have to stop him before he takes another life."

"*A chuisle*, if you continue this way, he'll take more than one life. It will be three."

She became still, the realization of what he'd said hitting home. "But if Taurnil dies…" She dipped her head, hiding her face in his shoulder. "I've grown quite fond of our young cousin. I couldn't bear to-"

"Cousin?" Dar felt her stiffen. "That's an odd way to refer to Taurnil."

Etain pulled back enough to look at him. "Well, he is."

Was she teasing him? Now? In this place? "How can you be related to an elf?"

She shrugged. "No direct blood relation. Strictly by marriage."

Something didn't ring true. "Did you discover this while in Nunnehi?"

"As a matter of fact, yes. Just this last time." She tried to pull out of his arms, but he held her tightly.

"Imagine that." He thought about it for a moment. "I thought your family was human. Which side of the family? Mother or father?"

"Neither, actually."

He nodded until he realized what she'd said. "Then how can you be related by marriage? Is your brother married?"

Etain pulled away. It was a struggle, but she gained her freedom and walked toward the balcony, standing at the door. "Not that I know of."

Dar cocked his head. "If everyone is human and your brother isn't married, how does that work?"

She ran a hand through her hair, turning toward him. "My husband."

"Aye?"

"Aye," she said, an expectant look on her face.

He rolled his hand in a gesture to get on with it. "Finish what you were going to say."

"I said what I meant to say."

"All you said was 'my husband'. My husband what?" He watched a blonde brow rise. Her thoughts finally penetrated his confusion. "For the love of Krymeria! What nonsense is this?"

She crossed her arms. "It isn't nonsense."

He stared at her, trying to digest the news. "Bullshit!"

"Why would Alatariel lie about something that important?"

Dar walked toward the balcony doors, standing opposite her. "How would she know anything about my family?"

"I don't know, Dar. Maybe because she *is* your family."

He blew out a breath. "*My* family? Where? How?" He needed to move. Walking away a few steps, he turned to her. "When? Why didn't I know of this?"

Etain shifted her weight to the other hip. "Well, let's see if I can answer most of your questions. Where? I can't say for sure, but chances are it was Krymeria." A shadow of a smile touched her lips. "How? That one I *can* tell you." She gazed out the balcony doors. "Your grandmother on your father's side was an elf." Dar huffed, bringing her gaze back to him. "She fell in love with a handsome Krymerian and married him, but her twin sister…" She paused, watching the expressions on his face change from outrage to dismay, "chose one of her own to marry." Etain hugged herself. "When? Well, it was obviously a long time ago."

"I don't understand why I wasn't told."

"Your father didn't want *anyone* to know about your mixed heritage. For your sake as much as his. He made Alatariel's family swear a blood oath to keep it secret. I guess he wanted to save you the burden of knowing you weren't pure Krymerian."

"We're wasting time here. We need to go." He moved toward her, but she stepped back.

"What're you gonna do, Dar?"

"I'm *gonna* save Taurnil's life…" He swept an arm around her waist. "Then I'm *gonna* have a little chat with my cousin, the Queen of the Elves."

Etain soon realized things were not going to go as she had anticipated. "Dar, why are we *here*? I thought you were going to-"

"I have another matter that requires my attention." He walked across the room and flipped on a light.

"But, Taurnil-"

"Will not expire before I arrive."

Standing in the living room of the small cottage, she wondered what matter could be so important he would risk the young elf's life. "I don't understand."

"You will…"

Alarm bells rang in her head. She watched him walk toward her. "What're you doing?" She stepped back.

He stopped and held out his hand. "Come to me, Etain."

Giving him her most indignant look, she backed farther away. "I don't like the look in your eyes."

"I imagine if I were in your shoes, I wouldn't like it, either." He reached for the dagger in his boot.

Her eyes widened, pulse racing. "What the hell, Dar?" The wall at her back, she darted to the side, just missing his grasp.

"Come to me, Etain."

"You can go to hell." She hoped to stay out of his reach long enough to get to the front door, but he cut her off. She pulled up just out of reach. "You're going to make your back worse. Why don't you sit down and I'll get Swee."

Although he smiled, she wished he wouldn't. "Thanks to our little excursion, it doesn't hurt so much. Now, come here."

Electrical charges sparked around her body in preparation of a shimmer.

"Wherever you go, *a chuisle*, I will follow. Shall we go to the Laugharne courtyard, share with everyone there?"

"No!" Afraid he might be having another terrible vision, she turned and ran into the bedroom. His footsteps behind her, she dashed into the bathroom, slammed the door, and engaged the lock. "Go away, Dar. Go to the house. Save Taurnil."

The door gave way with two good kicks. "Not until I know you're safe."

Etain almost laughed. "I'll be a lot safer when you put away that dagger."

His gaze went to the blade, then to her. "It serves a purpose."

She drew her sword. "Go save Taurnil."

He dropped his dagger and reached for *Nim* with both hands, running his palms down the length of the sharp blade. Etain gasped at the blood he left behind. With the flick of a finger, he commanded, "Release." *Nim* vibrated. Etain had to use both hands to hold onto it. The vibrations transformed into a white heat. With a shriek, she released the sword, watching it fall to the floor.

By the time she looked up, Dar moved in, pushing her back into the shower stall until she felt her back against the wall. She screamed. With bloodied hands, he grabbed the collar of her shirt and ripped it apart, buttons flying in every direction. His right hand pushed her head back as he dipped down and bit into the mark on her chest, drawing her blood to the surface. He reached over with his left and dragged the blood across her chest as his right slid down her face, each leaving a bloody path.

"With our blood, I bind thee to me, so we may always be one."

"No!" she screamed, remembering what he'd done to Faux. "Not like her." The harder she fought, the stronger he became.

His left arm pushed into her neck as he reached down and released the button of her trousers. Etain grabbed his arm. Tried to pull it away. The trousers fell victim to his overpowering strength and drifted to the floor in shreds.

"Don't!"

His intent set her blood on fire. Her heart pounded with a mixture of fear and desire. His eyes bored into hers as he shoved a leg between her thighs. "Touch me." He pushed his body into hers, forcing her hand to his crotch.

With shaky hands, she unbuttoned his fly, releasing his rock-hard cock. He groaned at her touch, picked her up, and spread her open for his penetration. "With my seed, I bind thee to me, so you will never leave my side."

Their hot breath blended as one, the friction of their bodies burned. He crushed his lips to hers, then made the final declaration. "With my lips, I seal your fate with mine."

In that moment, his mind, as well as his heart, opened to her. This wasn't an act of domination. This was Dar baring his soul, revealing his desperate need to keep her safe, to protect her, their family, their future. She clung to him, feeling his hot release deep inside her.

"Forever and a day, my love."

Later that evening, Dar left his sleeping wife in bed while he went to Taurnil. Alatariel jumped up from her seat when he opened the door.

"Dar! Thank the stars. Did you find Etain? Is she all right?" She rushed toward him as he came into the room.

"I did. She is. How's Taurnil?" He nodded at Chelri and Sylvan as he walked toward the bed.

"High Lord…" Sylvan dipped her head. "We're running out of time. Did you locate the demon?"

Dar sighed. "We have a demon…" He looked up from the sleeping elf to the Sorceress. "Not the one we were hoping for, but hopefully you won't be disappointed."

Sylvan smiled. "Never, High Lord. Shall we get started?"

"Please be seated, milord." Chelri indicated the chair Alatariel had recently vacated. "It will not take long."

The healer placed two bowls on the bed beside Taurnil. Each chose from a variety of herbs and plants displayed on a nearby table, breaking them into the bowls.

"How is it you know what to do?" Dar asked the Sorceress.

"When Chelri and Lady Swee were unable to determine an

antidote for the poison, Chelri consulted with me in the hopes I would know of a potion. I searched our records for anything that resembled the prince's symptoms and eventually came across an ancient Krymerian text, one we thought had been destroyed during the wars with the Draconians."

"Interesting. What does the text have to do with all this?"

Sylvan poured a few drops of oil into her bowl, but not into Chelri's. "I found an obscure reference to the poison used on Taurnil. Had I not known what I was looking for, I would never have noticed it."

"You read Krymerian?" Dar challenged, not quite convinced.

Sylvan caught the skepticism in his voice. "Yes, Lord Dar, I do. It has come in handy with my various spells and potions. The Krymerians were well versed in the arts and, fortunately, were thoughtful enough to keep a record of their pursuits." Dar waited for the last piece of the puzzle. "Your father taught me to speak and read Krymerian."

He raised his brows. "My father?"

"Yes," she said, lifting her chin. "We shared many spirited debates comparing Krymerian and Elven arts after I became apprenticed to the old Sorceress. He felt it imperative I learn the ways of both races to, at the very least, preserve the future of Nunnehi, if not Krymeria."

"Is that all he sought to preserve, Sylvan?"

"Dar, we haven't time for this." Alatariel interrupted. "Thanks to Sylvan, we can forget about the infernal demon." She motioned for the Sorceress to elaborate.

Dar listened, thinking what a sly fox his father must have been. He had speculated from time to time about the king's personal affairs after his mother's death, but never voiced his thoughts.

So, the apple doesn't fall far from the tree, he mused, remembering that it was his grandfather who married an elf.

"…Krymerian blood." Sylvan finished with an expectant look at Dar.

He realized he hadn't heard a word. Clearing his throat, he pretended not to understand. "Krymerian blood?"

"You haven't been listening," she said, perturbed at his apparent disregard. "The poison can be reversed with a few drops of Krymerian blood. You carry the Elven heritage that runs through Taurnil's veins, which will make it much easier. There will be no need for dilution."

Dar certainly heard that. Coming to full attention, his gaze cut to Alatariel. "About that..."

"First, High Lord, shall we draw some blood?" Chelri came around the bed, a freshly sterilized scalpel in one hand and clean bowl in the other. "If you will hold this bowl underneath your hand."

Dar took the offered bowl from the healer, not yet convinced it would work, and held his other hand over it. Chelri sliced across the High Lord's palm, the blood welling to the surface and dripping into the bowl. Once the bottom was covered by a thin film, the healer wrapped Dar's hand with a clean cloth. "That should do it."

Dar continued his conversation with the queen while the other two worked. "After the death of Alexia, Henrí, and Victoria, I spent *years* living in despair, thinking I was completely alone in the world. No family, no friends, nothing."

Alatariel appeared baffled. "I know all this, Dar."

"I spent over one hundred years traveling here and there, helping where I could with no commitment to anyone or anything."

All the while, Sylvan and Chelri pounded and stirred...one creating a salve, the other concocting an elixir, both containing the blood of the High Lord.

"Yes, Dar-"

"Until...," he said loudly, "my precious Etain. She changed everything. It took me *years* to understand what I felt was real." He leaned forward. "*Years* to admit my heart loved another. *Years* for me to see I could love again and live in happiness." He carefully unwrapped his hand and checked the wound, which was now healed. He leaned back, placing the cloth on the bedside table.

"Time after time, circumstances threw her into my life, then would rip her out just as quickly. I lied to myself repeatedly, saying it was because I felt responsible for her, that she was only in this world because of my error." His gaze met Alatariel's. "Then I realized the only time I was happy was when I was with her. It didn't matter if we were at odds or in a friendly chat. Having her with me was what made my heart sing, what *still* makes my heart sing."

"I'm so happy for you, Dar, but-" she started, but he held up a hand and stood.

He paced away a few steps, turned, then strode back to the bed. "Did it not occur to *anyone* during those one hundred years to possibly *clue me in* to the family I had around me? Family who stood back and said nothing of our connection. Family who left me in the dark with nary a word." Alatariel's eyes widened as he came even closer, his eyes ablaze with a golden fire. "Did you think so little of me? Was I not *good enough* for your precious Elven family? Was a half-breed too disgraceful for the royal family to claim?"

Indignant, she held her head high. "You were never a disgrace. I was forced by blood oath not to reveal your history. It was not common knowledge that your grandmother was Elven."

"Blood oath? Who in the name of Krymeria would do such a thing?" Although he knew the answer, he needed to hear it from her lips.

Alatariel squared her shoulders and looked him directly in the eye. "The King of Krymeria ordered it. The King of Krymeria, who himself was part elf, declared that no one would speak of his heritage, nor would his son be told."

Dar slammed a fist into his hand, making everyone jump. "My father has been dead well over one hundred years, Alatariel. Did you never think the promise died with him?"

"No, I did not. A blood oath does not die merely because the one it was made to is gone."

"It was *my* life!"

Anger sparked in her words. "Your father made sure your life was secure within the Krymerian realm. He knew there would be problems if anyone of pure Krymerian birth learned of your mixed blood. The challenges would have been endless. Your life would have been a constant battle."

With a grunt, he responded, "Have you not noticed my life, Alatariel? It *has* been a battle. Knowing I had family would've given me something to hold onto, something more than an idea or dream to fight for."

"Your father did what he thought best, and I honored his dying request."

"Then why tell Etain?"

"She was my loophole," she admitted with a shrug, her anger subsiding as the truth spilled out. "I couldn't break my promise to a dying man, and you were so distraught after their deaths, I didn't have the heart to burden you with information that could jeopardize your birthright. So, I kept my mouth shut all those years. I must admit, it was a relief when you disappeared. My guilt lightened as my attentions turned to ruling my kingdom. Then you crashed back into our lives… with Etain." She relaxed, lowering her shoulders. "You're right about her. She has changed everything. Not only for you, but for me, as well. I suddenly found myself freed from those bonds of long ago. She was someone I could speak to freely without reprisals or judgment. I felt she was someone who would understand my predicament."

"And so she did, milady." Suddenly feeling drained, he dropped into the bedside chair and ran both hands through his hair, watching as Chelri applied the salve to Taurnil's midsection. "I only wish I had known of my family ties sooner. I would've done so many things differently."

Alatariel moved to him, framing his face with her hands. "But if things had been different then, they would be different now. You may never have found your Etain."

Closing his eyes, he whispered, "Perhaps."

She gave him a warm hug. "I'm sorry, Dar. I wish I could make it up to you. Can we start anew today…cousin?"

"Aye. I'd like that." He opened his eyes. "I have another question.

How is it you have a book in your library of my family history written in both Elven and Krymerian?"

"High Lord, your assistance, please." Sylvan held up a small vial. "We need to pour a few drops of this elixir down his throat."

Alatariel stepped aside so Dar could help raise the prince as she explained. "Your grandmother kept the records of your family. She wanted the history, as well as the sacrifices, of both the VonNeshtas and the Krymerians documented for those who followed, so she wrote in both languages. After her death, your father made sure the book was sent to Nunnehi. Partly for safe keeping, but mainly to keep away from prying eyes."

"My grandmother was fluent in both languages?"

Satisfied with the amount given the prince, Sylvan nodded. They lay him back down.

"Your grandfather taught her Krymerian," said the queen. "They loved each other very much, Dar. The passion shared between you and Etain reminds me of their love."

"How is it you remember so much?"

"Your grandparents were my great-aunt and uncle. They visited us often when I was small. They were always so kind and loving."

"Seeing her and my grandfather at the honor ceremony reminded me of how much you look like her. Learning of our family connection sets several things straight in my memories."

Alatariel's gaze roamed to her son. His eyes glistened with unshed tears. "Taurnil." Dar stepped aside, switching places with the queen. "Son, how long have you been awake?"

He shrugged slightly as his eyes moved to Dar. His mother gave him a questioning look but seemed to understand. "Dar, I think he wants to speak with you." She and the High Lord switched places again.

He leaned down, placing his ear close to the elf's lips. All Taurnil could muster was a faint "E".

Dar placed a hand on his shoulder. "Relax. Let me come to you."

Taurnil settled back, his gaze holding Dar's, as the High Lord gently melded his mind with his cousin's. Within minutes, the two shared a silent conversation.

She's safe. The demon was nowhere to be found. He gave the young elf's shoulder a comforting squeeze. *To further ease your mind, she can't go anywhere that I won't be right next to her.* Dar tapped the side of his own head. *A little High Lord mojo.* With a laugh, he gave Taurnil a wink.

He felt the tension melt away from the young elf's body and was rewarded with a slight smile. Taurnil mouthed the words, *Thank you,* then closed his eyes.

"He's fallen asleep," Dar said, stepping away from the bed. "If I'm done here, I'd like to get some shut-eye myself. How soon will we know if it has worked?"

From the other side of the bed, Chelri raised his head. "We should know more by the time you wake, High Lord."

Alatariel walked him to the door. "Thank you, Dar. Please send my thanks to Etain, as well."

"We'll come by after breakfast to check on his progress. I fully expect to see him greatly improved." He kissed her on the cheek. "You should rest, too."

A slight smile touched her lips. "Not until I know he's out of danger."

"I pray it will be so. Good night, Rie."

"Good night…cousin."

Dar chuckled as he closed the door behind him and strolled down the hallway toward his bedroom. Once inside, he groped his way to the bed, looking forward to a long sleep next to his beautiful wife, and possibly a little pre-breakfast activity. As he unbuttoned his shirt, he thought the room rather quiet, and stopped, even holding his breath to listen. His heart beat erratically, realizing the bed was empty. He switched on the bedside lamp, wondering if perhaps he'd missed something with his binding spell. Worse, had she outwitted him and discovered a way to reverse it? Where would she go? Surely, not back to the demon's castle.

"Damn you, Etain."

Buttoning his shirt, he rushed to the door and yanked it open when it finally occurred to him. He'd left her at the cottage. He quietly closed the door and leaned his head against it, breathing in and out. Tears welled up in his eyes.

Damn you, Dar.

He wiped his tears on his shirt sleeves and fazed to the cottage. Dark and quiet, he went straight to the bedroom. Again, he held his breath, listening. Never had he heard a sweeter sound. He let go the breath as he walked to the bed, unbuttoning his shirt and tossing it to the floor. The rest of his clothes soon followed. He slipped between the covers, snuggled up behind her, and nuzzled into her hair.

"Your snores are music to my ears, *a chuisle.*"

Near enough to sleep himself, he heard her snort lightly. "I don't snore."

His lips curled into a smile. "No, milady… Never."

11

FAMILY

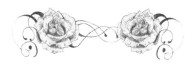

Etain woke later than expected, happy to be in the arms of her loving husband. His warm body pressed against hers felt exquisite. *I could get used to this.* Then she remembered the events from the day before and frowned. She understood his binding her to him, which basically blocked her from going to another realm unless he was with her. It was a nuisance, but she could abide it. What she wasn't sure of was if he'd also limited or taken away her powers, like he'd done to Faux. Midir said it couldn't be done, but-

"In that, he spoke the truth." Dar kissed her bare shoulder. "Not even I can bind your powers."

"I didn't mean to wake you." She turned to face him.

He stroked her hair, his eyes dreamy. "I'd rather spend my time with you awake."

She smoothed a finger over his lips. "How's your back?"

"Tight."

"So, how were you able to bind *her* powers?"

"I am her sire…" He trailed a finger along her shoulder, "which gives me power…" And down her arm, "over her. Faux needs to learn humility and to appreciate others."

"A bit brutal, don't you think?"

"She betrayed everyone. Not just in this castle, but across the realms. Considering the alternative, I think I was rather charitable."

"Do you think your actions toward me were 'charitable'?"

"Not quite." He looked away in thought, then brought his gaze back to her. "More like-"

"Overbearing?"

"Protective."

She pushed away and rolled out of bed. "Attaching me to your hip…" She slapped herself on the hip, "*stealing* my independence…" She waved her arms in the air, "is your idea of being protective?"

Propped on his elbow, his eyes positively glowed in appreciation. "Not that I see it the same way, but if this is how you've interpreted my good intentions…"

Etain recognized the look…his leer…and crossed her arms over her naked breasts. "Kiss my ass, Dar VonNeshta." She whirled away and disappeared into the bathroom, slamming the door.

"Come back to bed and I'll kiss more than just your beautiful ass."

Dressed in a loose blouse and skirt, she yanked the door open and hesitated, surprised by Dar, grinning in all his glory, just on the other side. "Prancin' around in the buff isn't gonna change anything."

He looked down at the bandages around his torso. "I'm not exactly 'prancin'…in the buff or otherwise."

"You know what I mean." She breezed past him.

"Where are you going? *What* are you wearing? I thought we would-"

"Think again, bucko." At the bedroom door, she stopped and turned toward him. *Damn.* Every ounce of bravado evaporated into thin air. Despite his persistent male dominance issues or the fact that he thought his way was the only way, he *did* strike an impressive figure, even with yards of gauze wrapped around him. Tall, lean, muscular, and…*Damn his soul…*a grin that melted her ovaries.

Wouldn't I love to pin you *in the shower and-*

"Such thoughts, milady," he said, sidling up close.

194

Etain placed a hand on his chest and swallowed. "No," she managed to say.

His hands engulfed her waist and pulled her to him. "I know you want to."

"*I* know I want to, but…"

He pressed his body into hers. "But?"

"Oh, well…" She didn't dare look him in the eyes – golden pools filled with promised pleasures. Instead, she focused on his mouth. His irresistibly, delectable mouth, begging to be consumed. "Goddamn you."

Ravaged, consumed, devoured. Her arms around his neck, he pressed into her, her back against the door. She had enough presence of mind to avoid his back, but his firm, round backside was fair game. Her heart thumped in rhythm with his. Their shared breaths hot and quick. Despite what happened the day before, it felt like ages since they'd been together - alone, passionate, in tune.

His hands were liquid fire, warming her skin through her clothes. She wanted to feel them on every inch of her flesh. Pulling the blouse over her head, she gasped as his lips encased an erect nipple, his tongue flicking, his mouth sucking. Had she ever felt this alive?

She reached for his cock, finding it hard, his balls tight, ready to explode. He moaned at her touch. Releasing her breast, his mouth came to hers again, taking everything she had to give. Their hands worked in tandem, raising her skirt. As he lifted her, his grunt melded into a shared moan of passion. Etain welcomed him in, gasping from the pure pleasure he brought.

He held onto her as fiercely as she held him, each giving and taking, loving one another, a much-needed coming together.

Awake, but not yet ready to face the day, he didn't open his eyes. His hand moved to his side, wanting to caress her fragrant skin. Nothing. Alarmed, he opened his eyes and turned his head. Where was she? It couldn't have been a dream. She had been there, in the flesh…warm, soft, comforting.

The room was dark. Unable to see, his other senses took over. Her smell drifted to him. Her warmth teased his skin. His muscles relaxed as supple arms engulfed him. Her firm breasts pressed against his naked chest, the growing roundness of her belly pushed into his as she moved, her strong thighs brushing against his.

"You didn't leave me," he whispered to his phantom lover.

"I am here." Her breath was soft and warm in his ear, his blood on fire. "Take me. Make me yours again."

He sensed something in the distance trying to emerge, but his mind pushed it away, fighting desperately to return to his sexy demon. He closed his eyes for a moment and she was gone. Searching hands reached out into the darkness. "Where are you? Come back."

"Freeblood, wake up."

Someone held his shoulders, shaking him. His eyes popped open. "Faux?" He blinked several times, unsure if he were awake or in another dream.

Straddling his hips, she sat back and sighed. "Where were you?"

"Am I awake?"

Faux pursed her lips. "Do you see any horns?" She pointed at her forehead.

He blinked again. "Uh, no."

"Then you're awake."

Freeblood rubbed his eyes, the memory of what happened between her and Dar rushing in. He pushed up onto his elbows. "You okay?"

She shrugged. "It's getting easier. What's up with you?"

With a pump of his hips, he dislodged her, then rolled onto his side, facing her. "Just a dream. Pretty mild, considering the things I've seen lately."

Stretched out beside him, a smirk lifted her lips as she trailed a finger down his chest. "What is it you've seen?"

He grabbed her hand and pulled her to him. "A beautiful woman in my bed, waiting for me."

"I wasn't *waiting* for you. Your bed's a lot more comfortable than the one at the cottage."

Freeblood laughed, accepting her lie for what it was. "Well, since *you're* here, and *I'm* here…how about we make the most of it?"

"Are you sure?"

"Yes, I'm sure." He frowned. "What's going on?"

She actually blushed. "Well, I'm just… This." She waved her hand, indicating her present state.

His eyes widened. "This?"

"I'm just a regular…person."

"There's nothing *regular* about you, my lady, in any shape or form. I love what's in here…" He lightly tapped her head, "and in here." Then her chest. "Other people might not see you, but I do. I also love this." He placed his hand on her belly. "We've created a new life… together. I hope you don't mind that I'm not a lord or some fancy-"

"Shut up and make love to me." She crushed her lips to his.

"Shall we pay a visit to our newly found cousin this morning?" Dar asked as he buttoned his shirt.

"I need to check on my brother, then I'll meet you in Taurnil's room. Okay?"

He stopped and watched her as she slipped into her blouse. "Is that what you're wearing today?"

"What's wrong with it?" she asked, straightening her skirt.

"It's not what you usually wear."

"I'm not usually pregnant with twins. My leathers are uncomfortable, and Swee told me I shouldn't wear tight clothing. So…" She walked up to him, giving him a peck on the lips, "I'm taking full advantage of it. This is so comfy, I might not ever go back to leather."

"Well, that would be a damn shame."

Etain laughed, walking to the door. "I'll meet you at T's in a bit."

Within a few minutes, she was at Robert's bedroom. Not hearing a response to her knock, she entered. Her smile disappeared as she walked toward the bed. An unusual odor hung in the air. A scorched smell that grew stronger as she neared her sleeping brother. His face in sweet repose, she found nothing amiss, but her intuition told her to take a closer look.

She placed a hand on his forehead. "Holy crap."

His skin was hot. She rushed to the balcony doors and threw them open to let cool air into the room, then hurried back to the bed, uncovering his heated body.

"What the hell?" She gently touched the brand on his belly. "How'd you get this?" Looking at his face, she saw his eyes open, piercing into hers, his black pupils encased in a green glow.

She stepped back into what felt like a stone wall. A muscular arm pinned her arms to her sides as a large hand clamped over her mouth. A deep voice chanted in her ear as she struggled against his hold, trying to thrust all her energy into transforming. She felt his will battling against hers, keeping her demon persona at bay.

A commanding voice spoke in her mind. *Etain.*

She looked at the bed. *Why is he using telepathy?* She blinked several times and shook her head, watching his face blur into that of the red-fleshed demon.

"Raum, bring her closer. Cut her. Quickly."

Who was he talking to? Raum? The name sounded familiar.

Overcome by the spell, Etain moved easily under Raum's manipulations. She watched him draw his dagger and slice into her arm, saw the blood well up and trickle down onto his master's lips. His hold on her unshakeable, Raum bent over Robert and worked his mouth so the blood flowed down his throat.

Once Dathmet had control of the facial features, his manservant pushed her arm down onto the caustic lips. Dathmet bared his sharp fangs and pierced into her tender flesh, taking a long drink. After a few moments, he pulled back with a noticeable sigh.

"Rub the blood over the mark. There must not be any visible sign left."

Raum smeared Etain's blood over Robert's belly. Within moments, the scorch marks, bruises, and blood disappeared.

"That's good. Now bring her arm back to me." He ran his tongue along the cut, sealing it. "Sit her down next to me and be gone. Hurry. The damn Krymerian will be here soon. Somehow, he knows something's amiss and is coming."

Raum pushed her down on the edge of the bed, then pulled the covers over Robert. He quickly reversed the spell on Etain as Dathmet melded into the young man's human form and closed his eyes.

The manservant vanished just as Dar burst into the room, dagger in hand.

"Etain."

He felt traces of evil, but saw only her, sitting on the edge of the bed, and Robert, asleep. He put away the blade as he walked into the room and placed his hands on her shoulders. "Etain?"

At his touch, she snapped out of the trance and covered his hands with her own. "Dar! What're you doing here?"

"Merely checking that you're all right. Taurnil is asking for you." He kissed the top of her head, then crouched beside her.

"I'm fine, my love. I was just talking with Robert." They both looked at the comatose young man. "Well, I thought I was." She chuckled as she shrugged. "So, the young prince has requested an audience with the High Lady of Kaos?"

Dar gave her an uneasy smile. He knew what he felt was real, but as long as she was well, he let it go. He stood, pulling her up with him. "Aye. He seems much improved. Let's leave your brother to his sleep. We can come back later." Walking arm in arm to the door, Dar glanced around the room one more time as she stepped into the hallway. "You've become quite fond of this new cousin. Is your interest merely for his welfare, or is there something else going on here I need to know about?"

She laughed, waiting for him to close the door. The sparkle in her eyes was a welcome sight, but he wasn't sure if it was because of him or his handsome cousin. "I've come to love him in his own regard." She took his hands in hers. "But mostly, it's because he reminds me of you. His golden eyes, the boyish grin, his courage, his spirit." Reaching up, she pushed back a stray lock of hair from his forehead. "He gives me a glimpse of what you were like when you were that young. So innocent, naïvely thinking every problem could be met with a bold show of bravado and a quick sword.

"However, my sweet husband…" She brought his hands up, pressing them to her lips, "it is *you* who quickens my blood and fills my heart so completely that mere words can never express what I feel for you." Tears shone in her eyes. "No one can *ever* replace you in my heart."

Humbled by her sincerity, he pulled his hands free and wrapped her in his arms. "Forgive me, *a chuisle*. I do not mean to doubt you. My true motivation is to keep you safe."

She laughed again. "Your true motivation is to keep me all to yourself."

"You know me all too well, milady." He laughed with her. "Shall we go?"

The prince faded in and out of consciousness most of the afternoon. Chelri, Sylvan, and Swee took turns checking his vitals and administering the blood elixir created from Dar's donation. They also made sure the donor received his fair share of attention. Swee changed his bandages, surprised at the improvement of his back. He grinned and told her it was all down to his Krymerian heritage.

Linq joined them for a short time, long enough to speak to Taurnil and share a few words with Dar. "If you're up to it, we need to put those funeral pyres to use. It isn't right that our dead haven't been honored."

"Aye. You're right, Linq. Have the bodies been prepared?"

"We're almost done. The pyres are completed and ready. Will you and Etain officiate?"

"We will, but we haven't the proper robes. I'll need another day or two."

"Dar…," Etain interrupted. "The faeries did a wonderful job on my wedding dress. Perhaps they'd be willing to help."

"Good idea, *a chuisle*." He turned to Linq. "How is Spirit? Has she been around?"

Linq shook his head. "I haven't seen her since the team returned from the blood castle."

"I'll speak with her," said Etain. Dar gave her a questioning look. "I'll tell you about it later."

"I need to get back," Linq said. "Are you coming down for dinner?"

"Aye, we'll be down soon." He walked him to the door.

"It'll be good for everyone to see you, Dar. Put a few minds at rest."

Dar lowered his voice. "Has there been talk amongst the clan about who will take over as chieftain?"

"Not that I've heard, but the mood, well… It's tense. We need Spirit to put them at ease."

"Do they not trust you?"

"It's not so much about me. She's the most direct link to Inferno."

Dar opened the door. "We'll get it worked out."

"Until dinner then."

Closing the door, Dar returned to Etain's side. "I think it best we attend."

She smiled. "I think it best *you* attend. If it's okay with you…" Her gaze turned to Alatariel, "and Rie, I'd rather stay here with T for a little while. It'll give y'all a chance to catch up with everyone else."

Alatariel gave her a nod. "I know he is in safe hands."

Dar hesitated. "I'd like to have you by my side."

Etain took his hand. "You'll be way too busy to even miss me. Please, go enjoy yourself. Everyone's looking forward to seeing you. You can bring me a plate later. If anything happens here, I'll let you know."

"I *will* miss you, but it would be rude of me to disappoint my fans." He laughed. "Ladies, it appears I've been given free rein." He offered one arm to Alatariel and one to Swee. "Shall we?" At the door, he looked back at Etain. "I won't be long."

"Take your time," she called after them.

Sitting on the side of the bed, she noticed an improvement in Taurnil's coloring and touched his forehead. His fever was gone. His golden eyes fluttered open. "Hey, T."

"Put them back," he whispered, his eyes unusually fierce. "Your hands... Put them back on my face."

Etain placed a hand on each cheek. He breathed a long sigh, closing his eyes. "Such a touch I have never known until I met you, sweet Lady Etain." With that said, he returned to his sleep, a smile on his lips.

Although somewhat daunted by his admission, she stroked his face and hair, noting how much easier he breathed. "Sleep well, T."

Downstairs, Swee pulled Dar away from the other diners. "We need to talk."

He didn't like her worried expression. "What's the problem?"

"Can we go somewhere more private? It has to do with Etain's brother."

Dar turned to Alatariel. "If you will excuse us for a moment, Rie." He followed Swee to the living room.

"There's something you should see, Dar."

"Why don't you just tell me? I need to-"

"You wouldn't believe me if I just told you. You'll have to see it for yourself." The plea in her eyes swayed him to follow her upstairs to Robert's room. On the way, she explained what transpired in their absence, how the young man was found splayed out at the foot of the stairs, seemingly dead to the world. They entered as quietly as possible. She carefully pulled back the covers. "I came in this morning to check on him before going down for breakfast. Do you know what burned flesh smells like?"

He gave her a puzzled look. Where was she headed with this? "Aye. All too well."

"Then this won't surprise you." She pointed at Robert but didn't look.

Dar followed her direction. "See what, Swee?"

Her brows furrowed as she looked down. "It was there this morning." Her confusion was obvious. "I swear, Dar. There was a mark on his belly."

"What kind of mark?"

"There were bruises here." Her hand moved in a circle over Robert's belly. "The edges looked like flames." Her eyes on the patient, she circled her hand in the other direction. "Around the bruises was another circle burned into his skin. A circle of swords." She looked up at Dar. "I know I saw it. I remember thinking I'd seen the mark before but couldn't place it."

He mulled over her words. While it would be easy to dismiss what others would consider ravings, he thought on other unusual events that had recently occurred within the castle, not to mention the high regard he held for this woman.

He unbuttoned his shirt halfway and separated the bandages over his chest. "Did it look like this?"

Her gasp and wide-eyed surprise were all the confirmation he needed. "It wasn't as crisp as yours, but yes. I knew I had seen it before. Etain has the same mark, doesn't she?" Her gaze returned to Robert's abdomen. "How can he have it, too?"

"I'm not sure." Dar buttoned his shirt. "And I don't know how it could disappear so completely." Replacing the covers, he took her arm and escorted her to the door. "Do not tell anyone of this. Understand? Not even Etain. Give me some time to sort this out."

"Dar, how do I look her in the eye knowing this and not say anything?"

"I'm only asking you keep quiet until after the Ceremony of Valor. Let's get through that before we move on to the next intrigue. Please, give me that long. Can you do that?"

She hesitated. "Okay."

They returned to the dining hall and parted company. Dar joined the dinner line behind Ra for his turn at the sideboard laden with choices for the evening meal. As he waited, his mind wandered to Etain's sleeping brother. *What could cause such a manifestation? And how? Could Etain have done something?* He quickly dismissed the thought, knowing that even if she had shared her blood with the man, it wouldn't cause such a mark. Then he remembered what he'd felt that morning...

"Ahem. Dar." Aramis, standing behind him, cleared his throat. "The food isn't going to jump onto your plate, man. You'll need to help it along, I'm afraid."

Shaken from his reverie, he gave the man a strange look, then recalled his whereabouts. "Sorry, Aramis. I guess I was daydreaming." He moved forward, grabbing two plates.

Aramis laughed. "I wouldn't do too much of that around this crowd. You may starve to death in the process."

Dar smiled as he filled the plates and placed them on a tray. Topping off one mug with ale and another with milk, he noticed Sylvan at the doorway, watching him with knitted brows.

"What has you so perplexed, milady?" he asked, walking to her.

"Apologies, Lord Dar. I did not intend to be rude. I've only just realized the resemblance between you and our prince. It's quite remarkable."

"It's only since Midir's death that I've assumed my true appearance. I suppose our reunion brought out the Elven blood."

"That's true."

"Would you please give Alatariel my apologies for not joining her for dinner? Something has come up."

"Of course, milord."

Dar moved past her to go upstairs, then stopped and turned. "Sylvan, an intrigue has arisen and I think you might be the one to help me unravel it."

Her demeanor brightened. "An intrigue? How fascinating. I would love to delve into a new mystery."

"Let's speak after the ceremony."

"Yes, milord," she said, bowing her head slightly.

Cherise had a special dinner prepared and sent up to Spirit and the children. Having the opportunity to eat in their mum's room made it all the more exciting. The boys spread blankets on the floor, while the girls tossed pillows around. Spirit stoked the fire in the fireplace, lit several candles, and turned off the lights. Everyone shared in a concert of "Oohs" and "Ahhs" at the magical transformation.

Spirit found comfort in her children. She noticed the sadness in their eyes, but after the initial crying fest of finding out their father had passed, they'd kept brave faces, doing their best to keep her spirits light.

Tegan sat close to her mum, munching on a handful of chips. "Mama, where Wuby?"

Spirit nearly spilled the plate she was handing to Seth, but he caught it and took it from her hands. She gave him a weary smile, then placed an arm around her smallest daughter. "Oh, lass, Ruby's gone with your da to the Other World. She couldn't let him go alone."

The little girl chewed on a chip, considering what she'd said. "Wuby a good girl. Now Da no be sad."

"They're probably hunting rabbits like we used to," said Seth. "We oughta go out, Mama. We haven't been in a long time."

Spirit filled another plate, handing it to Molly. "Well, it won't be anytime soon. The weather's turned cold and the rabbits have gone to ground. Maybe in the spring."

"Mama?" said Molly.

"Aye, love?"

"Are we having a ceremony for da and Ruby?"

"I expect we will."

"Can we go?" asked Dylan.

"Aye, Mama," added Tegan. "Can we go?"

Her breath caught in her throat. They were so small, yet so grown up. Where would she be without her children to keep her together? Tears burned in her eyes, but she blinked them away. "Aye." Her voice was low and heavy. "You will. Your da will rest easier knowing you've wished him well."

Tegan screwed up her little face. "West? Him huntin' with Wuby."

Spirit's laughter made the children laugh, except Tegan, who looked at them with a degree of disdain. It felt good to laugh again. Perhaps with the children at her side and the support of the clan, she would make it to the other side of losing Inferno after all.

12

ROBES OF VALOR

Early the next morning, Etain woke to the sound of knocking. Alone in bed, she called out for Dar, but he obviously had awakened earlier and left her to sleep. She grabbed her robe and padded to the door.

Aeval and Bwca, Spirit's faerie friends, fluttered at the door with scissors, measuring tape, notepad, and fabric in hand. "*Bore da*, High Lady," said Aeval, giving her a small curtsy. "The High Lord sent us. We're here for a fitting."

Etain's eyebrows scrunched together. "Fitting?" A sudden yawn made her cover her mouth. "Sorry, ladies."

The two giggled politely. "There's been a lot of that lately. Early mornings and late nights," said Bwca. "May we come in, milady?"

Etain stepped aside. "You said you're here for a fitting? What're we fitting?"

The ladies laughed again as they fluttered into the room. "A Robe of Valor, milady," answered Aeval. "The High Lord has started working on his and has asked us to prepare one for you. I hope you don't mind."

"Oh, aye. I mean…no, I don't mind. I assume the robe is for the funeral service." The ladies nodded. "You said Dar's making his?"

"Aye, milady…," Bwca said as she and Aeval winged their way to the center of the room. "He's quite adept at handling a needle and thread. He's made many a wonderful robe in the past."

Etain closed the door. "Well, he does have a light touch…when it pleases him. Where do you want me?"

"By the fireplace should be fine." The faeries placed their tools on the small table between the chairs. "We'll just take a few measurements for now. The High Lord told us of your condition, so they may be somewhat different than normal."

Etain raised a brow. "He did, did he?"

Aeval blushed deep crimson. "Oh dear. I've said too much."

Seeing she was truly upset, Etain smiled. "It's okay, Aeval." She placed her hands over her belly. "Please, don't tell anyone. We want to make the announcement at the right time. Can you keep our secret just a little longer?"

Tinkling laughter filled the room. "Of course, milady. You can trust us." Aeval stretched out her measuring tape. "Ready, Bwca?" The other faerie nodded. "I thought an Empire waistline would be best, milady, if you're in agreement."

"An Empire waistline?"

The small ladies exchanged a glance. "It comes just below the breasts, milady." Aeval held her hands underneath her own ample chest. "Then flows to the floor with no uncomfortable constraints across your tummy."

"Oh, aye. That sounds lovely."

They spent the next half-hour measuring and jotting down notes, the tiny women chatting away.

"Robes of Valor are a very old Krymerian custom. I don't know the last time one was worn," said Aeval.

Bwca remembered. "I do believe the last ones to wear such robes were the High Lord's parents when he was but a wee child."

Aeval's eyes lit up. "That's right. Ack, his mother was very beautiful, and his father… Such a handsome man."

The mention of Dar's parents pricked Etain's ears. "You met his mother?"

"Aye. She was a lovely lady. Always so kind," said Bwca.

Aeval billowed the fabric over the bed. Mesmerized by its richness, Etain noticed it already had form.

"Since we're pressed for time," said Aeval, "we've taken the liberty of piecing something together. I used your measurements from the wedding gown and added a bit here and there. There isn't much difference from what I used and what we've taken today. Shall we try it on?"

The coolness of the black silk felt delicious against her warm skin. With a rounded neckline, the bodice hugged her full breasts, showing off her cleavage. Underneath the bodice was a silk sash of crimson from which yards of gathered black silk flowed down to the floor. The long sleeves skimmed down her arms, gathering just above the elbows and into an angle cut trimmed with crimson silk to match the sash. Attached to the upper portion of each of the sleeves were three red runes.

"Y'all weren't kidding. It's almost perfect," Etain said, marveled by the lovely gown.

"Since the ceremony is today, it's a relief we won't have to worry about making changes. It should be fine." Bwca smiled, admiring their handiwork.

"Today?" Etain felt her throat go dry.

"Aye, milady. Did the High Lord not tell you?" asked Aeval.

"You're looking a little pale, milady. Would you like to sit down?" Bwca fluttered into the bathroom and soon returned with a glass of water, handing it to Etain.

"Thank you, Bwca." Etain took a few sips, then set the glass on the table. "I'm okay, just surprised. I thought I had another day!" The three shared understanding smiles. She peered down the side of one sleeve, then the other. "What're these for?"

Aeval pointed to the right sleeve. "These stand for justice, honor, and valor." Then pointed to the left. "The others represent love, compassion, and truth."

"Did Dar's mom wear a gown like this?"

"Similar, milady, but she wasn't as striking as you." Bwca ran her hands along the sleeves, smoothing the fabric.

"What did she look like?" Etain asked, anxious to learn more.

Bwca's expression turned melancholy, her memories coming to life in her mind's eye. "Her hair was a rich brown."

"With golden highlights," added Aeval.

"Aye. I remember how it would sparkle in the sunlight, like flashes of golden fire." Bwca fluttered to the floor, folding up the hem of the gown and pinning it in place. "She wore it long." She looked up at Etain. "Like you, milady. But she wasn't as tall as you."

"Her skin had an olive tint that set off her dark eyes." Aeval sighed.

Etain let several seconds pass before she asked in a soft voice, "When did she pass?"

Both faeries stopped and glanced at each other. Aeval nodded to Bwca, who answered. "The High Lord was a babe himself. No more than two or three."

"He had just turned three. 'Twas before his meeting with the priests," Aeval said softly.

Etain knew Dar's story. He was a bright child, full of promise, but at the age of three, signs of darkness began to show. One moment he would behave like an angel, doing as he was told, accepting the guidance of his parents and instructors, a loving child. In the next, he was the devil himself, ranting unintelligible words in his small voice, beating his tiny fists against those closest to him. He was manageable for a time, but when his powers began to manifest and cause serious injury to others, a desperate King Dari consulted with the Krymerian priests. The boy could not inherit the kingdom if he continued in this way.

After an interrogation by the priests, it was decided an exorcism would be performed to rid him of the growing evil. Although Dar survived the ritual, several priests lost their lives, and Midir came into being. The darkness to Dar's light.

"Emalyn-" Bwca began.

"The queen," Aeval added.

Bwca sighed. "As I was saying... Emalyn was having a difficult time with her second birth." She shook her head, a frown on her lips.

"They were so worried about their little prince," said Aeval.

"Oh, to think on those days." Bwca settled on the floor, a swath of fabric in her hand. "He was full of troubles."

"His mother's pregnancy was difficult?" Etain prompted the women.

"Aye." Aeval nodded, coming back to the original story. "She went into labor the day they took Dar to the temple."

"Oh." Etain could only imagine the trauma of that day. To have your three-year-old son taken away for purification, then to be in labor, a difficult one at that, and unable to be with him, to hold his tiny hand or give him comfort. She covered her belly with her hands again. To never know...

"Milady fought so hard." Bwca swiped away a tear.

"But she wasna strong enough," added Aeval.

"Poor Dar. To lose his mother and his..." Etain looked at the faeries. "Was the baby a girl or a boy?"

A tear in her eye, Aeval smiled. "'Twas a lass. Dark hair and amber eyes, like her great-grandmother."

"Her great-grandmother?"

"Aye. Natare," answered Bwca. "She had amber eyes, too, and dark, dark hair. Much darker than Emalyn's."

"Did they name the baby?" Etain wondered if Dar knew he'd had a sister.

"Illiana," Bwca whispered. "The most beautiful little girl in the world."

In a solemn mood, Etain walked into the bathroom to get a full view of the gown. "I'll do my best to live up to the legacy. Thank you for the extra care you've taken to create this for me."

They blushed in the face of her graciousness. "Oh, now, such carryings on," Bwca said. With one last look and a tuck or two, they decided it was ready to complete. Returning to the bedroom, Etain removed the Robe of Valor, placed it on the bed, and put on her regular robe.

Just then, the door opened. Dar peeked in, a cheeky grin on his face. "Is it safe to enter?" Not waiting for an answer, he disappeared for a moment, then stepped into the room, a loaded breakfast tray in his hands. "I've brought a bite to eat for my beautiful lady."

The faerie seamstresses tittered, their cheeks blushing bright pink. "High Lord! We weren't expecting you. Apologies…" Aeval darted away as he approached.

"Tck! It is I who's interrupting." He carried the tray to the bed, set it down, and kissed Etain on the cheek. "Have we made any progress?"

"Oh, now, you're not interrupting a thing." Bwca picked up their tools.

Aeval ventured closer, carefully folding the gown and tucking it over her arm. "We're done here, milord. Just a few little tucks and milady's gown will be done."

Etain smiled at him. "What about *your* gown, milord? Is it completed?"

Dar laughed. "Now that you ask, it's not quite ready."

Fluttering toward the door, Bwca stopped. "No?" She glanced at Aeval, then back at Dar. "Would you mind if we…"

Etain's eyes lit up. "Please, feel free. I'm sure the High Lord is much too distracted to do his any justice." She turned to Dar. "Is yours handy?"

She noticed one of his brows twitch. "You honor me, ladies. I've left it in Inferno's study."

Giggling and batting their eyelashes, the faeries said they would retrieve the robe and left the room. Their chatter could be heard all the way down the stairs. Dar chuckled and winked at Etain.

"You didn't mention that the ceremony is today," Etain said, crossing her arms.

His grin never wavered. "Probably because you were asleep when I left this morning."

She raised a brow. "Aren't I a lucky girl?" She tried to maintain a stern look but found it impossible. Shaking her head, she dropped her arms. "Are you ready for this evening?"

"Aye. We've wasted too much time. They should be laid to rest." Dar picked up the tray and joined her, placing it on a table between the chairs in front of the fireplace. "Are you hungry?"

"Starving. Have you checked on Taurnil this morning?"

"I have." Dar chewed on a piece of toast, his gaze a million miles away. "He's much improved."

"You've been a busy man." She shifted in her seat and touched his hand. "What's running through that head of yours?"

Her touch brought him back to her, an apologetic smile on his lips. He lifted her hand and placed a kiss across her knuckles. "I'm going to make his Black Blade status official."

Her eyes widened as she took her hand back, sitting up straight. "Oh, Dar. It will mean so much to him. He's worked hard."

"He has impressed me with his strength and presence of mind. He's ready."

"When?"

He poured himself a cup of coffee. "It will be in a few days. Both ceremonies are important and should be separate. Besides…" He sipped the hot liquid, "I need time to forge a black blade to present to him."

Etain frowned. "Dar, you've only just started to get better. Forging a blade isn't like sewing a-"

"It's what I need to do."

"You have dozens of men downstairs. Surely one or two know how to forge a blade."

He shrugged. "Not just anyone can make a black blade, especially for the Prince of Nunnehi. It must be forged by a Mastersmith. To my knowledge, I am the only one present."

She rolled her eyes. "Have you asked? You don't know every single person here." She didn't like the look in his eyes. "Dar…"

"Etain…" He obviously was not intimidated by her sternness.

"Then have someone help," she said, leaning back in her chair. "I'd like to have my husband whole again so we can get on with it."

His grin returned. "Get on with it? I like the sound of that."

Etain couldn't help but chuckle. "You're such a pervert." She shoveled a forkful of eggs into her mouth, got up, and headed to the wardrobe.

"Milady, is that any way to speak to your husband?"

"It's your own fault," she called out from the wardrobe. She heard him crunch into his toast as she shuffled through several hangers, looking for something to wear. A bag on the floor caught her eye. The one she'd packed when she and Spirit had gone to Texas. It seemed like ages ago. "How'd you get here?" She clearly remembered Midir's interruption and having to leave it behind. Curious, she reached inside, then gasped and yanked out her hand. "Ouch."

Dar was at the door in a flash. "What's happened?"

Her finger in her mouth, she mumbled, "I was looking inside my bag and cut my finger on something." He came into the wardrobe. "I left it in Texas. Any idea how it got here?"

He took her hand from her mouth, inspected the cut, then kissed it away. "After Midir kidnapped you, your house was my second stop. I knew you needed clothes, so I brought it with me."

She kissed him on the cheek. "Aren't you sweet? How thoughtful."

He released her hand and peeked inside the bag. "What is it that cut you?"

She reached in again and pulled out the silver journal. "This. It's weird. I don't remember it having sharp edges."

Dar took the book from her hand, thumbing through the pages. "Oh, aye. It cut me, too." He returned it to the bag. "Isn't it a journal?"

"My dad gave it to me when I was a kid."

"Why are there no entries?"

"Well…" She hesitated, not sure why she hadn't written anything.

"I was really young when he gave it to me." She ran a hand through her hair and noticed another bag in the corner. "Oh, my gosh. My backpack…"

Dar turned, watching as she picked up another bag from the floor. "How many bags does a woman need? When did you use that one?"

"In Deudraeth, when I went to find my brother. Here's Spirit's damiana." Etain placed the bundled herb on a shelf. "And this is for you." A smile on her face, she pulled out a box and handed it to him. "Considering all that's happened, I wish I'd given it to you sooner."

"Why is that?"

"Open it."

He removed the top of the box, tucked the bottom half into it, and stared at the contents for a long moment, then looked at her. "It's beautiful."

Pleased by his reaction, she reached into the box. "It's onyx…" She picked up the necklace. "The sales clerk said it protects against evil."

Dar chuckled as he eyed the impressive piece. "It would've been good to have…then."

Etain undid the clasp and placed the chain around his neck. His hands on her waist, she pressed her body to his as she looked over his shoulder. With it latched, she pulled back.

Dar looked down. "Does it suit me?"

She cocked her head and sighed. Her insides felt gooey and warm. "It's perfect…just like you."

"I understand the onyx, but dragons?"

She shrugged. "There's no particular reason." She ran a finger along one of the dragons. "I liked the way they're nose-to-nose with their tails intertwined. I see the fierce love between them."

His gaze came back to hers, making her heart skip.

He has no idea the depths of-

His lips on hers shattered her thoughts, stealing her breath, his hands sliding up her back to bring her closer. The tingles in her belly spread through her body, the pulse between her legs demanding attention.

"I feel it, too," he whispered, freeing one hand to address the pulse. She thought she would melt right there and then.

"Ahem," came a voice at the wardrobe door.

"Not now!" Etain yelled, every cell in her body tingling. "Go away, Freeblood."

Dar held onto her, resting his head on her shoulder. "Apologies, my love. I asked him to come."

"He could've knocked," she said to Dar, then raised her head and looked over his shoulder. "You could've knocked."

Freeblood kept his back turned. "I *did* knock." He turned his head to the side. "Several times."

"Get dressed, *a chuisle*, and join us," Dar said, letting her go, then licked his lips. "We'll pick this up later?"

Etain turned her back. "Perhaps. I'll be with you in a few."

Dar walked to Freeblood, who turned with a smile. "Excuse us for a moment." Dar closed the wardrobe door in his face. He returned to Etain and stood close behind her, running his hands down her arms. "I'll make it up to you." He lifted a section of her heavy mane and lightly kissed her neck. "I promise."

God! Could her nipples be any harder? She shivered. "Can't we talk to him later?"

"We need to know what happened between Faux and the demon. I hadn't planned on-"

"Obviously not." She turned and gave him a thorough kiss. "The sooner we chat, the sooner he leaves. I'll be out in a minute."

Etain smiled at Freeblood seated before the fireplace. He gave over his chair to her and pulled up a footstool to sit on.

She placed a hand on his knee. "How are you?"

He shot a glance at Dar, then back at Etain. "I'm good," he said, waiting for the other shoe to drop. When she continued to smile, he added, "Sorry about the intrusion."

She leaned back in her chair. "It's okay. I was taken by surprise, that's all. Have you seen Faux?"

"I have."

She raised a brow. "And?"

"I waited. She came to me." A warm smile passed between them.

"Now you know," she said.

"I don't how long it'll last, but for now, I know."

Dar cleared his throat. "We were talking about the demon."

"Sorry, Dar. As I was saying, we ran into him in Germany."

"I thought you discovered the demon here in the castle," Dar said.

"Actually, the *first* time I met him was in Japan. I thought he was just another comic-con wannabe."

Dar leaned forward, his brows knitted. "What is this 'comic-con'? Is it significant?"

Freeblood smiled, giving Etain a glance. "Only in the fact that it'd been over for a month. I know they love their anime over there, but this guy…" He shook his head, chuckling. "He took it to a whole other level."

Dar turned to Etain. "What in the hell is he talking about?"

"It's where people dress like superheroes and meet other people dressed like superheroes," she explained.

"For what purpose?"

"Entertainment." At Dar's doubtful expression, he shrugged. "Never mind. It doesn't matter. But, like I told Etain, he showed me how to manipulate my gem. Guess he never thought he'd see me again."

Dar leaned back. "I'd say he underestimated you."

Freeblood sat up straight, not used to receiving compliments from the big man. "Seriously?"

"Aye. We've all been guilty of that. But it ends today. We've received news that the Alamir Ambassadors, all of them, will be here for the ceremony. I won't have time to greet them properly when they arrive. Will you take care of that for me?"

He stared at Dar, not sure he'd heard him right. "You want *me* to greet the Ambassadors?"

Dar stood up and slapped him on the back. "Excellent. Go find Thoric and Cappy. They can give you the details." He headed toward the door and opened it. "Make sure you don't embarrass us."

Freeblood looked at Etain, who appeared as surprised as him. "But what about Faux and Dathmet?"

Dar walked to the young man, took him by the arm, and helped him to his feet. "Doesn't matter now. She won't be causing any trouble..." He walked him to the door, "and we know where to find him if we need to. Make sure you find Thoric or Cappy. They'll be a big help." He closed the door on a confused face.

Dar turned to his wife. "Now... Where were we?"

Etain chuckled, watching him from her seat. "Are you okay?"

He walked toward her, his intent clear. "We haven't had much time together since this debacle began." He held out his hands. "I've done about all I can do to clean up, help out, and bring closure." She placed her hands in his and stood. "Now it's *our* time...before another problem comes up that requires my attention."

"Shall we lock the door?"

"Done." He pulled her close.

"What about Taurnil's sword?"

"Handled."

"When?"

He grinned, bringing his face to hers. "The main component..." He brushed his lips along her cheek, "is in Krymeria." He hovered at her mouth. "I've dispatched someone to obtain what I need."

Breathless, she asked, "What is it you need?"

"You." At first, his kisses were light, playful, but soon took on a deeper purpose.

Etain leaned away for a breath. "Your back."

"I am."

She rolled her eyes. "Your *back*," she said again, touching it lightly.

"Will heal much faster knowing I am a happy man. I need you, *a chuisle*. I've missed you terribly."

The castle came alive as people emerged from their snug havens in search of a hearty breakfast. Zorn and Felix were the first to head downstairs to check on the smokers and big grill for the delicacies Chef Alaster had planned for the celebration feast. Wolfe, Elfin, and Dalos checked the various funeral pyres once again, just to be on the safe side.

Those entering the dining hall were greeted by the smell of freshly brewed coffee. Naturally, there were several hot topics to discuss – Dar, Taurnil, the trip to the blood castle, who would step up as chieftain of the UWS clan, and of course, the upcoming ceremony. Linq, with the help of Cappy and Thoric, passed amongst them, giving assurances that all was well.

Some of the younger Black Blades, having never seen a Ceremony of Valor, asked Linq what to expect.

"I've not attended a *Krymerian* ceremony. I didn't meet the High Lord until sometime after he left his people." He grinned. "I'd never even *met* a Krymerian until then." Several laughed with him. "But I doubt it's much different from an Elven ceremony. I expect the High Lord will preside. The name of every fallen soldier and civilian, if there are any, will be spoken as the pyres are lit. I think there is singing in there somewhere."

Toward the end of the morning meal, all eyes moved to the doorway when Dar and Etain entered the room. Aramis was the first to his feet. "Dar, Etain, we weren't expecting you, but we're damn glad to see you." He pushed others aside, moving down a couple of chairs. "Come, join us."

The couple bid good morning to every person they passed, taking the seats between Aramis and Linq.

Not long after their arrival, Spirit appeared at the door, escorted by her oldest son, Seth. Etain pushed from her chair and met them at the door. "I'm so glad you've come down." The women shared a hug. Etain smiled at Seth. "Look at you! So grown up."

Although his cheeks tinged pink, he stood a little taller and lifted his head. "*Bore da*, Auntie. May we sit with you for breakfast?"

She exchanged a glance with Spirit, trying not to smile. "Of course! I'm sure these fine gentlemen won't mind moving."

As they approached, the men at their end of the table stood, bidding them good morning. Etain made sure Spirit sat next to her. "How are you?"

"Struggling, but the children have made a big difference. Thank you again for bringing them home."

"I'd do anything for you. You know that." Etain smiled, giving her another hug. "Are you ready for today?"

"Aye. It will be hard, but…"

Seth seemed to sense her distress and placed his hand on hers. "We'll stand with you, Mama."

Etain gave him a nod, adding her hand to theirs. "Aye. You aren't alone. None of you."

Dar leaned forward. "All of us…" His gaze roamed around the table, then came back to Spirit, "are here. We stand together, or we don't stand at all."

In agreement, others in the room shared their condolences and heartfelt wishes with Spirit and Seth. In time, everyone settled in their seats to continue their meals.

Seth leaned toward his mother. "Mama, who is that man next to Auntie 'Tain?"

"Hmm?" She leaned forward to see who he spoke of. "That's your Uncle Dar."

His eyes sparkled with excitement. "Really? Can I meet him?"

She gave him a perplexed look. "Have ya not… Oh, goddess of us all. You haven't. I'm sorry, son. Would you like me to introduce you?"

"No! Uh… No, Mum." He quickly swiped a napkin across his mouth and scooted his chair back. "Thank you. I can do it."

She smiled proudly and watched as he tentatively moved toward the big man.

He stood behind the couple, watching Dar in his conversation with the others. Etain turned from Spirit and, without giving Seth any notice, touched Dar's arm, bringing his attention to her. She smiled and slightly tilted her head toward the boy.

He turned. "*Bore da*, young man. How may I be of assistance?"

Seth had to clear his throat. "*Bore da*, milord. I'm Seth."

Although Dar smiled, he glanced at Etain with a raised brow.

"Seth is Inferno's oldest," she explained.

His golden gaze came back to the boy, who stood straight as a board, an expectant look on his face.

Seth watched him unfold from his chair, having to crane his neck to take in all seven feet of the big man. His mouth fell open.

Dar stuck out his hand. "Seth, it is an honor to meet you."

He accepted the offer, watching his small hand disappear within the big man's grasp. "May I call you Uncle Dar?"

Dar released his hand and bowed his head. "I hope you will."

Seth grinned and turned away, then quickly turned back. "It's an honor to meet you, too… Uncle Dar." A blush in his cheeks, he returned to his mother's side.

Dar smiled at his wife and touched his chest over his heart. Before he could sit, Freeblood showed up with Etain's brother.

There were murmurs around the room as they slowly made their way to the table. Happy to see her brother on his feet, Etain didn't notice the scowl on her husband's face. "Robert! Are you sure you should be down here?"

Freeblood helped him to a seat across from Etain. "I needed to get out of that room for a while. See new things."

Assured her brother was seated comfortably, she went to the sideboard and picked up a couple plates. Back at the table, she handed them to Robert and Freeblood. Everyone watched as they filled their dishes, amazed by the amount of food between the two.

Spirit looked at Seth, then turned to Etain. "We'll give you some privacy."

"No, Spirit," she said. "Please stay."

Spirit stood and picked up her plate as Seth did the same. "I need to speak with me clan before the ceremony." She glanced at Robert, then Dar, and back at Etain. "We can talk later."

"Mind if I join you, Spirit?" asked Linq.

She cocked her head to the side. "Aye, you should. It concerns you, too."

"I'm off, as well," said Aramis. "I have a clan needs tending to."

Dar leaned toward Etain. "I have other things to tend to, as well, my love. I'll find you later when you're less engaged."

"Really? You're just gonna abandon me?"

He gave her a sideways smirk. "See it as time well spent with your brother."

"Go take care of your business." She rolled her eyes. "I'll see you when you're done."

After sharing an ardent kiss, he stood and left her to babysit. Her eyes followed him, admiring the way his hips moved as he walked, the ripple of muscle when he raised a hand in greeting, how his electric smile made her lose her senses. Once he stepped around the corner out of sight, she sighed and turned to her brother and Freeblood, who were busy clearing their plates.

"Freeblood, why isn't Faux with you?"

His head came up. "She's not quite ready for a public display, and I'm not going to make her do anything that causes her more stress."

"So you decided to check on my brother and bring him instead?"

He relaxed and grinned. "Hell no. I was on my way down when I found him struggling on the stairs. I couldn't leave him there. He might've fallen."

She nodded, seeing the practicality of his reasoning. "Robert, you're looking better. How you feeling?"

"Not as spry as Dar, but getting there."

"Well, he *is* Krymerian. They heal faster than we do."

"Hmph," he said, turning his attention to his plate.

She watched him for a moment. "There's something I've wanted to ask you since we returned." She pulled a leg up under her and leaned on the table, chin in hand. "How did you come to be in the blood castle?"

He looked up from his plate, his mouth full, and slowly chewed his food. Swallowing, he drank some juice, then leaned back in his chair, and wiped his mouth with a napkin. "I was taken a few days before Dar showed up. I'd been searching for plants in the woods. Next thing I remember is waking up in a cold, dark dungeon."

"Days?" Her gaze went to Freeblood, who shrugged. "I didn't realize the *Bok* had moved so early."

Robert didn't look at her, but answered, "Apparently so."

"Were you in the same cell as Dar?"

"Not at first. I heard them torturing him, trying to find out where you were. When he wouldn't talk, couldn't talk, they started in on me."

"I'm so sorry," she whispered.

"After that, they threw me in with him. I guess they thought he would talk to me. But Dar was too far gone." He closed his eyes. "One day…" He choked up, then opened his eyes and continued. "It was the day you came… They took him out. I didn't understand what was going on until Freeblood found me." He sipped his juice again. "He felt nothing, Etain. He was out of his mind."

"I know. I spoke with him many times, but he never recognized me."

His brows knitted together. "You spoke with him?"

"That's how I found him. We have a connection, the two of us. Have had ever since he shared his blood with me."

"That's a story I'd like to hear."

She eyed her brother for a long moment. "Funny… In all the times we spoke, I never saw you. Not even at the end."

He suddenly coughed, choking on his food. Freeblood slapped him on the back as Etain leaned across the table, grabbed Robert's glass, and pushed it at him. "Wash it down." Taking a drink, he gulped, coughing a few more times. "You should take smaller bites."

"Noted," he croaked and took another drink. Breathing in, he leaned back and wiped his napkin over his face. "Guess I *should* slow down." He looked at Freeblood. "Would you help me back upstairs? I feel like lying down."

Etain placed a hand on his arm. "I'll go with him, Freeblood. You should take some breakfast to Faux."

"She ought to be hungry by now. You sure you got him?"

"Aye. Tell her she was missed."

"Thanks, Etain. I will. It'll help." He grabbed a clean plate from the sideboard and got to work filling it.

Arm in arm, brother and sister left the room. Walking up the stairs, she said, "Now that it's just you and me, why would this Dathmet take you if you were Midir's ward?"

"Not a clue. What I do know is that he's a sadistic son of a bitch who loves torturing people."

She stopped in the hallway and faced him. "Dathmet is Midir's *son*. Don't tell me that was your first time meeting him."

He held her gaze. "I never met him before and hope I never see him again." His body began to shake. "I shouldn't have gone downstairs. It was too soon."

She held onto him until they reached his door. "Shall I help you-"

"No!" He took a deep breath and gave her a sheepish grin. "No. I can manage on my own. I'll see you later." He stepped into the room and quietly closed the door.

Having moved to Inferno's study, Spirit, the UWS clan, and Linq pursued their discussions on the succession of chieftain. Several names were mentioned, but no single one could be agreed on unanimously.

"It has to be someone who's familiar with all of us and knows who's most suited for which role," said Wolfe.

Elfin cuffed him on the shoulder. "You know us all quite well, Wolfe. Why not you?"

"Me?" He looked horrified. "No, thank you. I like my freedom. It might as well be you."

His friend laughed. "Only if it involves daily trips to the pub."

Linq stepped in at this point. "I think we can all agree that yourselves, as well as Zorn, are a tad young to take on such a responsibility." Everyone in the room seemed to agree, including the three mentioned.

"Why not you, Linq?" Zorn asked. "You've known the clan for a long time. You know where Inferno wanted to go with it."

"I also didn't agree with him." Linq turned to Spirit. "Apologies, milady, but you know as well as I we did not see eye to eye."

"There were many times even *I* didn't agree with him, love." She looked around at every face in the room. "Inferno was a great leader. He knew his people and always seemed to know what was best for the individual and the clan as a whole. But…" She hesitated, taking a moment to collect her thoughts. "But times change and so must we. I'm aware of everyone's confidence in Linq's leadership skills." She smiled at him. "You are a true friend. One we can count on in good times and bad. But this is not something I can ask you to do. You have a different life now and shouldn't look backward. You must continue to move ahead." She went to him, giving him a heartfelt hug. "Thank you for everything you've done, my friend." Pulling back, she said, "I'll take over from here."

Linq held her gaze and smiled. "It has been my pleasure, milady." He turned to the others. "You know where I am should you need me." With a bow of his head, he left the UWS clan to decide their fate.

The last words he heard spoken as he closed the door were, "Then that leaves us with only one choice."

He smiled to himself, knowing who he would choose.

Robert closed the door, stumbled across the room, and sat on the edge of the mattress. As he ran a hand through his hair, Raum came into the room. "That was not a wise move, milord. You've not regained enough of your strength-"

"Shut up, Raum. My little foray downstairs has acquired some interesting information."

The servant helped him back into bed. "What is that?"

"As we suspected, my sister and her husband share the mind speak. The bitch was in touch with him the entire time. That explains why she was at the house. She was looking for something."

Raum pulled the covers up, making sure of his master's comfort. "What could she hope to find, milord?"

"I'm certain it had to do with the opening of the portal." Robert laid his head back on the pillows. Closing his eyes, he pinched the bridge of his nose. "What I don't understand…" He opened his eyes and lowered his hand, "is how she found the right words. They aren't written in any book, and even if they were, she didn't have time to search every single one in my library."

"You need another infusion, milord. The demolition of the blood castle has taken too much from you. Let me get the woman. Her blood will put you to rights."

"They're having some stupid ceremony today, Raum. Something about their dead. She and her deadbeat husband are officiating, so I doubt you'd be able to take her without someone noticing. I'll be fine for now, but if you see an opportunity, take it."

"Master, have you considered the other one? Doesn't the same blood run in her veins? They are sisters, after all."

"I would agree had the bastard not stripped her of her powers. I don't know that her blood would be strong enough now." He fell silent, mulling over the idea. "If we can't get Etain in the next couple of days, we'll go for the other one. She'll suffice in the interim."

13

KRYMERIAN VALOR

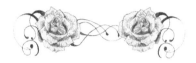

A half-hour later, Etain found a freshly showered and shaved Dar in their en suite, a towel around his hips. "Here you are. I've looked everywhere for you."

He grinned, catching her gaze in the mirror. "Just making myself pretty."

She leaned against the jamb, a smile on her face. "You're doing a fine job. I believe you'll outshine everyone. Shall I plait your hair, or would you prefer to go natural?"

He gave it some thought, patting his face dry. "It *is* a solemn affair. Perhaps it should be tamed. You don't mind?"

Etain grabbed a nearby stool. "Sit. Let's see what I can do." Once he was seated, she grabbed a comb from a drawer and worked it through his thick, blond hair. "So, High Lord of Kaos, I'm pretty sure what your duties are today. Please enlighten me as to what is expected of the High Lady of Kaos."

"Our ceremonies are full of tradition, as you know."

She nodded, setting the comb on the counter. "Where would we be without tradition?"

"Etain…" He gave her a rather fatherly look. "Tradition stabilizes civilization. There would be utter chaos without it."

Focused on parting his hair, she rolled her eyes. "Oh, aye. Utter chaos."

Unable to see her response, he seemed satisfied with her words. "There is an old Krymerian burial song that should be sung, as well as the ancient song of valor. Since you have such a lovely voice, I thought you should sing."

She lifted her head, meeting his gaze in the mirror. "I don't know those songs."

"Not to worry, They're very simple. I'll teach you."

"You're gonna teach me two Krymerian songs in the space of… What? An hour?"

He merely grinned, obviously not worried in the least. "You should also say a few words about our fallen heroes." Sensing her reluctance, he hurried on. "Don't worry, *a chuisle*. You'll be fine. Just speak your heart."

"Hmph. Says you." She resumed crossing the heavy sections. "What about our robes? Do you know if they're ready?" He started to nod, but she pulled his hair. "Stillness stabilizes braiding. Unless you *want* a wonky plait."

Grimacing, he sat still. "Apologies, milady. Aye, our robes are in the bedroom. I've spent a portion of the morning with the lady faeries, applying the finishing touches. I think you will be impressed."

"I wondered what took you away from me."

Coming to the end, she separated a small section of hair from the rest, then flipped the ends through the opening, finishing the plait without the use of a leather strip. "There. All done." She placed her hands on his bare shoulders and smiled at him in the mirror. "The handsomest man in all the land."

He covered both her hands with his, then brought each one to his lips, leaving a soft kiss on the palms. "Only for you, my love."

She rested her head on top of his. Their gazes locked in the mirror as their fingers intertwined. After all this time, he still made her pulse race and filled her belly with butterflies. Before she'd even started to dream of a perfect mate, he had been there - tall, handsome, and somewhat intimidating, only because he seemed so perfect for her. But who was she to believe he could be hers? That he would want to be hers? A man with so many options.

"*Is mise mo anam...mo chroí. Is breá liom tú* (You are my soul...my heart. I love you)." He leaned his body into hers.

She smiled and hugged him to her. "I love you, too."

"I could stay here forever with you, *a chuisle*."

"And I, you, my love." She lifted her head and let go of his hands. "But we have a Krymerian Ceremony of Valor to officiate. Why don't you show me our beautiful robes and teach me the words to those songs?"

He stood, took her hand, and led her into the bedroom. "Aeval and Bwca did a beautiful job. The workmanship. The details..." He practically gushed. "These truly honor our heroes."

The robes, placed over the backs of the chairs, were the first things she saw. "They're beautiful, Dar." She looked up into his beaming face. "Everyone will be honored by the care you and the ladies have taken with these."

His hands on her waist, he lifted her. "This is a grand day, milady. Thank you for having them finish our robes."

She leaned down and planted a warm kiss on his mouth. He slid the vixen down the length of his body, which caused his towel to slip to the floor. Her fingers trickled over his smooth skin as his lips blazed a trail of hot kisses down her neck.

"Dar," she rasped, "as much I love your attentions, I need to try on my robe."

"Not as much as I need you to love me." Opening her top, his kisses traveled farther down.

"But the songs-"

"Can wait."

"Don't you ever get enough?" she whispered, resigned to his attentions.

"Never of you, my love."

As the sun set the sky on fire in its descent, the High Lord and High Lady of Krymeria, dressed in the Robes of Valor, took their places on a dais built for the ceremony. To their right were the Black Blades and the Royal Guard dressed in full regalia. The Alamir Ambassadors, attired in their finest raiment, were to their left. Directly across stood the UWS and Dragon clans with the rest of those Alamir still housed at Laugharne. Clustered outside the outer castle walls were the funeral pyres, testaments to those who fought against the *Bok'Na'Ra,* alive and dead.

Queen Alatariel watched from a balcony with Taurnil, who sat in a chair beside her. Behind them stood Chelri, Swee, and the queen's handmaidens, all dressed in their best. Robert, Etain's brother, and Faux remained in their respective rooms. Freeblood, dressed in blue leathers made especially for the occasion and acting as Dar's emissary, stood with the Ambassadors.

Unlit torches lined the front of the castle. A nod from the High Lord set the two most experienced of the Black Blades into motion. Torches in hand, they approached the dais, whereupon the High Lady lit each one with a touch of her electrical charge. In turn, the Black Blades lit the row of torches, beginning at the outermost one and coming toward the center, then ended with the placement of their own torches into brackets attached to the dais on either side of the High Lord and Lady. With a salute, the two returned to their fellow Blades.

Etain met Dar's gaze. A warm smile on his lips, he gave her hand a squeeze. Just as she took her first breath to sing the Krymerian burial song, a powerful voice rumbled through the gathering like thunder before a storm.

"Desist with these proceedings."

A hush fell over the gathering. Everyone looked at each other, curious as to who would interrupt such a momentous occasion. A shimmer of light appeared before the dais. Dar squeezed Etain's hand again as the light formed into a doorway. An old man appeared, dressed in an ancient robe similar to Dar's, and stepped onto the dais. His white beard was nearly as long as his white hair. The deep lines on his face spoke of his age, but his ice-blue eyes revealed a contradictory youthfulness.

"Dar VonNeshta, High Lord of Kaos." His voice boomed over the gathering, his gaze piercing. "A ceremony such as this is forbidden."

Etain looked at her husband. "Do you know this man, Dar?"

He gave the old man a steely eye. "Aye. I know him. This is Lothous, the Krymerian priest I told you about. What is this nonsense?"

Lothous turned to Etain, smiling as he reached for her hands. Reluctantly, she submitted and gasped at his warm touch. "A ceremony such as this is forbidden without the proper crowning of the king and his queen." He looked at Dar. "You know that, boy."

"I am no longer a boy, priest."

"I do apologize, High Lord. I tend to forget." He winked at Etain. "Old age, you know."

"How do you propose to perform a crowning with no crowns? They were destroyed long ago."

Lothous continued to smile at Etain. "DarMidirets, Lady Alara, will you join us, please?"

Another shimmer appeared. Two figures stepped from within, each holding a silver crown encrusted with five jewels. Lothous held onto Etain's hands, but it was Dar who was shaken at seeing his grandparents again. He managed to keep a noble countenance that belied the pounding in his chest. They smiled at the young couple but did not speak.

Etain released one of the old priest's hands and reached for Dar. "These are your grandparents, aren't they?"

He looked at her in wonder. "How did you know?"

"For one thing, you're the spitting image of your grandfather. It's no wonder she fell in love with him. And your grandmother... If I couldn't see her standing on the balcony, I would swear she was Alatariel." Dar looked over his shoulder. The Elven Queen stood next to her son, a warm smile on her lips.

His gaze came back to his wife. "Do you think they can see them, too? Or is it just us?"

Etain shrugged.

Lothous spoke just loud enough for Dar and Etain to hear his words. "I am proud of you, Dar VonNeshta. You have overcome incredible odds and mastered the darkness within." His gaze came to Etain. "And you, young one." With a glint in his eyes, he feasted on her features. "My, how you have shaken things up. Your mother and her ancestors, well…" He trailed off, as though he'd lost his train of thought.

Etain shifted, stealing a glance at Dar, who looked just as uncomfortable. Louthous carried on with no explanation of his comment.

"The crowning of the King will be my last act as High Priest of Krymeria. Then and only then can this Ceremony of Valor be carried out in the proper manner." He stepped back. "If you both will kneel."

Lothous accepted the crown from DarMidiret's hands, then held it over Dar's head.

"As the High Priest of Krymeria, I crown you, Dar VonNeshta, as King of Krymeria. I charge you with the responsibility of maintaining the ways of our people, never forgetting that Kaos rules us all. We are the dark and the light, the very essence of Kaos itself. The good, as well as the evil. We are the balance that must be kept.

"Be strong in the face of adversity, show compassion for those in need, rule with honor, truth, and a fair hand. I further charge you to remember that your good fortune comes from above and to honor Him and his Goddess in all you do."

Lothous lowered the crown onto Dar's head as he completed his charge of duty. "I bless you, my son, King VonNeshta of Krymeria. Rise and crown your Queen as I speak the words of blessings upon her head."

Dar rose to his feet. Lothous took the crown from Alara's hands and passed it to Dar. In imitation of the priest, he held the crown aloft as Lothous spoke. "As the High Priest of Krymeria, I declare you, Etain VonNeshta, as Queen of Krymeria. I charge you with the responsibility of upholding the ways of the Krymerians, never forgetting Kaos rules us all. We have become the dark and the light, the very essence of Kaos. The good, as well as the evil. We are the balance that must be kept.

"As the High Lord's partner, you will be strong in the face of adversity, show compassion for those in need, rule with honor, truth, and a fair hand. You are the future of the Krymerian race. Remember, your good fortune comes from above and to honor Him and his Goddess in all you do."

He motioned for Dar to place the crown, identical to his except smaller, on her head. "I bless you, my daughter, Queen of Krymeria. Rise and stand beside your King."

Etain placed her hand into Dar's and stood. Her eyes glistened as Lothous said his final words.

"The fate of the Krymerian race is sealed with your union, Dar and Etain VonNeshta. I pray you have many years of happiness and your love for each other will pull you through the adversities you may face." The old man pulled a handkerchief from a pocket in his robe and wiped his face.

Etain and Dar reached for him at the same time, each holding an arm. "You should sit down, milord," she said softy.

He chuckled. "After this, I will have plenty of rest, young one. My time has finally come to an end. I can now rest in peace, knowing the future of our people is in good hands. Many blessings, my lord and lady."

Lothous, DarMidirets, and Lady Alara faded in a mist. Their remnants swirled away on a sudden breeze. The Black Blades and the Royal Guard lifted up a cheer, beating their swords against their shields.

"Long live the King of Krymeria! Long live the Queen of Krymeria! Who-hah!"

Holding Etain's hand in his, a surge of pride touched Dar's heart as he looked over those gathered around them. "Thank you, Black Blades and Royal Guard of Nunnehi. You honor us greatly with your faith and loyalty. As sad as this day is, it has brought us closer. The lines between Krymerian, Elves, and Alamir have thinned. We have become friends, as well as family."

With the skies turning dark, Dar raised his hands to bring the gathering back to its original intent. A slight breeze lifted the tails of his robe. Although his was similar to Etain's, with regard to the runes and crimson trim, it differed in its structure. Made of the softest cotton woven by faerie hands, the length extended to his feet with the front open, a small set of buttons in the center, starting just below his breast and ending above his belt buckle.

"Today, we honor those who fought against the *Bok'Na'Ra*. Those who lost their lives, as well as those who were fortunate to return to us. As long as any one of us breathes, the *Bok* shall never rule." Another cheer rose from the crowd.

Etain stepped to his side and began softly singing the Krymerian burial song in acapella, then from across the yard, the strings of a fiddle accompanied her sweet voice. Zorn appeared, stroking his violin with his bow, Felix at his side. Her voice grew stronger, infusing the song with heartfelt emotions. Together, they breathed new life into the age-old tune.

Dar noted the connection between the two, but also recognized Zorn as the rampart she needed for this particular performance. He squelched his impulsive jealousy and closed his eyes to enjoy her song.

At the end, she spoke her own words of tribute to the mighty warriors. "Would someone please bring me a bottle of Inferno's finest wine and a glass?" No sooner was her request spoken than one of the Deudraeth women appeared with both in hand, the bottle already uncorked. Etain smiled and thanked the young woman, then poured her own glass and raised it to the Alamir standing in front of the dais.

"To those who fight for the honor of the Alamir." She turned to her right. "To those who fight for the honor of Nunnehi and the High Lord." To the Ambassadors, she said, "To those who govern for the sake of us all." Lifting her chalice higher, she continued. "To those valiant warriors who gave their lives. I salute you all. Were it not for such noble lords and ladies…" She looked at Felix with a small smile, "and canines, our world would not exist."

She drank, then turned to the man next to her. "To my husband, Dar VonNeshta, High Lord of Kaos, King of Krymeria. You are the rock on which we stand. You have shown love, not only to me, but our friends, our compatriots, and even those who have challenged you every step of the way." Her gaze swept over the company and came back to Dar. "To you, King VonNeshta. Long live the King!" As the crowd laughed and cheered, she drank from the cup, her eyes never leaving his.

Overcome by her public show of appreciation, he took the chalice from her hand and raised it high. "To our High Lady and my queen." With a smirk, he drank the rest.

Returning the chalice to his wife, he took on a more serious air. Quiet overtook the crowd. "It is time for the naming of the warriors who have passed as we light their funeral pyres. Linq, Black Blades, Alamir, and Spirit, come forward and take a torch. Each and every name of the fallen shall be spoken here tonight."

One by one, they approached the line of torches, each taking one to light a funeral pyre as they called out the name of a fallen comrade. Their tributes burned hot, lighting the night skies with glowing fireflies.

When Spirit approached Inferno's pyre, the final one, everyone fell silent. She stared at his body wrapped in its death shroud, tears in her eyes. She touched the torch to the kindling and stepped back as it flared, the flame quickly consuming the dry wood.

Etain tried to pull away from her husband to go to her, but he held her fast at his side, shaking his head in the face of her anger. It broke his heart to see the pain in her eyes. "She must do this alone, *a chuisle*."

Spirit's lone voice spoke above the roar of the flames. "*Nid yw marwolaeth ddim rhyngoch chi a fi. Rwyt ti fi a fi ydw i chi. Beth bynnag yr oeddem yn dal i fod yn wir.* (Death is nothing between you and I. You be I and I be you. Whatever we were still holds true)." She paused, the grief almost too much to bear. Tears rolled down her cheeks. Taking a deep breath, she composed herself and continued. "*Rydych chi wedi mynd i wlad arall yn unig. Rwyf wrth fy modd i Inferno Gallimore, a byddaf yn eich caru am byth yn fwy* (You have merely wandered into another land. I love you, Inferno Gallimore, and will love you forever more). Wherever you be, my love, I pray our Ruby be with you."

Dar kissed his wife on the head and whispered, "It is time for the song of valor."

"Would you hold me as I sing? I'm not as strong as Spirit." Although unconventional for such a ceremony, he could not say no. He stood behind her and wrapped his arms around her waist, letting her lean into him. Strengthened by his closeness, her voice rang out, sweet and true. Once again, Zorn picked up on the tune, joining her in the moment of honor.

No longer did boundaries exist between these people who stood together at Castle Laugharne. They were brought together by a common cause, forever bound by the blood spilled. New bonds of friendship emerged and renewed allegiances formed as the early evening transformed into night. A full moon glowed overhead, adding to the brightness of the yard. At the end of the proclamation of valor, the group broke and made their way toward the back garden for the feast prepared by Alaster and his staff.

Dar helped his wife from the dais so they could speak to Spirit and her children. Etain gave her a hug. "How are you?"

Spirit lifted her chin. "He's with me here." She touched her chest over her heart. "Thank you for the beautiful ceremony."

"Is there anything we can do for you, milady?" asked Dar.

"Not at the moment. It's time we get on with it and move ahead."

His gaze went to the small ones around her. "Good evening, Seth. I'm glad to see you again."

Seth stood a little taller. "Hi, Uncle Dar." He glanced at his siblings, each one watching the exchange with their mouths open and eyes wide.

Dar flashed a big grin. "Who do we have here?"

"This is my brother, Dylan. Molly and Tegan are my sisters. Tegan's the little one."

They continued to stare up at the biggest man they'd ever seen.

"Kids, this is your Uncle Dar," Spirit said. "Stop being rude and show him you have manners."

"You're so big," Dylan said, his head cocked all the way back.

Molly held back, not sure what to make of the fair-haired warrior towering above her. She tried to push her little sister behind her skirts, but Tegan swatted her hand away and waddled around her toward their new uncle. She cocked her head back and lifted her arms, wiggling her tiny fingers. "Up, up."

Thoroughly charmed by the small girl, Dar leaned down and scooped her into his arms, bringing her soft hazel eyes in direct line with his. "Hello, Tegan. Good to meet you, little one."

Her eyes widened as she glanced down at the ground, her little mouth forming an "o". She brought her gaze back to Dar, took his face in her chubby hands, and gave him a good look over. She smiled, patting his face. "Angel. Angel." She laid her head on his strong shoulder, sticking her thumb into her mouth as her brothers and sister giggled behind their hands. At that moment, Dar lost his heart to the little girl and made a silent promise that evil would never touch this family again.

"It's time for you lot to go upstairs," Spirit commanded.

"But, Mama!" they whined, except Tegan, who seemed content.

Spirit held her arms out for her smallest child. "Come on, my sweet girl. You've had a long day."

Tegan lifted her head and gave Dar a drowsy smile. "Night, angel." After leaving a kiss on his cheek, she happily went to her mum.

"Get your bums moving." Watching them walk away, Spirit leaned toward Dar. "The time will come when we'll have to face this bastard again. I want to be there."

Dar bowed his head, unsure of how to respond. Linq joined them at that moment, offering his assistance to Spirit. "Shall we get the children settled and join the celebration?"

"Bless you, Linq." Spirit turned to Etain. "We'll be right down."

"We'll save you a seat." Dar watched them as they followed the children into the castle. He reached for his wife's hand and laced his fingers with hers. "Should we be worried?"

"About Spirit? Nah. I would feel the same. I *do* feel the same."

"It's just a shock, seeing her like that. I can't envision her as a warrior."

"She was, in her early Alamir days. Inferno told me stories of when they first transitioned. To hear him tell it, she was fierce."

"Motherhood seems to have mellowed her. Perhaps-"

"Forget it, bub. I am a warrior. That will never change. I will live as a warrior, and my children will live as warriors."

No further words were spoken as they watched the funeral pyres burn, their thoughts on those lives lost. His gaze still on the fires, he whispered, "The weight of the crown is not too great?"

She stared ahead, mesmerized by the dancing flames. "For the moment, it sits fine with me."

Her words made him smile. "May it be an eternal moment. My friend. My partner. My wife. Thank you for all you've given me." His eyes followed his hand as it traveled down to rest on her growing belly. "They *will* be warriors." He turned her to face him, a hopeful rush making him feel a bit lightheaded. "Would you mind if I made the announcement tonight? About our children?"

He knew it was probably too soon to say anything. She looked away and lifted her hand to her mouth, resting a finger in the groove that curved from her nose toward her lips, obviously deep in thought.

Tartarus, I need her to say yes. His entire being vibrated from the joy of the news. *But if she does not, I'll honor her decision…though it will take every ounce of my will to-*

"I think it will be fine," she said, cutting into the monologue in his head. "Otherwise, I'm afraid you just might scare the life out of everyone with that outrageous grin on your face."

Once Spirit and Linq joined them at the table, Dar stood, the same grin in place. "Friends, if you will bear with me for a few minutes…" Everyone stopped talking and turned to listen. "There is news I'd, well…*we'd* like to share with you. News that, we hope, will bring you joy." He glanced at Etain, who chuckled and stood with him.

He smiled so big his face hurt, but he couldn't help himself. "This beautiful woman, my wife, my Queen, has honored me with the greatest gift of all." He smiled at her, his heart full of love, joy, and pride. "We are pregnant!" He laughed out loud, tears threatening to spill down his cheeks. "We're having twins!"

Etain blushed and laughed with him. A smile shone on every face, some breaking into laughter to see a giddy High Lord. Congratulations came from every direction. There were handshakes for Dar and hugs for Etain, all accompanied with well wishes.

Freeblood's grin was almost as big as Dar's. "Congratulations! I know what this means to you, Dar. I'm really happy for you both."

"Thank you, Freeblood. I hope our children will be the best of friends."

"We'll make sure they are." After hugging Etain, he said, "I've got to get back to Faux. She worries when I'm gone too long."

"How is she doing?" Dar asked.

"She's adjusting, looking forward to the baby."

"And you? Are you adjusting?"

Freeblood shrugged. "I can handle anything. Just wish I could help her more."

Dar slapped him on the back. "I understand the struggle, but about all you can do is be there for her, son."

Freeblood smiled. "I am that. Always. I'll see you two later."

Spirit waited until most everyone had their say before she wrapped Etain in a warm hug. "Oh, lass. I'm so happy for you." She pulled away, a sad smile on her face. "What a blessing."

Linq came from behind Spirit and surprised Etain with a hug. "Congratulations to you and Dar." He grabbed Dar's hand and pulled him in for a hug and pat on the back. "Always the showstopper, aye?"

"Aye." Dar laughed, but found himself at a loss for words, feeling a touch of melancholy. To have these people, who not so long ago thought of him as a demon, the enemy, accept him as family.

Etain placed her arms around him and smiled. "It's been a long time, hasn't it, my sweet savage?" He gave her an inquisitive look. "Since you've had a family." She hugged him close, laying her head on his shoulder. "Welcome to my world, Lord Dar. Welcome to my family."

After a hard swallow, he found his voice, albeit husky. "I love you, milady." Taking her face in his hands, he kissed her lips reverently and hugged her tightly. "I love you with all my heart and soul."

Linq cleared his throat. Etain turned her head and smiled, but Dar would not let her go.

"It's wonderful news," the elf said.

"Thank you, Linq. You, better than anyone, know what this means to me. What this woman means to me."

"Any idea of your due date, lass?" Spirit asked.

Etain stared at her, then blinked and turned to Dar. "Nine months?"

Dar and Linq laughed.

Etain raised a brow. "What's so funny?"

"Krymerian babes develop faster than humans," Dar said. "You're going to see a lot of changes in the coming days, my love."

"How long do I have?"

His eyes cut away for a moment, then returned to her. "Normal term for a single child is about six months. With twins, I believe it is five."

"Five?" she choked, her face turning red.

Spirit quickly filled a glass with water and shoved it into her hand. "Here. This will help."

Etain took a few sips. "*Five* months?"

"Closer to four by now." Dar chuckled. "That's why we must get our business here done as soon as possible so we can go home and prepare for our family."

"Holy crap. I think I need to go to bed. I'm feeling really tired all of a sudden."

Amidst the ensuing laughter, the happy couple bid everyone goodnight and left them to their party.

With the ceremony completed and no apparent danger in sight, the Alamir Ambassadors and Arachnia decided to leave after breakfast the next morning. Not wanting to disturb Dar's rest, the Ambassadors left strict instructions with Spirit to pass along their well wishes and congratulations.

Arachnia added her own sentiments. "They were surrounded by so many people last night, I didn't want to intrude. Please tell Dar and Etain to let me know when the twins are born. I would love to visit and get to know Etain better."

As she walked them out the door, Spirit assured them the couple would get their messages and thanked them for attending the ceremony.

After a short audience with Queen Alatariel, Commander Crom released two-thirds of his Black Blades to return to Nunnehi. Along with the Blades, the queen allowed all the War Wizards to return home, as well.

The Dragon chieftain, Aramis, sent most of his clan back to the Dragon Lair, but he and Ra chose to stick around for a few more days, having personal business they wished to discuss with Dar.

Alaster offered to stay on until a new chieftain for UWS was decided. Spirit gratefully accepted his offer, happy to leave the running of the house in his capable hands.

Linq, having become somewhat restless as of late, enlisted Aramis and Ra in an afternoon of hunting in the nearby woods. He set each up with a bow and a quiver of arrows. Spirit, wanting to keep busy, took the children out to the estuary for a picnic.

Close to noon, Dar finally stirred, waking before Etain. He quietly slipped from bed, pulled on a pair of jeans, and after a light kiss on Etain's cheek, padded downstairs in search of something to eat. The unusual quiet of the castle made him uneasy. How could such a large place with so many people be this silent? He walked into the kitchen, expecting to find Alaster busy with some new concoction, but it was empty. However, someone did have the foresight to keep the coffee brewing.

"Looks like you're on your own, Dar, my man." He poured himself a large cup, then set to clearing the refrigerator of any breakfast worthy ingredients. As he diced tomatoes, cheese, and ham, he soon heard footsteps in the hallway. A tousle-haired Freeblood came into the kitchen wearing only a pair of jeans, looking rather barbaric.

"Rough night?" Dar asked.

Freeblood ran a hand through his wild hair and laughed with a blush. "Just a very long one." He stood across from Dar, the island between them. "Want some help?"

Dar ignored him for a moment, then gestured toward the rack of knives. "Grab one and dice some potatoes and onions."

Freeblood nodded, grabbed a knife, and set to cutting potatoes. The two worked side by side in silence for a time.

"Faux is here…in the castle." Dar's only response was a grunt as he mixed batter for pancakes. "She wants to come home."

"Does she think everything will be forgiven and forgotten?" Dar asked, beating the batter harder than necessary.

"Maybe not forgotten, but at least forgiven." Dar gave him another grunt. "Come on, Dar. That demon would've come whether she helped or not. She was used as a pawn, just like you were." The

Krymerian turned to him, eyes narrowed, but Freeblood continued before he could speak. "I'm not trying to insult you. We were *all* duped. He used everyone to get to Etain and damn near succeeded."

He refused to back down from the steaming Krymerian, but his voice carried a slight waver. "You're lucky, Dar. You have someone who truly loves you and will do anything to keep you safe." His sincere words began to have the intended effect. "Even sacrifice her life to save yours." He turned back to the business of the potatoes. "I know Faux has a good heart. I've seen it. In her own twisted way, she thought by working with the demon she was saving me."

Dar's anger snapped. "And in the process, nearly caused the annihilation of everyone else."

"She was tricked, Dar. Don't you see that? The only thing she's really guilty of is being naïve and susceptible to his charms."

"It's a damn good thing Arachnia arrived when she did, boy. Otherwise we wouldn't be having this conversation." Batter in hand, he moved to the stove and poured out several medallions, then glared at the young man. "Forgiveness will not come easily. She has a lot to answer for."

"She will, Dar. She really is sorry."

That said, the conversation turned to more mundane subjects, neither of them wanting to pursue the issue any further. They discussed Freeblood's growing interest in horse breeding and what it entailed. Would Dar be open to such an enterprise once they returned to *Sólskin*? Would he be willing to teach Freeblood everything he knew?

With nothing set in stone, they prepared the trays for their respective mates. Dar held the door open for Freeblood. "Let's talk later today. You, Faux, Etain, and I. Set a few things straight before we go home."

"As long as no more accusations are thrown in her face. She's as delicate as Etain right now. I don't want her upset any more than she already is."

Dar followed him down the hall to the stairs. "I'm well aware of her condition. That's the only reason she's still alive and allowed to stay." He left him at the foot of the stairs.

"Well, with that said," Freeblood watched the big man, "the talk will have to wait. I'm taking Faux west, out to the coast. Maybe we'll find some sunshine."

Dar waited until he was on the landing before he looked over his shoulder. "See you when you get back." He disappeared down the hall.

Freeblood ruminated over his words as he headed up to Faux. Walking into their bedroom, he saw her, stark naked, exiting the bathroom. "Are you okay, babe?"

"I'm perfect. What have we got here?" She walked toward him. "It smells delicious."

He grinned. "Me and Dar made breakfast."

Her eyebrows lifted. "And you still have your head? How'd you manage that?"

"I think I'm starting to wear him down."

"I'd like to see that," she chuckled, turning to walk to the bed.

"Looks like you're doing pretty good without your tail." His eyes roamed over her backside. He much preferred it minus the extra appendage.

She patted the bedside table. "Put that tray here before you hurt yourself."

The changes in her body became more apparent with each passing day. Her breasts grew heavier, the once light pink areolae and nipples now a dusky shade of brown. He noticed how much her belly protruded, making him wonder just how long before this child of theirs would be ready to emerge into the world. He looked at her with a warm smile and his own obvious protrusion.

Once his hands were free, she kneeled on the edge of the mattress, gripped the waistband of his jeans, and pulled him to her. She engulfed his mouth with hers, opening his fly at the same time.

"Just like you, always changing the subject." He moaned as she freed him from his jeans and closed his eyes in response to the intense pleasure of her lips on his skin. Pushing the pants over his hips, her mouth trailed farther down, encasing him within its warm, wet confines.

"Oh god," he muttered, his fingers digging into the flesh of her shoulders. "Holy fucking mother of us all!" he yelled, feeling the climax build, gathering strength. He closed his eyes and submitted to the pure pleasure as it rolled through him, reveling in the vibrations he felt in every fibre of his body.

Once his breath returned, he cradled her head in his hands and crushed his mouth to hers. "You drive me crazy." She uttered a small shriek when he suddenly shoved her back onto the bed. "Second course is mine."

"Not before I eat!" she laughed, scrambling away.

"Ya wee wench," he teased. "I've half a mind to drag ye away to another kingdom."

"If you had any mind at all, we'd already be gone," she joked.

Settled against the headboard, they interspersed nibbles of breakfast with nibbles of each other, making a mess of not only the bed, but of them, as well.

"Seriously, we're leaving today." The smile on her face told him he'd made the right decision. "I'm taking you to the western most point of the land. A place called St. David's."

"And what do you propose we do once we get there?" She popped a piece of fruit into her mouth.

"Whatever we wish."

Dar expected to find her in bed, but it was empty, the covers in total disarray. A muffled scream snapped his gaze to the balcony where he saw a naked Etain in the arms of another man. He dropped the tray and rushed toward them. "Let her go, Raum!"

The man placed his dagger at her throat. "You stay right there. I have what I've come for. No need for things to get messy."

Dar knew the demon servant could quite easily slit her throat before he could get to her. "Do you really think I'll let you leave with her?"

He laughed darkly. "You will if you want her to live."

"He won't kill me," Etain said, breathless. "If Dathmet's anything like his father, he wants more than just my blood."

"Now that's where you're wrong." Raum jerked her back toward the balcony. "Your blood is all he's ever desired. Incest is one thing my master has no taste for."

Etain looked at Dar. *Incest?*

Dar tried another angle. "If you slice her throat here, she'll bleed to death before you can get out. Her blood will be wasted."

Raum considered his words. "Perhaps you're right." He moved the blade down to the mark on her chest, sliding it slowly around her left breast. "If I stick her here, she'll live long enough to get to our castle where I can bleed her dry. Her blood will restore him and her heart will give him all the power he'll ever need."

Etain sucked in a breath as the cold blade slid over her skin.

Dar struggled against the rising alarm in his own heart. He hoped to appeal to whatever humanity may be left in the demon who was once a man. "Raum, she's pregnant."

His eyebrows lifted as a lascivious smile spread over his face, cupping her breast. "I knew you were more luscious than the last time we met."

It took all Dar's strength of will to keep from blasting the bastard with his ultimá solar. If only she weren't in the way, the demon would be toast.

Raum looked up at Dar. "Her blood is rich with the life of two. I can serve the master both hearts." The demon pulled her farther onto the balcony, making every attempt to faze. Disconcerted by the fact he couldn't exit with his prize, his grip loosened.

Etain took advantage of the slip and jabbed her elbow into his gut, doubling him over. She pushed away and ran toward Dar, who was halfway to her. Raum had enough presence of mind to grab a handful of silver hair.

Dar lunged. Raum hurled his knife. Etain screamed as Dar staggered and fell to the floor, the blade buried in his chest. Raum tried to leave again, his gaze on Dar. His eyes, white with the solar, glared back. The demon pushed Etain at him and disappeared. The Krymerian's solar faded as his eyes closed.

Etain scrambled to him, crying as she caressed his face. "My Dar! Oh, baby. Please don't die." So overcome with grief, she didn't notice his eyelids flutter.

"*A chuisle*, please… Remove the blade from my chest. It hurts like hell."

"Huh? What?" She blinked, dumbfounded.

"The blade." Trying not to move, he indicated with his eyes. "Take it out."

"Are you nuts? You'll bleed to death. Let me get Swee."

"Don't worry, love," he whispered. "Remember the jewel Lothous placed in my heart…" He slowly breathed in, "to separate me from Midir? The dagger must have hit the jewel. If you will pull it out…"

"Are you sure?"

"Aye."

She took hold of the hilt and quickly removed it. Dar grunted, but otherwise seemed all right. She pulled the bandages away from the wound and found only a small trickle of blood.

"I'm fine, my love."

"I think *my* heart's gonna burst from all this."

He pulled her down on top of him. "I love you," he said, tasting her salty tears as he kissed each eye, then ran his hands over her body. "Did he hurt you?"

He listened carefully for any hint of distress in her voice. "He only tossed me around and scared the hell out of me."

Dar continued to stroke her body, taking great pleasure in feeling her respond to his touch. "I can't tell you how it made me feel, seeing his hands on you," his voice was soft, but edged with anger. "Now we know you are no longer safe here. The sooner we leave, the better."

A growl came from her stomach. "Can we eat first?"

He gave her his boyish grin. "Aye. I've worked up a raging appetite myself this morning."

"Why, Lord VonNeshta, whatever have you been doing?"

Laughing, Dar carefully got to his feet and offered her his hand.

"How's your back?" she asked. "That fall couldn't have helped it."

"No, it didn't."

"Let me have a look. Turn around."

He did as requested and looked over his shoulder. "How is it? Is there any blood?"

"I don't see any on the bandages, but we should have Swee check, just to be sure."

"I'll find her after breakfast."

While Etain dressed, he salvaged as much food as he could and set the tray on the small table near the fireplace. Although cold now, it in no way deterred the hungry couple from digging in. Dar smiled, happy to see her with a healthy appetite.

They ate in silence for a time, but when Dar sensed a shift in her mood, he leaned back in his chair, noting the crease between her brows. "Tell me, love."

"Hmm?" Roused from her reverie, she gave him a blank look.

"Something's on your mind. Tell me."

"I was wondering…" She leaned over the arm of the chair toward him. "Does the protection spell still surround the house?"

"Aye. Can you not feel it?"

"No. I never could." She narrowed her eyes. "How was Raum able to get in?"

He sat quietly, his hands steepled under his chin. "Good question."

A few moments passed in silence. "Dar, you're being weird."

"I have a question for you."

"Okay."

He rested his hands on the arms of the chair. "Were you aware your brother suffered an injury while you were gone?"

She sat back. "No one mentioned it."

"Oh, aye. He fell down the stairs and was out cold for quite a while."

"Are you sure? He didn't say anything at breakfast yesterday."

"Don't you find that odd?"

"What I find odd is that no one, not even you, bothered to tell me sooner." She stood, grabbed her boots from the side of the bed, and returned to her seat.

"Where are you going?"

Lacing her boots, she didn't look up. "I'm going to see my brother. He was probably waiting for me to say something."

"Listen to what I have to say first."

"Maybe if you'd said something yesterday…" She turned her head to him, "I would've listened. But today?" Her boots fully laced, she stood and looked down at him. "Forget it. I've neglected him too long."

"Have you noticed any bruises on him? Any marks at all?"

"No. But he wasn't moving so well, either."

"There were marks the other day."

Her gaze snapped to his. "What? Who told you that?"

"Swee's been keeping an eye on him."

"Well, she's mistaken. It wouldn't be the first time." She had a wild glint in her eye. "You saw him, Dar. His skin wasn't marred in any way."

"Don't you think that unusual? A fall like that would leave *some* bruising. Hell, he's lucky he didn't break his neck. I saw the look on Swee's face when she took me to his room. She's telling the truth."

"When was that?"

"The other day," he said again.

She placed her hands on her hips. "What did she see? Bruises? Cuts?"

Dar separated the bandages around his chest and pointed at his own mark. "This, except his was over his stomach, partly in bruises and partly burned into his skin."

She flinched. "*Burned* into his skin?" Running a hand through her hair, she paced back and forth. "You said she took you to his room?"

"Aye."

She stopped. "What did *you* see?"

"I didn't see anything."

She threw her arms up. "Well, there you go. Swee's losing it. I think all this is proving too much for the poor girl."

"*I* think a cloaking spell has been cast to hide it."

"Who would do that?"

"Robert, for one."

"You can't possibly believe my brother has the capacity, the ability..." She turned away, striding back and forth. "Damn, Dar. He was tortured and left for dead."

"Etain, it's a fact he was raised by Midir. He has the capacity *and* the ability," he said patiently.

"Then why?" she practically yelled, flinging her hands in the air again. "Why hide his injuries? Holy crap, why was he even out of bed?"

"You're not asking the right questions, Etain."

She stopped and glared at him. "Then what's the fucking question?"

Dar stood, but didn't move toward her. "Of all the marks one can get from falling down the stairs, why does he bear the mark you and I share? How does that happen? How does it disappear in a matter of hours?"

An idea bloomed. "Oh, my god. Could it be a delayed reaction? Like Taurnil? He didn't show any symptoms at first."

His heart lurched to see her so torn. "It isn't the same thing."

"The same godforsaken demon who attacked T attacked my brother. He's playing a cruel joke to make Robert look like he's as evil as Midir."

What she said made some sense. But it didn't explain why. With Robert as Midir's protégé and Dathmet his son, surely the two knew each other, or were at least aware of each other. "Sylvan may know of a way to make the mark reappear. I must see it for myself."

"How do we do that? Robert isn't just gonna let her perform some mojo on him."

"If the elves can knock out someone like me, I'm sure they can handle a human."

"Well, you aren't doing it without me. I figure she's in T's room. Let's go have a chat."

14

TO SAY THE LEAST

A walk down the hall found them at Taurnil's room. Erudessa opened the door and smiled, then curtsied. "High Lord, High Lady, good afternoon."

"Dar! Etain!" Alatariel called from inside the room. "Come in. Come in." She appeared from around the corner, a smile on her face. "Please. Taurnil has been asking after you both. We heard your wonderful news. Congratulations!" She hugged Etain, giving her a kiss on each cheek, then turned to Dar, doing the same. "Twins! It's so exciting."

"Thank you, Rie. How is Taurnil?" Dar asked.

"Judge for yourself," said the young elf, walking from the attached room.

"T!" Etain rushed to him and wrapped him in a warm hug. "Look at you. Are you sure you should be on your feet?"

He grinned, leaning on her more than he normally would. "I have to take it slow, but I'm getting better."

Dar noticed the paleness of his face and joined them. "Let's get you in a chair."

"You should be resting, too, Dar," Taurnil said, gratefully taking a seat.

"I'm good. I have the best nurse in the world." Dar grinned, glancing at his wife.

Taurnil laughed. "I should be as lucky."

"Is Sylvan around?" Etain suddenly blurted.

As if on cue, there was a light knock on the door and the Elven Sorceress walked in. "Milord, milady," she said. "Pardon my abruptness, but it's time for the next application."

"Of course," Dar answered, stepping aside.

She leaned down to take hold of his shirt, but Taurnil batted her hand away.

"I'm well enough to do it myself, Sylvan…later." His eyes cut to the High Lady.

The Sorceress smiled as she straightened and handed him a small jar. "Apologies, milord. I've become so accustomed to my nursing duties, I forget myself." She turned to Dar and Etain. "I hear congratulations are in order. News like yours is exactly what we needed."

"Thank you, Sylvan," said Dar. "I hope we've raised a few spirits around here."

"You most certainly have." Alatariel sat in the chair across from her son. "Did you stop by just to check on Taurnil, or is there something more you need?"

"Mother." The young elf gave his mother a stern eye, to which she merely shrugged.

"Both." Dar acquainted everyone with the details of Robert's illusive mark without elaborating on the connection with his dead brother or the demon. "Can you make the mark visible?"

Sylvan considered his request. "It's possible, but not guaranteed. I will need the assistance of a dark elf. Their ability to reveal the unseen will be of great help."

"A dark elf?" Dar raised both brows. "I've only met one in my lifetime, and it wasn't a pleasant experience."

She smiled courteously. "No, I don't expect it was. They never had much use for the Krymerians."

"Where do we find one? Don't tell me they live in Nunnehi."

"They do not," said Alatariel. "However, we *do* have one in the Black Blades." His eyes widened at this revelation. "Yes, Dar. There is a dark elf in the Blades. She is astute in the art of warfare and has proven herself a valuable warrior."

"She?"

"Her name is Renme. I believe she's one of the Blades who remained here. How soon-"

"I would prefer we get this over with as soon as possible." He turned to the Sorceress. "We'll need a few drops of the Living Dead Draught."

Sylvan bowed her head. "As you wish, milord."

"I will speak to Commander Crom and have Renme meet you at the young man's room," said Alatariel.

"Thank you, ladies. Sylvan, if you will get with Swee, I believe she has the easiest access. He won't suspect anything coming from her."

"We will need some time," said Sylvan. "Shall we meet at his room in an hour?"

Dar's gaze went to the queen. "Alatariel, does that give you enough time to speak with Crom?"

"I guess it will have to," she said, her eyes going to her son.

"We'll stay here, Rie," Etain said. "Until we're ready."

"I'll be fine, Mother. Please, go ahead and find Crom. We have to solve this mystery." Taurnil moved to stand up, but his mother waved him back.

"You stay put." She looked at Etain. "Thank you. I'll be back soon. Sylvan? Shall we get on with it?"

An hour later, a silent group consisting of Dar, Etain, Swee, Sylvan, and Renme, the dark elf, met at Robert's bedroom door.

Swee's hand on the knob, she said, "I gave him a cup of tea not long ago. Let me go in first to make sure it's taken effect."

As they waited for her return, Sylvan introduced the Blade.

"Good to meet you, Renme," Dar said. "Thank you for your assistance."

"Milord," she responded with a sharp salute.

Aware of the disposition of dark elves toward Krymerians, Dar's curiosity was piqued. "How is it you come to my Black Blades?"

"I come by way of my father, sir," she said respectfully.

His brows lifted. "Your father? He is a dark elf."

A faint smirk curled one side of her mouth. "Aye, milord, as was my mother."

"I'm sorry to seem so dense, but I find it hard to believe a dark elf would join an organization so immersed in Krymerian custom. I was in league with a dark elf many years ago and found him to be quite unruly," he stated, crossing his arms over his chest.

Her smile widened. "Yes. I must admit, my father found Krymerians a rather…adverse race." Dar looked at Etain, then back at Renme. "My father was Shalan."

His body tensed as memories flooded in. Etain noticed the change in him and placed a hand on his arm. "Renme…," he said, finding it hard to meet her gaze. Shalan lost his life to the High Lord during Dar's battle for his sanity. "I cannot apologize-"

"We do not blame you, High Lord," she said solemnly. "Your brother…" She cast her gaze to the floor. Clearing her throat, she brought her gaze back to Dar. "My father is why I joined the Black Blades."

"You have a brother… Garrick?"

Dar noted the admiration in her eyes. "Yes. Garrick studies to be a War Wizard, like our father."

"Shalan would be proud to see his children pursuing such noble occupations." Dar waited a moment, his eyes on the young woman. "Thank you."

She seemed to understand what his gratitude encompassed.

"My admiration for your father will continue all the days of my life, Renme, although I never voiced it directly to his face. He was much too stern for such admissions."

"To say the least," she said, smiling.

Swee appeared at the door and motioned them in.

"Shall we see what we may see, ladies?" Dar stepped aside for the women to enter.

Renme snapped to attention. "After you, milord." She followed Dar into the room and closed the door.

The five stood around the bed. Renme watched Robert's face for a few moments before she pulled the covers down to his hips to expose his upper body. Closing her eyes, she murmured a chant to invoke her powers.

Etain glanced at Dar and slipped her hand into his.

Renme opened her eyes, which now glowed electric blue. She moved her gaze to Robert's belly as her words became more forceful, imploring the powers of light to assist. A faint blue tint appeared on his skin. As the chant continued, the light brightened, forming the outer circle of swords first. Etain took hold of Dar's arm. The flaming sun appeared in the center of the crown of swords. However, Dar noticed another mark suddenly appear, as well. One only he recognized for what it truly was. Just below Robert's navel was a small mark in the shape of a sickle.

"Is it what you thought?" Etain whispered.

Releasing her hand, he bent over the young man for a closer look. "Has your brother always had this mark?"

She looked at where he pointed. "I'd forgotten about that." She looked at Dar. "He was born with it. How funny I didn't think of it sooner."

"I would say it's been cloaked all this time."

Etain emitted a small laugh. "Well, that doesn't make any sense. Why hide it?"

Renme blinked once, breaking the spell. "So his enemies would not recognize him."

"Enemies?" Etain echoed. "What enemies?"

Dar looked at Swee and Sylvan. "Would you ladies please excuse us?" Clearly taken by surprise, the women nodded silently as he grabbed Etain's hand and pulled her toward the door, addressing Renme over his shoulder. "You know what to do, Blade."

"Yes, milord." She saluted as they left the room.

Once in the hallway, Etain dug in her heels, bringing them both to a jarring halt. "Wait a minute. What the hell is going on, Dar?"

"I'd rather not discuss this here. Come with me." He pulled her down the hall.

Twisting her wrist, she slipped from his grasp. "No. You tell me right now."

"We will not discuss this here, I said." He clamped onto her arm, making her yelp. "Sorry, love, but this is not the time to defy me."

Unable to wrench free, she reluctantly accompanied her husband to their room, then turned on him the second the door closed. "What the bloody hell? Why would my brother feel the need to cloak his birthmark?"

For a brief moment, he gazed at his raving wife, thinking how absolutely delicious she looked with her eyes flashing and the color high in her cheeks. By the gods, he'd love to silence that luscious mouth with a passionate kiss, rip off her clothes, and take her right here on the floor. However….

"Dar," she said loudly. "Answer me."

Shaken from his thoughts, his eyes cleared and focused on the now.

"Me."

She rolled her eyes. "Are you serious? He's my *brother*, Dar! This jealously has got to stop."

Running a hand over his face, he took a deep breath. "Etain. He has good reason to hide that mark."

"Bloody fucking hell." She rushed at him and shoved him back against the door, then spun around and stormed to the balcony. Her body taut, she grabbed the rail, squeezing and releasing several times.

Dar strode across the room and stood just inside the balcony doors. "I do not say this lightly. Robert is not the boy you remember."

She turned to face him. "Why can't you just accept him and let us have what you and Midir never did?"

"This has nothing to do with jealousy. I don't begrudge you a brother, Etain. You know me better than that."

"I know you don't trust him."

"Up until now, it's been only a gut feeling." She huffed and looked away, shaking her head. "But I've seen that birthmark before." His comment caught her full attention. She looked back at him. "Midir had the same mark on his lower back."

Although he was fully clothed, her gaze automatically moved down his body.

"It was unique to him. I never had a mark."

"Me, either." Her eyes moved back to his. "Is it possible for two people to have the same mark and not be related?"

"I'm no expert on such matters. All I know is that it's an exact match to Midir's."

Etain tossed her hair over her shoulder. "Well, how the hell could that happen?"

Dar shrugged. "I can only think of one."

She placed her hands on her hips and leaned toward him. "You are full of shit." She turned her back to him, gripping the rail with both hands again. "My mom loved my dad. She would never betray him." She spun around again. "My mom would never let someone like Midir *ever* touch her."

Dar watched her, unconcerned with their momentary difference of opinion. "Midir considered humans beneath him. I can't see him fraternizing with a human woman, even your mother. But I have no other explanation. My instincts tell me all these occurrences are connected."

"And you think my brother is part of it."

He leaned against the door jamb. "I know he is. I don't know how yet, but he is."

"I don't want to discuss this right now. I'd rather go sit with him." Turning, she stepped past Dar into the bedroom, headed toward the door.

"You won't be able to," he said almost apologetically. "He's under guard now."

"That was quick." She stopped and turned to him. "I can't see my own brother?"

"No, you cannot."

"I am the High Lady and I *will* see him." With a glance over her shoulder, she left the room.

Dar shook his head. He knew full well his Black Blades would respond only to his orders. Once given, not even the High Lady could usurp his authority. He followed her into the hallway.

Etain regally walked down the hall and paused at Robert's door. The two Blades stationed outside were respectful when she spoke to them, although they never relaxed their stance. However, as she moved to enter, they sidestepped toward each other, standing shoulder to shoulder.

Her head snapped up, eyes blazing. "Do you know who I am?"

The Blade to the left answered. "Yes, High Lady, but you cannot enter."

"Oh, I can…and I will," she said, looking every bit a queen with her head held high.

The Blade to her right responded this time. "Not today, milady. We have orders from the High Lord."

"Orders?" Her eyebrows lifted. "This is my brother, my family. I have every right to be with him."

"Not without the High Lord's approval, milady."

She looked from one Blade to the other, then turned and quietly walked to the stairs, ignoring Dar's presence in the hall. He followed her downstairs and out the front doors. She stood in the center of the courtyard, her back to him. Wings fully extended, she lifted off and curved around toward the side of the castle where Robert's room was located. It wasn't long before he heard a loud shriek, then saw her soar past him, headed for the horizon.

Curious, he walked around the corner to check out the situation himself. Four Black Blades were stationed on the balcony, standing shoulder to shoulder. Seeing the High Lord, the Blades snapped to attention with a salute. Dar saluted in return.

Considering the events of the day, he turned, prepared to go after her. However, before he could spread his wings, Aramis and Ra stepped out the front doors.

"Dar! Just the man I was looking for," Aramis said.

"Hello, Aramis, Ra." He greeted each man with a handshake. "What can I do for you today?"

"I assume you and Etain will be returning home soon," said the Dragon chieftain.

"There are a few loose ends we need to tie up here, but aye, I expect to be leaving before too long."

"We've heard you have a sizeable estate," Ra said.

He crossed his arms, looking from one to the other. "Sounds like someone's been telling many a tale about me and mine. What're you Dragons about?"

Aramis cleared his throat and dove in. "As you know, our clan is one of the smaller ones of the Alamir. With the *Bok* becoming active again, I don't know how safe our lair will be stationed so far away from the other clans. We've been looking to make a move, but nothing's been right."

"Until now," Dar finished the thought.

"We think so," Aramis agreed. "Not only would it secure the safety of our clan and families, we could help patrol the estate. And, of course, assist with whatever else needs doing."

"How many are we talking about?" Dar asked.

Ra gave him the numbers. "Seven clan members. Including family members, it's no more than seventeen total."

Dar gave him a fixed look. "Give me some time to think it over. I'll get back to you by the end of the week."

"Thank you, Dar," Aramis said. "We'll let you get back to it."

Dar turned toward the estuary as Aramis and Ra walked off. The idea of Etain alone prompted him into action. Sensing her nearby, his wings extended and he took to the air, headed toward the coastline.

A dark energy entered his radar as he closed in on her location. He touched down quietly, then tucked his wings in close and stood still, alert to every nuance. Moments passed as he looked to his right, then left.

Eyes closed, he concentrated on the energy. Its evil danced around him, taunting, daring him to fight. His temples thrummed. His brain felt as though it were being squeezed in a vice. His heart raced. The demon inside hungered to strike out, the warrior demanded action, but he knew to resist the evil would give it the power to defeat him. With a great force of will, he let the dark swirl about his body in its attempt to consume his soul.

A soft sigh cut through the noise in his head. Although his brain felt like it would explode, his eyes slid to the side. Etain lay on the sandy shore, asleep, her wings wrapped around her. The tide washed over her, rising with each incoming surge. He wondered why she didn't wake.

I must get to her.

The evil pressed around him like bands of steel, holding him in place. Darkness crawled over his skin. Meanwhile, the tide came farther up the shore, covering Etain with each wave.

"To hell with this," he murmured, gathering his anger into his gut. Just as the dark began to penetrate, his rage erupted in a white heat, lighting his ultimá solar. He threw his head back, pushed his wings out with all his might, and released a bloodcurdling war cry.

Dar blazed with the flare. The sand beneath his feet turned to glass. Rocks exploded. The evil withdrew, disappeared. With a flap of his great wings, he rose into the air and was at Etain's side in seconds. His touch roused her.

"Dar…"

Another surge of water washed up, nearly drowning her this time.

He scooped his sputtering wife into his arms and soared into the sky. Bypassing the castle, he flew to the small cottage. As he touched down, he instructed her to retract her wings as he did his own.

He fazed them into the bathroom, where he gently set her on the countertop. "You sit here for a sec." He grabbed a couple towels from the side of the tub. "Let's get you out of that wet dress." Laying the towels to the side, he unfastened the buttons down the front and pushed it over her shoulders and down her arms. She shifted her hips so he could pull the dress from under her, then tossed it to the floor and wrapped an oversized towel around her. She shivered as he dried her hair with the other.

"What were you doing out there?"

"I had to get away…to think. I didn't realize I was so close to the water. What're we doing here?"

"You probably weren't that close when you sat down. The tide came in while you were asleep. We came here because I think we need time to ourselves."

"This is getting to be a habit, you bringing me here."

"Sometimes I feel it's the only place we can connect and not be interrupted."

"Laugharne *is* a busy place. But it's filled with people who care about us."

"Aye. It would be nice if they'd care farther away, though." That made her smile, which helped him relax. "It was a strange place to fall asleep."

She shrugged. "I don't remember feeling sleepy or even lying down."

"What *do* you remember?"

"I was pissed at you."

He smirked. "I got that. Did you go there to think or to plan?"

"To think…" Dar raised a brow, "of a plan," she confessed. "It was just starting to form in my head when something interrupted my thoughts."

He stopped drying her hair. "What?"

"I guess that's when I fell asleep."

"Interesting." Laying the towel aside, he scooped her up again and carried her into the bedroom. "How about we talk in bed?"

"But it's early and I'm hungry," she said, wrapping her arms around his neck.

"I'll fix us something in a while." He set her on the bed, then sat next to her with a groan.

"Aw, baby…" She ran a hand through his hair. "How's the back?"

"It catches now and then, but mostly, I'm ready to get home," he said, removing his boots. He set them aside, then pushed her back onto the bed. "And get our house in order."

Before she totally succumbed to his attentions, she pushed him away. "Wait. I'm mad at you."

"Be mad at me later. Right now, all I want to do is concentrate on you and me." He dipped his head, nibbled on her ear, and blazed a trail of kisses along her neck.

"Oh," she said breathlessly. "I guess I can do that."

After their departure from the unusual meeting in Robert's room, Sylvan and Swee returned to Taurnil's. They found the young elf sitting up in bed, his hair freshly combed, his eyes bright, and a big smile on his face. Sylvan noticed the pale blues of his aura deepening, the edges darkening to his normal violets. She checked his eyes to ensure there were no lingering effects hidden in their depths.

A satisfied smile on her lips, she declared, "Prince Taurnil, I believe you will recover completely."

"Thank you, mistress. Your abilities are truly legendary."

"Actually, it was by pure luck that I found the cure."

He dismissed her words with a wave of his hand. "No matter. You, Chelri, and Swee shall always be remembered in the saving of my life."

"You're looking quite well," Swee said, smiling.

He turned his electric smile on the young healer. "You're a marvelous nurse and friend."

"Since you're doing so well and in excellent hands, I'll take my leave," Sylvan said. "Be well, milord."

"Off to Nunnehi then?"

"Not just yet. I've heard of a rare, exotic herb in a little town on the northern coast. I have hope the local apothecary will be able to assist me."

Swee gave her a hug. "You will be missed, Sylvan. Thank you so much."

"You are a great student, Swee, and are always welcome in my home." She hugged her in return. "Please, thank Ms. Spirit for her hospitality and give my apologies to Alatariel for leaving without saying goodbye."

"She'll understand, milady," Taurnil said.

With a bow of her head, she stepped back, murmured a chant, and disappeared in a mist.

Swee sat on the edge of the bed next to Taurnil. "So, what are your plans once you're fully recovered?"

He leaned back into the pillows. "I haven't thought that far ahead, Swee." A curious look on his face, he asked, "Have you?"

"Oh, nothing serious." She blushed. "I've been waiting to see how all this turned out before I made any plans."

"Is that so?" He placed his hands behind his head. "Any ideas on how you'd like it to turn out?"

"You're laughing at me."

"No. I truly want to know," he said, continuing to smile.

She gave him an *I'm not so sure* look, but just as she opened her mouth, Alatariel and her entourage walked into the room.

"Taurnil, you're awake." She rushed to the bed. Swee stood and offered her place to the queen. "Son, you're looking better by the minute. Thank the heavens for Sylvan and Chelri."

"And Swee, Mother. If it weren't for her personal attention-"

"Yes, yes. And Swee." She leaned toward him and kissed his forehead. "Where is Sylvan? I was sure she would be here."

"She sends her apologies, but she felt me well enough she could leave."

Alatariel's eyes sparkled. "Chelri, how soon can he travel?"

"Mother..."

Swee moved farther back, working to hide her embarrassment.

Chelri bowed his head. "Your Highness, I would say a few days of good bedrest and he should be strong enough for a trip."

"Perfect." She issued orders to her handmaidens. In all the commotion, Swee quietly made her way to the door and slipped out unnoticed, except by Taurnil.

Perturbed by his mother's rudeness and her total disregard for his wishes, he used what little strength he had to raise his voice. "Queen Alatariel." Taken aback, she looked at him expectantly. "*I* will decide when I am ready to return to Nunnehi." The crestfallen look on his mother's face made him relent. "Mother, please. Let me get back on my feet for longer than a few minutes, then we can discuss where to go from there."

She quietly nodded at her son's request, then regally asked everyone to leave the room. Once they were alone, she took his hand in hers. "I'm sorry, *sonur*. Here I am, treating you like a child." She reached out, smoothing his hair with her fingers. "Excuse me for being a mother. You scared the hell out of me."

He gently brought her hands down to his lap. "I don't mind you acting like my mother, but you were rude to Swee. She has worked harder than anyone for my recovery."

Alatariel sighed. "*Sonur…*" She pulled her hands from his. "You must remember who you are and what you mean to our people. I appreciate what she has done-"

"Then I expect you to *show* her your appreciation. She has become a close friend. I will not have her disrespected, especially by my family."

"Taurnil-"

"Mother… Your Highness…"

She held up a hand. "Let's not argue. It has been a long day. We can talk about this later. Agreed?"

He raised a brow. "As long as you show her the respect she deserves."

Alatriel bowed her head. "I will make amends tomorrow." She stood, then kissed him on the cheek. "Good night, *sonur*."

"Good night, *móðir*."

Dar woke early the next morning. "Wake up, my tasty morsel," he whispered in Etain's ear.

Her eyes closed, she swatted at him and rolled away. "No. Sleep."

He pulled her back against him. "I'm afraid not, *a chuisle*. You cannot be alone anymore. Too much has happened."

"I can take care of myself," she murmured.

"Perhaps…" His hand glided over her smooth skin as he pressed his hips to her backside. "But I'm not leaving anything to chance now. Until we go home, you will be accompanied by someone at all times."

With a great sigh, she turned in his arms to face him. "Is that really necessary?" She stroked his body, her hand moving down between his legs.

Her touch was a delicious distraction. His grip tightened on her when her actions intensified. "I mean it, Etain," he growled.

Pressing her lips to his, she breathed him in. "I know, my love." She seared his mouth with her kiss. "But I'll suffocate if I'm watched like that."

"Not watched," he said with great effort. "Protected."

Unable to hold back any longer, Dar pushed her back, sliding into her warmth and taking her with an unexpected urgency. She welcomed him in, her passion meeting his with the same intensity. The lovers clung to one another. Her, driving him to plunge deeper, to become a part of her. Him, matching her dare, giving her his everything, uniting them once again.

Assured of her contentment, he rolled to her side, trembling from the intensity of the encounter, and pulled her close. "You are my addiction," he whispered. "But you will not sway me in this. You will be in the company of at least one other person at all times."

She frowned prettily. "If it makes you feel better, okay. But does it have to be so early?"

He grinned and hugged her tightly. "I have a sword to design for a Black Blade. It's no easy feat."

"I suppose I can find something to keep me busy." Etain swirled a finger over and around his nipples. "Maybe find Spirit and the kids since I'm not allowed to see my brother."

Dar shivered, tempted to take her again. "I'm sure they can keep you entertained while I work in the forge." But duty called. He rolled out of bed. "If you behave, perhaps I'll take you to see your brother this evening."

She sat up, her skin aglow from their lovemaking, her lips an inviting red. "If *you* behave, maybe I'll let you sleep with me tonight."

Dar chuckled. "Such a wicked invitation, milady. I'll certainly try my best."

"Hmph." Etain walked behind him into the bathroom.

Catching her eye in the mirror, he grinned. "Get your bonnie arse in that shower and let's get moving."

With a laugh, she obeyed his orders and pulled him in with her.

15

A BLACK BLADE FOR A BLACK BLADE

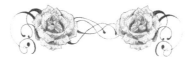

Just as the sun peeked over the horizon, Dar and Etain walked into the Laugharne courtyard. "Jeez," she said, shivering. "When did it get so bloody cold?"

"Winter's late this year," Dar said. "I hope we can get home before the snows come; otherwise we'll have to stay till spring."

"Why would we have to stay? We could just shimmer home." She moved closer to share his warmth.

"Because we aren't going back alone. I want to establish a Black Blade Academy and will need others to help. Besides, an estate doesn't run itself."

"Oh. Guess we have some work ahead of us."

He spotted Linq stepping out the back door and steered them in his direction. Etain made him stop and look at her. "I think the academy is a wonderful idea. Whatever I can do to help, I will."

"That's very generous, my love. Your support is important." He caressed her face, his admiration for her sparkling in his eyes. "After the children are born, perhaps you can demonstrate some of your signature moves to my students."

"With pleasure."

Linq met up with the couple. "*Bore da*, Etain, Dar. I was looking for you."

"*Bore da*," they said at the same time. "Was it me or Etain you needed?"

"You. But since she's here, let's start with the lady."

Etain's gaze darted between Dar and Linq. "Why?"

"I'm aware you may not know how it happened with Inferno, but-"

"Isn't it enough that we accomplished what we set out to do?"

He considered what she'd said, exchanged a glance with Dar, then shifted his stance. "I can do that if you tell us about the second trip. No one has said a word."

Dar moved a step closer to Linq and turned toward her. "Good point. I've been too distracted by other things to even think on it. Why don't you share that with us now, my love?"

"Well…" She looked away. "I wasn't alone…as you know." The men stared at her, neither giving an ounce of response. A ghost of a smile flashed on her lips. "Yeah." She ran a hand through her hair. "So, when we didn't find the demon, I destroyed the castle. Spirit helped."

Linq continued to stare at her. Dar raised a brow.

"It truly was a blood castle. Every drop ever spilled in that place was absorbed by the monstrosity. We tore it down…and blasted it to hell."

"You and Spirit?" Dar asked.

"Mostly me…but her magic reinforced mine." The men looked at one another. "You're wrong about Inferno." Their heads snapped to her. "I know what happened."

"How?" Dar said. "I saw your reaction when you found him. You were devastated."

"I was." Her hand went through her hair again as she turned to the side, then turned back. "It was Ruby." Dar raised both brows. Linq furrowed his. "What was left of her. Dathmet kept her head."

Linq lowered his gaze, unable to speak. Dar placed a hand on his shoulder and opened an arm for Etain. She stepped into his embrace, wrapping her arms around him. The three stood in silence. Each one knew how much Inferno loved his wolfhounds, Felix and Ruby. Seeing her head mounted was an atrocity he would not have been able to bear. The demon had obviously taken advantage of his momentary weakness.

Anxious to lighten the mood, Dar noticed his scabbard in Linq's hand. "What's that you have there?"

He seemed surprised but held it up. "Riko gave me this after their return from the blood castle. I thought I'd repair it for you."

"What happened here?" Dar asked, indicating the cut leather straps.

"He didn't say."

Dar turned to Etain. "Would you know?"

She stared at the straps. "Dathmet."

He glanced at Linq. "After you're done with the scabbard, maybe I could interest you in helping design a sword for a certain future Black Blade?"

"Has Túrë returned from Krymeria?"

"I'm expecting him any time. I want to be ready when he does."

"Sounds a plan."

"I'll leave you to your designs," Etain said. "I'm off to find Spirit and the kids."

Dar grabbed her by the arm before she could get away. "Not so fast, milady."

Etain narrowed her eyes and tried to pull free. "I don't need a guard to walk me into the house. The door is right there."

"Humor me, my love. Linq, go ahead to the forge. I'm going to escort my lovely wife upstairs. I'll meet you in a few."

"Of course, Dar." He bowed his head to the lady. "Etain. I hope to see you at breakfast."

"Oh, aye. I'll be the one with an entourage up her bloody ass."

Linq chuckled as they headed toward the kitchen door.

"You have become quite the handful lately," Dar said.

"You haven't seen anything yet."

The house was quiet as they walked through the kitchen. "It appears everyone decided to sleep in today," Dar said, opening the door to the hallway.

"Lucky them." Etain walked through and waited for him.

"The morning is the best part of the day, my love."

"For sleeping." She frowned and linked her arm with his. "I think I could sleep for a week."

"Soon, you can sleep as long as you wish."

"I doubt it. Let's face it, Dar. Our lives will never be the same once the babies are born."

He stopped and lifted her chin, looking her in the eyes. "It will be better, *a chuisle*. I'll be there every step of the way."

She gave him a nervous smile. "I know, and it will be wonderful, but it's still daunting. I kinda wish we could take Spirit with us."

He gave her a light kiss. "Like scores of other parents who came before us, we will manage."

"Oh, that reminds me. We need to discuss names."

"Fric and Frac? Mutt and Jeff?" he laughed, guiding her toward the stairs.

"Ha-ha, funny man," she pouted. "It's very important to choose the right names for our children, Dar."

"Aye, love. I am aware."

"Shall our son be a Junior?"

"Definitely not. We've had enough DarMidirets in our family. I've always liked the name Harley."

She gave him a dry look. "Hardly."

He shrugged. "Had to start somewhere. What was your father's name?"

"David James," she said. "Your mother's name was Emalyn, wasn't it?"

"Aye. How do you know?"

"The faeries."

He wasn't surprised by the admission. He knew how the ladies loved to talk.

"Would you mind if our daughter carried her name?"

His heart swelled, proud to have this woman as his wife. "My mother would be very touched to know her granddaughter was named for her."

She touched his arm. "It would help me feel more connected to your family."

"What was your mother's name?"

She placed a foot on the first step. "Aurelia."

"A beautiful name, as well. Are you sure you don't want to use it?"

Etain leaned back against the stair post, a thoughtful expression on her face. "Emalyn Aurelia VonNeshta… How does that sound?"

"Emalyn Aurelia VonNeshta. I like it. It has a regal sound to it."

"I like it, too."

They continued up the stairs toward Spirit's room. "Talk about our son's name tonight?"

"I look forward to it." He wrapped her in a warm embrace. "Our son. I never thought anything this wonderful would happen for me again. Thank you, milady."

She snaked her arms around his neck. "All I did was fall in love with a handsome warrior with a most endearing grin."

"Ah, so that's it. All this time," he looked down, "I thought it was another endearing quality of mine."

"You rogue," she laughed, following his gaze. "It was definitely the smile. At first."

"I love a lusty wee wench, especially when she's mine." He leaned down and shared a passionate kiss.

"Forever and a day, my love," she whispered.

The door suddenly opened. "I'm pleased to remind you there are children on the other side of this door. If you aren't going to get a room, please take it to a different door." Spirit laughed at the shocked expressions on their faces.

"I'm sorry, Spirit," Etain said, blushing. "I guess we got a little carried away. Did we wake you?"

There was a sparkle in her eyes. "Sleeping late is not an option when you have children. You'll learn that soon enough. Is there something you needed, or was this a random tête-à-tête?"

"Well, it's been decreed that I shall not go anywhere alone, so my jail-"

Dar interrupted, a flush in his own cheeks. "Due to extenuating circumstances, my lady will have an escort wherever she goes until we leave for home."

Spirit's brows knitted together. "What circumstances?"

Etain rolled her eyes. "I'll tell you in a minute." She turned to Dar. "I know you need to get to the forge, but if Spirit and the children go with me, am I allowed to visit my brother? Will you please call off your guards?"

He considered her request for a long moment, looked at Spirit, then Etain. "With the Blades in the room and Spirit in attendance, it should be fine. But don't stay too long."

"Thank you, my sweet." She gave him another kiss and a hug.

"I'll stop by his room before I head to the forge. See you at breakfast?"

Etain batted her eyelashes. "Why, Lord VonNeshta, I'm mighty sure you will." The women's laughter followed him down the hall.

"Lass, you bedevil the poor man," Spirit said, opening the door so Etain could step inside.

"Well, he bedevils the hell out of me, too."

The children rushed up, greeting their Auntie 'Tain, each one vying for her attention.

"Hey, y'all. How are you?"

Tegan stomped her little feet, her hands in the air. "'Tain! 'Tain! Pick up me!"

Etain laughed, scooping the small girl into her arms.

Molly tugged on her dress. "Auntie 'Tain, I saw you at the fires. You were so pretty."

"Thank you, Molly. You were very pretty, too." She turned to the little girl in her arms. "So were you, Ms. Tegan."

Both girls giggled. Molly thanked her, but Tegan gave her a cheesy grin.

"Mama made us come up here to eat," added Dylan, a frown on his little face.

"Dyls, it woulda been boring down there anyways," said Seth. "Nothing but grown up stuff."

"Still, I wanted to sit with Uncle Dar."

Etain smiled. "Believe me, Dylan, you didn't miss a thing."

Spirit placed her hands on her hips. "Well, there was one thing."

"What, Mama?" Molly asked.

Dylan and Seth joined in. "Yeah, Mama. What? What did we miss?"

Etain gave Spirit a confused look, clueless to what she referred to. "Please, do tell, *Mama*." Tegan clapped her hands, laughing at Auntie 'Tain's silliness.

Spirit cleared her throat, eyeing Etain's belly. "Actually, it's more like two things."

"Oh, gosh! Aye!" She gave the kids a sheepish grin. "Me and Dar are going to have twins."

The kids went quiet and looked at each other. Tegan's brows came together as she took Etain's face into her hands. "'Tain, what twins?"

"Twin what?" echoed Dylan and Seth.

Molly scratched her head, trying to sort it out.

Etain laughed again. "Babies! We're going to have a boy and a girl."

Molly's eyes widened and a huge smile lit her face. "Babies!"

Tegan's small mouth rounded into an "o", her eyes as big as her sister's. "Babies?"

Seth and Dylan were crestfallen. "Yuck. You can't even play with 'em," Seth said.

"You will, in time." Etain smiled.

"No way. I don't even like babies. All they do is cry and poop." Seth walked across the room and threw himself into a chair. "I'm not babysitting, either, so don't ever ask me."

Dylan watched his brother, then looked at Etain, crossing his arms over his chest. "Me, either." He followed in his brother's footsteps and fell into the other chair, a pout on his face.

Molly rolled her eyes. "Boys. I'll babysit for you Auntie 'Tain."

"Me, too. I big girl," said Tegan. "I wike babies."

Etain hugged her tightly. "Aye, you are a big girl. Thank you, Molly. I'm sure I'll be asking for help before you know it." Her gaze came back to Spirit. "In the meantime, would you mind going with me to visit Robert?"

She looked around at the children. "I don't mind going, but let me get one of the boys to take this group. They might make things worse."

"Okay. I don't see how, but it's up to you."

"Give me a minute to hunt down Wolfe and Elfin. The kids love 'em."

On their way to Robert's room, Spirit asked, "Tell me why you're having to ask to visit your own brother."

"Apparently, my brother fell down the stairs while we were gone. No one knows why he was out of bed or where he was going. He was found sprawled on the floor at the bottom of the stairs."

"Crikey! How is he?"

"Well, he seemed to be fine, except for some bruising."

Spirit stopped walking. "What does that have to do with-"

"It's not what you'd expect." Etain detailed the styling of the bruises and the burns. She hoped it would be enough intrigue to keep Spirit from asking more about why she had to have an escort.

"Burns? For fuck's sake, how did that happen?"

"Good question." They continued down the hall. "If I hadn't seen it for myself, I'd have called Dar a liar. Then there's the birthmark below his navel."

"Who has a birthmark?"

"My brother."

Spirit gave her a confused look. "Is it important?"

Etain ran a hand through her hair. "I'm not sure. Dar says it looks exactly like one Midir had."

"Are you sure it's a birthmark? Maybe it's a scar."

Coming to Robert's door, they gained easy entry and found him sitting on the side of the bed in the middle of a catlike stretch. Etain did her best not to sound anxious. "Robert? Are you sure you should be doing that?"

He smiled, motioning her to come in. "Etain! I feel good. A little weak, but much better. Hello, Spirit."

Coming closer, Spirit peered over his shoulder, noting the faint scars on his back. "Hmm…" She stood back, taking his face in her hands. "I see the nose is healed, too. The bruises are almost gone."

"Really?"

"You stay there," Etain said when he started to stand. She dashed into the adjacent bathroom. "There should be a hand mirror in here somewhere."

She returned shortly and handed it to him. He inspected his nose from every angle. "You can't even tell it was broken."

"Aye," Spirit said, giving Etain a suspicious look. "Amazing, isn't it?" She then scrunched up her nose. "Would you like us to send someone to help you bathe?"

He lowered the mirror, a puzzled look on his face, then realized why she looked at him the way she did. He sniffed himself. "I guess I *do* need a bath. I can handle that by myself. How is everyone else?"

Etain and Spirit pulled up a couple chairs. "Everyone is good. I'm sorry you weren't well enough to attend the ceremony the other night. It was really nice."

"I doubt I was missed." He turned to Spirit. "Please accept my condolences for your loss. I didn't have the chance to get to know your husband, but everyone speaks highly of him."

"Thank you," she whispered.

Eyeing the guards in the room, he leaned toward Etain. "What's with all the heat? Are we afraid there might be another attack?"

It wasn't a conversation she was prepared to have. "You can't be too careful. It's merely a precaution. We're all on alert."

"What else's been going on?"

"We're making plans to return to *Sólskin*, Dar's home…I mean, our home. I hope you'll consider coming with us."

"Gotta get the nursery ready, huh?"

Etain hesitated. Robert wasn't at the dinner the other night, and she hadn't said anything to him since she'd found out she was pregnant.

"Oh, aye," Spirit said, filling the awkward silence. "The lass has a lot to do to get ready." Etain gave her a strange look.

Robert smiled. "Such great news! Are you hoping for a girl or a boy?"

Etain suddenly stood. "We should let you get that bath. Are you sure you can handle it by yourself?"

"Very sure." He glanced at Spirit, then Etain. "Shall we talk later?"

"Of course." With that, she and Spirit left.

In the hallway, Spirit pulled her past several doors before she spoke. "Lass, if he knows you're pregnant, he should know you're having twins."

"I don't know how he knows anything, Spirit. I haven't told him and doubt anyone else has. Maybe he overheard a random conversation?"

"Or maybe he's been talking to someone he shouldn't."

She couldn't possibly know about Raum. "Like who?"

Spirit shrugged. "It's been different around here since we've come back from Nunnehi. I'm sorry to say, Etain, but I don't get a good feeling from the lad. You need to let Dar know."

"I'm sure it's just a misunderstanding."

Spirit took hold of her arm. "Etain, tell Dar. He must know."

"Okay! I'll tell him." She pulled away. *Like Robert doesn't have enough against him already*. "Now, would you like to go with me to see Taurnil?"

"I'll walk you there, but I should get back to the kiddies. And I have another clan meeting today."

"You aren't avoiding him, are you?"

Spirit tried to laugh it off but wouldn't look her in the eyes. "Where do you get these ideas? Why would I do that?"

"Because he saw what happened to Inferno." She touched her on the shoulder. "Don't you want to know?"

Spirit shrugged off her hand and stepped back. "I know enough. I helped prepare his body. I saw what the bastard did to him."

"I didn't mean to push. I'm sorry."

Her shoulders slumped as she closed and opened her eyes. "You have nothing to be sorry for, lass. Me nerves are just that frazzled."

"Well, maybe you and the kids should get away." Etain linked arms with her and steered her down the hall. "Have y'all decided what to do about the next chieftain?"

"I'd rather not say just yet."

"It must be hard. I'm sorry you're having to deal with that on top of everything else."

"It only serves to make me stronger. Aye?" Coming to Taurnil's door, the women hugged. "I'll leave you here."

"See you later." She watched her friend walk away, then knocked on the door. Not hearing a response, she knocked again. Several minutes passed before the door opened. Taurnil leaned against it, pale and wobbly.

"T, what are you doing out of bed?" She placed his arm around her shoulders as she held him by his waist, turning him toward the bed. "You're not ready for this."

With a weak smile, he leaned heavily on her. "I have to start sometime, E."

"Not by yourself. You've been through a lot. It'll take time to get your strength back."

"Then help me. The others ignore my requests."

"Requests for what?"

"If I can't stand on my own two feet at my induction and wield my own sword, I won't go through with it." With her assistance, he sat down on the edge of the bed, then grabbed her by her arms. "I mean it, E. I won't be humiliated."

"T, this is temporary. Everyone knows the fight you've been through. You have no reason to feel humiliated."

"Are you going to help me or not?"

She rolled her eyes. "You are as mule-headed as your cousin."

"Which one?" A grin came to his lips. "I'll take that as a yes."

Sitting next to the Cheshire cat, she took his hand in hers. "I suppose it is; otherwise you'll end up hurting yourself and make me feel responsible for it."

"Guilt is a great motivator."

"Why do I put up with you?" she laughed, punching his arm lightly.

"Watch it. I'm still very tender," he chuckled, but his expression turned serious. "How is Spirit? I thought I heard her voice earlier."

"She had to get back to the kids." She couldn't tell him the truth. "She tries to stay busy, but I know she's struggling." Etain gave the young elf a long look. "I've been thinking on what you said about Inferno."

His brows knitted together. "What is that?"

"How he was distracted by something in the room."

"Oh, aye. It's beyond me."

She squeezed his hand, mostly as a way to bolster her courage to say the words. "I know what it was."

"How could you know? You weren't in any-"

"When we went back - me, Freeblood, and the others - for the blood to save you..." Her eyes came up to meet his, "the castle wasn't happy about the intrusion. It threw everything it had at us…at me."

"E…" His hand gripped hers. "What happened?"

"Do you remember the weapons displayed on the walls?"

"Aye. They were everywhere."

"The demon was gone, but his castle had a mind of its own. I don't understand it…" She ran a hand through her hair. "It sounds insane, but that place was alive. Every one of those weapons came at us."

"I'm so sorry, E. You shouldn't have-"

"Do you remember meeting Felix?"

He looked perplexed. "Felix?"

"Inferno's wolfhound. He was with Zorn that night we went to Laugharne, after the battle."

"Vaguely. There was a lot to take in."

"He had another wolfhound. Her name was Ruby…because of her red fur." Tears welled up in her eyes. "Felix and Ruby, along with Zorn, disappeared the night of our wedding. They were missing for several days. Eventually, Zorn and Felix returned, both bloody and torn up. Ruby never came back." She felt responsible for what happened and had to look away, afraid of what she might see in his golden eyes. "I don't know that Zorn's shared his experience with anyone."

Taurnil squeezed her hand again. "E, look at me."

She didn't want to, but she did.

"What does that have to do with Inferno?"

"At the blood castle, it was Ruby's head that led the snake of weapons. That's what he saw that day. Ruby's head mounted on the wall."

"By the stars!" His eyes widened and he pulled her to him, holding her as she cried. "I'm so sorry. If only I hadn't been so stupid, acting like an idiot, thinking I could save the day."

"Not you." She pulled away. "Me. You and Linq were right. I was too focused on the godforsaken demon. I let them corral me in that room, cut me off from you and Freeblood. It was me."

Taurnil pushed her hair back from her face. "I didn't get the chance to know Inferno very well, but from what I experienced in my short time with him, the last thing he'd want is for you to blame yourself. We have to learn from this and move ahead. We'll get this demon."

"I hope so." She wiped the tears from her cheeks. "Let me wash my face and we'll get to work." As she walked into the bathroom, she asked, "Before we start, where is Swee? More importantly, where is your mother?"

He raised his voice to be heard over the running water. "Swee is working with Chelri to learn as much as she can while he's here. My mother left for town yesterday and hasn't returned. Since my recovery, she's been preoccupied with going home…me in tow."

Etain came back into the room, dabbing her face with a towel. "Sounds like you're not in agreement with her."

"Absolutely not. I've told Dar I want to go with you. I have more I want to learn from him."

"Well then…," she said resolutely, "we don't have much time before the ceremony. Let's get started. Are you ready?"

"Ready, Commandant. I'm all yours."

"We'll see how you feel about that in a couple hours." She grunted as she helped him stand.

They spent the next few hours working on his walk. This being his first day of exercise, Etain allowed him frequent breaks, always encouraging him to keep working the muscles in his legs, slowly building his strength.

By late afternoon, he was completely exhausted, his body drenched in sweat. Despite his protests, Etain ended the session. "That's enough for today, T. You sit down and let me run you a bath. Do you think you can walk that far after all this?"

He grimaced as he sat on the edge of the bed. "Aye, I think so. Would you pour me a glass of water first?" Doing as he asked, she handed him a full glass to drink while she tended to his bath.

When she returned, she escorted him into the bathroom. "Do you need help getting into the tub?"

He blushed brightly. "No, I'll be fine. Just give me a minute."

She turned her back until he was safely ensconced in the warm water. His modesty intact, she kneeled at his side and wet a washcloth, drizzling water over his broad shoulders. He pulled his legs in and rested his head on his knees. "Thank you, E."

"Aww…" She reached for the soap, lathering it into the cloth. "You looked so pathetic. How could I not help?"

His head snapped up. The grin on her face made him laugh. "Heartless, picking on a defenseless elf."

"When have you ever been defenseless?"

They laughed together.

He rested his head on his knees again. "I would help you, too," he whispered.

"I know." She gently washed his back. "I asked Spirit if she wanted to talk to you…about what happened to Inferno."

"Since she didn't come in with you, I'd say she's not ready."

"She knows what happened to him." Taurnil lifted his head. "The wizards invited her to help with preparing him for the ceremony."

He nodded and lowered his legs into the water. "That must've been hard."

"She went with us to the blood castle, too."

Taurnil raised his brows. "She did?"

"Oh, aye. She was impressive, too. A woman in charge of herself, and her destiny. After that, I thought she'd want to know."

"Grief is a strange thing, E."

She stopped and looked him in the eye. "You said you'd not lost anyone close to you."

An echo of a smile lifted a corner of his mouth, then disappeared. "Have you ever met my father?"

Of course, he had a father…somewhere. She opened her mouth, but had no words to express her embarrassment or explain her thoughtlessness. "I'm a self-absorbed idiot. T, I'm-"

"It's all right, E. My mother has such a strong presence, she leaves no room for another parent. I imagine it comes from losing him when I was small."

"Do you remember anything about him?"

"Not really. There are times, though, when I feel something here…" He touched his chest over his heart, "and here…" Then his head. "A warm certainty that tells me I've done well. I never met him, but I know he loved me."

"How did you lose him?"

"War...with the *Bok*."

She raised both brows at the news. "Really?"

"Aye. They've been around for a very long time."

"My dad used to tell me stories about them and the creation of the Alamir, but he never mentioned how long ago it was."

"Grief has been in my life since I can remember."

"I'm sorry, T.

"Don't be. It's just how life is sometimes. Now, get out of here so I can finish my bath."

Etain rinsed out the cloth, then handed it and the soap to him. "I'll wait in the other room until you're done. Just holler when you're ready and I'll come get you."

Standing outside the door, she heard the water splash as he washed.

"E," he called out. "Tell me of your home. Is it a big place? A castle like this?"

She closed her eyes and envisioned her new home, trying to remember as much as she could. "Let's see. It's not a castle. More of a large manor house built of pure white stone."

"All white? Sounds boring."

She smirked, hearing the smile in his voice. "Do you find Nunnehi boring with all its white?"

His silence told her he was considering her question. "Well, no. Okay, so it's not boring. What else?"

"During the day, the sun gleams off its surface and changes the color of the stone. In the mornings, it can look pink or orange, turning white at mid-day. In the evenings, it glows gold. It's so beautiful. Dar has a rose garden, too. So many different colors. He loves working in it."

He was quiet for a moment. "What do you love doing, E?"

The question took her by surprise. "Uh, well… I've never thought about it."

Taurnil suddenly appeared, wrapped in a deep blue robe, looking refreshed. "Maybe it's time you did."

"Dar wants to create a Black Blade Academy. I can teach the sword."

He laughed. "Between feedings and diaper changes?"

She took his arm and helped him to the bed. "That won't last forever. I'm sure I'll come up with something."

His expression turned serious. "Do something for you, E. Don't lose yourself in Dar or your children." He touched her arm. "Always remember who *you* are and be her."

She held his gaze. "I will."

Resting back into the pillows, he patted the side of the bed. "Sit with me a bit longer and tell me more of your beautiful home."

"Only for a bit. You need to rest."

"But you'll be back tomorrow, right?"

Sitting beside him, she nodded. "Of course. I told you I would help. But we need to devise a plan to keep everyone out of our business while we work."

"That's easy," he said. "I must have my afternoon rest and will insist on perfect silence, which means no one else in the room. I'm sure Swee will take advantage of the time to study, and Mother, well… She'll occupy her time with preparing for my triumphant trip home."

"She'll be so disappointed that you're not going with her."

"Queen Alatariel will be fine. I believe I can explain it in such a way that she'll see my point."

"Bloody sure of yourself."

A soft knock interrupted their conversation and the door slowly opened. Swee peeked in. "Etain, there you are."

"Were you looking for me?"

She came into the room, closing the door. "I ran into Dar earlier. I thought you were with Spirit."

"Well, I was, but she had clan stuff to do, so I thought I'd visit T for a while."

"I didn't mean to interrupt," Swee said. "I can come back later."

"Don't be silly. Join us. We were conspiring on how to keep T here when his mother returns to Nunnehi."

Swee laughed. "There's a challenge."

Without a knock, the door suddenly opened and the High Lord entered. "Etain…" He sounded quite relieved, then pulled up short, realizing she wasn't alone. "I've… Swee… Taurnil…"

Taurnil turned the awkward moment around. "Dar! How good of you to come by."

Dar eyed the three as he walked toward Etain. "I've come to escort my wife to dinner."

Taurnil stole a look at the clock on the wall. "I didn't realize it was so late."

Dar placed an arm around her waist. "You didn't show for breakfast and no one remembers seeing you at lunch."

Swee added her opinion. "Etain, it's hard enough having one baby, but with two…" She reached out, taking one of her hands. "They'll get whatever they need from you to the point where it could make you sick. You have to eat, and eat healthy, to stay strong."

Etain didn't see Dar's smile of thanks. "You're right. I'll try to do better." She looked up at her husband, who now wore a stern expression. "It's not on purpose. I get busy and forget."

Swee laughed. "I don't think that'll last much longer. After hearing how quickly Krymerian babies develop, it won't be long before you'll be eating all the time."

Etain frowned. "Looks like I'm gonna need a few more dresses. Big ones."

16

ESCORT SERVICE

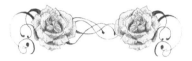

The next day, Dar started with the same morning routine, waking Etain early, but he made sure they shared a light breakfast before he escorted her to her brother's room. There, she met her new escorts, two Black Blades assigned specifically to her. Leaving her with a kiss and whispered endearments to the babes, Dar charged her with making sure she ate during the day, then left for the forge.

Etain looked at her Blades. "Okay, gentlemen. Looks like we're stuck with each other until we leave this place, so how about we drop the formalities and get on a first-name basis?"

"We cannot do that, High Lady. It would be disrespectful," one Blade said.

"As the High Lady, I'm giving you permission to call me by my name."

"It is not allowed, milady," the other explained.

She looked from one to the other. "Hmm… Well… Am I allowed to address you by your names?"

"If you wish, milady."

Happy to know she wasn't required to act like a high and mighty aristocrat, she smiled. "Excellent." She turned to the Blade to her right. "What is your name, sir, and how long have you been a Blade?"

With a courtly bow, he introduced himself. "Eol Tulcakelume, at your service, milady. I have been a Black Blade for just a short time, but I would say nigh on fifty years."

"So nice to meet you, Eol. Fifty years?" She grinned at her own naiveté. Neither elf appeared to be any older than Dar. "I forget that time is different for elves."

She turned to the other Blade, who also bowed. "Milady, I am Galdor Helyanwe and have been in the Black Blades almost as long as Eol."

"Very nice to meet you, Galdor. Have you gentlemen had breakfast?"

"Yes, milady," they said at the same time. Galdor cleared his throat. "We rise early, High Lady."

"It seems to be a habit around here," she said. "Well then, you're all set. Excuse me while I visit with my brother."

Completing a full restoration of a black blade, Dar moved to the sharpening stone. Sparks flew as he applied the metal to the spinning stone, drawing it slowly down one side, then the other. A prickling of the hairs on the back of his neck made him stop. In the next instant, a hand slammed an object on the table next to him.

"A black blade for a Black Blade."

Seeing a dark metal block, he realized it was Túrë. "It's about time, man." He turned his head. "What took you so-" He stopped mid-sentence, taking in the elf's disheveled appearance. "*Tartarus*! What in the hell happened to you?"

Covered in mud and sporting multiple scratches, Túrë gave him a weary look as he leaned against a post. "Took a little more work than I expected. Everything has shifted there."

Dar turned off the sharpening wheel and set down the sword. "Shifted? Not too much I hope."

"About six feet. Not too bad, but still exhausting."

"Let's get you inside and cleaned up. Some of Alaster's home cooking will make you feel better." Dar draped an arm over his shoulder as one of the younger Black Blades dashed into the forge.

"High Lord," he said, breathless. "You must come at once, milord." Doing a hasty salute, he continued. "It's the High Lady, sir."

"What is it, Blade?"

"She's drawn her dagger against the commander and is threatening to, well…" He stumbled over his words as a bright blush tinged his cheeks.

"I see…" Dar turned to Túrë. "Looks like you're on your own, my friend."

"No worries, High Lord," Túrë said. "It sounds important."

The Blade led the way up the stairs and straight to Robert's room. Linq was at the door, shaking his head. "Good. He found you."

"Aye." Dar had to work his way through a small group at the door. He found Etain standing beside the bed, brandishing her dagger, eyes aflame and body aglow.

"Stay back, Dar," she warned. "I meant what I said. No one will come near my brother until I say."

He leaned to the side and looked around Etain. Robert was sitting up in the bed. He looked pale but well enough. Dar's gaze met hers. "What's going on here?"

Her eyes darted between Dar and the others. "He's too weak for their interrogations right now, Dar. He needs to get well first."

"High Lord, sir," Commander Crom blustered. "He's a suspected traitor and should be treated as such."

Etain turned on the commander. "He is a guest of this house, Crom. I suggest you keep your opinions to yourself."

"May I remind you, milady, he has been involved in suspicious happenings of late and cannot be trusted."

Her eyes narrowed as she prepared another rebuttal, but Dar

interceded. "I'm sure all this yelling isn't doing him, or you, any good." As he stepped toward her, she turned her blade on him.

"I will not be challenged in this."

"Etain," Robert said from behind her, his voice weak. "Please stop."

"I will not," she said to him without looking back. "Everyone here is so quick to accuse, just because you're a stranger and know nothing of our ways." Her last words were directed at the commander. "They will keep their distance until *I* say you're ready, then they can speak with you in a civilized manner."

"Etain," Dar said softly. "Please, calm down."

"No," she snarled. "How can you condone this…this mob? If it were me, would you let them treat me this way?"

He turned to the small group. "Commander, clear the room."

Crom glared at Etain, gave the High Lord a salute, then turned and waved toward the door. "Blades, ladies and gentlemen…"

Dar closed the door after the last person stepped out and returned to Etain, extending his hand. She held his gaze, unsure whether to submit or resist. He waited. In the end, she handed over the dagger and collapsed onto the bed next to Robert.

She blew out a breath. "I won't let them bully him."

"But you know there have been a few strange occurrences of late."

"You can't possibly blame him for all of them."

"Etain, we have enough to warrant an investigation." He crouched in front of her. "Have you considered that their questioning could prove his innocence?"

She leaned toward him. "I'm scared, Dar. I've seen what a group like that can do…both good and bad."

"As have I, my sweet," he said, taking her hands. "I'll make sure it's fair."

"I know you have your doubts, but if you say it, I know it will be."

"It's nice to know where I stand with you two," Robert said.

Etain turned. "You need to understand what you're up against. It won't be easy."

He touched her arm. "With you as my champion, how can I lose?"

"She is an ally to be reckoned with." Dar stood and placed a kiss on her head. "I have to get back to the forge."

She squeezed his hand. "I'm gonna stay here a little longer. Can I have my dagger back?"

His gaze moved to Robert, then back to Etain. "It's in need of sharpening. I'll give it to you tonight," he said, sliding it into his belt. At the bland look on her face, he reached into his boot. "Here…" He pulled his own dagger free and handed it to her. "You can have mine until then."

She gave him a thankful smile and accepted the blade. "When you go down, would you ask Alaster to prepare some soup for Robert?"

"As you wish, milady." Dar looked over her shoulder. "Rest well, Robert."

"Thank you, Dar."

The guards resumed their positions as Dar left the room. He stopped in the kitchen and asked Alaster to send a tray, adding a little extra for Etain, then headed to the forge, anxious to get back to his new creation. Linq showed up not long after.

"How can you be so relaxed?"

Bent over a makeshift desk, he added a few strokes to a drawing of a blade. "Am I?"

Linq stared at him. "You're not?"

"I am…to a degree."

"My gut tells me trouble's brewing. I have every faith in the Black Blades, but if he pulls something, are they going to get to Etain in time?"

Dar remained focused on his plans. "I wouldn't worry too much about Etain."

Linq cocked a brow. "Why is that?"

"I took her dagger…for sharpening." He looked at his friend, a grin on his face. "I gave her mine."

"Hmph. There's something you aren't telling me."

"Etain's unmatched with a small blade, but in case her brother proves more capable, the spell will finish whatever he starts."

"Spell?"

Dar's grin grew bigger. "Oh, aye. I cast it before giving it to her."

Linq laughed. "I don't know why I ever worry about you and yours."

"Me, either, but don't stop…just in case."

The remainder of the day passed much like the day before. After her visit with her brother, Etain helped Taurnil with his exercises. This time, she brought a pair of Dar's black jeans and a white t-shirt.

"I don't know how well these'll fit, but I think you'll find them more comfortable than your regular clothes."

Taurnil stared at the clothing. "I've never seen such things."

Etain chuckled. "These are jeans." She held them by the waistband, letting them unfold. "Trousers, if you will. And this…" In the other hand, she held up the shirt, "is a t-shirt. Dar has become quite fond of them."

"Shall we give them a test run?" Taurnil grabbed them and disappeared into the en suite. In a few minutes, he stepped out. "How do I look?"

"Not bad, except the shirt's backwards. The v part of the neckline goes in the front."

He looked down, then pulled his arms into the shirt and twisted it around. "Ah…" He shot her a grin. "The elusive v." Pushing his arms through the armholes, he smoothed the fabric over his torso. "Better?"

She looked him up and down. "They suit you, T. A little big, but not bad."

"Do I look like Dar?"

"Let's not get crazy," she laughed. "What do you think?"

He rolled his shoulders and looked down his frame. "They might work. Let's try them out."

They sparred for the rest of the morning. Etain pushed him harder than the day before and was impressed by his resilience. Come mid-day, the young prince made sure a healthy lunch was provided, refusing to return to his lessons until she'd eaten a fair share of the spread.

As the day wore on, Alatariel and her entourage, ladened with packages, returned to the castle. She detoured by Taurnil's room, but sent her handmaidens on to hers to make preparations. She found him in high spirits and stayed only a moment.

"Taurnil. What is this you're wearing?" She smirked, waggling a finger at his attire.

"They are called jeans and t-shirt, Mother. It seems to be the latest thing."

Alatariel laughed. "Oh, son, you are a comic. Please do not wear such things in public." She kissed him on the cheek, gave Etain a hug, and hurried to the door. "I promise I'll be back tomorrow and we can have a nice long visit."

Once she was gone, Etain turned to Taurnil, giving him the stink eye. "Surely you do *not* intend to embarrass the royal family-"

"The look on her face!" He laughed. "People think being the prince is a piece of cake, but let me tell you... By the stars, E."

"So, no jeans or t-shirts in your future?"

"What kind of ruler would I be if I did that?" He feigned a serious face. "Please tell me they come in other colors. I'll send my valet out tomorrow to buy one of each!" Etain snorted a laugh, which made them both laugh all the harder. "You think Chelri has something to ward off the evil eye of a mother?"

Etain laughed, placing a hand on her belly. "If he does, don't let these two hear it. It seems to be a very useful tool."

Not long after, Swee showed up with a dinner tray for herself and Taurnil but invited Etain to stay. "No. I'll leave you two alone. Have a good night, and I'll see you tomorrow." Hugging each of them in turn, she left with her escort, stopping to check on Robert again. She found him fast asleep, so went in search of her husband, chatting with Eol and Galdor along the way.

Dar smiled, seeing her beautiful face at the door of the forge. Assured of her safety, the Blades left the High Lady in her husband's capable hands.

"Are y'all near a stopping point?" Etain asked. "Supper should be ready soon."

Covered with sweat and soot, Dar quenched the emerging blade in a vat of water, cooling the surface quickly. "Aye. I think we've done enough today." He looked over his shoulder. "What say you, Linq? Ready to shut it down?"

"I believe I am. I may forego dinner and go straight to bed. This day has taken its toll on me, I'm afraid." He set down his work and turned off the sharpening stone.

"Well, make sure you grab something on your way," Etain said. "You'll feel better for it."

"I shall, milady." Linq bowed his head as he put away the blades. "Will you be joining the others in the dining hall?"

Closing the forge, Dar caught Etain's eye and winked. "I think I'll bypass the communal dinner tonight and spend a private one with my lovely wife."

"I'll see you in the morning then." With a wave, Linq jaunted to the house and disappeared inside.

Etain linked an arm with Dar's. "I've missed you this afternoon."

"I've missed you, as well, my love. Tell me what you've been up to."

"Spreading good cheer mostly. After Robert, I spent the afternoon with T." They walked through the hustle and bustle of the kitchen amidst delectable aromas of pork roast and freshly baked bread. She pulled Dar aside. "Why don't you go on up? I'll fix us something and be right behind you. Is that okay?"

"Just don't take too long." Giving her a kiss, his eyes darted around the room. With so many of Alaster's crew in the kitchen, he felt confident she would be safe and left her in the chaos.

Etain stepped out of the way of an oncoming tray of fresh vegetables, followed by one heaped with several loaves of bread hot from the oven. The movement of the kitchen staff reminded her of a symphony with Alaster as the conductor, pointing here and there, instructing without a single word, setting in motion a most unusual opus of cooks stirring pots, assistants filling platters, and servers delivering trays to the diners next door. In the midst of it all, Alaster noticed Etain pressed against the wall, doing her best to stay out of the way.

Putting aside his chef duties, he joined her. "Impressive, isn't it?"

"It's awfully busy in here."

His laugh deep, he considered the activity in the kitchen. "Yes, ma'am. Lots of people to feed and keep happy."

"You're doing a grand job, sir."

"What can we do for you, milady?"

"Dar and I would like to-"

"A quiet dinner alone, is it?" She nodded, amazed by his intuitive abilities. "Come over here. We'll get a tray ready in no time." Taking a seat at the island, she watched him in action as he filled a warming platter with pork roast, lightly buttered boiled potatoes, and seared asparagus. He added a fresh loaf of bread and a small crock of homemade butter. All this was then covered by a large silver dome.

"Bessie, please fill a pitcher with ale and grab two mugs." He finished off the tray with dishes, silver, napkins, and two pieces of apple pie for dessert.

Etain's eyes widened. "Heavens, Alaster. We'll never eat all that."

"I've seen that man eat," he laughed. "As hard as he's been working these past two days, I seriously doubt there'll be much of anything left after he's done."

She laughed in return. "If you say so."

"You grab that pitcher and the mugs. I'll take the tray up for you." Lifting it, he turned toward the door.

"You are too kind, sir."

"From your lips to the gods' ears." He walked out, Etain behind him.

Upstairs, she stepped in first to make sure Dar wasn't taken by surprise but found the room empty. "I believe he's in the shower. Come on in."

He carried the tray to the small table between the chairs in front of the fireplace and turned to survey the room. "I'll be right back."

"Okay…"

Within minutes, he returned, toting a proper table with fold-down sides, followed by Bessie with a red tablecloth, two silver candlesticks, candles, and a lighter.

"Really, Alaster…"

"Think nothing of it, milady. You can't possibly eat from this… stool." He set up the table and unfolded the tablecloth with a quick flick of his wrists. It billowed out like a great red cloud, floating down over the table. Bessie placed vanilla-scented candles in the candlesticks, then set the dishes and silver while Alaster retrieved the pitcher and mugs from Etain.

With the candles lit, they stood back to admire their work. As his last act, Alaster stacked logs in the fireplace and lit a cozy fire. "Magnifique."

"You think of everything. Thank you."

"Enjoy, milady."

She closed the door behind them and turned the lock. After dimming the lights, she sat in one of the chairs to enjoy the romantic scene before Dar returned and consumed all her attention. The flickering light against the silver cast reflections across the room. Hypnotized by the beauty of the fire, her thoughts went to Taurnil and his determination to live a simpler life for a time, which led to her brother. The work she was doing with T would need to be applied to Robert, as well. Those thoughts brought her around to the friction between him and Dar.

Proving a distasteful course, she shifted to more pleasant avenues. Life with Dar and their children, the plans it would entail, so much work to get done before they arrived, a boy's name…

Jarred out of her reverie, she realized Dar still hadn't made an appearance. She walked to the bathroom and pushed the door open.

"Dar, are you okay?" His form was merely a dark shadow in the steam-filled room.

"Mmm…," he groaned. "Hot water. It's liquid magic."

She stripped off her dress and opened the shower door. "Hard work, huh?"

He grunted. "Aye. Huh." He turned his head and looked over his arm resting on the wall.

"Give me the soap and don't move." Rubbing it between her hands, she applied the thick lather across his shoulders and over his arms, then set the soap aside. She kneaded into the tight muscles, glad to see his back was nearly healed, although there would be scars where the worst wounds had been. She moved down his back to his buttocks and down each leg. Once done, she instructed him to turn around and did the same up his front. To finish off the special treatment, she shampooed his hair, circling her fingers into his scalp, which elicited a deep sigh of approval. As she reached up to rinse out the soap, Dar wrapped his arms around her. "Your turn."

She wiggled in his grasp to get free. "Dinner awaits, my sweet."

"You keep wiggling like that and we'll never get out of the shower."

"I thought you were exhausted."

"You could make a dead man come to life, *a chuisle*." He kissed her. "I have spent all afternoon trying not to think about you waving that dagger, the flash in your eyes and hair flying. Can't tell you how thankful I was today for the leather apron I wear in the forge." He gave her his signature grin. "You set me on fire. Give me another kiss."

Her arms slid around his neck while his hands traveled along her back. He cupped her buttocks and lifted her up. "Oh," he said, his voice somewhat strained. "It seems you've taken me up on my advice."

"What advice?"

He breathed out. "To eat."

Settling onto his hips as she took him inside her, she quipped, "Don't blame me, mister." Their bodies moved in concert. "They're *your* children."

Not long after, wrapped in lush terrycloth robes, the couple sat down to their intimate dinner by the fire. Etain dished out the delicacies as Dar poured the ale, commenting on the perfection of the evening – the food, the setting, his dinner companion. He raised his mug to his beautiful wife.

"To say I love you is not easy for me.
　You have my heart, my soul,
　I hope you can see.
　You are always on my mind.
　I am immersed in your love.
　Our hearts, our souls are forever intertwined.
　You are the exceptional woman I have searched for all my life.
　You…are the one…which is why I made you my wife."

He extended a hand across the table, taking hers. "I came across the poem some time ago and memorized the words, waiting for the right moment."

"My heart is yours, completely. I hope you know that." She tapped his mug with her own and drank to the toast.

He released her hand and sat back in his chair. "You say you visited with Taurnil today?"

"I did."

"All afternoon?" he asked, cutting into his pork.

"Aye. We're getting him ready for his induction."

He raised a brow. "What exactly does that entail?"

Watching him eat, she described the work they'd accomplished in a short time. "He's improved remarkably."

"Of course. He *is* my cousin."

Rolling her eyes, she laughed. "Of course." She relaxed back into her chair. "Tell me about the sword you're making for him."

"I thought a katana would be appropriate - sleek, slim, and elegant. Naturally, it will have the signature black blade, but I'm thinking of carving the hilt from jade. What do you think?"

"Sounds beautiful, but won't that take too long?"

"Probably add a day or so. I'm almost done with the blade." Her eyebrows lifted at this. "After thinking of you all day, I had to get my pent-up energy out somehow. Nonetheless, it will be a powerful sword of the highest quality, I assure you."

"I never doubt you, my love." She gave him a wink. "Oh…" She leaned forward, her expression serious. "Our son needs a name."

"Aye. Anything come to mind?"

She shook her head. "No. I was hoping you had come up with something."

He chuckled. "Well, you didn't like my idea of Harley, so I haven't given it another thought."

"Dar, this is our son. Surely, you can think of another one."

"I'm playing it smart." He tapped the side of his head. "You did a wonderful job with our daughter's name. I have all the faith in the world you'll be just as creative with our son's."

She stood and walked around the table. Sitting in his lap, she snaked her arms around his neck. "You are a rascal, but I love you anyway." The mere touch of their lips ignited the fires that constantly simmered just below the surface. His free hand moved down to loosen the sash of her robe and slipped inside, caressing her warm skin.

"Give me another day to think on it. I promise I'll have some ideas by tomorrow evening," he whispered, his eyes following the trail of his hand. "Right now, I'd rather discuss dessert."

She closed her eyes. "We have apple pie," she whispered, gasping as he rubbed his thumb over the sensitive tip of her breast.

"Later. I have something else in mind." His voice thick, he dipped his head, tasting her sweetness.

"Would you be opposed to having your dessert in bed?" she asked breathlessly.

"As you wish."

He carried her across the room, stood her before him, slowly removed her robe first, then his own, each one dropping to the floor. "Your skin glows in the candlelight." He pushed her hair back over her shoulders. "Sometimes, this feels like a dream. You, here with me." He traced a finger along her jaw. "My wife. Mine."

Her gaze held his. "I have loved you for a very long time. You filled my dreams as a child and have been in my heart since I can remember." She moved closer to him. "You are my dark knight and my angel of light. I can do anything with you by my side. *We* can do anything." Caught in the current pulsing between them, they drew closer to one another, a hair's breadth apart. "I have never loved anyone the way I love you, Dar."

He framed her face with his hands and kissed her gently, then pulled back just enough to look into her eyes. "As I love you, my precious one."

A shy smile lifted the corners of her mouth as her hands covered his. "Kiss me again." Dar consumed her mouth with his, then swept her into his arms and deposited the breathless vixen easily onto the bed.

He lay behind her, molding his body to hers. "If you don't mind, my love, it seems the day has finally caught up to me."

She smiled and glanced over her shoulder. "It's okay. Just don't let me go."

"Never," he whispered and drifted off.

Dar rose early, anxious to get back to work on the blade. Dressed, he leaned over his sleeping wife to wake her, but her peaceful countenance stayed his hand. Instead, he decided to let her sleep, which presented another problem. How could he get her escort here without leaving the room?

"Looks like you'll have to get up, my sweet," he said softly. Just as he reached out to rouse her, there was a knock on the bedroom door.

He breathed a sigh of relief to find Eol and Galdor. "Your timing is perfect, Blades."

Saluting the High Lord, Eol said, "We know you like to start early, milord. Is the High Lady ready to visit with her brother?"

Dar glanced over his shoulder. "No. I thought I'd let her sleep in today."

"Yes, milord." Eol tilted his head in acknowledgment. "Shall we remain in the hallway until she wakes?"

"It's been quiet these past few days. She should be fine in here alone, but keep your ears open for anything unusual."

"Yes, milord."

Dar closed the door and returned to the bed. He leaned over her to leave a kiss when two blue-eyed slits peeked out at him. "Good morning, my sleeping angel."

She slipped her arms around his neck. "*Bore da*, my sexy savage." She pulled him down. "Come back to bed."

"I would love to, but I must get to work." He gently removed her arms. Etain twisted out of his grasp, took hold of his wrist, and plunged his hand underneath the covers onto a very warm and willing breast.

"You have work to do here, milord," she breathed, gliding her tongue over his lips. "You fell asleep on me last night."

"I beg a thousand pardons for that," he groaned, feeling her nipple grow hard in his palm. "But I must finish this job so we can go home."

She slid down against the pillows, holding his hand in place. "Have I lost your interest already?"

"By the Krymerian gods," he growled. "You are a temptress." He let go of her breast and dove his hand into her tousled hair as he bruised her lips with his. "Tonight, my fiery vixen, I'll show you just how much interest you stir in me." He released her and straightened. "For now, get some rest. You're going to need it."

The last thing he heard was her delicious chuckle as he stepped out the door.

———

Brusquely shaken awake, Etain found herself, covered in a cold sweat, in Taurnil's strong arms, pressed tightly to his muscular chest.

"E, you're safe. It was just a dream."

She tried to push away, but his grasp was firm. "What're you doing in here?" Behind him, she saw Eol, Galdor, and Swee, concern on their faces. "What's all this?"

"You were screaming bloody hell, E," Taurnil explained. "We could hear you from my room."

"I was screaming?" She held the sheet over her and pushed again. This time, he let go. "I don't even remember dreaming."

"From what we heard, I guess it's best," Swee said, handing her a glass of water.

Etain realized how dry her throat was and greedily drank it down. "Thanks, Swee." Her eyes cut back to Taurnil. "I'm sorry I alarmed everyone."

"Are you sure you don't remember? It was a spine-chilling scream. Hard to believe there's no lingering trace."

"No. Not even a creepy feeling."

"Very strange," he said, eyeing her closely. "You know what you need?"

"What?"

"To get out of this place." He laughed. "Swee's going into town today. Why don't you and I join her?"

"Should you? I mean, you've just now gotten back on your feet. I'm surprised you made it this far."

"Don't worry about me. I've been working at night. I'll be fine."

She turned to Swee. "You're okay with this?"

"I'm surprised, too, but he's doing a lot better, Etain. I think it would be good for both of you to get out of here for a while."

"Okay." She wagged a finger in Taurnil's face. "But if you get the least bit tired, we rest. No arguments."

"No arguments." Standing, he took Swee's hand and looked down at the disheveled High Lady. "We'll meet you back here in a half hour."

For the first time, she noticed Taurnil's state of undress, clad only in a pair of jeans. "Take your time. I'll need to check on Robert and let Dar know where I'll be." She turned to the Blades. "Eol, Galdor, will you be joining us?"

"Indeed, milady," Galdor said. "We are your shadows."

"Indeed," she murmured. "Well then, everyone clear out so I can dress. T, Swee, I will meet you downstairs. Eol, would you please consult with the stable boy to ensure we have the proper mounts?"

"Yes, milady." With a salute, he was gone. Galdor escorted Taurnil and Swee out the door, closing it behind him to give Etain her privacy.

She stretched her arms overhead and fell back onto the pillows with a happy sigh. "A day of shopping is exactly what I need." She pushed the sheet down to her hips and placed her hands over her protruding belly. "Perhaps I can get some ideas on how best to set up your room, little ones, or maybe even uncover a unique name for you, Junior."

She felt a fluttering sensation inside, as though dozens of butterflies had taken flight. She held her breath for a moment. Tears in her eyes, she smiled. "My babies, my precious little ones. Hello to you, too. Let's go shopping."

17

UNANTICIPATED

Donned in loose-fitting pants and flowy top, Etain grabbed her cloak and, escorted by Galdor, headed to Robert's room. Greeting the guards stationed outside his door, she entered the room and ran straight into a hurried Linq. Both were stunned by the impact. Quick to react, he grasped Etain by her arms to keep them both on their feet.

"Linq, I'm sorry…" A sudden wave of nausea rose up into her throat. Her easy smile disappeared as she pulled away and ran into the bathroom, slamming the door shut and kneeling in front of the toilet.

Once her stomach settled, she leaned against the wall. "Definitely revulsion," she muttered, feeling a chill down her spine. She'd never felt anything so vile in her life…except for Midir's touch. Shaky, she crawled to the sink and pulled herself to her knees. Looking at her reflection in the mirror, her hands trembled as she pushed back her silver mane.

"What is wrong with you, Etain?" She pushed herself up, turned on the cold water, rinsed her mouth, and splashed her face. Dabbing her face with a towel, she braced herself with a deep breath before joining her brother.

Back in the room, she noted the concerned looks from the Blades. "Darn morning sickness." She walked to the bed, noticed the dirty dishes on the bedside table, and sat next to Robert. "How you doing today? I see you've had breakfast."

"Kinda weird actually. That elf friend of yours brought the tray up."

"Linq?"

"Is that his name? The one you ran into coming in?"

Perplexed, she held his hand. "You don't remember him? He was with me in Deudraeth. The two of you left together."

"Oh. I don't remember. Guess that fall you said I took shook some stuff loose."

"I suppose it's to be expected after such a tumble. But you're looking much better. Your color's returned and your eyes have a sparkle I haven't seen in a while."

He smiled. "I *am* feeling better. Chelri's been helping me with his special potions. Today, I think we're going to work on getting me out of bed again, if he thinks I'm strong enough."

"Really? Well, take it easy and don't overdo. No need to rush anything."

"We'll take it slow."

"I hope so. I remember how stubborn you can be once you've set your mind to something." Etain reached out, smoothing his hair.

"Me? Stubborn? Never."

Chelri came into the room heartened by the laughter shared between brother and sister. "I see our patient is much improved today. *Bore da*, milady." He bowed to Etain, then performed his daily duties of checking Robert's vitals.

"*Bore da*, Chelri. He looks wonderful. I don't know what you're doing, but keep it up."

"A strong will is half the battle." Seemingly content with his findings, he looked at Etain. "Will you be joining us today?"

"I would love to, but I've been invited on a shopping expedition."

She smiled at her brother. "I stopped by to let you know so you wouldn't worry."

"Is Dar going with you?" Robert asked.

"Oh, hell no." She laughed. "He hates shopping...unless it's for manly things."

"You aren't going alone, are you?"

"Are you kidding? I'll be lucky to get out with the few I'll have with me. Just T, Swee, and my Blades."

Robert touched her cheek. "The fresh air will do you good, Etain. Have fun."

She left a sisterly kiss on his lips. "You take it easy." He nodded as she stood. Turning to Chelri, she gave him a piece of advice. "Watch out for this one, sir. He's as stubborn as they come."

Chelri smiled. "I've dealt with some patients who were set in their ways, milady. One of whom I believe you're quite familiar with."

She raised a brow and grinned. "Compared to him, this should be a walk in the park."

"Thanks for the vote of confidence, sis," Robert said, pretending to be hurt.

"Anytime." Etain winked and headed to the door, giving him a wave before she closed it.

***

Galdor assisted Etain with her warm cloak before they stepped out into the cold air of the morning. Not seeing Taurnil or Swee in the yard, they walked to the forge to tell Dar of their plans. A blast of warm air met them as they went inside. Engrossed in the hammering of the black blade, Dar merely glanced up, then realized who it was. His face lit with a welcoming smile. He plunged the blade into the water barrel, grabbed a nearby towel, and walked toward her as he cleaned his hands and face.

"What a pleasant surprise," he said, giving her a kiss. "To what do we owe this honor, my beautiful wife?"

"We?"

Linq stepped up from behind her, smudges of soot on his face and hands. "*Bore da*, Etain. You're looking well this morning."

She gave him a strange look. "Better than before."

"Before what?" Dar asked.

"When I saw Linq upstairs."

"Upstairs?" the elf echoed.

Dar chuckled. "Linq's been here all morning."

She glanced from one to the other. It was hard to believe that even Linq could move that quickly, but she knew she hadn't dreamed it. She shook her head. "Never mind. I'm going into town with Swee and Taurnil. I know you'll be busy out here for most of the day, but just in case you came looking for me, I didn't want you to worry."

"Very thoughtful, my love. Thank you. It's not too soon for Taurnil?"

"He's been working hard and going nuts being confined to his room. I'll make sure he doesn't do too much. The first sign of fatigue and we're off our feet."

"The same goes for you, milady. Do not overdo it."

"Of course not, milord." She smiled sweetly.

"Since Galdor is here, I assume Eol will also be accompanying you?" he asked, despite the fact Eol had advised him of the expedition earlier

"Oh, aye. I certainly wouldn't want to leave my new best friends out of the fun," she said, giving Eol a wink. He ignored the familiar gesture. "Will you be done with the blade today?"

"It's nearly finished. Just a little fine tuning, then I'm off to find the perfect piece of jade for the hilt."

"Off to where?"

"Not far. Spirit has agreed to let me root through Inferno's private stash of stones. She said it would be an honor to be a part of such an important sword."

"It can't be easy for her."

"It isn't, but I think it helps." Dar gazed at her for a moment. "Are you sure you're up for this today?"

"Of course," she said, looking flustered. "Why do you ask?"

"You seem paler than usual."

"I had a touch of morning sickness earlier."

His brows furrowed. "Morning sickness?"

Etain shrugged. "I guess it can hit at any time."

Brushing back her hair, he whispered, "I know carrying twins isn't easy." His hand moved down to her belly. "Take it easy today."

She framed his face with her hands. "Stop worrying, Dar. I'm fine. You'll see. By tonight, I'll be the picture of health. Shopping does wonders for a girl."

"So I've heard." He smiled, giving her another kiss. "Don't be gone too long. Remember what I told you about tonight."

"How could I forget such a promise, milord?" She and Galdor left the forge to meet up with the others.

Dar turned to find Linq's eye on him. "Do you really think that's a wise move?"

"No, I don't," he admitted, returning to stoke the fire. "But I have to give her some breathing room. Etain isn't a woman to be influenced by an iron fist. She's in trusted company and won't do anything to jeopardize the children." He picked up the blade, inspecting his handiwork. "My Blades will let me know how the day went."

"Where do you find the patience?" Linq laughed, turning back to the blade in hand.

"It's called love, my friend, and it gives you the power to do many things you didn't think possible," he replied with a grin. "Which brings something else to mind. What are your plans after all this?"

"Haven't really made any. You know me. I go where the wind blows."

"Perhaps I can persuade those winds to blow in our direction?" Dar asked as he put the final touches to Taurnil's blade.

"I'm listening."

"I've decided to open a Black Blade Academy once we get home. One open to Alamir, as well as elves." The announcement was followed by complete silence. Dar looked over his shoulder and found the elf staring at him. "What?"

"Open to the Alamir?"

"Aye, the Alamir. I've met many who have proven their worth and should have the opportunity."

"I'm not saying there aren't those who are worthy, but you know how diverse the Alamir kingdom is. What's to keep a *Bok* subversive from infiltrating?"

"Granted, we'll need more stringent standards of acceptance with full background checks and unquestionable references, but I believe that will make our group all the more exclusive. Only the best of the best will be allowed into the academy."

"Have you discussed this with Alatariel?"

"I have not and do not intend to. The Black Blades are my creation. She had no say in the beginning and she'll have no say now." Dar turned back to his work.

"I apologize, Dar. Being an elf myself, I tend to think of the Black Blades as an Elven institution, not Krymerian."

"No. You're right," he conceded. "Your response gives me a taste of what I'll run into once the formal announcement is made. I need to be ready for that. Thank you for your honesty." Driving the blade back into the water barrel, he walked over to Linq. "I want you to help me with the academy. You're an excellent judge of character and talent, as well as a good turn with the sword. I need someone I can trust without question."

"I'm no teacher, Dar," he balked.

"Ridiculous. If you can teach a stubborn Krymerian new moves, you can certainly teach a group of novices. I've seen you work with Etain. You have a natural ability that I fully intend to exploit."

The big grin on Dar's face made him laugh. "Bloody Krymerian. Never understood why I put up with your conniving arse."

Dar clapped him on the back. "It's my dashing good looks and irresistible charm."

"Actually, I'm thinking of Etain. She'll be busy with the children and won't have time to keep an eye on you. Someone has to keep you in line."

"We're going to have great fun, my friend, and build an amazing force." He walked toward the door. "I'm off to choose a piece of jade for the hilt. I'll come back later to help you finish up."

"Don't bother, Dar. I should be done here in another couple hours. Maybe catch up to you at dinner tonight?"

"Stranger things have happened," he laughed.

Upon their arrival in the small town, Galdor saw to the stabling of the horses while the rest of the group leisurely walked on to the apothecary shop. Along the way, they passed a fabric shop, its windows laden with new arrivals in the latest colors of the season. Etain's eyes lit up. Without giving Swee or Taurnil another glance, she walked toward the door.

"Y'all go ahead. I'll catch up in a few."

The always observant Eol moved quickly to open the door for the High Lady and followed her in. He chose to stand by the large plate glass window where he could see Etain and watch for Galdor at the same time. Oblivious to his watchful eye, Etain walked through the aisles, flitting from one bolt to another, the vibrant colors and rich textures enticing her deeper into the store.

At the apothecary shop, Taurnil trailed behind Swee, touching a bottle here, a vial there, doing his best to appear interested. Swee did her best to ignore his attempts as she approached the counter for assistance. His mind elsewhere, Taurnil inadvertently bumped into her.

"Oops. Sorry."

Swee gave him a stiff smile. "Why don't you go check on Etain? I'm sure she would love to spend more time with you, Taurnil."

"You think so?" A smile spread across his face. "We haven't had much time to just hang out. Can you handle the packages on your own?"

"Yes, I can manage. Go." She shooed him toward the door.

"Come find us when you're done." Giving her a kiss on the cheek, he left the shop.

As he meandered down the street, he checked out the wares in each window he passed, intrigued by some, bored by others. At long last, he came to the fabric shop, peering through the window.

It was at this time Etain stepped out of the store, unnoticed by her cousin. She leaned over his shoulder. "Anything of interest?"

The young elf jumped. "E! You scared the life out of me."

She covered her mouth, laughing. "I'm sorry, T. I didn't realize you were so captivated."

"I wasn't..." He grinned. "I was trying to find you without having to go in."

"Not a man of the cloth?"

"Never and no way in either case."

Etain looked up and down the street. "Where's Swee?"

"I was in the way, so she sent me to you."

"Poor T." She cocked her head to the side. "Not into shopping, eh?"

"Well, not for things that interest women."

Etain raised her brows. "Really?"

"Really."

"I know what we can do." She turned to Eol and Galdor, who had joined them. "Would one of you Blades please go assist Ms. Swee with her purchases? I'm sure she could use the help."

"With all due respect, milady...," Eol began, but Etain linked her arm with Taurnil's and walked away.

"I guess I'll just have to explain to Dar how his Blades refused to assist a good friend of his. I hope he'll understand…" Arm in arm, Etain and Taurnil walked up the street.

Eol closed his eyes and motioned Galdor to find Swee, then caught up with the other two.

"Where we going, E?" Taurnil asked.

"You'll see. We're almost there." Within moments, the three stood in front of the armory shop where Dar had shown off his warrior moves so many months ago. "Here we are. I think you'll enjoy this." She walked into the darkness of the shop, leaving the men to follow.

Taurnil's face brightened as he ogled the wonders inside - swords, daggers, axes, every accoutrement of battle known to man, and elf, in all sizes, shapes, and colors.

"*Mon dieu, dame douce,*" he exclaimed, amazed at the assortment of weaponry. "How did you ever find such a place?" He was drawn to a Scottish claymore, its hilt in the shape of a dragon's head.

His glee made her smile. "Dar found it on one of our trips into town. He was as impressed as you."

Taurnil reached for the claymore, but had to use both hands. Tired after only a few moves, he unintentionally slammed the sword back onto the table, lost his balance, and fell over the blade.

Etain placed a hand on his arm. "Are you okay?"

He took a moment to catch his breath. Then a huge grin appeared. "I am in heaven." He pushed up from the table, ready to move on. "Show me more."

"How about we try something a bit more lightweight?" She walked down the aisle to a set of fencing foils.

Taurnil peeked over her shoulder. "What have we here?"

"Follow me." She winked and headed to the back of the shop.

"Where you going, E?" he asked, following her. "I don't think there's room enough in here to…" His words trailed off as he stepped into the outside enclosure. "Incredible."

"Last time we came to town, Dar showed me some of his moves out here." She removed her cloak and slid a glove onto her right hand.

"Would that be why we're expecting Jack 'n Jill in a few months?" he teased.

"Ha-ha. I forget just how funny you think you are." But she grinned, handing him a glove and foil. "Here. Put this on and let me show you some of *my* moves, smartass."

"Music to my ears, milady. That I have lived to be privy to the High Lady's personal moves."

"Have you ever fenced, Lord Big Mouth?"

"Never," he laughed.

"First we must salute each other." She showed him the correct execution, then took her stance. "Then your arse is mine. *En guarde!*"

Mimicking her stance, he grinned. "I would give you free rein over my entire body, sweet lady, if only you would accept the offer."

"You best hope my husband doesn't hear your words of invitation, milord," she warned, tapping his foil and lunging. "You may find yourself missing more than just your arse."

"A price worth paying for but one intimate moment with milady." Although untrained in the art of fencing, the young elf caught on quickly, blocking her parries, advancing and retreating in concert with her every move.

Etain retreated. "T, you know that will never happen. Dar is my heart and soul."

Lowering his foil, he lifted his chin. "I am aware of the connection you share with my infamous cousin. Everyone in the entire kingdom knows of it." He swept out his arms. "But I, too, feel a connection with you. These past few days have brought us closer together. I know you feel it, too."

She went to him and stood before the young man so much like her husband. "Aye, darling T. We have a very special connection that I value above all others…" He raised a brow. "Except Dar's. I would die without him at my side." With a soft look, she gazed into his golden eyes. "What about Swee?"

"She's a special lady," he admitted. "But it's different."

Etain tilted her head, eyeing him more closely. "Is she special to you in the way a woman is to a man? Or as a friend?"

"We're great friends. She doesn't judge. She accepts me, warts and all."

A small smile lifted the corners of her mouth. "And how about you?"

"She has no warts." His face lit up. "She is perfect."

"Then stop mooning over an old married woman and put your energies where they'll be most appreciated. I've seen how she looks at you and vice versa." Etain leaned toward him, kissing his lips lightly. "To call us friends is a gross understatement. We're so much more, but we have separate paths to travel. You and Swee are an excellent match. Give her your love. I doubt you'll ever regret it."

"Damn you, E." He smiled. "You're so right, which makes me love you all the more. No wonder Dar's so lost in you. He's very lucky."

She laughed. "We'll see how lucky he thinks he is in another month when I'm the size of a barn and cranky as hell. Which reminds me. I need to find the facilities." She picked up her cloak. "Then, how about lunch?"

"Works for me. Meet you at the door."

He took both foils and gloves and followed her inside. They walked past Eol, who watched from the doorway, a stern look on his face. Once inside, Etain cut to the left in search of the toilet, while Taurnil went to find the shop owner. Eol strolled toward the front door, checking various weapons along the way, waiting for the High Lady's return.

The small toilet proved strictly utilitarian, but to Etain's relief, it was clean. A slight breeze billowed through a tiny window situated over the toilet as she quickly finished her business. Washing her hands, she heard the deep resonations of men's voices through the window but paid no attention to what was said until the voice of a child in distress chimed in.

Concerned, she carefully climbed onto the seat of the toilet and peered out into an alleyway. There were two large soldier types menacing a boy of about nine.

"Look, brat…," the soldier on the left held out his hand. "We'll let you go if you give back the ring before the sergeant shows up. Otherwise, you're dead meat."

The boy shrank against the brick wall at his back.

Etain jumped down, threw open the door, and stormed outside, wrapping her cloak around her.

The other soldier moved in closer, but stopped when the boy's eyes widened, looking past him. Both soldiers turned at the same time, surprised at the sight of the beautiful, silver-haired lady. The men straightened their shoulders and stood taller than before.

Etain noticed that while the boy was wary, he wasn't afraid of these brutes. She spoke directly to the green-eyed urchin. "Are you in need of assistance, milord?"

His eyes flashed as he straightened to his full height. "These creeps took something that belongs to me. I was just taking it back."

"Shut up, kid," the right soldier snapped. "This is none of your business, woman. Be on your way."

She ignored their glares as she stepped between the soldiers, standing in front of the boy. She smiled at him and winked, then faced the men. "What exactly are we talking about?"

A hand shot up from behind her, holding a silver, jewel-encrusted ring. "This belonged to my father and they took it."

"It was confiscated in the raid of a known traitor," blurted the man to her left, "and given to me as payment for my services."

The boy peeked out from behind her cloak. "You're a liar. My father wasn't a traitor."

The soldier reached for the boy. Etain grabbed his wrist with one hand, drawing her dagger with the other. Using her full body weight, she shoved the would-be assailant as she twisted him into the brick wall and jammed the blade against his throat. "If you want to live, you'll leave this alleyway…now." The other soldier moved to help his comrade, but Etain dug the edge deeper into his skin. "You really want to-"

"What do we have here?" Surprised by a third voice, Etain looked over her shoulder. "Another Alamir?"

An impressive officer stood not far away, his arms crossed over his chest and a bemused smirk on his face.

"I think the lady should remove that pie sticker from my soldier's throat."

She narrowed her eyes. "Assure me and my ward safe passage and I will."

He dropped his arms as he walked toward them. "We both know this boy is no ward of yours. You'd be well advised to be on your way."

"Only if the boy comes with me."

The sergeant moved around to her side, keen on any sudden movements from the boy. Having a full view of her face, he nodded with a grim smile. "I was going to say our business is none of yours, but I'm feeling generous all of a sudden."

"Don't come any closer," she warned as a trickle of blood ran down the soldier's neck.

"Perhaps you can help us," said the sergeant, walking back the other way. "We've come in search of an outlaw."

"An outlaw?" Etain struggled to keep him in her sights. "What would I know about that?"

"On second thought, I believe we've located the culprit and should be departing soon," he said, his eyes intent on her face. "That is, if you will kindly release my soldier."

"You found your man?"

"I never said it was a man," he laughed.

She looked the *Bok* officer in the eye. "Surely, you don't mean this boy?"

He looked her up and down. "This outlaw is no male by any stretch of the imagination... Lady Etain."

Her captive growled when her hand jerked, cutting deeper into his flesh. "On what charge?"

"Aside from the treacherous act you're currently involved in, you are charged with interfering with the apprehension of a murder suspect."

"What murder suspect?" Her mind raced, trying to remember a time she may have interfered with any dealings of the *Bok*. "You're mistaken."

"Another incident on which we do not agree," he said, placing his hand on the hilt of his sword. "Or have you already forgotten the *Bok* patrol you decimated outside Deudraeth?"

"Wait a minute…" She tried to make sense of his words. "*I'm* considered an outlaw for interfering with my own capture?"

"As well as for the murder of several *Bok* soldiers."

"They were going to kill us." Enraged by his accusations, her dagger slipped farther. The soldier beneath her blade glared at his sergeant.

The officer wrapped his fingers firmly around his sword's hilt. "Come now, Lady Etain. Do you really think I'd take the word of a known assassin and outlaw?" His laugh echoed off the brick walls. "You, milady, are under arrest."

He and the other soldier drew their swords. As the sergeant brought his blade up, Etain twisted, her blade slicing into her captive's throat. The soldier clamped his hand over the cut, his eyes bulging as he slumped to the ground.

In the next moment, an ear-piercing clang rang in her ears. A blade blocked an attack inches from her body.

"That's the problem with you *Bok*. No manners," said Taurnil, forcing the officer back. "The Lady Etain leaves with me."

"You stupid elf." The soldier glared at him. "You will not interfere with the arrest of a known criminal."

From behind, another voice joined in. "Believe we already have, *Bok*." The sergeant whirled around to Galdor and Eol, their black blades ready for battle.

Taurnil grinned. "Step aside, *Bok*, so the lady may pass."

The sergeant puckered his lips and whistled, loud and shrill.

At the same time, the boy scrambled away, running toward the end of the alley. Taurnil couldn't get to him due to the *Bok* in his way but saw Swee at the entrance and yelled, "Swee, grab that boy."

Able to catch him by the scruff of his shirt, the sudden impact spun them both around.

"Get out of here. Get Dar!"

A full *Bok* patrol descended from the other direction. Without hesitation, she grabbed the boy's arm and pulled him into a run.

"Get that woman," the sergeant commanded, pointing at Swee with his sword.

Etain stepped back behind Taurnil and returned her dagger to her boot, then silently called to *Nim'Na'Sharr*. A smile touched her lips when the solidness of the hilt filled her hand.

After his raid on Inferno's stash of precious stones, Dar felt a strange sensation creep over him. Although he knew Etain was out for the day, he stopped by their bedroom. "Etain?" He peeked into the room and laughed at himself, but as he closed the door, the empty sheath for *Nim'Na'Sharr* caught his eye.

That's unusual. He walked into the room. She didn't have the sword with her when she left. As he reached for the scabbard, the sound of a vehicle crunching on the gravel drive made him stride to the window. The sword forgotten, he headed downstairs.

Dar opened the large front doors just as Spirit jumped out of the Hummer. "I wasn't aware you had gone away."

Spirit stretched her arms over her head, twisting and turning. "I took the kids out. We needed some nature time." Dar walked to the back of the vehicle to unload while Spirit helped the children out of the back seat. "All things quiet here?"

"It has been peaceful this morning." Dar smiled, watching the children file out of the vehicle, one by one.

Spirit gave him a doubtful eye. "With a pregnant Etain in the house?"

"Well, she's gone into town with Taurnil and Swee."

Spirit smiled. "That explains it."

In the midst of their conversation, Swee and the young boy arrived in a cloud of dust, her horse sliding to a stop in front of the Hummer. Dar dashed around the vehicle, grabbed the bridle, and gently rubbed the horse's neck, trying to soothe the excited animal.

"Whoa, boy. You're home now." Dar's calm demeanor helped the horse settle. "What's the rush, Swee?"

"The *Bok*...," was all she said.

Dar took the boy, then helped Swee down.

He turned to Spirit. "Find Aramis, Ra, and any Blades who aren't on guard. Linq's in the forge. Tell them to get to town as quickly as they can."

Dar spread his wings, soaring straight up into the air, then turned toward the castle. He disappeared through a set of balcony doors and just as quickly reappeared, flying toward town with his blades, Burning Heart and Day Star, on his back.

The children gasped, seeing his transformation. All except Tegan. Her face lit up with a big smile and a sparkle in her eyes. "See? Angel."

Swee turned to Spirit. "The *Bok* showed up. Taurnil told me to run with the boy, to bring him to Dar."

"How many?"

"Lots."

"Stay here with the kids, Swee. I'll be right back." Spirit headed for the doors in search of the Dragon clan and Black Blades. Before her feet hit the steps, a loud noise from overhead caused everyone to turn and look. A Black Blade crashed through the balcony doors of Robert's room, landing heavily on the ground below.

"Holy shite!" Spirit changed directions.

"Kids, stay here." Swee ran after Spirit. Tegan waddled to the nearest person, the boy who had recently arrived, slid her hand into his, and returned her thumb to its former occupation. The boy eyed the little girl warily, but held onto her tiny hand and sighed.

Spirit and Swee recognized the fallen Blade as Renme, the dark elf. She bled profusely from a deep slash across her belly and multiple cuts on her arms and legs. Spirit gently laid Renme's head in her lap as Swee leaned over, trying to make out her words. Her lips were so swollen, she could barely mumble.

"Robert..."

Swee held her hand. "Save your strength." Although she knew she would be dead before nightfall.

"No." She swallowed, the effort making her cough.

Spirit looked at Swee. "Get some water. There's a canteen on the front seat of the truck." Swee ran to the Hummer and returned in seconds. Her hands shaking, she removed the cap and helped the Blade drink.

Renme leaned her head back against Spirit. "It's Robert."

"Is he hurt?" Swee asked.

She grabbed Spirit's hand. "I won't be...around later. We both... know that." She coughed again, sputtering blood. "All the Blades... Robert's guards...are dead."

Spirit looked at the broken balcony doors, as though they alone could confirm her claims. Another squeeze of her hand returned her attention to Renme. "Robert is gone."

"Is he dead then?" Spirit asked.

"No. Dathmet."

Spirit's eyes widened. "Dathmet?"

"He is..." Renme coughed again. Swee gave her another small sip of water. Gratitude shone in her eyes as she drank. "Dathmet," she whispered, holding her gaze.

"Spirit," Swee whispered, neither woman believing what they were hearing.

"For fuck's sake. The demon's taken her brother again. Dar needs to know."

"What do I do?" Swee asked.

"I'll stay here with Renme, try to make her as comfortable as possible. Linq's in the forge. Tell him what's happened."

Swee jumped to her feet and sprinted around the corner of the house.

Spirit looked at her four children and the boy staring at the injured Blade. "Seth!" she barked. All five sets of eyes snapped to her. "Find Freeblood, Zorn, anyone who can help move her. Hurry!"

"Aye, Mama!" The little boy ran into the house, followed by his brother.

"Molly, go tell Alaster we need the dining hall set up like a hospital. Tell him someone is bleeding badly." Tears welled in the little girl's eyes. Spirit reached out to her, beckoning her closer. Her arm around her daughter, she spoke softly. "*Mae'n iawn, un bach* (It's okay, little one). Now, go. Hurry!"

Molly ran off toward the rear of the castle in search of Alaster.

Renme coughed again.

"We're going to move you, lass. Hold on. Hold on."

In minutes, Zorn and Felix rushed out the front door, several members of the Royal Guard behind them. Alaster arrived at the same time, a folded sheet in his arms. "Let's get her into this." He unfurled the sheet onto the ground next to the dark elf.

She cried out despite their efforts to shift her as gently as possible. Each took hold of an edge and carried her into the castle, carefully laying her on the prepped dining table.

Spirit, Tegan, and the boy walked inside together, Tegan's hand still in his. As they walked, Spirit asked, "Do you have family?"

He looked at her with sad green eyes and shook his head.

Spirit chewed on her bottom lip for a moment. "Do you have a name then?"

"Austin."

"Nice to meet you, Austin. I'm Spirit and this is Tegan, me youngest. This is our house. Welcome."

"Are you going to take me to the *Bok*?" he asked timidly.

"Goddess of us all! Never! You'll stay here. At least for the night. Let's see what we can do for our Elven friend."

"Nothing," Austin suddenly said. "Dathmet hates dark elves. He hates *all* elves."

The *Bok* surged into the alleyway, splitting the allies apart. Galdor and Eol held the opening, but Taurnil and Etain were caught up in the midst of the *Bok*. The enemy worked together to cut Etain off from her comrades. Taurnil slashed and jabbed, doing his best to keep track of her movements by shifting in the same direction. Etain recognized the tactic but wasn't able to work her way back down the alley.

A lucky strike by a *Bok* soldier caught Galdor by surprise and brought him down with a thundering crash. The *Bok* turned to the others in a concentrated rush. Eol was able to move closer to Taurnil, the two working together, back to back. Taurnil tried to catch sight of Etain but couldn't locate her.

He spoke over his shoulder. "Etain is surrounded. We've got to get up that alleyway. We can't let them take her."

"Any ideas on how we get past all these demons?"

"I'm working on that." He stabbed into a particularly ugly demon and parried another jab from the side.

The *Bok* were so thick around the High Lady she had no other recourse than to keep moving up the narrow passage. She hoped to reach the entrance without capture, then make her escape. Her *Nim* continued to destroy any demon foolish enough to get close to her. However, the actual *Bok*, those traitorous Alamir turned dark, proved to be more elusive. It wasn't long before she realized she couldn't hold them off much longer.

Sweat poured down her back. Droplets of blood began to rain onto the cobblestone path as she continued to fight, her strength waning with every block. The *Bok* pressed their attack, driving her farther away from the safety of her friends.

Breathing heavily, Etain stopped. "I cannot-"

A strong, protective arm slid around her mid-drift and pulled her back against a solid, muscular body. She slumped into the welcomed support, dropping her sword arm to her side. A tiny warning twinged deep in her mind, but she was too tired to care. She felt safe within the strong arms.

She glared at the murderous *Bok*, but realized their stares were focused on the savior who held her. With a smirk of satisfaction, she leaned back, grateful for the intervention.

"That's right. Be afraid."

A soldier of obvious rank spoke. "Release the woman. She is *our* prisoner. She will answer for her crimes."

From the corner of her eye, she caught the movement of a great arm sweeping through the air, a lethal red-bladed sword in the hand.

Where have I seen that before?

A deep voice answered the challenge. "This woman belongs to me. You will not interfere."

Etain's weary brain could not compute. The voice was familiar, yet different from the one she expected.

He must be injured. His arm is covered in blood.

She knew he was a big man, but realized he wasn't as big as Dar.

If this isn't Dar, who is it?

She couldn't recall anyone as big as this man. But once the heat from his body seeped through her clothing, warming her skin, she knew.

The *Bok* moved into their battle stance, prepared to attack, as her savior shouted, "You know the power she carries. This woman is my sister and will do as I bid. With one word, she will send you all to hell." His declaration caused a stir among the soldiers.

His words sank in. "Your sister?" She twisted to look behind her and felt the color drain from her face, staring at the red skin and flaming hair.

"No!" she screamed as they disappeared.

ALSO BY NESA MILLER

NOTE FROM THE AUTHOR

If you read my books, whether you love it or hate it, please be kind and leave a review.

ABOUT THE AUTHOR

Nesa and her husband live in Derbyshire, England. When not working her day job in commercial insurance, she enjoys short walks on wonky pavements, driving on the straight and well-proportioned roads of the area where the exchange of single digit hand signals has become the latest fad, and the long, hot English summers. At other times, it's reading, writing, watching TV, or creating and selling her glitter glassware at local markets. Nesa has three children and four grandchildren living in Texas and hopes to, one day, move back home, so they can all spoil her more rotten than she already is.

You can find Nesa Miller here:

https://ladyofkaos.com/

f facebook.com/AuthorNesaMiller

twitter.com/LadyofKaos

g goodreads.com/LadyofKaos

CPSIA information can be obtained
at www.ICGtesting.com
Printed in the USA
BVHW072108110319
542338BV00001B/146/P